A Slow Moving Target, The LST of World War II

By

Joseph Francis Panicello

© 1996, 2001 by Joseph Francis Panicello. All rights reserved.

No part of this book may be reproduced, stored in a retrieval system, or transmitted by any means, electronic, mechanical, photocopying, recording, or otherwise, without written permission from the author.

ISBN: 0-7596-6924-4

This book is printed on acid free paper.

1stBooks – rev. 01/24/02

Other Books by Author

The Great Sicilian Norseman: North Hills Publishers
Vindicated: North Hills Publishers
Brian's Comet: www.1stBooks.com
The Wheeler-Dealer: www.1stBooks.com
How To Be A Successful Engineering Manager
A Man Of Destiny

Supported by The American Fiction Society

Member of the United States L.S.T. Association
Member of The American Legion
Member of the National Writers Association

Edited by Pamela Dumble

Acknowledgments

I would like to thank my wife, Barbara, for her patience and encouragement to complete this historical novel. I also want to thank Barbara's daughter, Pamela Dumble, for her outstanding endeavor in editing *A Slow Moving Target.*

Dedication

I'm dedicating this book to my brothers, Carl J. Panicello and Thomas B. Panicello, who served in the Army during World War II from 1942 to 1946, at separate intervals. Carl became a successful Drill Instructor as a Staff Sergeant, training new recruits in the art of combat and survival. He was later transferred to the Canal Zone to protect the Panama Canal. When the German war ended he was scheduled to fight in the Pacific against the Japanese.

Tommy was in the second wave of the Normandy invasion and was later wounded in the Battle of the Bulge, receiving the Purple Heart and other distinguished medals. He was also scheduled to go to the Pacific to fight against Japan. Tommy died in 1997 at the age of seventy-three.

I'm also dedicating this book to the many men and women who did not survive the war. It is astonishing how soon the American public forgets about the men and women who were killed fighting for the freedom of this wonderful country that we enjoy today. Hopefully their names will be remembered forever when they appear in the National WW II Memorial in Washington D.C.

Credits

To ensure accuracy on the invasions described in this historical novel, I have referred to several books, videos, magazines and newspapers which are all listed in the bibliography section. Some of these references are; *To Foreign Shores* by John A. Lorelli, *The GI War* by Ralph G. Martin, *Anzio* by Wynford Vaughan & Thomas, *Guadalcanal* by Richard B. Frank, *Iwo Jima* by Bill D. Ross, *Naval History of World War II* by Bernard Ireland, the *Scuttlebutt* newspaper printed by the U.S. LST Association, and the *Dictionary of American Naval Fighting Ships* in the Appendix of Volume VII and published by the Department of the Navy, Washington D.C.

Preface

A SLOW MOVING TARGET, The LSTs Of World War II, is a historical novel that contains many authentic stories about the turmoil and hardships that the Amphibious Fleet endured during beach invasions in World War II. To enhance the military adversities, the story revolves around the personal lives of five young fictitious sailors who, in 1942, enlisted in the U.S. Navy to defend their country against the Axis.

They come from different parts of America and meet in the same boot-camp at Bainbridge, Maryland. As a result of the difficulties they encounter in boot-camp and in the war they become life-long buddies. After boot-camp is completed they are transferred to the dreaded and perilous Amphibious fleet of LSTs (Landing Ship Tank), a *Large Slow Target* having the reputation of a brief life during an invasion.

In this historical novel each principal character in the book presents his own unique and unusual experiences. The main character of the novel is John Maroni, who attempts to keep the group together and to preserve their friendship throughout the war. They call themselves *The Five Phibies.*

The Five Phibies are later split up and are transferred to different LSTs, which compelled them to fight in separate campaigns in both the Pacific and Atlantic theaters. They continued to communicate with one another via one central location in the States. They send their mail to John Maroni's kid sister, Angela, in Queens, New York, who rewrites the letters by relating their war experiences, their health, and anything new about their personal lives, but deliberately leaving out any unpleasant ordeals, then sending the letters on to the Phibies.

Phibie No. 1 is John Maroni, who was born in Queens, New York. Phibie No. 2 is Dan Bletcher, born in Dover, New Jersey. Phibie No. 3 is Andre Robbier, born in Chicago, Illinois. Phibie No. 4 is Rich Hienman, born in Dallas, Texas. Phibie No. 5 is Bob Olsen, born in Boston, Massachusetts.

Understandably, most historical World War II novels are written around large fighting vessels such as aircraft carriers, battle ships, cruisers, destroyers, and submarines. Very little is written about the LST and their amphibious operations of beach landings and unloading troops and cargo. It was not a glamorized fighting ship. The book relates many authentic LST battles, which are depicted through the fictional characters presented in this novel. I tried to encompass the five Phibies in several authentic battles, even though their characters and experiences were created by my own imagination.

The LST played a very important role involving the military operations in the islands in the Pacific, and during the invasions of France, Italy, and Africa. Without the LST and its ramp, the delivery of cargo to the beaches during an assault would have been extremely difficult and time consuming. The LST was not the most elegant looking ship to come out of American shipyards but it was designed for a purpose, to deliver men and cargo to an invading beach as quickly as possible, and to support the Allied troops ashore with ammunition, tanks, jeeps, trucks, artillery, medical supplies, and, most critically of all, food and water. Without these back-up goods the war may have been extended a year or more, which would have cost many more American lives.

The LST and the other Amphibious forces must be recognized for being one of the most essential components of World War II, and should be commended for their efforts in the invasions of hostile territories both in the Pacific and in the Atlantic theaters. This novel attempts to do just that. The novel does not cover, in depth, the land struggle after an invasion because the ground assaults have already been covered by other authors, and to repeat them here would serve no other purpose but to reiterate their achievements.

Because LSTs 142 through 156 and LST 85 through 116 had their contracts canceled on September 16, 1942 and were never built, I took the liberty of using their numbers as part of the fictitious LSTs used in the novel. I did this so as not to offend anyone by using LST numbers improperly. If I have used an LST in a particular assault incorrectly, I apologize. Many different LSTs are mentioned throughout the novel but I do not cover all of their invasions.

I spent two years on LST 533 after the war in the engine room gang, and used the experiences I accumulated to describe the operations of the ship and the crew's responsibilities. Actually, LST 533 was one of the first *Slow Moving Targets* to land on Omaha Beach in the Normandy invasion. In my research I discovered a picture of my LST on the Omaha beach in the December 1994, issue of the American Legion magazine. I also found the history of LST 533 in the Dictionary of American Naval Fighting Ships, Volume VII, in the LST Appendix.

The United States L.S.T. Association refers to the LST as a *Large Slow Target* and a Bronze Sculpture bearing this title was dedicated to the men of the LSTs in Washington D.C. on October 26, 2000, and can be seen at the Navy Memorial on Pennsylvania Ave. In addition, on December 12, 2000, 29 World War II veterans (average age 72) sailed the partially restored LST 325 from Gibraltar across the Atlantic to Mobile, Alabama, so that people may view this wonderful craft. The LST 325 was given to Greece in 1964 and used by the Greek Navy for 35 years. LST 325 entered Mobile Bay two months after sailing from the island of Crete and nearly one month from the Strait of Gibraltar. The LST 325 was commissioned at the Philadelphia Shipyard.

A Slow Moving Target, The LST of World War II

1. The Day of Infamy

In a small home in Queens, New York, on December 7, 1941, a young Italian-American boy, Johnny Maroni, was looking over the help wanted ads in the Long Island Daily Press. Jobs were scarce during those depression years and he was hoping to find employment to help the family make ends meet. His sister was also present doing her homework. At the family dining room table they were listening to the Glenn Miller Orchestra from a small table radio that was playing *Moonlight Serenade* when suddenly, and for no apparent reason, the music was suspended.

After a short pause an announcer came on and said, "Flash! We interrupt this program to bring you the following bulletin. Today, the Japanese government suddenly and without warning attacked and bombed Pearl Harbor in Hawaii. Tomorrow, the president of the United States will be making a statement to congress about the attack which will be aired over this station."

As the music came back on Johnny turned to his sixteen year old sister, Angela, and said, "Did you hear that, Ann?" Angela was engrossed in her homework at the time and wasn't paying much attention to the radio.

Angela looked up, somewhat preoccupied and said, "Hear what?"

Johnny repeated the announcement, "The Japs just bombed Pearl Harbor in the Pacific."

She didn't seem at all surprised. "So what? They've been bombing Pacific islands for years. So what's another harbor?"

Johnny was a bit disturbed by now and said, "You don't understand, Ann. Pearl Harbor belongs to the United States. It's in Hawaii. We are being attacked! This is war against our country!"

They stared at each other in bewildered silence, waiting for additional news. An unpleasant thought went racing through

Angela's mind. If there's a war, she realized, her brother will be drafted and he might be killed.

The house that Johnny and Angela lived in with their parents was an attached two story brick home and about 1,000 square feet. The width of the house was only 16 feet. The downstairs rooms were sometimes called railroad rooms because they followed one another. The entry room was a 12 foot wide by 15 foot long living room with stairs on one side close to the entry door and a large window facing the street.

The second room was the dining room, which was in the center of the house. It was the largest room, 15 by 15 foot square. It had a window in the rear, on one side, overlooking the storm doors to the cellar. In the center of the room was a large dining table, 6 by 6 feet, with a buffet cabinet on the side. That's where they kept their small table radio.

The kitchen that followed was much narrower due to the entry path to the storm cellar door. It was approximately 7 by 15 feet long with a window on the side of the cellar entrance between the attached homes. It had a back door leading to a small garden followed by attached garages. There was enough room for a small kitchen table which the family used during weekday meals. Sunday's meal was always at the dining room table. This table was used by Johnny and Angela to do their homework because Mama was always in the kitchen cooking, washing or ironing. Washing was done by hand on a wash board in a big tub. The ironing board was fixed in a small closet which opened up in the center of the kitchen.

Upstairs were two large bedrooms with a toilet in the center. Johnny and Angela had to share one of the bedrooms which annoyed Angela, not having the privacy she wanted. Angela's father promised her that he would some day put up a wall separating the two of them. Sadly, Angela understood she wouldn't be needing that partition if Johnny were drafted.

She finally said, "Maybe you made a mistake, Johnny. Maybe you heard it wrong."

A Slow Moving Target, The LST of World War II

The next day, at the dinning room table, the music stopped once again and the radio announcer said, "America, here is the president of the United States, President Roosevelt."

"Ladies and gentleman of America. Yesterday, December 7, 1941, a date which will live in infamy, the United States of America was suddenly and deliberately attacked by the naval and air forces of the Empire of Japan..." His continued announcement was strange and baffling to them and to the entire country.

Johnny, after hearing the announcement said, "Did you hear that Ann? I'm sure to be draft bait. Hell, if I'm drafted I certainly don't want to go into the army marching twenty miles and living in a cold wet trench. I'd rather enlist in the navy. At least I'll have a dry warm bunk for awhile, that is, as long as we don't get sunk."

"Don't talk that way, Johnny." Angela didn't care to hear those remarks because she was concerned for her brother. She said quietly, "Don't be hasty to enlist, Johnny. Wait till you are drafted and then enlist. It may be years before you are called to serve."

Johnny replied excitely, "But our country is being attacked. I can't just sit by and let others do the fighting. I have to help. I love this country. Anyway, look at my situation. I don't even have a job. What am I going to do around here with a war going on. I have no money and Pop is just barely scratching out a living at the shoe factory. If I volunteer now it'll be one less mouth to feed."

Angela couldn't dispute his last statement. What he said was basically true. With the depression continuing throughout the country it was tough for a young man to find work, any kind of employment. With the war on it might be easier. But no firm would take a chance of hiring a man considered draft bait.

Johnny was nineteen years of age. He had graduated from high school one semester later than normal in June, 1941. He was six feet-one and weighed in at 190 pounds. He had brown wavy hair like his dad but hazel eyes like his mom. He was

Joseph Francis Panicello

definitely a good-looking boy. He was also very athletic, a three letter man in high school, making the varsity teams in basketball, baseball, and football.

He had to repeat his last semester of school because he didn't pass the New York State's Regents Examination in History. To graduate from a New York academic school, in those days, a student must pass all State Regents Examinations on every major subject. This put a burden on Johnny's dad who was hoping his son would finish school and find work to help the family out. It created many arguments between them.

When he failed to graduate his father said to him, "*Giovani*, you must quit school and help me support the family. They have cut my pay at the shop and it's getting harder for me to pay the bills."

Johnny's mom insisted that he should finish. Mr. *Giovani* Maroni was not an educated man himself, and before he migrated to America he worked as a laborer on an olive farm in Sicily. His wife, Patricia, was Irish-Italian-American born and she did have a high school diploma. Her father was from Ireland but her mother was an Italian descendant. She knew that without an education her son wouldn't have a chance of finding employment. Mr. Maroni would never go against his wife, so young Johnny was able to finish high school in the next seven months by just barely passing the history Regents Exam.

In the past, Johnny bounced from job to job, only to be released for lack of work. He tried all types of employment. He worked as a mechanic's helper at the Green Bus Line in Queens, then pumping gas at a gas station, and even as a carpenter making wood window frames. He once applied for a position for the Department of Sanitation in the City of New York but there were one thousand applicants for only ten positions. Times were bad then and many men had to work for the WPA just to make ends meet.

In the early thirties, many men tried to enlist in the army just to get a square meal but they were refused because the country was still at peace. When the European conflict started in 1939

A Slow Moving Target, The LST of World War II

the military began accepting only selected volunteers, which did help a few. Johnny knew that the news of Pearl Harbor had changed everything. For the first time in his life he could see his future, serving the country he loved.

Before Pearl Harbor, the war was raging in China, and the Japanese tried repeatedly to provoke America into an armed conflict. In early 1941, the American ambassador to Japan, Joseph C. Grew, wrote: "American churches, schools, universities, and hospitals throughout China have been bombed by the Japanese despite flag markings on the roofs. American missionaries and their families have been killed. There can be no doubt that these attacks were planned to provoke America into a war."

Even the deliberate sinking of the USS *Panay*, a small gunboat patrolling the Yangtze River to protect American civilians, failed to arouse America into a conflict. On October 17, 1940, General Hideki Tojo became prime minister of Japan. Tojo was resolved to prepare for war with America, a nation he hated intensely.

Tojo, nicknamed "Razor Brain," was barely five-feet-four and wore oversized horn-rimmed glasses which gave him an owlish appearance. Tojo had a reputation as a brilliant organizer and administrator, and as a skilled and daring military strategist. He was the principal architect of an operation plan designed to unleash the most devastating blitzkrieg in history, one that would extend the Japanese Empire from Manchuria to Australia.

First, a bold sneak attack would be launched to destroy or severely cripple America's fleet at Pearl Harbor, freeing the powerful Japanese navy to dominate the Pacific and achieve ground coverage for its military to control many Pacific islands and Asia. Tojo's plan for the conquest of Asia and America was approved by the Supreme War Council September 6, 1941.

Plans for the attack on Pearl began in 1931, when each graduating class at the Japanese naval academy had to answer the final examination question: "How would you carry out a surprise attack on Pearl Harbor?"

Joseph Francis Panicello

In America, with two broad oceans to protect the United States from Japan and Germany, Americans weren't interested in getting involved in any kind of conflict. "Keep out of other people's quarrels!" was the slogan.

In Japan, Admiral Isoroku Yamamoto was against war with America and said, "It is a mistake to regard the Americans as luxury-loving and weak. I can tell you Americans are full of the spirit of justice, fight and adventure. Do not forget American industry is much more developed than ours—and unlike us, they have all the oil they want. Japan cannot beat America." However, Tojo convinced Emperor Hirohito that the war must happen, so Yamamoto had no choice but to plan the attack on Pearl Harbor.

The U.S. Government knew there would be a war but they didn't know where. They knew because they broke the Japanese secret code with a small group who acted under the heading of MAGIC. On Nov. 27, 1941, the U.S government alerted the Pacific bases: "Japanese future action unpredictable but hostile action possible at any moment."

Except for a few carriers out at sea, the United States Pacific Fleet were a sitting duck in Pearl Harbor. The vunerable ships were the battleships *Arizona, Tennessee, Maryland, Pennsylvania, West Virginia, California, Nevada* and *Oklahoma*. Also in the harbor were an assortment of cruisers, destroyers, submarines and many other vessels. There were seventy combat ships altogether and twenty-four auxiliaries all with one boiler lighted, but they did not have enough steam generated to make an emergency exit.

Early Sunday morning—at 5:30 A.M.—Capt. Mitsuo Fuchido and his armada of forty "Kate" torpedo bombers, fifty "Val" dive bombers, fifty-one "Zeke" and "Zero" fighter planes, and forty-nine high-level bombers headed for Hawaii. They arrived at 7.00 A.M., outside of the Oahu coastline apparently undetected and attacked at approximately 8:00 A.M.

The sudden attack, planned for ten years, had been devastating. Within thirty minutes Captain Fuchido and his pilots

A Slow Moving Target, The LST of World War II

had achieved their primary goal, the destruction of the United States Pacific Fleet's battle line.

During this period, other Japanese aircraft had bombed Army and Marine Corps air bases on Oahu. In a few minutes thirty-three aircraft had been destroyed on Ford Island, and at the Marine field at Epa nearly all of the fifty parked planes were demolished. Twenty-seven of the thirty-three Navy Catalina patrol planes based at Kaneohe were wrecked. The three Army airfields on Oahu—Hickman, Wheeler and Bellows—were almost destroyed, and their planes were blown to smithereens.

In the days that followed the attack, Johnny listened to news constantly. On December 11, 1942, because of an earlier Axis agreement between Japan, Germany and Italy, Hitler and Mussolini declared war on America. In a few days came the announcement Johnny had been expecting and actually hoping for. The bulletin broadcast over the radio announced, "All men whose ages are between 18 and 38 must register for the draft."

The Selective Service Bill became a law on Sept. 16, 1940, and in two weeks 16,313,240 men between the ages of 21 and 35 registered for the draft and were given lottery numbers. The draft board had now extended both ends of the age limits by three years. Those drafted were summoned by induction notices that cheerfully began, "Greetings."

The first lottery number called was 158, which was held by Robert Bell, a 21-year-old fireman in the District of Columbia. His mother wept at hearing the announcement. She was proud, but fearful of sending her son to war.

Every one of the 6,175 draft boards in the country had at least one number 158 drafted. In New York, he was a Chinese laundryman who couldn't wait to get his hands on "the dirty Japs" for what they were doing to his homeland. In San Diego, he was a zookeeper; in Trenton N.J., a midget who'd been a Munchkin in *The Wizard od Oz*; in Cleveland, a newspaper reporter; and in San Francisco, a meteorologist.

Col. D, J. Renneisen (Ret.) of Jasper, Ind., said that being number 158 was "the only lottery I've ever won." After

Joseph Francis Panicello

reporting he said, "Our first issue of uniforms included some leftovers from World War I and from the CCC (Civilian Conservation Corps) outfit. We were ashamed to be seen in town in those garbs."

Among the men whose numbers were called early in other lottery selections; actors Jimmy Stewart, Henry Fonda and Wayne Morris; the swimming star Buster Crabbe; the baseball player Vince DiMaggio; and the singer Lanny Ross. On the 18th number pulled from the lottery was our future president, John Fitzgerald Kennedy.

Joseph P. Ellis, of Elmont, N.Y. remembers being called 5 months after number 158 and said, "At Camp Wheeler, Macon Ga., we trained with broomsticks and other make-believe arms. I was shipped out to the Pacific in January 1942, and was paid $21 a month for fighting a war. I was making more than that a week as a civilian."

One of the cartoons that commented on the draft was, "Superman was ruled 4-F (unfit for duty) because of his x-ray vision. During his induction physical, he read the eye chart in the next room by mistake."

In 1940, the federal government had spent only $9 million on military expenditures. By 1945 this figure would sore to $40 billion. When the war began the whole nation literally rolled up its sleeves for the war effort. After Pearl Harbor, the people were now 100% behind the war and many left their private jobs for defense jobs.

Johnny had no intentions of waiting to be drafted. His plans had been made in the moments following the news of Pearl Harbor. He was ready to carry them out.

A Slow Moving Target, The LST of World War II

2. Johnny Enlists

The following Monday morning December 15, 1941, Johnny went to the post office in Jamaica, Queens, where an emergency recruiting station was set up. He stopped momentarily to observe a marine poster that portrayed a marine in battle, with the American flag waving in the background. The words at the bottom of the poster read, "Fight the Japs as a Marine and save your country."

Johnny was impressed with the slogan and almost went into that station but quickly composed himself. The marines were no better than the army, he figured, and walked on down the hall to the naval recruiting station. When he entered the room there were twenty men in front of him. The first thing he did was yell out loudly, "Hey, what's the hold up?"

A huge Chief Petty Officer walked up to him and said, "The navy don't need jerks like you. If you don't like the wait go join the army."

This was the first time anyone, besides his dad, had told him off and got away with it. He was about to walk out but then decided to wait it out. The chief looked hard at him and knew that the navy would either make or break this kid. He had seen this kind of spoiled brat before. He would fall in line or end up in the brig.

Johnny was a tough kid. Whenever there was a problem in the neighborhood from other gangs his buddies would call on him to lead the fighting. He was their leader and wasn't afraid of anyone. Under different circumstances, Johnny would have punched this chief out but instead he stared right back at him. They scrutinized each other with anger in their eyes for a full minute. Finally, Johnny turned away and began looking down at the floor. He got his first military lesson. One cannot fight the whole damned navy, he realized.

He eventually got to the desk and after answering a few questions he was told he had to have his father's signature on the

Joseph Francis Panicello

application, and in person, because he was not twenty-one yet. Later, family approval was only required for 17 year olds.

Johnny stepped out into the hall and mentioned his dilemma to another guy standing there. The guy said, "Go downstairs to the Army induction center. Hell, they'll take anybody as long as he can breath. You can forge your dad's signature, they don't care. The navy's too damned fussy."

"Thanks, but no thanks. I'll get my dad to come here and sign me in. I still want to be in the navy." He was determined.

Asking his Dad, however, became a stumbling block for him because his dad refused to sign him into the navy. He said to Johnny, "*Giovani, mio figlio*. If you go into the service you will be fighting against your *cugino*. You could kill you own cousins."

"But Pa, they won't be sending me to fight in Italy. I'm of Italian descent. I'm sure they will send me to the Pacific against the Japs." His father wasn't impressed and still refused.

Johnny, to his displeasure, had to register for the draft. As weeks passed many of the boys in the neighborhood were being drafted. Johnny once again went to his father and explained, "Look Pa, all of my friends in the neighborhood are being drafted into the army. Is that what you want me to be, a soldier? Living in a fox hole and freezing to death. Don't you see, in the navy I'll have a dry bunk and eat regularly. In a week or two I'll be drafted anyway and then I won't have a choice."

Mr. Maroni thought about what Johnny had just said and after a moment he agreed and said, "Okay, lets go down to the Post Office and take care of this matter."

On January 15, 1942, Johnny was sworn in together with a room full of recruits. A Navy Chief announced to them, "Go home and say goodbye to your families for the last time but be at the Penn Train Station in Manhattan at 10:00 AM tomorrow morning. Bring only a few toilet articles with you and not too much cash. There's nothing you can buy where you're going."

That last evening had to be the most dismal time in the Maroni home. Johnny's mom cried periodically. His sister stayed close to his side, trying to control her emotions. His dad tried to read the Italian newspaper, *The Progresso*, to avoid shedding a few tears, himself. Johnny sat at the dining room table, not saying a word. He was numb. He had never left home before and now he was leaving for parts unknown, unsure of what the next few days would bring. He had a sleepless night.

The next morning, Johnny traveled to Manhattan on the subway with Angela. She insisted on coming along. When they were on the station before he entered the train, Johnny kissed his sister goodby on the cheek and said, "Goodby, Sis. Don't worry about me. I'll be fine."

She hugged him and began crying as he stepped off the platform and onto the train. As he walked down the aisle of the car he saw many young recruits looking out the window saying goodbye to their loved ones. One recruit had watched Johnny and Angela through a window before Johnny boarded. When Johnny sat down next to him the recruit said, "Boy, that girlfriend of yours is some looker. Is that the best you can do, kiss her on the cheek?"

Johnny simply answered, "Are you kidding? She's my sister."

The young man turned away for a moment in deep thought. He looked out the window once again and observed Angela with complete admiration. He couldn't believe his eyes. "She's gorgeous," he said to himself. To Johnny he said, "Hi. I'm Danny."

Daniel Bletcher was born in Dover, New Jersey. Danny was a wild guy in school. He was a big boy, about six-foot-four and over two hundred pounds. He was good-looking in a manly way, with dirty-blond straight hair which was parted in the middle and sometimes fell over his ears. His ancestry was mixed European, mostly German. Like Johnny, he couldn't find work in the state of New Jersey, and began a life of petty larceny by breaking into stores after midnight and stealing whatever he thought was resalable. He finally got caught by a local cop, Officer O'Brian, who happened to be a personal friend of the family.

Joseph Francis Panicello

The cop said to him, "Danny, I won't turn you in if you enlist in the service. You're no good, Danny. Maybe the service will straighten you out. Well, what's it going to be, jail or service?"

"What choice is that?" he asked. "All right... I'll enlist."

Danny could care less about the war or who won it, but since he had no choice he enlisted in the navy to save his family the embarrassment of visiting him in jail. He chose the navy because he didn't like the idea of marching in the rain. He also considered joining the marines because he did like a good fist fight, especially in bars and in pool halls, but he settled for the navy. His parents had driven him to Manhattan over the George Washington bridge and dropped him off at Penn Station.

At nineteen, he had never cared much about anything or anyone. When Danny saw Angela, he felt like a ton of bricks had fallen on him. He was completely captivated by her. As the train began moving out, both he and Johnny were glued to the window looking out at her. While Johnny waved to his sister all Danny could do was stare at her as though she was a special vision of sainthood. Her beauty struck a chord in his heart, and brought an onrush of emotion he had never experienced before.

Angela was indeed very beautiful. She stood about five foot five, and was very slim of figure with an above normal bust size. Her long hair was naturally curly and was reddish brown in color with streaks of blond running through it. She resembled her mother in looks being half Italian and half Irish herself. Angela's alluring large eyes were a captivating pale blue. She had a small, turned up nose, a mouth with appealing full lips. Her skin was very white with freckles on her arms and a few on her forehead. She seldom went to the beach, though Johnny practically lived there. Her prepossessing smile revealed straight white teeth and when she smiled people were invariably captivated.

Angela slowly turned her head from Johnny and looked at the other boy in the window. Her eyes focused on his for a moment with sympathy. There was something peculiar about his eyes that revealed, she thought, a lonely pathetic boy. She felt

A Slow Moving Target, The LST of World War II

pity for him, not having someone to see him off. She dabbed her own eyes with a handkerchief as she watched the train move down the track, wondering when she would see Johnny again. She took a deep breath, turned and headed for the subway platform that would take her back to Queens.

When the two boys could no longer see Angela from the train window they sat back and made themselves as comfortable as they could. After a few minutes of small talk Danny could no longer hide his interest. "What's your sister's name?" he asked Johnny.

Johnny was aware of the way Danny had stared at his sister but he was not angry or upset. There were so many boys in high school that were smitten with her. Even though she was voted Campus Queen as a junior, she rarely dated and wasn't impressed with any of the schoolboys.

Angela didn't even want to go to Johnny's senior prom with one of his friends, but had finally agreed because Johnny asked her to, and because his friend was shy and didn't have a date. She wouldn't date the guy afterwards, though.

Angela was a very practical girl and was not interested in getting serious with any schoolboy because she saw how rough it was for her mother and father who were struggling to make ends meet. Angela was definitely not going to marry early and follow the same pattern. In her requisites for marriage she decided she would marry only Mr. Perfect. There were no Mr. Perfects in John Adams High School where she and Johnny attended.

Johnny answered Danny by saying, "Her name is Angela. We call her Ann."

Johnny watched Danny turn his head away and stare out the window. Another love struck boy in love with his sister, he thought. Johnny grinned to himself. He was used to this behavior over his sister with several of his classmates at high school.

Johnny and Angela had had many conversations together about life in general and marriage. He knew Angela's feelings about marriage and that she wouldn't get serious with any man until she was in her late twenties and well established herself.

Joseph Francis Panicello

She was definitely not going to live the same life style that her parents did, trying to survive day by day.

Johnny grinned again, knowing he had not heard the last from Danny about Angela. Danny sat quietly, lost in thought about a girl he had seen briefly from a train window. He closed his eyes and allowed the train to rock him to sleep. When Danny woke he found Johnny anxious to talk. They related the general facts of their lives to each other, quickly feeling a sense of comradeship.

On the same train car and across the aisle was another recruit. His name was Andre Robbier from Chicago, Illinois. Andre was not a tall boy, only five foot-five. He weighed in at one-hundred and thirty pounds. Even though Andre was short he wasn't afraid of anyone. He was good-looking in his own way with black hair and brown eyes.

Andre's family migrated to the United States from Canada in 1921, a year before Andre was born. Andre's father was a medical doctor in Canada and before he could practice in the U.S. he had to go back to school. It took his father another two years before he was able to obtain his license and open up his own practice in the U.S.

Andre's father wanted his son to follow in his footsteps but when Andre turned eighteen he was not interested in going to college. After high school, he ended up working in a drug store as a soda jerk for a year and helped the druggist with prescriptions. He was exceptional in chemistry but he didn't have the drive to become a doctor like his dad. His future didn't look promising.

When World War II began for America, Andre, at nineteen years of age, enlisted in the navy like many of the boys in the neighborhood. When the recruiting Chief questioned him about his past and the fact that his father was a doctor, he recommended that Andre become a medical corpsman. Andre wanted no part of that position. He turned the Chief down.

On the train Andre became interested in Johnny and Danny. He liked the way they clowned around. Johnny was bragging about how great he was in football and Danny was boasting about the barroom fights he had had. Danny certainly looked like he could handle himself in a fight. He was a big boy.

Johnny glanced across over the aisle and saw this little recruit watching them so he asked him to come over. "Why don't you join us, sailor?"

Andre was elated and answered, "Gee, thanks. You guys seem pretty regular." He had a enthusiastic smile on his face. Andre moved across the aisle and sat next to Danny. "My name is Andre Robbier. Thanks again for inviting me."

Johnny could tell right off that this kid was well mannered and educated. When Andre mentioned that his father was a medical doctor, Johnny knew for sure that this kid was more than the average recruit. Andre had gone to private school and seemed to posses an intelligence that set him apart from the other recruits.

When the subject of corpsman came up, Andre explained, "I just want to be a regular sailor like you guys and do my part."

Johnny didn't think he would be strong enough, especially if he had to fight in a hand-to-hand combat situation. He didn't pursue the issue and, as the hours passed, they became good friends.

When Andre went to the head (bathroom) Johnny said to Danny, "You know, Danny, we're going to have to look out for that little guy. He's too puny to take care of himself." Danny agreed.

When Andre came back and sat down again, Johnny made a toast with a coke, "To the three of us, who will stick together throughout the war, wherever we go." They all responded together with, "Cheers." The bond for these three was now solidified, never to be broken.

3. In The Navy Now

The train came to a stop in a remote area in Maryland. All of the recruits bailed out of the train and were told to line up in a single file. As their names were being called out, each one had to acknowledge their presence by stepping forward. They were then marched to a temporary barracks about a mile from the train.

Before they could receive any chow they were first marched to a barber shop and their hair was cut right down to the scalp. One navy barber insisted that Johnny sit at his chair. He said, "I want that kid with all that wonderful curly hair."

He was licking his chops and had a broad smile on his face as Johnny was being ushered to his chair. Johnny became a little sick as he watched his hair falling out in front of him. The barber began singing while cutting his hair, "You're in the navy now. You're in the navy now," and began laughing and having a merry old time while disposing of Johnny's locks.

After they left the barber's shop they began lining up again outside. The Petty Officer then announced with a smile, "Welcome to the navy, skinheads." He then marched them to another barracks close by where they received their navy clothes.

"What do we do with our old clothes?" one of the men asked the Petty Officer.

"Throw them away or send them back home. You won't be needing them for many years. They'll probably no longer fit you, anyway, after we fatten you up and put some muscles on your flabby bodies."

The rest of the day was spent being pushed and pulled in a dozen directions, seemingly all at once. The pace left the raw recruits feeling dizzy and all of them were ready for lights out at 10:00 PM.

The next full day at boot camp was different. As far as Johnny was concerned it was hell. Getting up at 0500 hours was stupid he thought, with someone yelling "Reveille, Reveille" and banging his bunk with a night stick. They were marched to their

A Slow Moving Target, The LST of World War II

permanent barracks a few miles away while carrying all their clothes and a hammock, in a large seabag that weighed close to eighty pounds. Andre was having trouble with his bag, and when Danny tried to help him the Petty Officer reprimanded him.

"He carries his own gear," he commanded. Between dragging and carrying his seabag and falling behind, Andre was finally able to reach the barracks.

After they settled in, they were marched to the chow hall for breakfast. It wasn't too bad, Johnny thought. There was no waiting at all. His impression of the navy at this point was that it wasn't all bad. After chow, however, the day was spent making beds, scrubbing the deck, cleaning the head, and washing windows. By evening Johnny was convinced it was the Navy's job to bore him to death.

The recruits were marched to the chow hall as usual for dinner but this time they were lined up outside. There must have been twenty companies lined up waiting to enter the chow hall. It was cold that night and, as expected, it began to rain.

Danny said to Johnny, "This is stupid. Why can't we wait inside?"

He was answered with a question from Johnny, "Who said the navy was bright?"

Johnny saw some of the other sailors reversing their caps to protect their heads from the rain, so he did the same. The peacoat he was issued helped but it was wintertime, and the weather was very cold and the rain felt like icicles beating across his face. His legs and feet were getting stiff from the cold rain and he began jogging in place to help his circulation. It took at least an hour before his Company, 21, was called to enter the chow hall.

The next night when they lined up at the chow hall Johnny sneaked over to another company that was ready to be called. Andre tried to stop him and pleaded with him, "Don't do it, Johnny, they'll hang you for it!"

Johnny simply answered, "Bug off."

Joseph Francis Panicello

He got away with this for a week until he was caught. Cleaning greasy pots and pans in the chow hall for a week, after a full day of marching and going to classes, was exhausting but worth it, Johnny thought.

Danny and Andre never screwed off. They went about their duties and never squawked. Andre said to Johnny after he got back to the barracks at 10:00 PM, "I hope you've learned your lesson."

Johnny again responded, "I told you before, don't bug me. I'm exhausted," and quickly fell asleep.

The next several evenings, Johnny decided to forgo dinner at the chow hall and went to the canteen and ate cold sandwiches every night until his money ran out. At least he was warm for a spell before serving his extra duty at night.

Andre caught a cold and went to the sick bay. He was told he had "Cat Fever" which was just an expression in the navy given to all sicknesses, especially when the diagnosis was uncertain. He had to be admitted to the base hospital for a few days, where they gave him shots in the buttocks every four hours with a new drug called penicillin. Fortunately, he was able to rejoin his unit but many of the other recruits who became ill were reassigned to different units. Cat Fever almost became an epidemic at the base.

One boot, not feeling too well, said to Johnny, "I went to the sick bay and they told me I had walking pneumonia, but because I didn't have a fever the doctor couldn't admit me to the hospital. Navy policy, he said."

A week later this boot was shaking in his bunk so severely that the company commander had to call an ambulance. The latest scuttlebutt Johnny heard was that this boot died in the hospital. Johnny's opinion of the navy sank to a new low.

"What stupid rules," he thought, and decided then and there that he was going to survive this damned navy one way or another.

Johnny, like so many young recruits, couldn't see the point in the tedious activity of classes, drilling, and marching that just seemed to keep the recruits busy. He was anxious to get into the

A Slow Moving Target, The LST of World War II

war, to do something important. To Johnny, every day at boot camp was one less day to add to the war effort.

Andre showed a willingness to adhere to the regulations and routines of the navy training that Johnny could not seem to muster up, and secretly admired a little.

The recruit that surprised Johnny, though, was Danny. Danny went at everything without squawking and a resolve that Johnny couldn't understand, considering Danny's lax-a-daisy attitude.

Between them, Andre and Danny kept Johnny focused on getting beyond the next several weeks, keeping him out of trouble. His major scrapes were his responsibility and many times he pulled extra duty because of them.

Joseph Francis Panicello

4. Liberty

At the beginning of 1942 the Allies were on the defense in all the major theaters of war. The upheaval brought great changes to the United States.

Early in 1942, the Office of Price Administration (OPA) issued ration books for sugar, meat, coffee, fats and oil, butter, cheese, shoes, and canned goods. Because only two pounds of beef were allotted weekly, horse-meat and buffalo-meat began appearing on the restaurant menus. Quoted in a magazine, "Although it isn't our usual habit, this year we're eating the Easter Rabbit."

Because of gasoline rationing, many family cars were home in the garage and were hoisted onto wooden blocks. The "A" ration sticker was for families who were only allotted 3 gallons a week. It simply wasn't worth driving with only three gallons so they put their cars away and used local transportation. The "B" sticker was for War Plant workers, and the "C" sticker was for doctors, clergy and those in small business.

Nylon and rayon stockings were rare so the girls used the new product "stocking fizz" that put a line down the back of their bare legs and looked like stockings. The fizz manufacturer claimed, "The most scrutinizing pair of masculine eyes cannot distinguish it from sheer hose."

Women started wearing slacks on the street. Clothing became a scarce item on the home front. The "Zoot Suit" was the first to go because it had wide shoulders, wide pants that were voluminous at the waist with pinched ankles and deep pockets of which one contained a long chain with keys. To save material, skirts were shortened above the knee which pleased many a GI and cuffs were removed from mens pants for the war effort.

From the Scuttlebutt newspaper printed by the U.S. LST Association, Bob Stambaugh, of LST 757, recalls how it was fighting against the Zoot Suiters (Mexican-Americans from East Los Angeles). They preyed on men in uniform and after the Zoot

A Slow Moving Target, The LST of World War II

Suiters hospitalized one Marine they had enough. His Marine buddies came to L.A. seeking revenge and found some on a streetcar in downtown L.A. The Marines forced them to remove their Zoot Suits, then piled them up and burned them in the middle of the street. Los Angeles became off limits to service men after that incident, until the L.A. Police finally restored order.

Victory Gardens sprang up in such diverse spots as zoos, backyards, racetracks, and even jail yards. The American gardens were encouraged by the Secretary of Agriculture, Claude Wickard, to help in the war effort so that people could grow their own produce to supplement their diet and save war stamps.

Unemployment was no longer a problem. Millions of Americans, especially the very young, the old, and women, went to work in the defense industry to meet the production levels demanded by the military.

In July, 1942, the Women's Army Corps (WAC), began. This was followed by the navy WAVES (Women Accepted for Voluntary Emergency Service), the airforce WAFS (Women's Auxiliary Ferrying Squadron), the Coast Guard SPARS who were so named after the first letters of its motto, "Semper Paratus," and the Women's Reserve of the Marine Corps which began later in 1945. The service women were called "Petticoat Army" by military regulars. An army trainer, who was impressed by the women, said, "They learn more in one day than my male squads learn in a week." In all, 350,000 women served in the U.S. military in World War II.

A huge migration of people took place; more than 25 million people moved to be close to war plants. The relocation of 110,000 American-Japanese began for security reasons, but over 20,000 American-Japanese served in the Armed Forces, mostly in the European campaign. They proved to be great fighters.

More than 30 million men were registered for the draft. At least 15 million men and women would end up serving in the war. The least of their worries was introduced with the slogan

Joseph Francis Panicello

"Play it again SPAM." The GIs called it "cuisine a la foxhole." These were combined with the famous K-rations named after Ancel Keys who pioneered the stuff. The last entree that became popular in the service was chipped beef on toast or "S--t on the Shingle," while the American public was adjusting to rationing at the home front.

Boot camp was finally concluded for Company 21 and the boots were given a week leave. Johnny, Danny, and Andre headed for New York City, where Andre had to change trains for Chicago. Danny asked Johnny if he could go home with him and spend one day there. Johnny didn't think it was a good idea because he knew Danny wanted to meet his sister and he was sure Angela couldn't approve of Danny.

Liberty week at home for Johnny was great. He spent all his time with his family. He couldn't get enough of his mother's Italian cooking. The day before he was scheduled to go back to camp, the front doorbell rang and when Johnny opened the door he saw Danny standing there. "What are you doing here, Danny?" he demanded.

"Oh, I had a battle with my dad. I walked out of that fiasco this morning and I didn't know what to do with myself, so I came here." Johnny knew better. Danny had come to meet his sister, now sitting on a couch in the living room.

What else could Johnny do but introduce him to his sister and said, "Ann, I want you to meet my boot camp buddy, Danny Bletcher. Danny, Angela." Johnny wasn't pleased with this situation.

"Pleased to meet you, Angela. What a pretty name." Danny said and almost stumbled over his feet as he approached her. She shook his hand, overwhelmed by his size. Danny immediately sat next to her on the couch. Angela looked over at her brother for some sort of help but he simply shrugged his shoulders indicating, "You're on your own."

A hour later the doorbell rang again. This time it was Andre. "What are you doing here, Andre?"

Andre, looking sheepish, answered, "I was bored at home. My dad kept trying to convince me to join the medical corps and I got tired of all that baloney. You don't mind, do you, if I stay the night? I can sleep on the floor tonight."

"No. We've got plenty of room." After a pause Johnny said, "I want you to meet my sister, Angela."

When Andre saw her he was stunned. Danny immediately noticed Andre's reaction. Andre said, "What a pretty name," and sat on the other side of her. Before long both Danny and Andre were directing all their conversation toward Angela, each trying to impress her and outdo the other.

Johnny, shaking his head, went into the kitchen. He opened up the ice box and had a glass of milk. His mother said to him, "What's wrong, son. Why aren't you in the parlor talking with your friends?"

"I can't, Mom. Those two buddies of mine are monopolizing Ann. I don't know how they'll be able to get along back at the base."

Angela was very sweet to both of them. She was especially happy that Johnny had found two wonderful boys to be friends with. Every time she smiled, both Danny and Andre beamed. When she talked they just stared. It was love at first sight for Andre. Danny was already in love with her. He had been thinking about Angela for weeks, hoping this moment would come.

As Johnny wondered back to the parlor he noticed that Angela was having a great time talking with the boys. "What about Mr. Perfect?" Johnny wondered. He liked both Danny and Andre but he didn't think Angela could find much in common with either of them. They were young, without much direction, and Johnny knew the goals Angela had already set for herself. Andre had walked away from a family situation that might have opened a few doors for him. Instead, he joined the service. Danny had to join the service or do some time.

Angela was careful to divide her attention between the two boys. Having this much adoration directed at her wasn't new but

Joseph Francis Panicello

it was disconcerting. She was so happy at seeing Johnny home again that initially it had spilled over to include Johnny's new friends. As the afternoon wore on, however, she realized she was having a wonderful time.

Danny, she remembered, was the boy who had looked out at her from the train window the day of Johnny's departure. Up close to him she could see the beautiful shade of his blue eyes, the peculiar lost look still there, she thought. She felt another wave of sympathy pass through her as he sat next to her. She felt a sudden flush of shyness, then realized he was feeling the same way, which put her more at ease.

For the next hour they talked, mostly undisturbed, because Johnny kept wandering back and forth, first to the kitchen to see Mama, out to the garden where Papa was reading, then back again to the parlor to interject with some anecdote about boot camp.

Before Andre arrived Angela learned a great deal about Danny, more than Johnny could have guessed. The most startling fact she learned was that she herself had become a major influence in his life, more so than anyone he had ever known. As he quietly confided in her about his own feelings, her interest in this boy grew and she realized she was intrigued with a man for the first time in her young life. After Andre arrived she was moved in a different manner because Andre was more sophisticated, with a quiet and gentle demeanor. Their personalities were definitely different.

That evening mama cooked a special meal of *Lasagna* and *Braciola* (stuffed round beef tied in a roll). Danny and Andre sat on each side of Angela at the dining room table and couldn't get enough of her or the food. Papa *Giovani* was trying to be cordial because he knew that these boys would be in a war soon and might never come back. Normally, he wouldn't have allowed so much attention to be given to his daughter, especially by complete strangers. "Better here at home," he thought, grateful that his daughter seemed more mature than others her age.

A Slow Moving Target, The LST of World War II

It was a lovely evening, everyone was happy for the same reasons and different ones as well. By 10:30 that night Papa and Mama knew it was time to go upstairs to bed and insisted that Angela do the same. Mama brought bedding for the boys to sleep on the parlor floor while Johnny would sleep on the couch. Papa shook each boy's hand, Mama kissed them and invited them to come visit again.

Angela held out her hand, first to Andre, who took it gently but briefly. He said, "It was a pleasure, Angela."

As she turned to Danny she noticed a disturbing expression in his eyes. He held her hand and remained quiet. "Come back soon," she said to relieve the moment. She moved to Johnny, gave him a hug and whispered, "Be careful," then turned away and went up the stairs.

Danny and Andre gazed after her as Johnny moved towards the light switch. He turned back to see them still standing there in a trance. "Lights out, sailors," he said. As they laid into their bedding. Johnny said softly, "Angela, what a pretty name. Goodnight, you saps," turned on his side and went to sleep.

Joseph Francis Panicello

5. The Five Phibies

The next morning, without waking Angela, Mama and Papa, the three of them headed back to the base by train. On the subway and on the train all Andre and Danny could talk about was what a great time they had had the day before. Johnny had enjoyed his liberty in spite of his mates showing up. Johnny was a family man and enjoyed being home with his family. He wondered how it was over at Andre's and Danny's homes. Johnny could see how they enjoyed themselves at his parents' home but he knew that it had to be because they were enthralled with Angela. He wondered if this infatuation over his sister would come between them, preventing these boys from doing their jobs at sea. Johnny realized that it was out of his power and hoped that Angela would control the situation. As far as he was concerned these boys are his buddies and that's the way he would treat them.

The first thing they did when they entered their barracks was to look at a bulletin board to see what their new orders were. All three were scheduled to go to Norfolk, Virginia, but first they had to go to a Ship's Shore Station on the base temporarily to wait for their ship, LST 142, to arrive. Johnny said out loud, "What the hell is an LST?"

Another sailor answered, "Man, is that where you're going? Don't you know that an LST is part of the Amphibious Fleet, the worst duty in the navy. The Japs are sinking those amphibious craft like ducks in a pond. You guys sure got a raw deal. I'm going on the battleship Missouri," as he walked away, smiling with pride.

Two other sailors who were standing there looking at the bulletin board said, "Nuts. We're in the Amphibs, too."

Their names were Richard Hienman and Robert Olsen. After they saw their orders were the same as Johnny's, they went over and offered to shake hands with Johnny, Danny and Andre. The five of them struck up a conversation and became friendly.

A Slow Moving Target, The LST of World War II

Rich was from Dallas, Texas, and was very rugged at nineteen years of age. He was tall at six foot-two, with red hair, a slow mover and a slow talker. He looked like he'd be right at home in a pair of boots and a Stetson hat, on a horse, plodding alone through a Texas cornfield. Rich came from a typical mom and pop farm in Texas, raising cattle. They were relatively poor by New York standards but they ate well and were happy.

Robert Olsen came from Boston, Massachusetts and during summer vacations from high school he worked on different fishing boats, mainly lobster fishing beyond Nantucket Island and as far north as Maine. He became quite proficient in this trade, not only learning all the skills of fishing, but also steering and navigation of the boat. After he graduated from high school he worked at this occupation for another year with his father before he enlisted. Being of Swedish descent, Olsen was tall at six foot-two with blond hair, and weighed in at two hundred pounds. His personality was even-tempered but he could be aggressive if he had to.

The five boys hit it off instantly and were soon referring to themselves as the *Five Phibies*, a name that would follow them throughout the war.

The next day the *Five Phibies* were transported in the back of a canvas truck to another barracks several miles away. This new barracks was referred to as a Ship's Shore Station which provided sailors temporary quarters until their ship came in.

At this station they were required to work while they waited and their assignments sometimes weren't pleasant. It was as though they were still back in boot camp except here they were being marched to a work station every morning instead of to a class. At the shore station they would muster out in front of the barracks each morning and then were assigned to different tasks. After a few days of this nonsense, Johnny learned that if he lingered in the back of the marching crew he could easily slip away and spend the rest of the day in the canteen or just kill time walking around looking at the different ships in the harbor.

Joseph Francis Panicello

When he was caught a week later he was punished and given extra details, after hours, washing the barracks's windows.

Andre reminded him again, "It wasn't worth it, Johnny. Was it?"

Johnny again replied, "Don't bug me."

Johnny never learned and didn't care. He figured he had had a full week of grace from boredom, with no duties at all and it was worth it.

With the LST 142 still in the shipyard the *Five Phibies* had to stay at the Shore Station until September. They were getting fed up with this waiting but they did receive weekend liberty. No long leaves were allowed until their ship came in. The *Five Phibies* would spend the liberty weekends hitting the bars, and drinking beer. Virginia was somewhat dry with no hard liquor served in bars. In order to drink whiskey one had to bring his own bottle to a private club where they would provide set ups. The only problem these young sailors had was that they had to be 21 to purchase liquor at a state store.

When they finally got their orders to report to LST 142, things began to feel a little better. They were each given a four day leave before they had to report. Johnny had delayed going home the first day because he met a girl in town. He spent the day with her but later discovered she was married to a sailor who was out to sea. Johnny was still a religious boy and didn't like the circumstances so the next day he left for New York. Meanwhile, Danny and Andre had used their leave to visit Angela.

At home, Angela was torn between these two young boys. She cared for them both even though neither had a future or were even close to being a good prospect. The war does influence one's thoughts and values, it seemed. She felt sorry for both of them because they could be killed. She was unquestionably mixed up. She felt an emotional attachment to Danny and found him very attractive but at the same time she had an almost maternal instinct towards Andre and knew intellectually they were more compatible.

A Slow Moving Target, The LST of World War II

The competition between Danny and Andre over Angela was strong. On leave they both went to New York to see Angela instead of going to their respective homes. Danny traveled by train and Andre by Greyhound Bus. The train trip took about 11 hours while the bus took 12 hours.

Danny was first to show up at her home. Angela was very gracious and received him very warmly by kissing him on the cheek. She then asked, "Where's Johnny?"

"Oh, he'll show up in a day or so. He met a girl and wants to visit with her for a day."

Angela was surprised that her brother was seeing a girl but then asked Danny, "Why didn't you go home first, Danny?" she asked.

"I know I should have but I had to see you first. I'm..."

Just then the door bell rang. It was Andre. Danny was angry as hell, and yelled, "What the hell are you doing here, you little punk."

"Same reason you're here, partner," Andre responded back, with a broad grin on his face.

"Boys, let's be nice. I'm glad to see you both." she said somewhat pleased. "Now both of you sit down while I get you some lemonade." She also kissed Andre on the cheek as he came in, which really disturbed Danny.

Angela liked the attention she was getting from these two sailors, and was impressed with Danny for his size and Andre for his brains. She later thought to herself, "If Andre had Danny's physical size he would be Mr. Perfect." Together, she had the man of her dreams, except there were two of them.

Angela learned to share her attention with both of them. She always greeted them graciously, receiving them both with a kiss on the cheek. It took all of her skill as a woman to keep them from bristling at each other and each thought that he was the one she preferred.

That evening the three of them went to a movie at the fashionable Valencia theater, one of the most exclusive theaters outside of Manhattan. The Valencia was once an opera house and still had a ceiling with stars blinking and moving clouds. It was very romantic, a favorite of young men out to impress a date.

As Angela sat there gazing at the beautiful ceiling with a handsome young man on either side of her, she had never felt so admired or confused. She wondered if some day she might not have to choose between them. When the lights dimmed, she sighed and decided to enjoy the show. Time could sort it out. It was a peculiar situation but she was enjoying every minute of it.

Johnny showed up the next day and was surprised to see Andre and Danny there. The house was getting crowded these days, he thought. Quite a competition had developed between these two and though Johnny was amused by it, he felt he was in the way. Besides, he was having a good time on his own going out with a different girl each night. Johnny was not ready to get serious with any girl.

A Slow Moving Target, The LST of World War II

6. LST 142

In September, 1942 the war against Japan, Germany, and Italy was in full swing. On the afternoon of September 15, a peculiar looking ship began docking at a pier at the Norfolk Naval base. Some of the sailors on the pier, who were handling the ship's lines, were wondering what kind of a ship it was. It was certainly not a destroyer nor any sort of a transport that they have ever seen before.

One sailor said, "It's one of those new Amphibious ships. See the name on the bow, LST 142. I think it stands for Landing Ship Tank. I don't know all the details of its operation but it's supposed to be able to beach at the bow, open those big bow doors, drop a ramp to allow tanks and trucks to drive off and onto a beach.

"The alternate way of doing it was with transports that used large cranes to lift the tanks out of its hold below decks and onto small boats or barges that were in the water. All that took forever because small boats can only carry one tank at a time and barges had to be towed ashore.

"With this new line of Amphibious craft, in conjunction with the new APAs (Attack Transports), they can move troops onto small craft quickly. On the APAs, however, the troops will still have to climb down a rope ladder onto Amphibious Higgins boats. These new Higgins LCVPs (Landing Craft Vehicles Personnel) can be driven onto a beach carrying a truck, tank or personnel.

"During an invasion, the many different Amphibious craft, especially the LST, can put troops, tanks and other cargo on a beach in no time at all. The troops would then have backup food, ammunition, trucks, and tractors immediately available for them to mount a full scale land offensive against the Japanese or the Germans, right after they have established a beach head."

Joseph Francis Panicello

Another sailor asked, "You mean this huge ship will be beached just like those small amphibious craft we saw in those training films?"

"That's right. Like I said, I don't know all the details of how and when, but that's the way I heard it," responded the first sailor.

The second sailor was still not satisfied, "Well then, how do they get the ship back out into the water after it's grounded?"

A third sailor remarked, "Maybe they use yard tug boats, YTBs, to pull them out. Those tugs are pretty powerful."

It was obvious that these sailors were not altogether familiar with the different operations of these new LSTs.

The civilian crew who had sailed LST 142 to Norfolk were shipyard workers who were men in their forties and fifties. The captain was a 60 year old civilian pilot.

LST 142 was built by the Missouri Valley Bridge & Iron Works Company of Evansville, Indiana. The regular shipyards were loaded to the hilt constructing destroyers, battle ships, aircraft carriers and other warships, so new construction companies had to be found. After the Missouri Valley Company bid for the job they were one of five inland non-shipyard factories that were selected to build LSTs.

The Missouri Shipyard had to be rebuilt from scratch beginning in February 1942. They then had to work around the clock to meet a crucial delivery demand and were able to launch its first LST in September. After that first launching the Missouri Shipyard was able to launch an LST almost every day for the first month to meet the initial order. This yard built a total of 166 LSTs during the war, which became a record. All together the U.S. Navy built 1,051 Landing Ship Tanks in different parts of the country but 670 were constructed by inland builders.

In the construction of LSTs, prefabricated sections of the ship were built in other parts of the country and were assembled at the Missouri Shipyard. After the ships were commissioned the LSTs were launched from the yard side ways and into the Missouri river.

A Slow Moving Target, The LST of World War II

In another inland shipyard, LST 29 was laid down on January 8, 1943, at Pittsburgh, PA, by the Dravo Corp., was launched on May 17, 1943, and commissioned on July 10, 1943. On July 1, 1943, LST 29 headed south down the Ohio River with a civilian pilot and ultimately to the Mississippi. LST 29 was assigned to the Pacific theater and was involved in over five invasions and earned four battle stars.

Many LSTs had received a partial navy crew on board at the shipyard to bring it down the river themselves and later stopped at a New Orleans pier to pick up a combat crew. These ships were now ready to go to sea. LST 142, however, arrived at Norfolk to receive its full navy crew.

LST 142 was one of a block of numbers given to each ship yard, not necessarily the 142nd to be launched. It had to be sailed by a skeleton crew of civilians, down the Missouri and Mississippi Rivers, past New Orleans, and around the Florida Peninsula to Norfolk, Virginia, to be turned over to the Navy.

Norfolk, Virginia, is the home port of the Atlantic fleet. The Naval base is off the Elizabeth River, located at the mouth of the Chesapeake Bay, at Hampton Roads and the James river which empties into the bay. Thousands of navy ships are docked there or anchored in the bay. At any given time it could provide moorage at several piers for three battleships, five cruisers, four aircraft carriers, twenty destroyers, several submarines, and numerous other ships including thirty transports. The bay, by itself, could provide anchorage for thirty large vessels.

To the north, at the mouth of the James river, is the city of Newport News, which is one of the largest ship building centers in America, specializing in building aircraft carriers. It is close to the army base, Camp Peary, and nearby Langley Air Force base. Jamestown, on the James river north of Newport News, was the first permanent English settlement in North America, which was founded by colonists from the London Company in 1607. Further north up the James River is the city of Williamsburg and the capital city of Virginia, Richmond.

Joseph Francis Panicello

Just below Norfolk, on the West Branch of the Elizabeth River, is the Portsmouth Ship Yard located in the city of Portsmouth where many ships are built, repaired or refitted in dry docks.

The Chesapeake bay, by itself, is enormous and affords one of the greatest inland water ways to many cities. The bay is about 200 miles long and 30 miles wide. Just north up the bay are the cities of Hampton, Yorktown, Charles, Baltimore, and many other port cities. Several rivers run into the bay including the Susquehanna, James and the Potomac, which passes through Washington D.C. The Chesapeake is also one of the greatest fishing centers in the world because it is long and very wide. It is well protected from the open sea by the Charles Peninsula and has a variety of fish in its waters including clams, oysters, crabs, and soft shell crabs.

After LST 142 was tied down at the pier most of the civilian crew members began leaving the ship to travel back to Missouri by train to pick up another ship. They made this round trip venture over and over again throughout the war bringing many LSTs to Norfolk or New Orleans.

One civilian crew member remarked, "Well, we did our job, now it's up to the navy to use this ship on an invasion. It's kind of scary when you look at how vulnerable it is. I'm glad I'm not on it."

Another civilian remarked, "Yes, but look how valuable these ships will be when they land and bring tanks and artillery ashore in an invasion to support the troops. I understand the upper brass loves them. That's why we are building so many."

Three crew members and its captain remained on board LST 142 to maintain the ship and later transfer it to the navy. One of the crew members that remained operated one auxiliary engine which provided electrical power for the ship while they were in port. The civilian skipper did not leave the ship until an official navy captain took over her command.

After a week in port some of the navy crew members began showing up. The first members to arrive were the *Five Phibies.*

A Slow Moving Target, The LST of World War II

They were all green skinhead seamen, recently graduated from boot camp and didn't know anything at all about the operation of an LST. They had to wait months in a Ships Shore Station doing different duties, such as mess cooking and policing the grounds until their ship came in. Right behind them coming up the gangway was a huge Chief Boatswains Mate, Jack Turner, carrying a suitcase.

In no time at all, the chief began to show his authority by bellowing out, "Alright you swabs. Get your asses and your gear below decks. In a few hours I'll be calling muster and I'll want you all to fall in on the main deck, and on the double!" He then pointed to Danny. "You, big guy! Carry my suitcase to my quarters located in the starboard bow!"

His command was in a loud voice with a raspy sound to it which frightened Andre, who practically ran up the gangway with his seabag. The rest of the Phibies, who were still carrying their seabags, headed for a hatch that opened up into a large crew's quarters which could sleep approximately 70 men. Danny dropped his seabag and followed behind the chief, carrying his suitcase. He then went back to the crew's quarters, picked up his seabag and appropriated a bunk by pushing Andre aside and taking the middle berth. Andre didn't argue over it because he preferred the lower berth, being short as he was.

It took another five hours before eighty of the expected one hundred-five crew members arrived. Chief Turner then blew his boatswain whistle on the bridge over the loud speaker system to alert the crew and announced, "Now hear this," he roared, "All hands muster to the main deck and on the double."

All of the ship's sailors piled out of the crew's quarters and onto the main deck forming three lines. The Chief began calling muster (roll call), but pronouncing their names correctly was a major ordeal for him. His education was limited to grade school. He never attended high school, and was raised in a tough section of Brooklyn.

At the beginning of the war there weren't enough petty officers to go around to man the new ships that were being

Joseph Francis Panicello

massively produced by different shipyards. Promotions were given out indiscriminately to many veterans. Chief Turner joined the navy in 1936 and because of his ruggedness he was promoted early in 1942 and was given the temporary rate of Chief Boatswain Mate and assigned to LST 142. The navy needed strong men to train and control the new recruits and Chief Turner was perfect for the job.

Chief Turner was an ex-heavyweight boxer who had 40 fights, winning 30 by knockouts. He also lost 5 of his bouts by being knocked out himself. He was a big man at six-foot-four and now weighed 240 pounds. He was as tough as he looked. Because of his limited education, the Chief had a difficult time reading the names of the sailors as they appeared on the roster, so he proceeded to give them nicknames which made them easier for him to pronounce and would also allow him to recognize them later.

When the Chief called out Bletcher's name during muster he pronounced it, "Belcher." Hienman became "Hinny," Maroni became "Macaroni," Olsen became "Olly," and Robbier became "Robber."

At the time when the Chief announced Maroni's nickname, Johnny tried to correct the Chief by saying, "Chief, my name is Maroni, not Macaroni."

The Chief was visibly disturbed by this interruption and bellowed back in his usual strong, scratchy voice, "From now on it's Macaroni to me. If yous got any beefs about the ways I calls ya, we'll just step out onto the pier and settle it man to man."

Johnny Maroni didn't expect to have to fight over this stupid nickname so he just kept his mouth shut.

The chief added, "Anyone else who don't likes the ways I calls them has the same invitation." There were no challengers.

The chief continued, "Tomorrow morning all crew members not on duty are to report on the pier at 0900 hours. You will be taken on trucks to a conference room at the canteen where you will be lectured on the operation of this ship. Reveille is at 0500 hours. This gives you time to make your bunks and shave before chow at 0600 hours. After chow you will swab the deck and clean the head before you leave. Dismissed!"

"Oh, great." Johnny mumbled, as he and the other Phibies gathered together below decks. "School again."

Bob gave Johnny a disappointed look as he said, "We can't run a ship unless we learn how. You should sail more with the wind, Johnny."

Johnny laughed. "You sound like you're bucking for navigation, Bob."

Bob replied, "That's just what I have in mind." Turning to Andre he said, "What about you, Andre?"

Andre was uncertain and said, "As long as I don't have to work in a hospital or the sick bay, I don't care what duty I get." With a shrug he said, "I just want to be a plain seaman."

"I'm striking for gunnery school," Rich wistfully said. "I did a lot of hunting back in Texas and I love weapons."

Danny then chimed in, "That sounds like a Texan. I'm with Andre. For the first time in my life I'm where I want to be, except..."

"Except for Angela." Johnny finished for him. "Well, I guess the only thing left for me is to keep the ship running. It's down in the engine room for me. At least down there I won't be able to hear the name, Angela, every five minutes. Come on Phibies, let's get some chow."

Joseph Francis Panicello

7. Slow Moving Target

The following morning most of the crew, including the *Five Phibies*, went down the gangway and climbed on board the back of four trucks that were waiting there and were driven to the canteen.

In the conference room Chief Turner introduced the speaker. "Men, this is Lieutenant Goodday. He's going to lecture you swabs on all aspects of the LST. I want yous to take notes on any subject that pertains to your work station."

The Lieutenant stood up to the podium and said, "Thank you Chief. Men, I'm going to use slides to help me explain the operation of an LST. If you have any questions during my lecture, simply raise your hand and I will answer you as best as I can, right on the spot. I want this to be a group participation and not just a cold presentation from me.

"First, a few details about the LST. It's 308 feet long and has a beam (width) of 50 feet. It has a load displacement of 4,080 tons, and could provide accommodations for 13 officers and 106 enlisted men. Its sides are about 15 feet above the water line, but the bow is 20 feet high to confront the open sea.

"The super structure and pilot's house are located toward the rear portion of the ship as shown on this slide. There is a high navigation bridge or conning tower above the pilot's house to oversee the sea up front. The pilot's house, sometimes referred to as the wheel house, is below and in front of the bridge. The top forward main deck is flat and very long, and has the capacity to carry lighter cargo such as trucks, jeeps and even aircraft."

A hand was raised at this point and Johnny asked, "Sir, if aircraft are on board the main deck, how do they get them on to a beach?"

"Good question. The answer is they don't. The only reason an LST would carry aircraft on board is to transport them to a port. You see, the navy commanders don't like the idea of an LST going from San Diego to Hawaii empty handed, so they

A Slow Moving Target, The LST of World War II

may have aircraft and other cargo stowed on board to be delivered to a pier in Hawaii or even Australia where they will be removed with cranes by longshoremen. There are some LSTs that are modified to be equipped with a runway to launch a small reconnaissance aircraft, but this will not be discussed today."

Lieutenant Goodday looked around for more questions and since there were none he continued. "There are at least seven officers on board and each has a specific function. In the Conning Tower is the commanding officer's station or Captain. The Signal Bridge, which is located after the Conning Tower, is the communications officer. Below the Conning Tower and in the wheel house is the executive officer who is also the navigation officer.

"The rest of the officers are the gunnery officer in charge of the artillery and all weapons, the supply officer who is in charge of the ship's supplies and the stern anchor, the engineering officer in charge of the engine rooms, and finally the first lieutenant who is responsible for loading and unloading cargo. Some LSTs may carry up to 13 officers depending on the ship's assignment."

Danny asked, "Sir, who's in charge of opening the bow doors, and dropping the ramp?"

"If you are assigned to the bow doors and ramp switches, you will get your orders from the Petty officer in charge at that station who, in turn, will be getting his orders from the commanding officer in the Conning Tower over the intercom. At every station there will be an assigned seaman with earphones to communicate with the Captain and another seaman to operate the bow doors and ramp switches."

With no questions, Lieutenant Goodday continued, "The lower forward tank deck resembles a long tunnel which has the capacity to carry heavy duty vehicles such as tanks, tractor trucks, and artillery. During an assault, after all the lower deck vehicles have been discharged onto a beach, the upper deck vehicles will be lowered by elevator one at a time to the tank deck and subsequently driven ashore."

Joseph Francis Panicello

Another question from Johnny, "Sir, how many trucks can they carry on the main deck?"

The Lieutenant was pleased with the questions thus far and answered with a smile, "I can see you men are very much interested in the operation of this ship. I'm glad because it is a very important vessel.

"On the main deck the LST can carry thirty-three 2 1/2 ton trucks, or 17 DUKWS, or 17 LVTs. The trucks can be stowed five abreast on the main deck. If an LST is equipped with a special ramp between the tank deck and the main deck the DUKWS can drive up to the main deck when it is being loaded through the bow ramp from shore. Not many LSTs have this capability, however. Generally, an elevator is used to lower vehicles from the main deck to the tank deck. The tank deck can hold 10 heavy tanks, or 20 medium size tanks or 39 light tanks, three abreast.

"Some LSTs will carry an LCT on its main deck or they may carry prefabricated water tight sections of LCTs as separate parts for one LCT and a third of another LCT. These water tight sections will be assembled in the water close to their destination to become a complete LCT and ready for war. It's amazing what the navy can do using these LSTs."

"Sir, does the LST carry troops?" asked Andre.

"Yes it can. Along each side of the ship, under the main deck, there are two long compartments that provide bunks and toilets for up to 165 men and 20 officers of which some will man the vehicles that are on board. If necessary, these compartments can accommodate 300 fighting marines or soldiers. On short runs, over a hundred troops can be carried on the main deck.

"During an invasion these troops may be deployed ashore by either using small boats, tractor tanks, trucks, or on foot running down the bow ramp as you can see from this next slide. Those marines, as shown, are fully packed and will be running down the ramp and onto the beach as fast as they can to get out of danger."

A Slow Moving Target, The LST of World War II

Another question was asked, this time from Rich, "Sir, what protection do the marines have from enemy fire when they go down that ramp like that?"

"Unfortunately, they don't have any. They are wide open and exposed to the enemy counterattack coming from above the shore line. The only protection they could have is to follow close behind the tanks and DUKWS that are going up toward the beach ahead of them. These vehicles will be firing at the enemy as they move up the beach. Also, as shown on this slide, the LST does provide fire power against the enemy to support the troops from these gun turrets located above the bow doors.

"This particular LST, as seen here, carries seven single 40 mm guns and twelve 20 mm guns. Some of the newer ships carry many more guns. For further protection while cruising, as shown at the stern, there is a fog generator which can be used to create smoke screens to help the LST hide from an enemy ship or a submarine that is lurking in the area."

The lieutenant paused for a moment for a drink of water and then continued, "The crew's quarters are located at the stern of the ship and has the capacity to accommodate most of the LST's deck hands and engine room gang which consists of one hundred or more sailors. It is a very large compartment located under the main super structure and just under the upper deck but level with the side compartments. The galley is in another compartment located just forward of the crew's quarters.

"The deck hands use the bunks on the port side of the crew's quarters while the black gang, engine crew, lives on the starboard side. With these separations, I have to admit, sometimes there is friction between these two groups and, inevitably, it has caused some pretty good fist fights. If either side doesn't pass inspection, for example, liberty may be cancelled for all crew members. It wouldn't take much for a turmoil to flare up between the deck hands and the snipes (engineers) especially if liberty were cancelled.

"I don't understand why you sailors are always fighting. It is my experience that fighting between crew members is almost a

Joseph Francis Panicello

bi-weekly exhibition while in port. I can't understand why you hate each other. Maybe it's because you have been restricted on the ship too long. I don't understand it. As far as I'm concerned, we are all in the same navy but for some reason you always seem to get into fist fights.

"The seven or more officers on board, including myself, usually don't interfere with the fights because our state rooms are above decks and in the super-structure. We can't hear the commotion going on down below, and we don't particularly care to know. The only one that might be concerned is your Chief Turner. The last thing he needs is his men going to the sick bay on shore with broken noses and such."

The chief interjected, "I may have to bust a few heads myself if they wants to fight. You swabs had better save your fighting for the Japs!"

Bob piped up and said, "Why don't they just settle their disputes in the ring at the gym on the base?"

"Don't ask me," grinned the Lieutenant. "I notice that many of the fights begin over gambling. I must warn you that gambling is frowned upon in the navy." The Lieutenant looked over at the chief who simply shrugged his shoulders. He knew that it was impossible to stop the men from playing craps or poker.

The Lieutenant continued, "The standard LST has a flat bottom hull which allows it to be driven up and onto a sandy beach close enough to shore to deploy its cargo. Its bow doors would open before it reaches the shore and a huge ramp would be lowered to provide a solid path for tanks and trucks to be deployed onto a beach. Food and ammunition will also be unloaded either by hand or by trucks having the goods already stored in their beds."

Over the years in combat, the one weakness Amphibious craft had during an invasion was unloading their goods and moving them to a safe supply depot. It wasn't the design of the ship as much as the design of man. It seems, on many invasions, there weren't enough men available on the beaches to do this task because the fighting soldiers and marines considered

A Slow Moving Target, The LST of World War II

themselves warriors and not cargo carriers, and refused to unload. The sailors operating the small landing craft would simply drop their stores on the beaches and quickly leave for their own safety. Those few that remained to unload were constantly being fired upon by the enemy and were in a no win situation until the enemy was driven far enough inland to secure the beach. Unfortunately, in the early part of the war, the Generals and Admirals were more concerned about an invasion itself and never considered the menial task of unloading and storing the cargo.

The Lieutenant proceeded with his presentation, "Before an LST is to be beached during an invasion, a rear anchor will be dropped at the stern of the ship at a specific time as it approaches the beach. The object of this anchor is to help pull the LST back out and off the beach by reeling it in with a capstan, and with the support of the main engines running at full speed astern and its screws in reverse. This is the only way an LST can pull itself off of the beach and out into the open sea. It's quite an operation but it does become much easier after the ship is unloaded of its heavy cargo making the bow lighter and not wedged into the sand.

"Driving the LST onto a beach at full speed ahead is much more difficult because of prevailing winds, tides, and break waters. These factors will, invariably, push the LST off of its course and possibly beach itself at a different location intended. This task, of course, is the responsibility of the captain and his officers, so you won't be so much involved, but you should understand the circumstances.

"Notice the stern of the LST on this next slide. In back of the crew's quarters there is a huge motor powered capstan that is used to reel in the rear anchor. The cable for the rear anchor is a 900 foot galvanized wire halzer that has a mark every 100 feet. You must record how many marks, or every one hundred feet, have been released. This is important."

A sailor raised his hand, "How will we know when to drop the rear anchor, sir?"

Joseph Francis Panicello

"You will be notified over the intercom from the bridge. The officer at the wheel house will give the order to drop the anchor to the Supply Officer who is in charge of the stern anchor and he, in turn, will give you the signal to drop it."

With no questions the officer continued. "There are two large engine rooms located below the super-structure and tank deck which take about one third of the ship's lower area. The two engine rooms require almost the entire width of the ship. The main engine room is aft of center. Those engines indirectly drive the long shaft that is connected to the ship's propeller or propellers. The main engine room has two very large GMC eight cylinder Diesel engines that are connected to a gear reduction system which turn the screws that propel the ship.

"Some LSTs have twin propellers but your ship, LST 142, has only one screw. Twin screws do provide more maneuverability while docking and landing, but a single screw is more than adequate to do the job so you don't have to feel bad about being left out. If, however, your ship is equipped with twin screws, then one engine will drive the starboard screw and the other will drive the port screw. With this arrangement the captain can actually maneuver the ship using different engine speeds, with one propeller rotating faster that the other.

"The main GMC engines run at a very high RPM (Revolutions Per Minute) to create the necessary power for cruising and to beach the ship. By using the gear reduction technique the screw or screws turn at a much slower revolution thus providing a substantial mechanical advantage and torque from the engine to the propellers."

The chief decided to ask a question, "Sir, what's the difference between the operation of this engine compared with that of an automobile?"

"Good question, Chief. The same technique is used on many four cylinder automobiles. They increase their horse power at the wheels by using high RPM motors and a five speed transmission. On an LST it's called gear reduction instead, but the same principles apply."

A Slow Moving Target, The LST of World War II

The Lieutenant looked around for more questions, then continued with his presentation, "The gear reduction system on an LST is also used to reverse the main screws.

"Some amphibious craft are equipped with low RPM engines such as the Fairbanks Morse Diesel engines which uses little gear reduction. When these Fairbanks Morse engines are running at cruise speeds one can actually hear each cylinder firing. Some LSTs, such as LST 325, use two 12 cylinder Diesel engines for their main power. Other LSTs use twin Pielstick Diesels, which I'm not familiar with. I don't have a list of all the different diesel engines that are used on LSTs, but I'm told there are quite a few.

"Now, at this time, we will take a five minute break."

The men piled out of the conference room for a smoke or to drink a coke. Johnny had listened keenly to the lecture and said to Rich as they walked out together. "I guess there's an awful lot to learn about our ship. What'a you think, Hinny?"

"I'm just wondering who our gunnery officer will be. I hope he's a veteran and not a new dumb recruit," was his only concern.

"Yeah, but what about the operation of the ship? Don't you care about all the details he's telling us about? I think it's really interesting."

"What for? That may be your responsibility. Remember, I'm striking to become a gunners mate. It don't matter to me what ship I'm on. My job will be to shoot down as many Japs as I can. You guys worry about the ship's operation, just as long as we don't get sunk. This ship sounds more like a SMT than an LST."

Johnny, looking puzzled, said, "SMT? What's that?" thinking he had missed something.

"Slow Moving Target," Rich whispered, as they filed back into the conference room together. "Think about that, Macaroni!" he intoned, as they settled into their chairs so Lt. Goodday could resume the lecture.

Joseph Francis Panicello

8. Class Resumes

After the men settled in LT. Goodday continued. "The forward engine room contains three axillary engines that are used to provide electrical power to the ship. When the ship is normally cruising, only one axillary engine is fired up. During combat and beaching, a second axillary engine provides the power to electrically open or close the bow doors and lower or raise the ramp. When the ship is pulling out and away from the beach this same second engine provides the electrical power to reel in the rear anchor and help pull the ship out to sea. The third engine provides the electrical power to the many sea pumps that are used to ballast the ship for different maneuvers.

A question was asked, "Sir, why does the LST need all this ballast capability?"

"For several reasons. One is to trim the ship so that the bow is high enough for beaching. Another reason is to drop an LCI, for example, over the side by tilting the ship. Ballasting a ship is more of an art than a science, believe me, especially when dropping an LCI or an LCT.

"As I said, during normal LST cruising only one auxiliary engine is used at a time and they are alternately powered up to spell one another thus extending their operating lives.

"Overall, it's a complicated ship and the designers knew their business. Operating the doors and lowering the ramp during an invasion are very complicated tasks by themselves. All of these maneuvers have to be accomplished under duress because you will be fired upon by a hostile enemy. I don't wish to alarm you, but many LSTs become dead ducks during an assault. They are very vulnerable because they are large slow targets at sea, and while they are sitting on a beach they are a stationary target because of the slow process of unloading their cargo before they can evacuate the ship and get out of danger. This is war, men, and the troops on shore are depending on your cargo, so your captain will have to decide when to leave if you are being attacked." Johnny and Rich exchanged glances at this.

"The procedure to beach an LST is difficult enough and many conditions have to be considered. The captain must know the slope of the beach, the character and contour at the bottom of the sand, the surf condition, the tidal variations, the wind conditions, and finally if there are any obstructions on the beach such as disabled small craft. The captain also knows that the best time to beach an LST is at high tides. The variation of the tides are crucial when beaching a craft.

"To illustrate tide variations near the equator, let me explain an unusual experience I had. My LST was docking at Balboa, Panama, and I was the engineering officer in the main engine room. After the ship docked I decided to go ashore so I showered, shaved and dressed in my officer's whites. I headed for the hatch to go ashore, but to my surprise, I was staring at the dock pilings. I looked up and noticed that the gangway was now up on the pilot house deck and across to the pier. Late that night, however, after I returned from liberty, I noticed that the main deck of the LST was now ten feet above the pier. The variation in tide from the afternoon to that night was well over 25 feet." The men chuckled as the mental picture sank in.

Lieutenant Goodday continued, "Variation of 20 feet or more in tides are critical especially with small craft landing on a beach. Normally, when a small craft lands it immediately pulls out after it drops its cargo, so the tide is not a factor. But sometimes, when a small craft is heading toward a beach in an assault, the coxswain may be killed. He is very vulnerable when beaching because he has to be able to see where he's going with his head above the front ramp. When there is a counterattack he may have to duck down to avoid being hit by gunfire. This, of course, will obstruct his vision.

"Under these conditions, every once in awhile, the coxswain may rise up and peek to see if his craft is still heading for the beach and make the necessary correction. Unfortunately, sometimes he could get hit by a bullet. When this happens the craft may be stuck on the beach waiting for another coxswain to take over or be towed out. If it remains there too long it cannot be moved at all due to a low tide. It will have to wait for the tide to rise again because the boat will now be completely out of the water."

"Question, Sir?" coming from Bob. "Isn't there more than one sailor on board a landing craft who could take over the coxswain's position?"

"Not on the smaller landing craft such as the LCP. On larger boats such as the Higgins boats, the answer is yes, there are more sailors on board who can take over the coxswain's job.

"The LST, of course, has a similar problem with the tide, because it usually takes eight hours or more to unload its cargo. A 25 foot tide in the South Pacific is common, which could delay the LST's departure because half of the ship is now resting on the sand. But then again, it can change its ballast to raise the bow even higher and it might still be able to pull itself out.

"Now let me discuss what goes on aboard an LST during an invasion. When the LST is about three hours away from an assault, it will begin its procedure to prepare for a landing. First, General Quarters will be sounded for the crew to man their stations and their guns in case there is an enemy aircraft attack.

"The armored tanks and other vehicles below must be checked out and their engines started to insure that they will still operate after the long cruise from the States. This is accomplished by opening up 37 ventilators on the main deck that are connected to the tank deck and by turning on many huge exhaust fans to expel the CO^2 coming from the vehicle exhaust fumes. After the vehicles are checked out they are then shut down and its crew will go back to their quarters to wait for the final assault signal to be sounded.

"Any more questions?" There was one from the rear.

"Sir, why don't these men just remain there if they're in the process of an invasion?"

"Well, three hours is a long time to wait and in many cases the assault signal may be delayed even longer because of enemy

A Slow Moving Target, The LST of World War II

gunfire or some other reason. There is no need for these blowers and engines to be running if the assault is canceled, for example. That was a good question, by the way.

"During the time of cruising the LST is trimmed to draw 18 feet aft and 8 feet forward. When the ship is to be beached the 16 ballast tanks throughout the ship are used to trim it to 9 to 10 feet aft and 3 to 5 feet forward so that the bow is now high enough to slide across the sand. This maneuver, by the way, answers one of the earlier questions of why the LST needs all those ballasts.

"Let's take a break for lunch. Talk it over with the rest of your crew members and maybe you can come up with some more questions. It is very important that you understand every aspect on the operation of an LST, because your lives may depend on it. So far your questions have been good."

As the men walked through the doors and down to the canteen their voices filled the halls. Some hurried through lunch, eager to get back and hear more about this strange ship they were unfamiliar with. In their enthusiasm, very few were thinking clearly enough to realize what danger they would face when they finally took her into battle. There was a chatter of voices as they discussed the different aspects of this ship, the duties they were to perform and which assignments each would be given. They all had preferences so competition would be rough as they vied with each other over the coming weeks to secure the position each wanted.

The *Phibies* were subdued. Every now and then Johnny and Rich would exchange glances. Johnny couldn't forget those ominous initials, *SMT*, Rich had used when referring to the ship. Rich wanted more than ever to go to gunnery school. He was beginning to feel a fierce protectiveness about LST 142.

Andre, in spite of himself, was wondering about medical equipment and other procedures on the LST while Danny sat, already convinced that he should be the man assigned to operate the bow doors and the ramp.

Joseph Francis Panicello

Bob sat quietly, watching each man in turn. He had paid close attention to every bit of the lecture. He hoped to hell that this crew would be a credit to the ship.

After lunch the lecture resumed. "To prepare the doors to be opened, three men have to go down a forward manhole to undog the doors. This is a difficult task in itself because the ship is bouncing around and these men have to first unbolt the beams that secure the doors with large wrenches and then they have to use large ratchets that control a small crane to stow the beams out of the way. The last step they have to perform is to unhook the pelican hooks which keeps the doors from opening during cruising speeds and over high seas. All this effort requires strength and agility from these men because they have to swing from place to place in the bow like monkeys."

Danny decided to ask a question and stood up. "Sir, you say that these men have to be strong and agile? In that case, that lets out little runts like you on this operation, Robber," pointing to Andre with a smile on his face.

The crew began laughing but Andre wasn't. He raised his fist at Danny as though he was challenging him to a fight.

The Lieutenant, smiling, said, "Okay men, let's stick to the subject. When the bow doors are cleared and undogged, ready to be opened, a 'Condition One Mike' alarm is sounded. Army or Marine Corps troops will then man their armored tanks and trucks, but first they must remove all latching chains and stow them out of the way. They will start their engines again and be ready to drive down the ramp and on to the beach. The exhaust blowers will now be running continuously throughout the assault.

"When 'full speed ahead' is commanded by the captain, the throttle man controlling the main engines will respond to the captain's orders by using the chain driven return signal and slowly moving the throttle to a full speed position for both engines. A good throttle man will know when both engines are running at the same speed by the sounds of the engines and by observing the RPM gauges on the front panel. If the engines are

A Slow Moving Target, The LST of World War II

running at different speeds the throttle man will detect a hunting sound instead of an equal and continuous sound from both engines which will sound like there is only one engine. Is anyone here a throttle man?"

Johnny piped up and said, "I'm hoping to be, Sir. My name is Maroni."

The lieutenant asked, "Have you ever experienced this hunting sound of the engines while cruising?"

Johnny answered, "Yes I have, Sir. It's more of a feel than a sound, isn't it? I can't explain it unless one is down in the engine room and feels the throttles for himself and listens to the background noise. It does take a special talent."

"I thought so. Many engine men have told me this but I have to admit I've never experienced it. Thank you, Mr. Maroni. As you can see, men, it is even more important to control the engine RPMs when your LST is equipped with twin screws. Mr. Maroni sounds like he has what it takes to operate those throttles."

After Johnny sat down the Lieutenant continued, "The next thing that happens is the command for the bow doors to be opened. After it is accomplished the ramp is lowered to about 6 feet above the water line. Steering the ship to a particular landmark with wide open doors and with the ramp half way down, and using the ballast to keep the ship in trim becomes quite a chore for the captain and his quartermaster. The wind and surf also plays hell on a landing.

"The stern anchor is then dropped when the beach separation from the ship is 2 to 2.5 times the ships length or 600 to 750 feet away from shore. Every 100 feet of the rear anchor cable is recorded to insure that the 900 feet limit is not exceeded. If it is exceeded the LST will be dragging the rear anchor or it could cause the ship to stop too soon."

"Question, Sir. Has this ever happened?" coming from a sailor in the front row.

"Unfortunately, yes. It has happened quite often, especially when you're in a battle and in the middle of a storm. It's hard to

Joseph Francis Panicello

tell where the beach begins and the anchor could be dropped too soon or even too late, which is just as bad.

"When the LST is finally grounded and on the sand the bow ramp is then dropped completely onto the beach allowing the tanks to be driven off first, then the half tracks, followed by trucks pulling cannons."

Danny raised his hand and asked, "Sir, has there ever been a case where the bow doors didn't open or the ramp was stuck?"

"Yes, there has. On one ship that I was on the bow doors were only half open, so the crew had to use ropes and chains to open them and tie them back. I haven't heard of a ramp ever being stuck, however. The ramp is very heavy, and when it's released, gravity will bring it down pretty quick.

"After the vehicles have disembarked from the tank deck, the ship must be re-trimmed by shifting its ballast again because the load at the bow has now been reduced and the ship must be held down onto the beach so that the rest of the cargo can be unloaded from the main deck. While this is going on, the main deck vehicles are being prepared to be lowered to the tank deck, one by one, using its large elevator. These vehicles are then immediately driven off and onto the beach as well.

"This whole operation of unloading should take no more than eight hours but it sometimes takes longer, especially if the LST is being fired upon by the enemy or they are experiencing foul weather. We had one LST that took three days to unload because it had to leave the beach due to heavy gunfire from shore and then a heavy storm came up."

Another sailor raised his hand and asked, "Sir, what if a vehicle stalls in the tank deck and blocks the rest of the vehicles. What should we do?"

"Remove that vehicle as soon as possible either by pulling it to the side or by pushing it overboard. This does happen, by the way. We had a case where the lead tank stalled on the ramp and wouldn't start. The second tank simply pushed the first tank down the ramp and out of the way. We lost the use of that tank but we did manage to unload our cargo. On the tank deck the

A Slow Moving Target, The LST of World War II

vehicles are usually spaced in three lines across so if a tank is stalled in the line the others may be able to drive around it. But the ramp can only accommodate one tank at a time.

"When the beach has been secured, your LST may remain there to receive casualties, but if it's in danger the captain may give the order to pull out. This does happen often in an assault and many poor wounded soldiers or marines are left on the beach waiting helplessly for your LST or other small craft to return.

"This now concludes my presentation. Are there any more questions?" There were none. "In that case you are all dismissed."

The crew were then taken back to LST 142 by the same trucks. Most of the *Five Phibies* were impressed with the session, especially Olsen, who had a more serious attitude about the operation of an LST. He would make a good officer some day.

9. Early History

Amphibious assaults to a beach in the past have always been one of the most difficult tasks of all military operations. Their attacks go back to early Greco-Persian wars of the fifth century B.C. It was difficult then and it wasn't any easier at the start of World War II. The eminent British strategist Sir Basil H. Liddell Hart concluded in the 1930s that "technology had rendered future amphibious invasions almost impossible."

A small group of Americans disagreed with Sir Hart. They began developing a doctrine for a Joint Amphibious Operations and worked on a plan for conducting amphibious operations. A document was produced in January 1934, the *Tentative Manual for Landing Operations.*

Fleet Landing Exercises became an annual event off the Southern California coast which were conducted from 1935 through 1941. As a result of these exercises, in 1937, it was determined that special landing craft were needed because the ordinary small boats released from ships were unsuitable for the rapid landing and deployment of the large numbers of assault troops and vehicles needed.

Marine Lt. Victor Krulak, who was serving in China, reported that he saw how the Japanese were able to launch a full-scale assault on China with landing craft. If the truth be known, the Japanese were way ahead of the U.S. in landing craft design at that time. American bureaucrats said Krulak's report was the work of "some nut out of China."

In 1938, a "Special Boat Plan" was adapted and various types of experimental amphibious boats were being introduced. Marine Gen. Holland Smith was one of the first to be instrumental in the development of assorted amphibious landing craft. At that time most naval commanders were not anxious to go all out for amphibious craft because there were endless problems in landing them successfully. The navy's attitude against amphibious craft "made Smith's blood boil."

A Slow Moving Target, The LST of World War II

After Krulak witnessed how the Japanese built their landing craft, he built a wooden model of a ramp-bowed landing craft and showed it to Smith. Smith said, "That's it," and went to show it to his commandant. His efforts were not received well. *Time* magazine dubbed him as 'howling mad.' Eventually Smith won out.

The first landing craft was a small LCS (Landing Craft Support) which had armed machine guns mounted on it to provide fire support for other landing boats. The next was the small LCP(R) which had a ramp to deploy personnel, and later the small LCM or Landing Craft Mechanized which was used to deploy a tank, a truck or a tractor. The LCP(R) and the LCM were both built by Andrew Jackson Higgins. The Amphibious Boat and Tractor (LVT) was then developed by Donald Roebling. It could maneuver over water like any power boat and then drive onto a beach like a tank on its tract wheels, even over coral reefs. These became available in July, 1940.

As an interim measure, three medium-sized tankers were converted to landing craft with bow doors. They proved their potential in the invasion of Algeria in 1942, but they were inadequate and an all-out design was required.

A meeting was held between the Admiralty of England and America and it was decided that the Bureau of Ships would design the vessel.

From information printed in the L.S.T. Scuttlebutt newspaper, the preliminary plans initially called for an LST to be 280 feet in length, but in January 1942, the Bureau of Ships discarded this length in favor of 300 feet. The final configuration called for 328 feet in length and a 50 foot beam. The LST could carry a 2,100 ton load of tanks and vehicles. The bow door opening was 14 feet high to accommodate most Allied vehicles. The British Admiralty then requested of the U.S. delivery of 200 LSTs for the Royal Navy, under the terms of lend-lease.

The first LST was laid down in Newport News, Virginia, but the need for more was so great that steel fabrication yards were converted for LST construction. Of the 1,051 LSTs built during

Joseph Francis Panicello

World War II, 670 were constructed by five major inland builders.

In the L.S.T. Scuttlebutt newspaper, as part of an article written by Gene Owens, Jack Niedermair described his father's roll in designing the original LST.

He wrote; "Churchill desperately needed an ocean-going vessel that could take troops and heavy equipment right up to the beach. The British asked the United States for help in designing and producing such a ship. The request was forwarded to John Niedermair, my father, who was then with the U.S. Navy's Bureau of Ships. My father worked out the basic design in a half-hour. He took it home that night and in his private drawing room, he sketched out the details. The next day the plan was flown to England."

In 1945, the senior Niedermair was awarded the Distinguished Civilian Service Award, the Navy's highest honorary award. He also contributed to the designs of the Essex-class carriers and the nuclear submarines, but the LST was his most rewarding achievement. He died in 1982.

From the publication "Our Prairie Shipyard," the Chicago Bridge & Iron Co., claimed that a major contribution in the development of the LST came from Admiral E. L. Cochrane, Chief of Bureau of Ships. It's obvious that the Admiral, who represented the navy, worked with Niedermair on this project.

In 1941, a prototype LST landing craft was developed, as well as the LCI (Landing Craft Infantry) and the LCT (Landing Craft Tank). Later the LCVP (Landing Craft Vehicles or Personnel) became available which was originally designed by Andrew Jackson Higgins in New Orleans. It was sort of a floating cigar box that could carry 35 men in full gear or a vehicle right to the shore line and release them quickly. During the war 20,000 of these Higgins boats were built in New Orleans to hit the beaches in Normandy, Iwo Jima, Guadalcanal, and dozens of other Pacific islands. Today there is a D-Day Museum in New Orleans honoring these extraordinary Higgins Boats as well as other D-Day amphibious displays. In addition, a project

A Slow Moving Target, The LST of World War II

is currently under way to honor Andrew Higgins and his LCVP in his birth town of Columbus, Nebraska, sponsored by the American Legion, Post No. 84.

In an open letter to the L.S.T. Scuttlebutt, Joe Butcko, wrote: "Andrew Higgins does deserve credit for designing the LCVP but another man was neglected in many articles about that ship. He was Preston Tucker, owner of the Ypsilanti (Michigan) Machine Tool Co. This is the same man who introduced the Tucker Torpedo Automobile in 1951. A movie was made "Tucker, The Man and His Dream," portrayed by Jeff Bridges. Tucker's company was responsible for the development and manufacture of the Tucker marine engine for the Higgins LCVPs". Joe Butcko worked for Tucker in 1942 before he received his greetings from the government in 1944. In the navy he was assigned to LST 862 and became coxswain on an LCVP during an invasion.

The LCI was a British design but built in America. The LCI is 160 ft. long and 23 ft. wide. The LCT is 203 ft. long and 34 ft. wide. In 1943 the LSM was developed which was ocean going and could carry 5 medium tanks or up to 9 DUKWS (amphibian motor-lorries), sometime referred to as Ducks. An LST could stow on its top deck several LCAs that could be placed over the side using portable derricks, or it could stow a 203 foot LCT that could be put afloat by heeling the LST sideways with its ballast and dropping it into the water.

There were several LST variations used in the war. LST 776 was outfitted for launching and recovering spotter planes. LST 16 was used as an aircraft carrier with a long runway mounted over its main deck, used generally for army artillery spotter planes. LST 19 had an LCT on her main deck. Thirty-eight LSTs were converted to serve as hospital ships. On D-Day in the invasion of Normandy 41,035 wounded men were brought back across the English Channel on LSTs.

An LCT doesn't have the capacity to power itself across the ocean and has to be either piggy-back carried on an LST or towed close to the assault area. It can also be carried in water

Joseph Francis Panicello

sealed sections by an LST to be assembled closer to the target area.

LST 556 carried a pontoon causeway on her starboard side which was used to deploy cargo and troops when sand bars or corral reefs prevented the LST from reaching the beach. LST 341 also had a LCT on her main deck. LST 341 received the Navy Unit Commendation for its "gallant record of service" in transporting vital supplies to amphibious forces participating in the Solomon Islands campaign from March, 1943, to May 1944.

The LSTs could even carry the 160 foot LCI on its main deck and launch it into the ocean by tilting the LST on its side using its ballast pumps. The LCI was designed to deliver more than two hundred infantrymen directly onto the beach from its bow ramp. The LCI had its own power and the capacity to cross the ocean, which is not at all like the larger LCT that was designed to carry many more tanks and troops over a shorter distance.

At the start of the war, Secretary of the Navy, Frank Knox, called Admiral Ernest King to his office. When they settled down Knox asked King, "Ernest, I have something important to ask you. Now that we are in the war we need a Naval Commander to run the entire fleet in both the Atlantic and the Pacific theaters. He must be strong, able to work with the Army, Marines, and with the Joint Chief of Staffs here in Washington. Ernest, have you anyone in mind that you could recommend for this job?"

King thought it over for a moment and answered, "I can't say that I can, Mr. Secretary. It will be a major responsibility, whoever takes on the assignment."

Frank Knox then said kiddingly, "Well, since you can't recommend anyone, I guess I'll just have to give you the job. Congratulations, Ernest. I'm offering you the position of Commander in Chief of the entire United States fleet." The secretary was half-smiling.

Admiral King was astonished at the offer. He certainly didn't expect it. "I accept the job, Mr. Secretary." He thought for a moment then added, "There is one thing. I must insist that my headquarters be located here in Washington D.C., rather than out at sea."

"Fair enough, Ernest," replied Knox. "Anything else?"

"Well, yes. I also want to have access to the president's office at any time." He wasn't so sure this would be acceptable.

"It's fine with me, Ernest, but you'll have to get permission from the president. He may refuse you."

President Roosevelt was approached with this last request and readily agreed. At the same time, King was informed that Admiral Chester W. Nimitz would be his new Commander in Chief of the Pacific Fleet.

In 1942, King turned sixty-four and completed his forty-first year as a naval officer. His father was a seaman, a bridge builder, and later a foreman in a railroad repair shop. While working with his father, Ernest learned about the complexities of machines.

After graduating fourth in a class of eighty-seven from the Naval Academy, King pursued a career with surface ships, submarines, and naval aviation. He could be belligerent at times and somewhat tactless and arrogant to his subordinates, but was dedicated to any assignment given him. He once commented, "You should be very suspicious of anyone who won't take a drink or doesn't like women."

Charles Deison, in 1940, the previous Secretary of the Navy, was impressed by King's ability, and wrote to President Roosevelt that the Navy needed a new commander in charge, to forget about the "peace-time psychology." He wrote: "The man who could do it is Rear Admiral Ernest J. King."

Almost a year before the raid on Pearl Harbor, in January 1941, King was promoted to Rear Admiral of the Atlantic Fleet. Shortly after the Pearl attack, the new Secretary of the Navy, Knox, commissioned him to be the Commander in Chief of the entire U.S. Fleet, making him the naval leader of all United States Naval Operations throughout the world, including ship building.

Joseph Francis Panicello

King considered the war in the Pacific more important than the Atlantic but when Churchill came to town he swayed President Roosevelt by saying, "Mr. President, the German war should have priority. If we don't stop Hitler now he will have control of all Europe, Africa and possibly Russia. Now is the time to strike back."

Obviously, the British were more concerned with the German war because it was closer to home. Admiral King finally concurred with Churchill's approach that the defeat of the Germans should be first. However, in his heart, the Pacific was still more important to him. He also knew that he couldn't outmatch Churchill's diplomacy and the friendship he had with the President.

By March, 1942, 90,000 American soldiers were transported to the Pacific theater, 57,000 men went to Australia, while many more were sent to Hawaii. The North Pacific and the South Pacific commands were assigned to Admiral Nimitz and the Southwest Pacific command was under the jurisdiction of General MacArthur.

Admiral King was unquestionably the main authority over the entire fleet, in charge of all operational forces and the massive shipbuilding program. Later that month, King ordered Nimitz to San Francisco for their first of many wartime meetings.

He told Nimitz, "Chester, my first instructions to you, as the Pacific fleet commander, is to begin preparing for amphibious offenses in the Pacific."

Nimitz replied, "Thank you, Ernest. I've been waiting a long time for this. I'll begin planning as soon as I get back to Hawaii."

A struggle between the requirements of the Atlantic and the Pacific for amphibious craft began. When the U.S. joined the war General Marshall asked Lord Louis Mountbatten, "How can we get into this game as soon as possible?"

Mountbatten's reply was, "Double all the orders you've already given for landing craft." Mountbatten was obviously

A Slow Moving Target, The LST of World War II

describing the need for a special landing craft that could put 250 soldiers on shore at once which was the LCI, a British design.

President Roosevelt, in addition, ordered the construction of 300 Landing Ship Tanks (LSTs) and 300 Landing Craft Tanks (LCTs). The best estimate of assorted landing craft needed to land in France in 1943 was 765 ships. The Navy planners decided in 1942 that the Pacific alone would require 4,000 assorted landing craft. Unfortunately, in January 1942, landing craft in Washington remained number eight in priority, far behind destroyers.

President Roosevelt then exercised his authority as Commander in Chief, overrode the Pentagon, and directed the Bureau of Ships to deliver 600 LCTs by September 1, 1942. By July the need for landing craft increased again, to 12,000.

Training the Army and Marines in amphibious landing became the next most important factor. The original schedule for landing exercises was to take place on Cape Cod but, because there was a menace from U-Boats on the Atlantic shores, the landings were rescheduled to an area near the Chesapeake Bay. This plan proved unacceptable because army units were unable to land on their assigned beach due to the turbulent weather.

Admiral Holland Smith needed a better training site and selected the island of Bloodsworth, which was safely within the Chesapeake Bay and not affected by the stormy ocean seas. With this move, it became the first amphibious gunfire training range. Bloodsworth Island is in the center of Chesapeake Bay, in the state of Maryland. To train the amphibious craft on the west coast the Navy bought 132,000 acres of brush-covered California land and beach shore property north of San Diego, now known as the Marine base at Camp Pendleton.

The friction between the Navy and the Army continued. On March 26, 1942, Rear Admiral Richmond Kelly Turner, now chief of War Plans Division, wrote to King saying, "It is a far different matter attempting to establish advanced bases in the Solomons." He was, apparently, against assaulting the Solomons.

Joseph Francis Panicello

He was siding with MacArthur, who was against the invasion of the Solomons. Turner urged King to appoint a commander for the South Pacific and to provide him with amphibious troops. On March 9, the Joint Chiefs of Staff, composed of Admiral King, General George C. Marshall, and General Henry H. Arnold, all knew that General MacArthur had enormous national popularity which made him the obvious choice for such a command. King objected to giving this power to an army officer but no naval officer was acceptable to the army over MacArthur. It was almost a deadlock.

The first orders from King to Nimitz was to seize Talagi Island in the Solomon Islands. But before this could take place King found himself in a dispute about who should command this assault.

Douglas MacArthur, at this point, revealed his true intention of trying to take over the entire Pacific war. He submitted a plan to Roosevelt which read, "We should conduct a full scale offense that will be launched from Australia against the Philippines." His plan was rejected by the Navy and by King.

The Military Chiefs considered MacArthur's scheme impractical and beyond America's capability. MacArthur didn't believe that the Solomons were a suitable starting point. The arguments went on until General Marshall said to MacArthur, "George, don't you think you ought to fight the Japanese instead of the navy?"

It was finally decided that Nimitz would command the assault on the Solomons and New Guinea, and MacArthur became the commander of the South Pacific area, including Australia and the Philippines. The dispute was momentarily settled but MacArthur would not give in so easily on other assaults. The final decision was that General Marshall would give his orders to MacArthur for the army, and Admiral King would give his orders directly to Nimitz for the navy.

The assignments for the *Five Phibies* on LST 142, were given out by Chief Turner after they spent two months at the pier in Norfolk, Virginia. Bob Olsen became a deck hand and later a

A Slow Moving Target, The LST of World War II

coxswain. He was sent to navigation school and after he graduated he was classified a Third Class Boatswain Mate.

Because Danny Bletcher was big and strong the Chief said, "Belcher, your main assignment is operating the bow doors and ramp." This wasn't an easy task and required a man of strength and agility. Danny accepted the assignment with pride.

Rich Hienman talked to Chief Turner about his own preference, saying, "Chief, I've had a lot of experience with guns hunting in Texas, I'd like to be a gunner."

The chief, believing him, sent Rich to gunnery school to learn all there was to know about navy weapons. When he returned three months later he was rated Third Class Gunners Mate, assigned to be in charge of all of the ships artillery but still reporting to the Weapons Officer. He then had to use his talents to teach young, up-and-coming Gunners Mate strikers the art of shooting cannons and machine guns.

Rich was later regarded as the best crack shot in the Amphibious Fleet. The LST 142 skipper, Captain Quincy Hull, after finding out about Hienman's talents, treated him as though he was one of his officers and gave him special privileges such as never standing any watches and free liberty whenever the ship was in port. His marksmanship proved to be outstanding, and shooting down enemy aircraft during combat turned out to be his specialty.

Andre was a little guy, and not very strong. The Chief, at first, didn't know what to do with him. He found out, after questioning him, that his father was a doctor so he said to him, "Robber, report to Doc. Smith," actually the Chief Pharmacist Mate. A smaller vessel, such as an LST, doesn't rate a full-fledged medical doctor.

Andre Robbier didn't like this assignment. He had already refused to go to medical corpsman school. His reply to the Chief was, "But Chief, I don't want to work in the sick bay, I want to be a seaman." One growl from Chief Turner changed his mind rather quickly.

Joseph Francis Panicello

Johnny Maroni asked the chief, "Could I be assigned to the engine room gang, Chief? I did work in a gas station working on cars and in the garage as a mechanic's helper for the Green Bus Line in Queens, New York."

Chief Turner agreed with him and filled out the necessary papers for the captain to transfer him to the engine room gang. His assignment, as a fireman, would be to participate in the normal engine room duties while cruising but also to be the sole engineer on any small landing craft that was deployed by the LST during an invasion.

Johnny didn't make waves about his duties, especially the part about an invasion. He rather liked the idea of being with the troops during an assault. He also had to learn from Hienman how to operate the machine guns which were mounted on both sides of the small craft. He was later sent to Diesel engine school and graduated as a Third Class Motor Mechanic.

Some LSTs carried LCVPs Higgins Boats (Landing Craft Vehicles, Personnel) on board when the troop transports (APA) were not available. When these LCVPs were launched, Johnny would be assigned as the engineer. He would also have to fill in with other duties in case either of the gunners mates was killed or incapacitated. He even had to practice being a coxswain in case of an emergency.

There were usually four sailors on such a small landing craft; a coxswain, a starboard gunners mate, an engineer, and a bow man who was a gunners mate striker. The bow man's job is to release the ramp lock before beaching and then man the port machine gun before the craft hits the beach. All four sailors have to know the other man's job.

10. Heading For San Diego

On December 20, 1942, all leaves on board LST 142 were canceled. Johnny was disappointed because he had no leave after he finished Diesel Engine school, but was involved in the special training on board. He had been looking forward to going home for Christmas since he hadn't seen his family since he completed boot camp.

With no leave, Danny and Andre immediately began writing letters to Angela expressing their devotion to her. They promised to continue to write to her no matter where they ended up.

Rich also wrote letters to his mother and sister. Rich had two younger twin brothers under sixteen who would be eligible for the draft in a couple of years, and a sister a year older, whom he adored. She was exceptionally attractive but because she was needed to help work on the farm she neglected her appearance and never really had the chance to meet a boy. Most days she pinned her long blond hair in a bun, but when it was free it was shiny and silky. Her amber eyes sparkled with vitality and working outdoors left a permanent blush on her high cheek bones. Her lean body was strong and agile, enabling her to do all but the most arduous chores. She loved horses and spent any free time she could find riding over the vast, open land surrounding the ranch. The idea of victory gardens amused her because she had always had one and was proud of the produce she provided for the family.

Rich had had to assume most of the responsibilities on the ranch after his father died in 1938. He tried to limit the butchering of their own livestock because that was their only staple cash product. Through the years he became a proficient hunter and the pheasant, rabbit and deer he brought home were a welcome addition to the family diet.

By 1941 the ranch was running smoothly again. Rich was torn between his responsibility at home and his desire to be part of the drama unfolding overseas. His mother reassured him,

Joseph Francis Panicello

sending him off with a teasing remark, "In a year your sister will be the best rancher in the family."

LST 142 left port for San Diego at 1200 hours. Johnny noticed on the bulletin board that he had the 8 to 12 shift in the main engine room. He also saw that Rich had the same watch but in the Pilot House. At this particular time the captain didn't know he had a prize gunner and Rich was just another Gunners Mate on board. Johnny wandered over to visit with Rich on the port side of the ship and noticed a picture of his family on the inside door of his open locker. He asked, "Is that your sister, Hinny?"

Rich stood up and walked over to his locker, held the picture in his hand and replied, "Unfortunately, this is an older picture of Dolores. She's much prettier than that. She's one year older than me but we are very close. I hated to leave her with all the responsibilities of the farm, but my country comes first. My twin brothers, I'm sure, will help her."

Johnny, looking at the picture, was impressed. Dolores. "What a nice name," he thought. Out of work and no future to look forward to, Johnny had never gotten serious with any one girl. If he did fall in love his requirements would be pretty conservative. She would have to be a fairly religious person with strong family ideals. She didn't have to be beautiful. Her personality was more important to him than her looks. The girl in the picture was pretty. Johnny wanted to know more.

Rich explained, in his Texas drawl, how it was on the farm and how tough it was to make ends meet, especially after his father died. Quietly he said, "I never spoke of my father before. He was killed helping a neighbor farmer operate a new power tractor. The tractor flipped over an embankment and landed on my Dad. It was awful. Now that I'm in the Navy, the responsibility has passed to Dolores."

When Johnny walked away to his own bunk he began humming to himself a popular Bing Crosby tune, "How I love the kisses of Dolores. I, ya yaah, Dolores." He knew he was

A Slow Moving Target, The LST of World War II

acting peculiar. "Hell, I never met the girl," he reminded himself, "but she sounds wonderful."

LST 142 was now heading for the Panama Canal. She wasn't loaded with cargo at this point in time but at her final destination in California she would undergo a series of maneuvers to train the crew on beach landings, and how to deploy its cargo quickly. No one on LST 142 had ever beached a ship before so the task would be an experience for everyone, even the captain and his officers.

In Panama, at Balboa, the *Five Phibies* had liberty. They marched five abreast down the streets singing navy songs. They frequented several bars, drinking, having a great time. Danny became belligerent and began arguing with a marine. Within minutes the *Five Phibies* were in a fist fight with a bunch of marines. The Shore Patrol was called in and all the Phibies ended up in a brig.

LST 142 was to sail the next morning. It took some doing for the Executive Office of LST 142 to have them released. An LST has a much smaller crew than a destroyer and every man is essential. The Captain restricted the *Five Phibies* to the ship for one week after they hit the next port.

Johnny and Andre were sporting eye shiners from the ordeal. Bob thought he had a broken rib but it was only bruised. Rich was sure he had a broken jaw but Andre assured him it was just swollen. Andre then looked at Danny and said, "You started the damn fight and you don't have a mark on you. What gives?"

"Well, I know how to handle myself. You think I'm going to let a dumb marine mark me up. I'm saving my pretty face for Angela."

Andre then responded, "What would Angela want with a dumb, brawling ox like you?"

Danny was getting mad, "Listen, you little punk. Angela is my girl. Next time I catch you near her I'll punch your lights out."

Andre wouldn't back down, "Yeah, jerk. You don't scare me. There's a lot of equalizers around here. You come near me

Joseph Francis Panicello

with your fists and I'll crack your head wide open with a marlin spike."

Johnny jumped up and separated them. "Listen you guys. We're supposed to be buddies. Save your anger for the Japs."

Johnny, at this point, wished he had never introduced either of them to his sister. As things quieted down, Johnny turned to find Rich standing dumbstruck, a letter in his hand.

"Hinny, what is it? Something wrong at home?" Johnny asked.

Rich shook his head slowly, a dazed expression on his face. "Dolores has gone to California," he answered quietly. "She's living in a place called Burbank, wherever the hell that is, sharing a place with another gal. They work at Lockheed, an aircraft company, on an assembly line. Bombers, she says."

"What about the ranch?" Johnny asked.

"Everything's fine. The boys and Mom are handling it." Rich shook his head again, this time in anger. "When we hit port I'll get to the bottom of this, Johnny. She says she wants to get into the movies. The whole world has gone crazy, Macaroni!" he exclaimed, leaving abruptly.

Johnny, staring after him, began to smile. "Dolores in California," he thought, pleased. San Diego was going to be more exciting than he had originally thought. Suddenly he couldn't wait to get there. Humming "How I love the kisses of Dolores" he headed off for the engine room.

LST 142 finally made port in San Diego at the Coronado Island naval base. The Phibies had a week of restriction before they would be granted liberty.

Time passed slowly but the restriction did allow them to wonder around the base. The five of them headed down to the pier to observe all the different ships that were tied up there. They went to the Canteen to drink 3.2 beer or take in a movie. They spent the majority of their time swapping stories and playing cards with others on the base.

When the restriction was over the *Five Phibies* dressed in their navy whites and headed for a ferry to take them across

A Slow Moving Target, The LST of World War II

Coronado Bay to the San Diego harbor. Rich made a phone call, then called Johnny to the side and said to him quietly, "Macaroni. Let those guys go on alone. You know what will happen. They'll get drunk and Belcher will start another fight with the marines. I've got a couple of dates lined up. What do you say? Come with me."

Johnny was unsure. He felt responsible for all the Phibies. He wanted the guys to stick together. But he liked Rich a lot, so he reluctantly agreed. After the ferry landed Johnny and Rich sped off and picked up a bus that went to downtown San Diego. When they arrived at the bus stop they were met by two girls waiting for them, dressed to kill. One girl ran over to Rich and threw her arms around him, hugging him fiercely. She wouldn't let him go. Johnny assumed that she was Hinny's date and that the other girl was for him.

Rich and the girl finally separated and he said to Johnny, "I want you to meet my sister, Dolores."

Johnny was confused and visibly astonished. She couldn't be the little girl that he'd seen in that picture over Rich's locker. Rich then said to his sister, "Dolores, I want you to meet my best buddy, Johnny Macaroni."

She giggled and asked Johnny, "Is that your real name?"

Johnny explained, "No, that's just my nickname. My real name is Maroni. If you think that's funny, we call your brother Hinny." Both she and the other girl giggled together.

Dolores then introduced her friend and said, "Boys, I want you to meet my roommate, Mildred Stone."

Mildred was a knock-out with her long auburn hair laying on her shoulders and down her back. She was tall at five foot-eight and had a voluptuous figure. She was actually an aspiring movie actress and had had some parts in "B" movies. She came from a small town in Iowa, where she had helped on her father's farm. She met Dolores at Lockheed's plant and they became good friends.

When Johnny realized Dolores was his date his spirits soared. "She's so pretty," he thought. Her blond hair was no

Joseph Francis Panicello

longer in a bun as it appeared in her picture, but hanging free in soft waves. The same high cheek bones, great smile, and with those high heels Johnny was looking straight into her amber eyes, which mesmerized him. Johnny had not known the color of her eyes. At a loss for words he said, "Hi," and shook her soft hand with his firm grip.

He didn't want to let go but then warned himself, "It can't happen now. I can't fall in love at this point in my life. It's too soon. There's no future with me." He attempted to suppress his emotion, feigning a nonchalance he didn't feel.

Dolores glanced at Johnny and was impressed with what she saw. His cap, pushed to the back of his head, exposed his wavy brown hair. His tailor made whites fit perfectly, revealing a strong, muscular body. When her eyes rested on his hazel eyes she couldn't tell whether they were blue, brown, green or purple. Each eye had different shades of greens and blues and each time she looked into his eyes, she found it hard to look away.

Johnny was used to this. His eyes were truly unusual. One time, when he was on a bus going to Jamaica, a young lady walked up to him while he was seated and asked him, "Sir, I don't mean to rude but could you tell me what color your eyes are?"

Johnny, at first, thought she was trying to pick him up and replied, "I don't really know, exactly. I think they're hazel."

She continued to look deep into his eyes and finally said, "Oh," and just walked away.

Another time, a middle aged female doctor was examining him for a sore throat and after she gave him a prescription she left the room. As Johnny began putting on his shirt the woman doctor returned and walked right up to him and began examining his eyes. She place her hands on both sides of his face and began looking at one eye and then the other, back and forth. She then walked away. Johnny at first didn't know what to make of it but then realized she just wanted to see what color his eyes were. He grinned to himself.

A Slow Moving Target, The LST of World War II

At first he was embarrassed by the compliments he received from women but eventually he learned to shrug it off. His eyes seemed to have a powerful impact on women.

Dolores didn't say a word and eventually looked away. She could feel herself blush. She had vowed that nothing would interfere with her ambition to become a movie star. "This is not the time to get involved with a sailor who is going to sea and may never return," she thought, trying to convince herself.

Rich knew Johnny was captivated by his sister. He also liked Johnny a lot and if Johnny and Dolores hit it off he wouldn't mind a bit. He was actually playing the part of Cupid in this meeting, hoping something would come of it.

Ever since receiving Dolores' letter, Rich had been consumed with anxiety over the idea of Dolores on her own in California. Added to that was her ambition to break into the movies, an ambition that few realized. Dolores had never been an impetuous person and Rich wondered how long she had cherished this dream. He didn't want to interfere but he was hoping that perhaps with him and Johnny being close by he could watch over her.

Rich had another problem. He was immediately fascinated by Mildred. She was, without doubt, the most beautiful woman he'd ever met. As they chatted Rich realized their backgrounds were very similar. Mildred had a knack of putting him at ease and the conversation flowed easily.

The foursome took a cab to a restaurant on Harbor Island where the atmosphere presented a perfect setting for young people getting acquainted. It overlooked the bay which had a few private sail and power boats moored there. Johnny was having a hard time trying not to be too obvious, glancing over at Dolores occasionally. He couldn't help himself. She was definitely a pretty sight to behold.

When the small band at the restaurant began playing a fox trot, Johnny asked her to dance. Dolores looked at Mildred apprehensively. "What should I do?" her look said. Rich and Mildred grinned broadly and urged her on. Shyly, she accepted.

Joseph Francis Panicello

As she stepped into his arms she felt her shyness disappear. A feeling of warmth engulfed her, as his arms tightened around her. She heard him whisper "Oh my Dolores" as they began to dance. She cuddled a little closer and neither of them spoke another word.

Rich, pleased at the way things were turning out, said to Mildred, "It looks like my sister and Macaroni are hitting it off. You want to try it on the dance floor?"

She said, "I'd love to." Mildred wasn't as shy as Dolores and cuddled right up to Rich with her cheek touching his.

After dinner they went to the girls' hotel where they were staying overnight. While the radio played Mildred and Rich danced. Johnny and Dolores sat, hands entwined, listening to Frank Sinatra sing "It Had To Be You" with Tommy Dorsey's band.

Reluctantly, Johnny and Rich knew they had to bring the evening to an end. Both couples seemed totally oblivious to the other as they shared a last, few minutes.

Both men were smiling as they made their way back to the ship.

On the way back Rich asked Johnny, "Well, buddy, what do think of my sister?"

Johnny's answer sounded unsure and confused, "I think she's great, Hinny, and I could easily fall in love with her. But isn't it foolish? I mean, what if I'm killed or severely wounded. I can't get serious with a girl, at least not just yet."

Rich, more jovial, answered, "That's okay, buddy. I understand. I'm having the same problem with Mildred. Let's play it one day at a time. At least we have a girl to write to."

11. Wake Island

Wake Island is an atoll in the central Pacific Ocean, and before the war it was an unincorporated U.S. territory administered by the U.S. Air Force. After Pearl Harbor it was occupied by Japan from 1941 to 1945. The island group consists of three wishbone-shaped atolls; Wake, Wilkes, and Peale, which are less than 10 miles long and barely above sea level. Our government officially designated Wake as a bird sanctuary.

Wake Island was never assaulted by the American Amphibious forces during the war, but its story is included here because it is located in the Pacific and was originally controlled by American forces until they were invaded and conquered by Japanese troops right after Pearl Harbor. The island, after that, was controlled and maintained by the Japanese military throughout the war.

The Joint Chiefs decided to bypass these islands and invade the Solomons instead because Guadalcanal could be used by the Japanese as a military base to invade Australia. The problem was that the American prisoners on Wake were overlooked by the planners and were never rescued. After the Japanese invaded Wake Island they imposed a great deal of brutality on American prisoners captured there, and their story must be revealed lest they be forgotten.

In 1941, before Pearl Harbor, 452 U.S. Marines of the 1st Defense Battalion, commanded by Major James P.S. Devereux, were there to defend the island. Also on the island were Marine fighter squadron VMF-211, which was equipped with 12 Grumman F4F-3 Wildcats, lead by Major Paul A. Putnam, 71 Naval personnel, and 1,146 American construction workers, managed by Dan Teters, all under the overall leadership of Commander Winfield S. Cunningham. Their objective was to complete an airstrip and a defense fortification.

The morning after the attack of Pearl Harbor, on December 8, 1941, Wake Island was assaulted by the Japanese

Joseph Francis Panicello

Government. Wake Island is 2,000 miles west of Hawaii, and could have been used for American heavy bombers to strike the Japanese controlled Marshall Islands.

Without warning, 36 Japanese Mitsubishi G3M2 Nell bombers flying in three V-formations at two thousand feet began dropping their bombs and, using their machine-guns, tore the island to pieces. They were later joined by Japanese aircraft carriers who pounded Wake Island day after day. American Wildcats rose to meet them but, eventually, all of the American aircraft were destroyed. Fifteen days later, 10,000 Japanese naval infantrymen assaulted the island and were able to seize it.

Cunningham, as the ranking officer, seeing how hopeless it was to continue the fight, made the decision to surrender. In the attack, the Americans lost 88 Marines, 8 sailors, and 82 civilian construction workers. It cost the Japanese much more with two destroyers, one submarine, seven ships damaged, and 21 aircraft shot down. Approximately 1,000 Japanese men were killed. The Americans put up a good defense and imposed a great deal of damage on the infuriated Japanese.

Enraged by their loses, the Japanese treated their prisoners cruelly. The Americans were stripped of their clothing and jammed into two suffocating concrete ammunition bunkers. After a few days a Japanese commander returned their clothes and announced, "The Emperor has graciously presented you with your lives."

A Marine said, "Well, thank the son of a bitch for me!"

Later on, the real brutality began. Most of the prisoners were transferred to a merchant ship headed for China and were crammed into the ship's hold. On the merchant ship the prisoners were abused by the Japanese sailors, hit with clubs, fists, and heavy belts. The Japanese left 380 American prisoners on Wake Island to rebuild the islands defenses. They slaved for two years, until October 1943. At that time the Japanese garrison murdered them all.

On board the merchant ship, the brutality continued. Five selected prisoners were assembled on the ship's deck to demonstrate to the 150 Japanese sailors on board how Japan avenges their dead troops.

The Japanese commander announced to the prisoners, "You have killed many Japanese soldiers in battle. For what you have done you five are now going to be killed...as representatives of American soldiers."

They were then told to kneel down and one by one they were beheaded. Their bodies were then used for bayonet practice before being thrown overboard.

In China in a Shanghai War Prison Camp, 500 of these prisoners were routinely beaten and fed poorly. Each of the Wake Island prisoners lost at least 60 pounds. The worst Japanese offender was Isamu Isihara, a civilian interpreter who enjoyed beating the helpless Americans and, in some cases, killed them with a samurai sword.

A survivor, Sergeant Bernard O. Ketner recalls, "I was severely beaten by Isihara. He stuck me with his saber four times and kicked me twice in the testicles."

Many others died from illness, untreated battle wounds, and malnutrition. Some others died even more violently. In June 1942, a civilian prisoner was shot to death while a soldier was playing with his gun. Others were killed just for the joy of it.

Despite the fact they were prisoners, Major Devereux insisted on maintaining military standards for the men. He insisted they exercise regularly. Although the men disliked Devereux's methods, they eventually believed his efforts helped them stay healthy enough to survive until the end of the war. When Devereux confronted the Japanese about the Geneva Convention and the way his men were being treated, the Japanese claimed, "Japan did not sign the Geneva Convention."

The brutality continued until the spring of 1945, when Americans began receiving shipments of food and medical supplies. Their captors realized the war was winding down and the guards began making occasional friendly gestures to the prisoners. They were, obviously, afraid of American retaliation to the treatment American prisoners of war had had to endure.

Joseph Francis Panicello

In July 1945, Japanese officers invited American officers to a formal dinner. A senior Japanese officer stood up and proposed a toast and said, "To the everlasting friendship between Americans and Japan."

The American reply by Major Luther A. Brown was, "If you behave yourselves, you'll get fair treatment."

The "Bataan Death March" was another example of Japanese brutality where American prisoners were unmercifully beaten and murdered after they were captured in the Philippines. Before the Japanese invaded Bataan there were over one hundred thousand people in Bataan to feed, including civilian refugees. The caribou disappeared first, then 250 horses, then 48 pack mules followed by iguana lizards and monkeys.

American troops at Bataan surrendered on April 9, 1942, and the death march began. If a soldier fell to the ground from exhaustion he was shot to death. If a Japanese soldier wanted a GIs ring and he objected, the Jap simply chopped off his finger, ring and all. If a GI crawled out of line for a drink in a pool of water a Jap would smash his head with his rifle butt and split his head open. Some ten thousand American soldiers died on that march.

Unfortunately, many of these Japanese soldiers who had brutally beaten and killed Americans, especially on Wake Island, were never punished for their atrocities, as some Germans were for the war crimes they had committed in Europe.

The Geneva Convention rules of war were often violated by both the Japanese and Germans in World War II. Americans, on the other hand, were much more lenient with their prisoners and did not torture and kill them for pleasure. As a matter of fact, many German soldiers welcomed being captured by the Americans rather than being captured by the Russians so that they could get a square meal and be safely out of the war.

German prisoners brought to the United States because of their knowledge and skills in sensitive areas of industry were well taken care of while waiting for placement in jobs by their

A Slow Moving Target, The LST of World War II

protective sponsors. Later, it was quietly arranged to give these prisoners United States citizenship.

Since the end of the war the United States has shared diplomatic relations with these two countries and was instrumental in getting them back on the road to prosperity.

Even though the brutality against the Wake Island prisoners was known to the American military, American Amphibious forces did not assault Wake Island. Had they been invaded by the Americans the 380 prisoners left on the Wake Island may have been saved. Even though the U.S. continuously bombed the island they never assaulted it because it was no longer considered a strategic island by the JCS. In September 1945, Rear Admiral Shigematsu Sakaibara, the last Japanese commander on Wake Island, surrendered the island to America.

The prisoners of Bataan had to wait years for the American forces to recapture the Philippines. There was still fighting in the highlands when World War II ended.

---

*The author personally witnessed how well German prisoners were treated. Captured in Europe and brought to America between 1944 and 1945, they were all well fed, over-weight and were happy working in the chow hall of a Naval Hospital in Norfolk, Virginia, where the author was a patient. It certainly wasn't the way the Germans had treated American prisoners in Europe. The author's brother, Tommy, during the battle of the Bulge, witnessed how many American prisoners, hands tied behind their backs, were executed by the Germans.

12. First Amphibious Assault

On June 27, 1942 Admiral Nimitz issued orders to assault and seize two of the main islands in the Solomons, Tulagi and Guadalcanal. The assault would be known as Operation Watchtower. The Joint Chiefs split the Pacific into three sub-commands, the North, the Central, and the South Pacific. Nimitz retained direct command of the first two, and King requested that Nimitz recommend a naval officer for the South Pacific. Nimitz recommended Rear Admiral Robert L. Ghormley, still in London. King promptly selected the fifty-nine year old Ghormley as the South Pacific naval commander.

The responsibility for the assault in the Solomons was now on the shoulders of Admiral Ghormley who had no experience in amphibious warfare. His service career included destroyers, battleships, and many important staff assignments but never amphibious landings. His post in London was Special Naval Observer for the U.S. He was a large, dominating man, intelligent, and respected by his fellow officers. He was well liked, but was very reserved and didn't socialized much with the other officers. He had one major weakness. He too often sided with Gen. MacArthur instead of his naval boss.

The Solomon Islands were discovered by the Spanish Explorer Alvaro de Neyro, who named the islands. In 1893 a British Protectorate was established on Guadalcanal and Malaita. Before World War II, the Japanese captured the Solomon Islands and later fought the Americans bitterly for them in the Battle of the Coral Sea.

Admiral Ghormley agreed with General MacArthur's objections to the Solomon operation and they radioed their opinions, together, to the Joint Chiefs of Staff, "The situation of this operation is, at this time, without a reasonable assurance of adequate air coverage and during each phase would be attendant with gravest risk."

A Slow Moving Target, The LST of World War II

Both he and MacArthur stated that, "It would be a gloomy task because there would be insufficient air coverage and the Japanese capability of destroying the American air power and troops is, at this period, very successful."

They jointly sent a message to Admiral King and recommended that this operation be deferred. Also, Admiral Stark, who had been there before, said, "In no way was the Pacific Fleet to show any interest in the Solomons."

Admiral King would not budge. He told the doubters that the operation would work especially when Admiral Holland Smith said it would. In any event, Watchtower, the name given to this assault, would be a desperate gamble but King knew it had to take place.

Because of Ghormley's position, Nimitz relieved him of his command of Task One and it went to both Vice Admiral Frank Jack Fletcher and Kelly Turner, who had long sought action in Guadalcanal in the Solomons. Ghormley was given the command as Strategic Task Force in Person which designated the New Caledonia and New Hebrides area. It seemed that Nimitz lacked confidence in Ghormley's role in this operation which was, no doubt, a very great gamble. Ghormley considered "Watchtower" second in priority and he was not behind what he perceived to be a dangerous invasion of Guadalcanal. Going against his senior officers and siding with the army cost him his job.

Maj. Gen. Alexander Archer Vandegrift was given command of the 1st Marine Division and when he arrived in Auckland on June 12, he was told he had just six weeks to train his men. He was expecting six months. He responded by saying, "Maybe we can make up in guts what we lack in training." It turned out that loading and unloading the transports was their most difficult training exercises. This aspect of an invasion became a continuous weakness throughout the war.

Major General Vandegrift was fifty-five years old in 1942. He had a sturdy build and a handsome face. He generally spoke in a soft voice with a Virginia southern drawl. One of the first

Joseph Francis Panicello

things he did when he received his assignment was to consult an atlas to find out where he and his men were going.

Adm. King's timetable lagged behind because only five ships could be accommodated at the pier at Hawaii at one time and because there weren't enough longshoremen to load the ships. Three hundred marines, with no prior experience, had to be enlisted for that task. Loading became a nightmare when attempted around-the-clock, in the rain. The ships to be used for Watchtower originally came from different locations; San Diego, Norfolk, San Francisco and Pearl Harbor, and were to rendezvous at Karo Island in the Fijis because it was located only 1,100 miles from Guadalcanal.

Many officers were uncertain about this assault, which became a major concern with the army. On Guadalcanal and Tulagi, the Japanese strength was expected to have 8,400 enemy troops. To make matters worse, Adm. Fletcher announced that aircraft carriers under his command would provide only two days of air cover instead of the five that were needed to unload. He was scheduled to support MacArthur on the third day.

Vice Adm. Frank Fletcher was commander of Task Force 61, which led the convoy through the sweltering heat, while Marines below deck horned their bayonets, rolled dice, and played a record of "Blues in the Night."

Fletcher was leery about his new assignment after having lost two carriers, the *USS Lexington* and *USS Yorktown*. Both were sunk right out from under him.

Other problems came up. There was friction between Turner and Gen. Vandegrift on the number of marines to be used in the assault. Turner reluctantly agreed that he would give the transports and cargo ships four days to unload. Admiral Turner had 475 small landing craft stacked on his transports and only a third of the marines on board could make it into the limited number of small landing boats at a time. This meant at least two round trips had to be made by the landing boats to bring all the marines to shore. They definitely needed more landing boats.

A Slow Moving Target, The LST of World War II

The marines on the transports laid in their bunks, or nervously checked the cartridges in their machine-gun belts. They griped about the food, the heat, and the mission. One marine complained, "Whad'da we want with a place nobody ever heard of before?" Another marine said, "Yeah, who ever heard of Guadalcanal?"

A Marine sergeant answered, "Guadalcanal is part of the 900 mile long Solomon Islands, located in the South Pacific just east of New Guinea. If the Japs control it then we gotta take it from them. The Admiral knows what he's doing, so shut up!"

August 7, 1942, became the first American offensive of World War II. The navy planners decided that island hopping was the best way to go on the road to Japan. Guadalcanal was chosen to stop the advancing Japanese, who were building up to invade Australia.

Up until now the Japanese had not tasted a single defeat. They were invincible, it seemed. By now they had control of the Philippines, the Dutch in the East Indies, the British in Burma, Mayaya, Singapore, and Hong Kong. New Guinea and Australia were next. New Guinea is the second largest island in the world, next to Greenland, and up until now it acted as a buffer for Australia against the Japanese by having a large defensive force there. The island was an equatorial hell to fight in, with 16,000-foot mountains, Stone Age cannibals, and some of the thickest jungles on the planet.

The intent of the Japanese was to use Guadalcanal as an air base that would be within striking range of many of the eastern Allied controlled islands such as New Hebrides, New Caledonia, the Fijis, and Samoa.

MacArthur and Nimitz both finally agreed that the island of Rabaul in New Britain, located on the northwest side of the Solomons and next to New Guinea, was a Japanese stronghold that threatened Australia. MacArthur wanted to attack Rabaul directly, assuming he would have command of the assault. From the Navy's point of view, this plan would be disastrous because American aircraft carriers would be easy targets for the Japanese.

Joseph Francis Panicello

The Joint Chiefs of Staff in Washington solved this disagreement by separating the area of command into two tasks. Nimitz was to attack Guadalcanal and Tulagi while MacArthur was to seize the western Solomons including Lae and Salamaua.

Tulagi is just 20 miles north of Guadalcanal and is part of the Florida Islands. Tulagi is a small island about 2 miles long and half a mile wide. The island has been the seat of the British Solomon Islands Protectorate of Government structures including the Governor's House of Residency. The Japanese garrison in Tulagi consisted of 3,500 men under Commander Suzuki.

The assault on Guadalcanal and Tuiagi on August 7 caught the Japanese completely by surprise. Seventy-six assorted ships arrived off the shores of Guadalcanal, including twenty-three amphibious ships ready to disembark 23,000 marines. The first American amphibious assault of World War II began at 0613 hours when the guns from cruisers and destroyers began bombarding the coast of Guadalcanal.

Twenty minutes into the battery the order was given, "Land the Landing Force" which sent the marines clambering down rope nets over the sides of transports into the small landing craft below. The nets were made out of webbing rope which were used as a rope ladder for the men to get into amphibious boats that were bobbing up and down with the swells. It was quite a stunt for the marines carrying eighty pounds of equipment on their backs, trying to step into a bouncing boat.

Up to fifteen men could be accommodated on these landing craft which had been stacked on top of one another on board the parent vessel. These boats were early versions of the LVT, which could drive over offshore reefs, and by using their tracker type wheels, could travel beyond the beach to the tree-line. The Americans quickly adapted the LVT design as the most desirable small landing craft.

When all of these amphibious boats were in the water they were told to assemble in one area in the bay in a wide line formation. After the signal for all craft to attack was given, a flag of Red-Yellow-Red was displayed on the flag ship informing all the boats to head for the shore line. As they approached the beach many of the marines became seasick from the choppy seas.

To protect the marines from enemy fire, warships poured 1,500 rounds of shellfire into the area and additional bombs and gunfire came from dive bombers that knocked out Japanese gun positions, ammo, and supply dumps. Unfortunately, a few marines were also killed from friendly fire by the wayward bombs from the inexperienced American bombers. Despite all of the difficulties encountered, 11,000 marines landed on Guadalcanal. The American casualties were a bit high as one in ten marines were killed or wounded and one of our destroyers was demolished.

Once ashore the marines were faced with repeated counterattacks by the enemy. As the cargo was being brought ashore on a twenty-four hour basis, air raid warnings were sounded constantly throughout the day causing cargo ships to cease unloading and retreat out to sea. It was a tedious process to unload the transport ships. The cargo had to be lifted by crane out of deep holds of the transports and onto small landing craft. Once on the beach the cargo had to be hand carried from the boats to a temporary storage area.

One officer commented that unloading and storing was a picture of confusion and disarray. Coxswains mistakenly brought food rations to beaches marked fuel. Medical supplies and ammunition were mixed together. Sailors did not help because they maintained that their job was to bring the stuff ashore and it was up to the marines to get it off the beach. But the fighting marines refused to move the material. One marine said to a non-combating sailor that was helping unload the cargo, "Hell, we're combat troops. You unload the goddamn stuff."

By nightfall there were 100 landing craft on the beach waiting to be unloaded and 50 more laying off shore waiting their turn to land. Most of 1st Division's supplies were piled high

Joseph Francis Panicello

on the Guadalcanal beaches and became an easy target for Japanese aircraft.

Then the finger pointing began. One captain of a transport ship blamed the marines. The marines claimed there should be special organized details to do the unloading. No one was trained for this task. Troop commanders were more concerned with establishing safe beach positions than unloading the cargo. The transport ships were continuously being attacked and their unloading was disrupted by the Japanese raiders. An oiler had remained at sea and could not refuel the landing craft because they were in danger from Japanese air attacks. No one even mentioned the more serious responsibility of attending the wounded.

The 'Watchtower' assault on Guadalcanal became a hard lesson. Not only were the procedures for unloading inadequate but air support and cannon fire from the ships off shore, meant to protect the troops on the beach, were poorly carried out.

During the morning of August 9 a Japanese cruiser, under the command of Gunichi Mikawa, was able to elude American destroyers and came upon U.S. support forces. In three-quarters of an hour his cruiser was able to destroy four heavy American cruisers off Savo Island. Fortunately, Mikawa was happy with his strikes and left to save himself knowing that he would be attacked at daybreak. The U.S. Navy suffered the loss of the carriers *USS Hornet* and *USS Wasp*. Also lost was the *USS Juneay* which was carrying the five Sullivan brothers. After that catastrophe, brothers were not allowed to be on board the same ship.

To the delight of the American command, Mikawa did not attack all of those dead-duck transports or the smaller amphibious forces sitting offshore, unprotected. If the transports had been sunk, the 1st Marine Division would have been destroyed. Many of the sunken cruisers' crews were lost, buried at sea, but several hundred sailors survived.

Halsey was considered a hard drinker and a fighting sailor. After taking command he had a large sign erected on his ship

A Slow Moving Target, The LST of World War II

which read KILL JAPS, KILL JAPS, KILL MORE JAPS. He was definitely a mean-spirited person when it came to the enemy. He called the Japs monkeys. "I call them monkeys because I cannot say what I would like to call them." His presence alone would dramatically change the operation in the Solomons.

Admiral Kelly Turner learned the hard way from what happened at Guadalcanal and immediately set forth a series of orders to his amphibious forces beginning with; "Each will now hold four rehearsals before reaching the transport area. Shore parties will be the first men on the beach, to be drilled thoroughly in all aspects of preparation."

Guadalcanal was an important battle that taught the Navy and Marine Corps much about amphibious warfare. It also taught the Navy that unloading supplies using transports and small landing craft was not the best approach. The need for large landing craft, such as the LST, was essential, because it could land right on the beach to unload its tanks and trucks by carrying its stores in their truck beds.

On Guadalcanal the Japanese and American land forces battled for six months. In an unusual situation, one banzai Jap charged Gen. Vandergrift as he walked through the jungle but was shot dead by Vandergrift's clerk typist, who pulled out a 45 pistol in the nick of time.

Before Guadalcanal was secured by the Allies, they had lost a considerable number of cruisers, destroyers and carriers. However, the Allies forced the Japanese to revert to a defensive posture.

Guadalcanal became a huge cemetery. The Japanese lost 25,000 men, the Marines reported 1,420 killed, and the U.S. Army suffered 550 dead.

By February, 1943 Guadalcanal was won. After the war, many years later, independence was granted to the Solomans by the British on July 7, 1978.

Admiral Nimitz was deeply upset with the whole assault and decided to relieve Admiral Ghormley again and replaced him

Joseph Francis Panicello

with Vice Adm. Halsey. William F. Ghormley's continuous position of siding with MacArthur was Nimitz's last straw. He said, "If he wants to side with the army then, Goddamn it, he should have joined the army."

13. North Africa

In the Atlantic campaign, the first amphibious assaults were in North Africa in Algiers and Morocco, against the Vichy French who were in command and who had sided with the Germans to defend these lands against any invaders. It was a peculiar situation, Americans fighting against the Vichy French while the free French were our allies. The invasion of Africa was called Operation Torch.

After the Vichy French regime surrendered to the Germans they collaborated with them and rejected General Charles De Gaulle's call to arms. He was denounced by the Vichy leaders and was sentenced to death as a rebel. De Gaulle remained in England and formed the Free French movement. He dispatched his leader, Colonel Philippe Leclerc, to Africa on June 27, 1940, to fight against the Vichy French. The Free French caused quite an uprising opposing the Vichy French regime.

The Americans sent agents in submarines in advance of Operation Torch to determine whether the Vichy French leaders would allow the Allies to just walk in without worry. On Torch D-Day, November 8, 1942, Marshal Henri Petain, the Nazi puppet in Vichy France, broadcast a message to the French troops in North Africa.

"France and her honor are at stake. We are attacked and we will defend ourselves. That is the order I give."

Against the Americans, the Vichy French had 60,000 troops in Morocco, who were unsure of fighting against the Allies. The principal American commanders involved in the African campaign were Rear Admiral H. Kent Hewitt and Major General George S. Patton.

At a conference in Washington D.C., an unknown officer at that time, Major General Patton, had a poor view of the Navy's ability to put his troops on a predetermined shore area.

He told the assembled naval and civilian audience, "Never in history has the Navy landed an army at the planned time and

Joseph Francis Panicello

place. If you land us anywhere within fifty miles of the target and within one week of D-Day, I'll go ahead and win." His statement was probably the first time the media had ever become aware of the boastful personality of this great general.

Eisenhower, frustrated with the American performance at Kasserine Pass in Africa, replaced Gen. Fredendall with Maj. Gen. Patton. When Patton attacked he told his commanders the night before, "If we are not victorious, let no one come back alive." His advice to his men was, "Grab the enemy by the nose and kick him in the pants."

The landings in Africa were made when LSTs were still not available and the Allies soon learned why they needed those large amphibious ships to unload tanks and trucks quickly. In the African campaign, it was necessary to capture ports so that they could use their piers to unload the heavy armor from the transports, but as soon as LSTs became available the immediate need of capturing ports became unnecessary.

During the invasion, the French Vichy troops were in a state of confusion, but their shore batteries commenced firing thirty minutes after the first Allied landing and the Vichy Navy put up a good fight against the Allied Naval forces. The French battleship *Jean Bart,* although moored in the Casablanca harbor, was able to drop a salvo of bombs on the Allied ships. Several Vichy French cruisers, destroyers and submarines were ordered into action against the Allies.

The American battle ship, *Massachusetts* and the heavy cruiser *Wichita*, took care of the *Jean Bart,* but seven Vichy French destroyers and a cruiser headed to destroy American transports. Admiral Hewitt ordered the cruisers the *Augusta* and the *Brooklyn* and two destroyers to attack the French force. He then ordered the battle ship *Massachusetts* and the heavy cruiser *Tuscaloosa* into the action and they quickly blew up a French destroyer.

The rest of the French reversed their course and retreated but in the end the Americans were able to score heavily on the French Vichy Navy, reducing them to a single destroyer. The

A Slow Moving Target, The LST of World War II

rest were either sunk, beached, or out of the war. In the struggle, the Vichy French lost four destroyers, eight submarines, and 500 dead. Hewitt's carriers shot down 55 French planes.

As the Army was attempting to land, several landing craft received a heavy counterattack and many were destroyed. To save the remaining landing craft from further destruction the Navy beachmaster altered the landing plan but was criticized by Army commanders. General Patton intervened and said, "that beachmaster saved the whole Goddamned operation." Patton went ashore from the *Augusta* at 0800 hours on the 9th and found the situation on shore a mess, but on November 11, 1942, the Vichy French commander of Algiers, Admiral Jean Darlan, surrendered.

On May 13, 1943, the Allies captured Tunisia, taking 275,000 German prisoners. Later, Rommel would write of the Americans: "What was really amazing was the speed with which they adapted themselves to modern warfare. They were assisted in this by their tremendous practical and material sense and by their lack of tradition and disdain for useless theories."

In Algiers a new military group arrived. They were WACs. The girls were installed in an Algiers convent and the only men allowed within perfume-smelling distance were two MPs. They played bridge instead of craps and made their own fudge. They got up at 0630, and were bussed to headquarters at 0700 to work as typists, drivers, and even mechanics.

Joseph Francis Panicello

14. LST 142 in Training

As a result of the experiences encountered during the assault of Guadalcanal, the Navy, with its new LSTs, began training off the coast of Southern California and in the Chesapeake Bay. Sending amphibious ships into combat without proper training is precarious. Learning from experience is sometimes the only way to get things done. But the Navy was hampered in its attempt to set procedures by the dissimilar approaches of MacArthur, Nimitz, and General Vandergrift, the commander of the 1st Marine Division, concerning invasion tactics. Actually, at this time, no one really had any experience at all with amphibious warfare using LSTs.

On board LST 142 in San Diego, Bob Olsen was called into Chief Turner's quarters. The Chief sat Bob down and said, "How about a cup of jo (coffee), Olly?" Bob accepted it as the Chief continued, "Listen, Olly, we are getting ready to prepare this ship for war in the Pacific. They had a lot of trouble unloading supplies in the Guadalcanal invasion and we lost a lot of men, several transports and many small craft during the assault. I understand it was mass confusion. Our job here is to train our young sailors on the procedures of landing our LST and unloading the decks as quickly as possible of tanks, trucks, ammunition, troops, food and water.

"Olly, even though you're only a 3rd class Boatswain Mate, you will be in charge of all the seaman on this training exercise. I need you to train our young boots on the proper techniques in the art of making a landing. A 2nd Class Boatswain Mate will be coming on board next month but, right now, I'm counting on you. The other two 3rd Class Boatswain Mates and I will have to remain on board to run the ship, but I'm sending you and Belcher to take special classes and training for a week here in Dago, to learn all the skills necessary to land this ship and empty it. You will also be trained on how to handle a small landing craft. After you and Belcher return both of you will have to teach our own crew members what you have learned. Are there any questions?"

"Yeah," answered Olsen. "How long will we be here in San Diego and when will we be heading out to the Pacific?"

"We expect to be here about five weeks, so you will have four weeks to train our crew. As far as heading out, I don't know when or where. Do you think you can handle this assignment?"

"No problem, Chief," Olsen assured him, "except maybe for Belcher. You know him. He's strong minded and sometimes I have trouble ordering him to do anything. He even threatened to punch me out once." Bob was having trouble ordering his fellow Phibie around.

The chief smiled a little and said, "Don't worry about him. He's my kind of a guy, rough and tough. When the chips are down and the fighting begins, believe me, he'll do his part. My advice to you is, when you're both in class don't try ordering him around like he was a new recruit. Treat him as your equal. He'll do fine. I already had a talk with him and he is anxious to do his part. If he does well, I'm going to recommend he be promoted to Seaman 1st Class. Don't mention that to him, of course."

When Chief Turner read Olsen's background and after having numerous conversations with him, he knew that this was the man he was looking for to be his striker. His experience on the fishing boats taught him to take orders and he had learned a lot about seamanship. The chief originally thought that Danny would be the man to be his backup but he'd seen how rowdy he was. Danny wasn't as interested in Navy procedures as Bob was.

Olsen and Bletcher went to a special training session off the coast of the Coronado Island. An LST was beached there with its doors wide open and its ramp down on the sand. They went on board over the ramp, up the tank deck, and to the crew's quarters where they joined several sailors who were also being trained for LST beaching.

As they assembled together they all were wondering and discussing what the training was all about. Some of these sailors

Joseph Francis Panicello

were new recruits and knew absolutely nothing about the operation of an LST.

One sailor said, "God. This ship looks like a death trap. The first chance I get I'm going to ask for a transfer."

Another sailor remarked, "Forget it, sailor. You're here for the duration. Once you are in the Amphibs you're stuck with them for life or death."

Bob and Danny had some advantage over the other sailors. They knew the ship's basic operation because they came aboard their ship at Norfolk, sailed down to and through the Panama Canal to San Diego. Many of these new recruits came to San Diego by train right from boot camp. The other experienced sailors that were there came from fighting ships such as cruisers and destroyers and were, to their dismay, transferred to the Amphibs.

A Chief Boatswain Mate stepped into the crew's quarters, accompanied by a 2nd Class Petty Officer who immediately called out "Attention!"

The Chief then announced, "At ease, men. I'm Chief Brown and this here is 2nd Class Boatswain Mate, Avery. The object of this training course is to teach you men every aspect of landing an LST on a beach and unloading it. Unfortunately, we only have a week's time to accomplish this task. This training exercise should take a month but we are at war and time is essential. The Admirals need many LSTs in the Pacific as well as in Africa and Europe. Now, this job is not an easy chore. It means timing and cooperation from every crew member on your ship. Teamwork is absolutely essential during these operations.

"Each of you will learn a new task every day. Avery will escort you to a different station each day where you will be trained by experts who will demonstrate to you how that particular station works. Listen to these individuals carefully and take notes because you won't get another shot at it. After you have been sufficiently trained, the last two days will be devoted to an actual landing exercise onto the beach. What you learn here

A Slow Moving Target, The LST of World War II

you will be expected to pass on to your shipmates on your own LSTs.

"I'm leaving you in the hands of Avery. I wish you all the luck because you will need it during an actual assault sometime soon on an island in the Pacific."

The first day the entire class was shown how to operate the rear anchor; when it should be dropped, recording how much cable has been let out, and how to reel it in to pull the ship back out into the open sea. In the afternoon they were shown how to operate the elevator, lash up a vehicle, and lower it down to the tank deck. A truck was used to demonstrate the procedure.

Day 2, they were shown how to release and drop an LCM and LCVP over the side using portable derricks. The LCT and LCI are too large for the derricks and have to be dropped over the side by banking the ship. This task was not demonstrated, only explained. The Petty Officer in charge of the station said, "The Higgins LCVPs and LCMs each require a four man crew to man it; a coxswain, an engineer, a starboard rear gunner and a forward sailor who will release the bow door as they approach the beach. He will also act as a gunner on the port side during an assault."

The Petty Officer explained further, "The Higgins LCVP may carry a platoon of 35 troops or a vehicle such as a tank with its own crew on board right up to the shore line. The LCM can carry 100 troops and a tank. The LCT, the next largest amphibious craft, can carry 300 troops or several tanks. LCTs have their own power and its own crew to man it, but they do not have the range, however, to travel across the ocean. They have to be either carried on an LST or towed somewhere in the vicinity of an invasion.

"Placing a tank on these small craft is usually done from Liberty ships. After you drop these boats from your LST onto the water, the coxswain will drive the craft over to a Liberty ship where cranes are used to lower the tanks onto the boats. You may have as many as 300 marines or soldiers on board your LST

Joseph Francis Panicello

and they may have to go down rope ladders to board the small craft, or run down the ramp on foot after you have beached."

Day 3 was set up to learn the procedure of opening up the various vents above the tank deck and operating the fans to exhaust the tank deck of all the fumes coming from the different vehicles that are fired up.

The Petty Officer explained, "This operation is necessary to help the marines or soldiers check out their tanks and trucks in the tank deck before they launch an invasion. The fans will be on continuously, however, when the ship is approaching a beach."

On this day the class was also shown how to unlatch the tanks in the tank deck and on the main deck prior to the LST being beached. The instructor said, "Usually, the tank crew will do the unlatching themselves, but sometimes the ship's sailors have to do it because there is so much going on."

Day 4 was spent in the pilot's house where a quartermaster explained the duties of each control station. They were shown how to steer the ship into the beach and the things to be aware of, such as tide, wind, and waves. If there are reefs far from shore the LST may not be able to reach the beach, so it was explained how pontoons are used for the withdrawal of tanks, trucks and personnel. The instructor did have a short section of a pontoon on deck to illustrate their application. They were also shown how to change the ballast of the ship from the different pump stations.

On day 5 the men had to learn how to "Undog" and open the bow doors and drop the ramp. Four sailors at a time had to climb down into the manhole to be shown what had to be done to release the bow doors. Danny was especially interested in this assignment because he knew that he would be the one doing it. Each four man crew had to actually go through the procedure of opening the bow doors. After lunch they were shown how to load and fire the cannons and machine guns on board. The instructor fired one of the 40 mm guns at a target on the beach to demonstrate the procedure. All deck hands must learn to load and fire the various guns on board.

A Slow Moving Target, The LST of World War II

On day 6 the LST was taken out to about one mile at sea. At this distance the training captain gave the orders of "Half speed ahead," preparing for a beach landing. As the ship approached one half mile from the beach "General Quarters" was sounded.

Danny and three sailors had to go down through the manhole at the bow to release or, "Undog," the bow doors. At a certain distance from shore the "Condition One Mike" alarm was sounded and the doors began to open. When the Captain gave the command "Full Speed Ahead" the doors, by now, were opened to their full extent, and the ramp was partially lowered to about 45 degrees. As the LST approached 600 feet, or two ship lengths from shore, the stern anchor was ordered to be dropped and every 100 feet of anchor cable was recorded. This day Olsen was assigned to run the task of dropping the rear anchor.

After the ship hit the beach the ramp was then completely lowered onto the beach. Two tanks and a truck towing a cannon were driven off and onto the beach to demonstrate the proper procedure of unloading. A truck and a jeep were then lowered from the main deck to the tank deck by elevator and were also driven down the ramp and onto the beach.

The time it was supposed to take to do this exercise should have been no more than four hours, especially with only five vehicles on board. But in this particular operation it took the students four hours just to land the ship because there were so many mishaps.

After the exercise was over Chief Brown ordered all of the students to assemble in the crew's quarters that evening. He then read them the riot act.

"You dumb bananas. What the hell were you thinking about out there. It took you four hours just to beach this damned ship. Do you know what would have happened if you took that long during an actual assault. You would have been bombed out of commission by the Japs. You would all be dead, and worst of all, so would most of the invading marines or soldiers that were on board your ship. The object of this exercise is to dump your

Joseph Francis Panicello

stores as quickly as possible and get the hell out of there!" He was screaming so loud that he almost lost his voice.

After awhile, he calmed down and began speaking again in a softer voice. "Men, I know I sound desperate and vicious, but I can't help myself. I'm worried about you boys. You're all so young and you're going to war with limited training. You're about the same age as my two sons are. I want them to live just like I want you to live. I want you to support the marines and soldiers that will be hitting the beach, putting their lives in harm's way. I know it's not an easy task.

"It's imperative that every assignment that you and your fellow sailors are given must be carried out without any mistakes. We are teaching you the proper procedures so that everything goes as smoothly and as quickly as possible without any of the mix-ups that I have just witnessed.

"Now, tomorrow we will try it again. You will each be assigned to a different task from what you had today. Please, men. This is your last chance. Do it right. Tonight, think about your assignment. Make a mental picture of what you have to do, and in this way you will be ready for tomorrow."

The Chief paused a bit, looking over these young sailors, a frown on his face, and finally added, "You're all dismissed."

Danny and Bob walked over to their temporary bunks and Bob remarked, "Boy, was he pissed. What happened at the bow, Belcher. How come you guys were so late with the bow doors?"

"Oh. It was those other two sailors. The guy that was working with me to undog the beam on the port side dropped his wrench and he had to crawl down to the bottom to find it. I finished my starboard side first and then had to climb over to his side to undog his beam. It sure took a lot of time," Danny sighed.

"Then the guy who was supposed to use the ratchet to stow the beams away didn't have the strength to do it. I had to crawl over there and help him. What a mess. We definitely need stronger men for this task. We can't have any men working the bow doors that are as puny as Robber."

A Slow Moving Target, The LST of World War II

Bob thought about what Danny had said because he was assigned to be in charge of the bow crew tomorrow, and said, "I'm going to make sure that the guys that work with me tomorrow know what they are doing and are physically capable."

Danny replied, "Lots of luck," knowing full well that he'd need it.

The next day, day 7, they went through the same routine of landing the ship. This time the entire landing took them only three hours and the unloading took another three hours. The chief was still not satisfied but he had no choice but to dismiss them to return to their respective LSTs.

When they all left, old Chief Brown said to Avery, "It just ain't fair. To send these young boys out into an invasion with limited training is just plain foolish. These poorly trained sailors will now have to go back to their LSTs and show their own crew members how to beach the ship but they will probably have to learn the procedures the hard way, during an assault. They will get one more chance at it here in Dago but then it's off to the war. They ain't got a chance."

Avery noticed a trickle of tears coming down the old man's cheek. Chief Brown had been in the Navy thirty years and Avery thought it was about time the old Chief considered retiring. "He's become too soft," Avery thought.

After Bob and Danny returned to LST 142, they were greeted by Johnny and Andre. "How did the training go, Olly?" asked Johnny.

Bob answered, "Not too well," sounding despondent. "We really needed more time to practice. I'm on my way to see Chief Turner to report on what we have learned thus far. I don't think he'll be happy at the prospects of teaching our own men how to beach this ship with only one trial run. I hope he can convince the upper brass that we need more than one day."

"Where's Hinny?" Danny asked, looking around.

Johnny chuckled, "He's on his honeymoon. While you Phibies were working your tails off he ran off and got married to

Joseph Francis Panicello

Mildred. He's been seeing her every chance he could get, taking the Red car from San Diego to Burbank."

"That's love," said Andre. "Hell, it's a 4 hour trip, non-stop and on the Red car it's never non-stop."

The other Phibies laughed as Johnny continued, "Chief Turner gave him two weeks leave. He'll be back in time for shooting exercises."

Bob said quietly, "That's pretty fast work. Hope he knows what he's doing." He left to talk to the Chief as Danny beckoned Johnny aside.

"Macaroni, it looks to me like your buddy is being taken for a ride. I'll bet that his wife is in it only for the monthly allotment that she will receive and, if he's killed, she'll be awarded his ten-grand insurance policy instead of his mom. I heard about a girl who was married to three sailors at the same time, receiving three allotments. They finally caught up with her when two of the sailors showed up at her home at once."

"I agree, Belcher. But what can we do? It's too late now so let's not talk about this again. We need Hinny in combat without any distraction. He's already filled out the paper work and as far as the law and the navy are concerned she's his wife. Maybe it'll all turn out okay."

Danny looked skeptical, "Maybe. What about you and Dolores?"

Johnny brightened, "She's great. I think I'm really in love. It's foolish, though, isn't it? I shouldn't get serious about anyone."

Danny thought for a moment about Angela. "Just don't put Dolores on the spot, Macaroni. If you don't do anything stupid, then neither can she."

"Belcher, sometimes you're a lot smarter than you look." Both men laughed as they joined the others.

15. Letters to Angela

Dear Ann:

Hi, Sis. Everything is going well. The Phibies all have assignments and are trying like hell to master them. I'm a Third Class Motor Mechanic in the engine room but during an invasion I'll be the engineer for any small craft the LST deploys.

I met a wonderful girl, someone I'm sure you'd like. Her name is Dolores. She's Hinny's sister. I'm taking it slow, however. This is a bad time to get serious. She sure is great though.

I want to say thanks for the letters you've written to Belcher and Robber. It makes them happy though sometimes I have to stop their bickering over you.

Give Mama & Dad a hug for me and be good.

Love, Johnny

P.S. They call me Macaroni.

Dear Angela:

The first week of practice for LST 142 was operating the ship under different situations. We had to learn how to dock at a pier into the wind, stern first, to come along side and tie up to an anchored LST in the bay by coming in from the bow and then from the stern. We practiced how to transfer a wounded patient from one ship to another. We practiced first within the Coronado Harbor and at the end of the week we practiced out in the ocean under more severe conditions.

The second week was devoted to lowering an LCM over the side in the harbor with troops going down a netted rope onto the small craft. During this exercise one marine's leg was crushed between the LCM and the LST while he was trying to get into

Joseph Francis Panicello

the boat. I felt helpless. I learned a lot about first aid from my Dad but I couldn't do anything for him.

Chief Turner had warned the troop's commander that this could happen but he was ignored. If this happened out at sea with the boat bobbing up and down from the waves there could have been even more casualties. The troop commander became more concerned after this accident and cautioned the men to wait until the swell is at its peak before dropping into the craft.

Another method we use to load an LCM out in the bay is to lower the LCM as usual with the four crew sailors already on aboard. The coxswain then drives the LCM around to the bow of the LST which has already lowered its ramp. The LCM places its open ramp on top of the LST ramp. A tank then drives off the LST and onto the LCM. Troops follow and climb aboard the LCM over the LST ramp. The LCM is now fully loaded and ready for a landing on the beach. This task is not an easy assignment because of the waves and the winds could cause the LCM and LST to move apart suddenly. Pretty neat operation.

We didn't practice dropping an LCT over the side of an LST by tilting it. This exercise is one of the most difficult maneuvers for an LST crew and it needs special training over and above what LST 142 crew members are commissioned to do. We have enough problems just learning how to drop an LCM into the ocean and to man it.

When the LCM hit the water for the first time Olly, Macaroni, Belcher and I went down a rope before the troops did. Olly became the coxswain, Macaroni the engineer, Belcher was stationed at the stern and controlled the rear shackle that held the boat steady while I did the same at the bow. After the troops came down rope ladders and were all on board the boat, Belcher and I released the shackles freeing the boat. I had trouble releasing my shackle by hand so I kicked it with my foot.

Belcher then mounted the starboard machine gun on the LCM. When we were 50 yard from the beach I unlatched the bow ramp and then mounted the port gun. As we approached the beach Belcher and I began shooting at special dummy targets on

A Slow Moving Target, The LST of World War II

the beach. Belcher was pretty good at it but I scored poorly. I guess I need more training from Hinny. I don't know if the Chief is going to give me the chance, He's pushing me to work in the sick bay. It may be hard to understand, but I clearly do not want that position.

The rest of the week was spent teaching the entire crew about procedure for releasing the stern anchor, the bow doors, undogging the bow, changing the ship ballast, dropping the ramp and running the blowers.

I'll have to admit, Belcher is pretty good at all of it. Don't tell him I said so.

Thanks for writing.

Sincerely,
Andre (Robber)

My Angel:

I feel like I'm a million miles away from you, not 3,000. That is probably a good thing. I'm great at advising the other Phibies about not falling in love. There was no one there to protect me.

Hinny got back from his honeymoon 2 days late for target practice, in the third week of training. We thought for sure he would have to report to Captains Mass because he was AWOL. He was first up for target practice and he blazed away at the first target being flown by an airplane. He had some pretty good hits.

Later, and out of the blue, another plane approached and this time I was allowed to take a turn at shooting at its target. Then a third plane arrived with its target and another Gunners Mate striker was allowed to do the shooting.

The next day there was a tug boat towing a target on a raft. This time Hinny used his cannon and began blasting away at the target. The other gunner and I also had our turn with the cannon on separate tugs towing targets.

The third day we were shooting machine guns at targets on shore as the LST cruised by. In this exercise Hinny was on the

Joseph Francis Panicello

bow, I was amidships, and the other gunner at the stern. We were each assigned our own targets.

When the results were in the next day it showed that Hinny had hit the flown silk target 90% of the time and had a 80% kill at the target on the raft target. I scored 50% on both the silk and raft targets which was considered excellent, so you can imagine how good Hinny is. The other gunner had only a 40% hit on the silk and 30% on the raft target, which is average for most gunners.

Captain Hull realized he had a prize Gunners Mate on board. Hinny's score was the only one in all of those San Diego exercises that registered a 90% kill on silk and 80% on the raft target. The best score ever recorded before was a 65% kill on the silk and 60% on the raft target.

After Captain Hull read the report he dropped the charges against Hinny for being AWOL and there was no Captain's Mass. The Captain knows that a sharpshooting gunner like Hinny could save the ship and its crew when they are being attacked. Hinny will get away with murder now.

The last week of training was beaching the ship carrying one tank lashed down on the tank deck and a jeep on the main deck. Four sailors were ready at the bow to undog the doors. Robber was stationed at the stern anchor. Olly and I were in charge of the switch panel that controlled the blowers, opened the doors and dropped the ramp. Macaroni was stationed at the two throttles in the main engine room. Your brother sure has the touch at the throttles.

Hinny sat around in the galley drinking jo while his strikers manned the guns. He wandered onto the main deck just in time to witness the gun barrage from his men at some dummy targets on the beach as the LST approached the shore. When he saw how weak and clumsy they were with their efforts to load, reload and shoot the guns accurately, he decided that he had better take a more active role. He's terrific, but his men need practice.

The beach landing exercise took over three hours but because there were a few major glitches the LST never reached

A Slow Moving Target, The LST of World War II

the beach. The stern anchor was released too soon and it ran out of cable. It hooked itself around a large boulder underwater and caused the ship to stop too soon. The officer in charge of the bow activities assumed that the ship was beached and ordered Olly to drop the ramp.

The marine in the tank saw that the ramp was now lowered, moved his tank out and onto the beach, except there was no beach. The tank ended up in deep water and was sinking fast, water over its turret. The marine driver of the tank crawled out of the upper hatch, jumped into the water and swam back to the ramp, where he was rescued.

The Captain was furious. He wanted to have another go at it but we had our orders. We are leaving for Hawaii tomorrow morning. Right behind LST 142 is another LST waiting its turn to practice its own beaching.

Chief Turner was angry and read the riot act to the crew, especially to Robber who dropped the anchor too soon. Robber heard someone yell drop the line, but thought they yelled drop the anchor. Robber is not really cut out to be a seaman. He could be a lot more help in the sick bay.

Tomorrow I'll be heading farther away from you, yet if I close my eyes I can picture you right here. Be my Angel.

                                                        Love,
                                                        Danny

16. Pearl

In February, 1943, as United States marines and army infantry were being shipped to Guadalcanal LST 142 left San Diego and began heading for Hawaii. During the trip the crew had to practice each landing assignment over and over again, sometimes under rough seas. Rich Hienman was training his men to operate and shoot their cannons and machine guns out at sea with imaginary targets. One gunner fired at a dolphin for target practice. The dolphin was safe. He missed. Rich, after seeing this poor demonstration, realized his men were still not ready yet.

Bob Olsen was instructing his young boots on the procedure of handling a small landing craft as the coxswain, and what their duties would be during the LST beach landing. Danny Bletcher, who was now promoted to a Seaman First Class, assembled his strikers at the bow to go over of the details and procedures of how to undog the bow doors before a beach landing.

Andre Robbier was given mess-cook detail on this trip, which he hated, but when he was off duty he was at the stern of the ship instructing the new recruits on how to operate the rear anchor capstan.

Johnny Maroni had the twelve-to-four main engine watch and didn't practice anything because he was too bushed after working extra hours in the auxiliary engine room. One of the three auxiliary engines broke down and Johnny and another Motor Mechanic worked throughout the night to repair it. One cylinder had a stuck exhaust valve which caused it to have a very low compression.

When the LST was halfway to Hawaii a good size storm engulfed them. All practice on the ship was immediately canceled for fear of losing men overboard. The captain had enough trouble just keeping the ship afloat without losing his men. His last ship was a Destroyer Escort which he knew how to handle. The LST had a completely different ride to it during a storm. It was the wildest ride he and his Exec. had ever experienced.

There were 30 foot waves towering over them so the skipper ordered Olsen to steer the ship at a 45 degree angle to the port side. Moving into the waves, at that angle, would help prevent the ship from broaching. This meant he would have to periodically reverse the ship and steer it at a 45 degree angle to the starboard side in order to keep the ship on a straight course.

The angle of steering did help, but because of the distinctive features of the LST, with its flat bottom hull, any large wave that came toward it caused the bow to come up and out of the water at the crest of the wave. When the ship's bow came down again it would slap the water at the trough with such tremendous force it caused the ship and everyone on it, to be rattled vigorously.

After the wave passed under the ship it would lift the stern above the water line causing its screw to come out of the water and spin freely in air. With little or no resistance the propeller's RPM increased rapidly. As the ship's stern fell back in the water the screw would cause a twisting action of such tremendous force that it would yank the ship sideways. This jerking motion played hell on the crew. If a crew member happened to be walking on the port side of the crew's compartment, he might be thrown completely to the starboard side of the ship. The sailors on board quickly learned to hold on after the initial slap at the bow. They knew what was coming next.

Then, of course, there was the constant rolling of the ship, which didn't help those prone to sea sickness. Sometimes the ship would be cruising almost sideways as they came upon an unusually large wave where one side of the ship would be high above the other side. It was as though the crew were in free space, and if a sailor didn't hold on to something he could slide down across to the opposite side of the ship.

Johnny discovered early that there was less action in the main engine room during these turbulent storms. Beneath the water line and at the bottom of the ship in the engine room was the lowest pivotal point of the ship going side to side or front to

Joseph Francis Panicello

back. When he was off duty and felt queasy, Johnny would go down the two flights via a long straight ladder to the main engine room and sit under a blower that brought in cool fresh air from topside. Johnny never became seasick on any of these cruises but there were times when he felt poorly.

Johnny and Dolores had been corresponding quite a bit, although he was reluctant to express his strong emotions or make a commitment to her. Her letters were more intimate. Basically, she summed it up with a "why fight it" attitude. She had a bit part in a B-movie with a promise of other more demanding parts.

Rich wrote long, loving letters to his wife, Mildred. The other Phibies teased him but Rich didn't mind.

Both Andre and Danny wrote to Angela but the contents were somewhat different. Danny wrote as if he was sure of the place he held in her heart. Andre wrote letters any girl could read to her mother.

Bob was the only Phibie without a female distraction and it showed. He was dedicated and diligent in attending his duties. Except for sleeping, his whole day revolved around the ship.

When LST 142 landed at Pearl the bulletin board had liberty listed for two thirds of the crew. The Phibies were not listed for watch duty so they immediately made plans to head for Honolulu. Rich had to be coaxed by the other Phibies. As a married man he felt he should stay on board to avoid the Polynesian enticements in town.

The *Five Phibies* took a bus to Honolulu and when they arrived there were several Polynesian girls with leis waiting to greet them. Each sailor received a lei and a kiss on the cheek. Bob, however, kissed his girl on the mouth. The other Phibies were amazed. It looked like their officer in-training was breaking out.

The Phibies went to a local club with the girls and ordered beer. The place was crawling with American military personnel. The establishment was beautiful, with palm trees and other tropical flowers that presented an attractive setting, typically Hawaiian. At the club entrance there was a fountain in the center with orchids and lilies in a planter surrounding the fountain. The only Phibie that was enthralled with the embellishments was Andre. He paused to look at the fountain and Danny said to him, "Come on, Runt. We got some drinking to do."

The *Five Phibies* and the girls sat at two tables pushed together. They were having a great time, dancing and drinking beer, except Danny, who preferred Scotch whiskey. The group had their hands full controlling his natural tendency to act up. Later he disappeared with one of the girls and they didn't see him again until the next morning.

Rich drank his beer quietly and was only cordial with his date. She finally called him a "dead beat" and left him for a marine at the bar. He then slipped away from the crowd and headed back to the ship. He wanted to uphold his intentions of being true to his wife. He'd only gone to town to please his buddies. He definitely wanted no part in any activities with other women.

Olsen, on the other hand, was having a great old time. He was practically having an orgy on the dance floor. Later in the night he became inebriated. His date led him outside, helping him walk, wobbling, to a hotel nearby. The next morning he discovered that the girl was gone and the 100 dollars he had secretly stashed in his wallet was gone. The first thing that came to his mind was, "I've been rolled." He couldn't remember what happened. He didn't mention anything to his buddies about what happened that night. He was embarrassed over the money he lost and he didn't want to be laughed at. When he returned to the ship he kept his mouth shut about the whole affair. When Andre asked him how his date was he simply responded, "Not bad."

Andre had had a small problem at the bar that night. A large soldier was horning in on his girl. Andre had words with this doggy but then decided he was too big for a confrontation and let him have her. "What the hell, I still have Angela back home," he thought.

Johnny also lost his girl to a girene (marine) but he didn't care, either. His mind was with Dolores. Johnny and Andre

Joseph Francis Panicello

finally had enough at 0200 hours and headed back to the ship together with an arm over each other's shoulder singing, "We're in the Navy now."

As they approached a gate a Marine Guard was inspecting each sailor for a hidden alcohol bottle as they entered the main gate of the base. In front of Johnny and Andre was a plastered sailor who had a pint of Gin under his jumper in the back of his pants. The Marine whacked the sailor in the back with his night stick and broke the bottle. With the booze coming down the sailor's back he became enraged and took a swing at the guard but was knocked out cold by another marine's night stick. He was then dragged away into the building.

Johnny almost intervened but Andre grabbed him. Johnny yelled and said, "What a dirty thing to do. You goddamn Girenes are always beating up on us sailors!" The marine guard looked at him with determined eyes, ready to use his night stick again.

Andre pulled him away and said, "Come on, Macaroni. Let's get out of here."

Johnny never forgot that incident, and from then on he detested all marines. He didn't know what fate was in store for that poor sailor but he imagined he would have to serve time in a brig with other marines harassing him.

On the way to the ship Johnny was still complaining to Andre, "Why did you stop me? They could just as easily confiscated the booze from him. They didn't have to break the goddamn bottle, the bastards."

Andre assured him, "If I didn't stop you they would have put you in the brig. Those marines love beating up sailors. It's a form of training for them, using sailors for practice until they come up against the Japs. Being mean and ornery is bred into them at boot-camp. They are brainwashed into believing they are invincible. That's why Belcher always picks a fight with them. He wants to knock them down a peg.

"When Belcher was in the brig he said they had piss calls every hour. The marines would wake a sailor up by rapping on the bars with their sticks. They would hit him on the ass with

A Slow Moving Target, The LST of World War II

their belt buckle if he took a break while digging a ditch. He said it was chicken shit. All because he snuck a bottle into the base in his sock."

The next day LST 142 was being loaded with cargo. Liberty was given to the crew that were on watch the day before. Johnny and Andre were listed for duty but Danny and Bob could still go ashore. Rich always had free liberty but he remained on board, working with his recruits. Bob remained on board because he was broke after being rolled on his first night ashore.

As Danny was leaving the ship he and Andre got into a heated squabble. Andre accused him of screwing around, "You don't give beans about Angela back home."

Danny began yelling back, "Listen, you little punk. You mention one word about me to Angela and I'll put your lights out for good! This has got nothing to do with Angela."

Andre was quick to reply, "You don't scare me. Go ahead. Go out with your little whore, and I hope you catch the Clap!"

Danny was about to clobber Andre when Johnny intervened. "Leave him alone, Beltcher. Go on out and enjoy yourself. This might be your last liberty, and who knows when we'll see another girl again." Johnny was sure that his sister wasn't interested in Danny anyway, so why shouldn't he have a good time before they embarked for places unknown. Andre knew better but he remained silent.

Danny headed down the gangway, whistling. His thoughts were on that Polynesian girl, Tia. She was outstanding, better that any of the girls he'd had in New Jersey. After he took a bus to Honolulu he grabbed a cab. Her apartment was on the second floor and he ran up the stairs anxiously, anticipating another wild love encounter.

He didn't even knock on the door, just opened it and went in, unannounced. There was no one in the living room but when he entered the bedroom he saw her, nude in bed with another sailor. Danny went wild. He grabbed the sailor and began punching him. The surprised sailor fought back but Danny was too much for him. Tia was screaming for him to stop. She called the police

Joseph Francis Panicello

on the phone. They showed up just in time to arrest Danny before he had killed the guy.

They threw Danny into a cell which had no bunk and no blankets. He had to sleep that night on the ground, shivering from the damp cold cell, until the next morning when a Judge presided over his case. Word got back to the ship that morning and the Exec. had to drive over to the court house with a Jeep to plead his case before the Judge.

The Judge decided it was a navy problem, and since Danny didn't harm the girl he released Danny to the Exec. with a 100 dollar fine. He then reprimanded him on the laws of the city of Honolulu, "I will not tolerate such behavior from any military personnel, no matter how bad the war effort is going, do you understand?"

Danny nodded but kept quiet. The Judge looked down at this swab whose white sailor suit was now filthy from laying on the floor of the cell. He knew that this sailor, with many others, was about to embark on a combat mission and may not make it back alive. He reduced the fine to $50 and set him free with the Exec.

Danny was put under guard by an SP and, with the Exec. driving, they headed back to LST 142. Danny was restricted to the ship until further notice by the Captain. The Captain had put up the money for the fine so Danny's monthly pay of 25 dollars, as a Seaman 1st Class, was partially garnished until it was paid back, which took three months.

A Slow Moving Target, The LST of World War II

17. Heading to Sea

Bob and Johnny were drinking jo out on the main deck while watching the cargo being brought on board at Pearl Harbor. They heard the orders that were given out by Chief Turner to lower the large elevator down to the tank deck. They observed eight tanks being lowered by a crane, one by one, into the tank deck through the opening of the elevator shaft. Then four tank trucks were brought on board and also lowered into the tank deck. They were followed by four trucks and then four artillery cannons. All the vehicles were immediately shackled down to the floor of the tank deck and the trucks were hooked up to the cannons. The elevator was then raised back up flush with the main deck.

Four LCMs were then hauled on board and two of them were placed on both sides at the stern and under an overhanging crane. In this position the LCMs can be lowered into the sea by these cranes during an invasion. The other two LCMs were shackled to each side of the ship and on the main deck. These LCMs would have to be lowered into the sea using the mobile derricks on board. After the LCMs were placed in the water during an invasion, they would be loaded with troops, using a rope ladder. The rest of the troops would go out by way of the ramp when the ship is beached.

Four more tanks were brought on board and secured next to the LCMs but in the center of the main deck. After the tanks were tied down four Jeeps and four trucks were brought on board. The trucks were shackled down forward of the tanks in the center of the main deck. The four Jeeps were tied down alongside of the tanks.

This task was followed by bringing crates of food and medical supplies on board for the ships crew and the troops. While all of this was going on, one of the fireman was filling the fresh water tanks located at the stern of the ship below decks, and two other engine men were emptying several oil drums on the main deck by tilting them by hand and draining them into a

Joseph Francis Panicello

storage tank below decks through an uncapped hole on the main deck. This task alone took six hours.

While the loading of the supplies continued, 300 fully packed marines began coming on board. Johnny and Bob watched them struggling up the gangway carrying heavy backpacks, each looking over the ship as though it was a death trap. They all had that blank stare on their faces.

Johnny said to Bob, "God, they look like high school kids. What are they recruiting, babies?"

"Pretty close. The average age of these marines is eighteen years," Bob replied.

Ammunition for the LST cannons, the tanks, the artillery, and bullets for the machine guns would be hand carried on board by the entire crew, at an isolated location, for safety reasons. Each tank would be loaded with the required munitions needed for the initial assault on the enemy. Two of the truck beds would be filled with boxes of ammunition that would essentially support the troops, the artillery, and the tank guns after they landed on a beach. The other truck beds would carry food, water and medical supplies. The rest of the cargo would have to be hand carried ashore.

This dangerous cargo, including the ship's fuel, are the last of the freight to be brought on board, in a remote area, before they leave for the Pacific. For safety reasons, in case of an explosion, the smoking lamp would be out during these last chores. LST 142 would have to load its ammunition and diesel oil over at a special man-made island out in the bay, away from other ships.

The crew didn't particularly like loading ammunition because it was a slow process of hand carrying them on board. The ammunition to support LST 142 cannons and machine guns had to be carried down to a special ammunition locker below decks. It was safer carrying ammunition by hand than using cranes which could cause a spark and a fire. Even with the help of the 300 marines the task took the whole day on this remote island.

A Slow Moving Target, The LST of World War II

When Captain Hull of LST 142 received the message from his Lieutenant that all cargo was on board, and the vehicles secured to the decks, he gave the order to his quartermaster on the bridge to proceed directly due west into the Pacific Ocean. After they were an hour out at sea, Captain Quincy Hull and his Exec. went down to his quarters and, as was customary, the captain poured them both a small glass of brandy to commemorate their first cruise toward the war zone.

The captain said, "Here's to our first assault, John. I hope we both get through it alright. How's your family doing? I understand you have a boy at Annapolis."

Lieutenant John Lester answered, "Yes I do, Quin. He'll be graduating in June. I was hoping to be back there for the ceremony but it doesn't look that way."

The captain stared at his wife's picture on the desk and replied, "Unfortunately, Linda and I were not blessed with any children. It would have been nice to have a boy following my footsteps. You must be proud of your boy, John."

"I sure am," was his pleasant reply.

"Well, I guess we might as well get down to business. Here again to a safe trip, John," as they toasted and finished their drinks.

After that last toast the captain proceeded to open up his safe. He removed a sealed manila envelope and drew out its contents. For the first time since they came on board the captain was able to read the ship's orders and her destination. Now, they were both aware of where the ship was bound for.

The captain spoke, "It looks like we are to convene with LST Flotilla-7, already in the Pacific."

It was now March 1943, and Captain Hull's destination was to travel to New Guinea to support Rear Admiral Barbey under the command of General MacArthur. Barbey had just been given command of the amphibious forces in the Pacific. Adm. Kelly Turner was still in command of the amphibious forces in the North and Central Pacific.

Joseph Francis Panicello

On the long journey in the Pacific by LST 142, one morning Johnny and a fireman, nicknamed Red, were having a discussion at the galley table. The fireman said, "You know, Macaroni, it's easier to do time in prison than it is being in the navy."

"What are you talking about, Red?" questioned Johnny.

"I mean it," he replied.

"You gotta be nuts." Johnny started to get up. He wasn't interested in this bull talk.

"Wait a minute, Macaroni. Hear me out. I know what I'm talking about because I spent two years in the big house. I got out five months ago. The Warden told a number of us prisoners that if we enlisted in the military to fight for our country, the authorities would drop the remainder of our time in the penitentiary and give our citizenship back, including the right to vote. I had three more years to go in jail for armed robbery, so I readily agreed. I enlisted in the navy as soon as I could, but I didn't expect this crazy life we're having.

"Look at it my way, Macaroni. Out to sea we have three four-hour shifts twice a day; the twelve-to-four, the four-to-eight, and the eight-to-twelve. That's eight hours on duty a day. However, if we are not on duty during the normal work hours from eight in the morning until four in the evening, we are still required to work on special details.

"I now have the four-to-eight watch, so when I get off duty at eight in the morning I have an hour for breakfast, and then I have to turn to and clean out the head, swab the deck, do some painting, etc. I'm available for extra work details from nine in the morning until four in the afternoon when I have go to back to my four hour watch again. That means I could get stuck working fourteen hours a day, not counting lunch, for seven days a week with only eight hours of sleep, and on a ship that's bouncing around like a top on high seas. Now, is that fair?

"And, in addition, we're not allowed to use our bunks during the daytime to rest. So, if I'm not on a work detail during the daytime, I have to scrounge around trying to find a place to lay my head down and take a nap. Hell, in prison I only worked

A Slow Moving Target, The LST of World War II

from eight to four, with an hour for lunch, and after dinner I was back in my cell reading or listing to the radio in a nice, dry bunk, and the ground was not rolling around making me seasick."

Johnny argued back, "You got a point, Red. But in the navy you get to go ashore once in awhile and meet up with some pretty dames."

This didn't stop Red who said, "Hell, I'm married and every once in awhile my wife comes to visit with me at the prison and we are allowed a private reunion."

"Well, go back to prison. I don't give a damn."

Johnny was getting tired of his bellyaching and walked away. Red did make a point, but Johnny said to himself, "So what?" and headed to his bunk to relax, before his own twelve-to-four watch was due. When he got there he realized it was still daytime and he couldn't use his bunk. He said, "Damn!" and had to go down to the electrician's shop, where a mattress was laying on the deck for that purpose.

Back in December, 1942 there was a bitter struggle between MacArthur and Admiral King over who should command the South Pacific forces. MacArthur wanted the next major offense to be New Guinea, but King wanted to continue through the Solomons to the island of Rabaul. He didn't like the idea of MacArthur having control of his naval forces.

Adm. Halsey wrote a letter to Nimitz and called MacArthur a "self-advertising son of a bitch," After their first meeting together, however, he said, "I felt as if we were lifelong friends."

MacArthur returned the compliment to Halsey by saying, "He's the bugaboo of many sailors, and the fear of losing ships is completely alien to his conception of sea action. I liked him from the moment we met."

After several deliberations in Washington, a compromise was reached and MacArthur was given overall command, with Halsey cooperating, but fleet units were still under Nimitz's control.

Operation Cartwheel was the name given to both offenses. The entire operation was to be kicked off June 1, 1943. At this

Joseph Francis Panicello

point Admiral King had just assigned newly appointed Rear Admiral Daniel Barbey as commander of Amphibious forces of the Southwest Pacific.

MacArthur's first orders to Barbey was, "Your job is to develop an amphibious force that can carry my troops in these campaigns."

Barbey's dilemma was that he had to create a worthy amphibious force with only six months to train the crews of the landing craft. He also discovered that he only had one transport permanently assigned to him.

In April 1943, LCT Flotilla-7 and LST Flotilla-7 arrived and were ready for training. LST 142's assignment was to join up with LST Flotilla-7. Because there were no transports available for practice many of the LSTs had to simulate a cargo ship by slinging nets over its sides for troops to practice debarkation. The 1st Marine Division, having recently fought in Guadalcanal, was assigned for these training exercises.

MacArthur's plan was to occupy the islands of Woodlark and Kiriwina and the campaign was called Operation Chronicle. These islands were reported to be unoccupied. To make sure, two APDs were sent to scout the two islands ahead of time. Their job was to prepare the beaches for the landing force and on June 30, troop forces went ashore without any difficulty. The islands would now be used as a launching base to invade and bomb the other islands using aircraft bombers. The landing in Nassau Bay, New Guinea, was next.

To accomplish this shore to shore tactic, Barbey utilized a variety of small craft to transport 1,000 men of the 162nd Infantry Regiment, using three PT boats, 29 Higgins LCVPs, and one LCM. It was a forty mile run from Marobe to Nassau Bay.

Fortunately, the troops on the PT boats landed without a mishap and there was no counterattack from the Japanese. But in the process, because of the weather, 17 Higgins LCVPs were disabled and an LCM broached as it approached the beach.

As a result of the situation of shore-to-shore operation all of the LSTs would not be utilized. MacArthur now formed the

A Slow Moving Target, The LST of World War II

Army Engineering Amphibious Brigade, which consisted of 1,380 LCVPs, 172 LCMs, and 30 LCTs. It was a constructive assault brigade.

After Nassau was secured, LST 142 was ordered to support Admiral Halsey to capture Munda. The code name for this operation was called Toenails. The 43d Infantry Division would make the assault while the 37th Infantry Division would be held back in reserve. In addition to his present fleet, Halsey was now receiving new amphibious units consisting of LCIs, LSTs, and LCTs from the east. LST 142 now joined the newly arrived LST Flotilla-5 on the island of Noumea on May 14. Each of the new LSTs carried an LCT on her main deck, which would be launched by listing the LSTs to one side.

The many different slow moving LSTs that traveled from the United States took sixty days to reach their destination in the Pacific. The Flotilla-5 originally departed from New York harbor and stopped in Bermuda in the Atlantic. From there they went through the Panama Canal and then to Bora Bora. Engine breakdowns, near collisions, missed light signals, and ships falling out of formation slowed the procession. In Panama, two sailors deserted.

Another Flotilla of five LST replacements began heading west from San Diego to the South Pacific, each loaded with many marines. Unfortunately, the cruise across the Pacific on the flat-bottomed LSTs was pretty rough on the marines. The Flotilla war diary reads, "many of the Marines passengers aboard LSTs found the rail a comfortable and convenient place to stay."

Also in the diary, written about the Hospital ship *Doyen*, "daily instructions were held for hospital corpsmen and corpswomen in surgical techniques, advanced first aid, X-ray, and nursing." The medical officer's aim was, "to have every corpsperson capable of carrying out any function or duty assigned to him or her."

What Halsey learned from the problems they'd had in the Guadalcanal invasion was that they now needed to know in advance the Japanese situation on Munda. The 1st Marine Raider

Joseph Francis Panicello

Battalion was given the task of determining the Japanese defenses. They traveled at night, landing on the islands of Munda and Rendova, which were opposite of each other. The information Halsey received was positive and the schedule for the invasion was on.

Operating from his flagship, Admiral Turner's first priority was to speed up the system of unloading the ship's cargo. He didn't want a repeat of the Guadalcanal invasion. He assigned work parties for each vessel over and above their normal crew. Each transport was assigned a crew of 150 men, each LST, 150 men, each LCT, 50 men, and each LCI, 25 men. Seabees on shore were to support the army shore parties, establish supply dumps and remove cargo off the beaches. This all sounded good but when men are being fired upon nothing goes smoothly.

The plan, called Operation Toenails, was to land on Rendova first and to use this island for a shore-to-shore assault on Munda. LST 142 laid away from shore about one mile from Rendova while the other LSTs and Transports nearby were preparing to launch their own small craft. There were many LCMs, LCVPs, LCP(R)s that were ready to be dropped into the sea with troops, tanks and trucks.

LST 142 had originally disembarked the two forward LCMs at Noumea, which would be used to support the landing Flotilla. The other two LCMs at the stern had remained on board until the orders were given by the captain to lower those last two LCMs. Johnny, Andre, Bob, and Danny headed to the stern of the LST to assume their positions on one of the LCMs on the port side. The chief decided to give Andre one more shot at being a gunner.

Tensions were beginning to mount and rightfully so. This assault would be their first combat mission. They didn't know what was in store for them. Andre, especially, was acting anxiously and Johnny had to reassure him that the Phibies would stick together and make it through the battle. The fifth Phibie, Rich, was stationed at the forward machine gun turret on board LST 142 and was ready to defend the ship from any air attack.

A Slow Moving Target, The LST of World War II

He would also spray his gun at the shore line to protect the landing forces as the LST approached the beach.

The weather, however, did not provide the best conditions for the assault. It was raining relentlessly, and the waves were high and strong. When the port LCM hit the water the four Phibies shimmied down four ropes and into the boat. Bob took the position as coxswain, Johnny as the engineer, Andre as the port gunner, and Danny was stationed as the starboard gunner.

Fifty marines then followed them into the boat, carrying all their gear on their backs, climbing down rope nets that were draped over the side. It was difficult because the LCM was bouncing around from the waves. When the troops were on board, Bob drove the LCM to a rendezvous site where other landing craft were assembling.

The command came from the flag ship, *Libra*, by Admiral Turner for the destroyers and cruisers to begin pounding the beach with artillery. Two aircraft carriers launched their fighter bombers which began dropping a barrage of bombs above the landing site. This devastating assault went on for hours. Nothing on shore should have endured and survived such an attack, but the Japanese were well entrenched and prepared.

The command was then given for the Flotilla to begin their assault on the beach. Several PT boats went along to protect the movement. The air raid bombing continued but when the ships halted their artillery so as not to hit their own forces, a Japanese shore battery opened fired on them and hit one of the destroyers. It was a fatal hit. The destroyer was ablaze and the captain sounded the order to abandon ship. Sailors began jumping into the sea but several didn't make it. Those that were severely wounded and those already dead went down with the ship. One sailor was seen carrying a wounded sailor and they both jumped into the sea together. Most of the men were rescued. The turbulent sea drowned the rest.

As Bob and his LCM approached the beach with 50 troops on board, Andre panicked and began spraying the beach with gunfire, not knowing if the enemy were there or not. Danny

Joseph Francis Panicello

yelled across to Andre, "Robber. Stop firing at nothing and save your ammunition."

When they finally saw return gunfire coming from above the beach line both Danny and Andre opened fire. The counterattack from the Japanese was fierce and Danny was hit by a sniper just as the small boat landed and the ramp lowered. The troops began to disembark and several of the soldiers were hit as they struggled through the shallow water.

Andre, after seeing that Danny was shot, worked his way over to the starboard side to assist him. Olsen yelled at Andre to get back to his post. Johnny, realizing that they were now unprotected with no one firing either machine gun, crawled up into the port gun well and began shooting the gun in the general direction of the sniper. He witnessed a figure fall out of a tree and assumed he got one. He continued to shoot at the trees that were above the beach line and saw another body fall to the ground. All the marines disembarked and several made it to the beach safely. Bob decided to move his craft out of danger.

Unexpectedly there was an air raid from the Japs, who began dropping bombs on the Flotilla and spaying machine gun fire at LST 142. Hienman went to work and began shooting his 40 mm machine gun at the enemy. He scored one, then another. Later, he shot down two more. Captain Hull was cheering him from the bridge. It was like watching a good war movie, with the enemy taking a beating. The rest of the fleet took care of the remaining Japanese bombers but, unfortunately, they'd left a magnitude of destruction.

The Japanese guns had destroyed the piled-up American supplies on Rendova's beach, leaving sixty-four men dead and many soldiers and marines wounded. Several LCPs, LCMs, and LCVPs were sunk by the Japs but, luckily, most of the troops in these craft survived by discarding their cumbersome back-packs into the water. Those that couldn't, perished from the heavy load.

Danny was wounded badly in the left arm and was bleeding profusely. Andre immediately placed a tourniquet around

A Slow Moving Target, The LST of World War II

Danny's arm to stop the bleeding. His arm was shattered and broken. Danny would have died from loss of blood except for Andre's quick reaction.

Later, after LST 142 hit the beach and dropped its ramp, Bob moved his landing craft back to the beach again to allow Johnny and Andre to carry Danny off of the small craft and up the ramp of LST 142, through the tank deck, and up to the sick bay. There were more than a hundred wounded marines and soldiers being brought on board the LST that required immediately medical attention.

Medical Chief Smith was overwhelmed with the wounded and asked Andre to help him. Andre said he would do his best even though he was not trained for this assignment. The sick bay was too small to accommodate them all so the troops crew's quarters had to be utilized as an emergency ward. There were men laying everywhere. Still more wounded were being brought on board.

Andre was receiving an on-the-job medical training course. He had to stitch several bleeding marines and had to give morphine to those who were in pain. He had to provide IV blood plasma transfusions to several others. He also had to find time to assist the Chief on the operating table, removing bullets and shrapnel from the wounded and setting broken limbs.

From the L.S.T. Scuttlebutt newspaper, Rebecca Smith submitted some historical facts about LST 397 on behalf of Ralph S. Huff. She said, "LST 397 was laid down on September 28, 1942, at Newport News Shipping and Drydock Company. On June 16, 1943, the ship encountered its first action with the enemy when 120 Japanese planes attacked. Later, in a return trip from Cape Torokina to Guadalcanal in December, a torpedo passed under the ship amidship.

"During the time in the Pacific LST 397 saw action at Bougainville, New Guinea, Munda, Rendova, Hollandia, Philippines, Samar, and Leyte. During this period LST 397 evacuated over 1,200 casualties from hostile beaches. Her Surgical team # 9, called themselves 'Bring 'em back alive.'

Joseph Francis Panicello

"When the war ended LST 397 had to her credit 59 combat missions, had participated in 16 invasions and was getting ready for the big push on Japan. In all those missions it never received any serious damage. It was considered a lucky ship. LST 397 earned seven battle stars and the Navy Unit Commendation for World War II services."

On June 30, 6,300 American troops had landed on the island of Renova. The Amphibious forces did have some problems during the landing because of the foul weather. As the Flotilla approached, another problem was discovered. Many LSTs could not land because of the tight quarters on the beach. LST 142 was one that was able to land and in due time, their supplies were transported to the beach. Tanks, trucks, and cannons rolled out and onto the sand. The Seabees quickly removed the cargo from the beaches using the trucks that came off the LSTs, taking them to a special storage area.

When the shooting subsided and the men were back on board LST 142, Bob filed a report against Andre for relinquishing his post on the LCM as the port gunner, and leaving the boat and its crew of 50 marines in peril. After the islands of Rendova and Munda fell, Andre was directed to report for Captains Mass.

Johnny was furious at what Bob had done. He went to Bob and began yelling, "What the hell did you report him for, Olly. I took over his gun and it all worked out fine."

"Look, Macaroni, his job was to protect the troops and the crew. He cannot put the rest of us in jeopardy just to save one man. If he wants to be a gunner, then that's what he has to do. If he wants to be a medical corpsman then he shouldn't have volunteered to be a gunners mate striker."

This did not satisfy Johnny. He felt that the Phibies should stick together and help one another. Johnny kept yelling back at him and began pushing Bob around. Olsen pushed back and, ultimately, fists began to fly. Both of these men were equal in stature and both could handle themselves in a brawl. The battle went on for a long time until Chief Turner came crashing through the hatch and broke them up.

He began shouting at them. "What's the matter with you Goddamn swabs? Didn't you have enough fighting out there on the beach? What's the problem?"

After the situation was explained to him, the Chief became concerned. He had heard that Andre was on his way up to appear before the Captain but he didn't know why. He then bellowed, "You swabs hold off awhile or I'll punch you both out. I'm going up to see the Captain and sees what can be done."

He immediately left for the Captain's quarters. At the Captain's door in the passage way he observed Andre standing under guard, waiting to be called in. The chief pushed the guard aside and knocked on the Captain's door. He was allowed to enter. Chief Turner and the Captain deliberated a long time over Andre's fate. The chief finally came out and told Andre to go to the sick bay and attend the wounded.

"You're not to handle any more guns ever, understood?"

Andre asked, "What happened with the captain, Chief?"

This visibly infuriated the chief. He roared back, "I said, get your ass out of here!" Andre left on the double.

Joseph Francis Panicello

18. Danny Goes Home

Danny Bletcher needed more than just a cast. His arm was badly shattered and needed the expertise of a medical surgeon at a hospital. From the ramp of LST 142 he was able to walk over to a small craft which took him out to an APA transport that was scheduled to bring the wounded back to a military hospital in Hawaii. After one month in the hospital Danny was given leave to go back to the States.

With his left arm in a sling, he hitched a ride on a PBY to San Francisco and then continued his journey to New York via a navy air transport. On the aircraft he had to give a navy attendant one dollar to borrow a parachute. He thought it was peculiar but was told it was navy regulations. He landed at Floyd Bennett Field in Queens Saturday morning, and hitched a ride to South Ozone Park on the Belt Parkway.

Instead of going home, he went to visit Angela. She greeted him at the door, throwing her arms around him. She noticed that his left arm was hidden under his Pea-coat.

She asked, "What happened to your arm, Danny?"

Danny answered, "Nothing much. I took a bullet, but I'm fine now."

Danny was surprised by her embrace, but welcomed it and kissed her lips. They went into the house with her arm under his good arm and before he could remove his Pea-coat she began asking a barrage of questions about Johnny. Mrs. Maroni also fired a volley of questions at him.

"Everyone is fine," he assured them. "I'm the only one that got wounded. Johnny is doing fine, don't worry."

Mrs. Maroni went upstairs to pray to the Virgin Mary and thank her for protecting her son. She left Angela and Danny on the couch together. Angela asked him about his own wound, "Does it still hurt, Danny? Are you going to get well?"

Danny smiled, "Oh sure. Like I said, it's nothing serious. I'll probably be going back to duty in a couple of weeks."

A Slow Moving Target, The LST of World War II

He put his right arm around her and kissed her. Angela was swept off her feet by this huge sailor. He told her how much he loved her and how he missed her.

Angela, now eighteen and out of school, was working as a secretary for an insurance firm. She wasn't sure about Mr. Perfect anymore. She loved Danny. He was fun and thoughtful. She knew about his rowdy side but when they were together she felt cherished. They'd known each other such a short time but the letters they shared had established a bond she had never felt with anyone else.

They talked for hours that day and the next. Danny was impatient. He knew that he would be reassigned soon and didn't know when he would see her again. He decided to pop the question of marriage.

"Angela. You know I love you. Well, I'll be going to sea again and this may be our last chance to be together. I know it's dumb but since I have only a month leave coming, well, don't..."

He couldn't get it out so she helped him and said, "You want to marry me, Danny? If that was what you were going to ask me, my answer is yes."

He was thrilled. He jumped up from the couch, whooping and hollering. He couldn't believe she would agreed. He was the happiest guy in the world. He pulled a small box out of his pocket and, shyly, laid it in her hand.

"You bought a ring?" she asked, touched, as tears came to her eyes, "How could you afford it?"

Danny laughed. "I'm a pretty good card player, Angel. I want my wife to have a ring."

After Mr. Maroni came home from work that evening and they were all seated at the dining room table, Angela made the announcement. At first Mr. Maroni was stunned, but when he looked over at his wife and saw how happy she was over the news, he simply got up and shook Danny's hand and then hugged his daughter with tears in his eyes.

He went back to his chair and raised a glass of wine and said, "May you both be as happy as Mother and I have been."

Angela then burst into tears, followed by her mother, who put her arms around her. They cried together. Danny was as happy as a lark. He asked if he could use the phone and, with their approval, proceeded to call his own parents in New Jersey about the good news.

They were married the following Saturday morning in St. Clements Catholic Church. Father Donovan presided over the ceremony. It was a small affair. Danny's mother and father drove in from New Jersey. Meeting Angela for the first time, they could easily see why their son was so taken with her. They were pleased to observe the closeness between Angela and Danny.

They'd never seen their son so happy and this alone won Angela a place in their hearts. After the ceremony, with evening blackouts still in effect because of the war, a small luncheon reception was held at the Maroni home. The parents of the bride and groom had pooled their ration stamps and, with Mama Maroni's talent for cooking, the guests enjoyed a lavish meal. It was a gay occasion and when Danny and Angela danced together in the middle of the room to "People will Say We're In Love" playing on the phonograph, everyone applauded.

At Angela's insistence, after the reception, the two of them went to the Valencia theater. It wasn't until they were seated that Danny remembered the first time they'd been there together.

"You and I and Robber came here together," he said.

"Yes," she assured him, "and now it's just the two of us. It always will be."

When Johnny received a letter from Angela informing him of the marriage he was surprised, but resigned. His sister seemed happy. "That is the important thing," he thought to himself.

Andre, on the other hand, was annoyed. "How could she marry him?" he asked Johnny. "What can he possibly offer her?"

"What about you?" Johnny retorted. "Are you any better?"

Johnny struck a nerve. Andre went back to his bunk and laid there for a long time, thinking about what Johnny had said. He realized that his own life was going nowhere and would end nowhere unless he did something about it. He had no more of a future than Danny did.

He decided, if he survived this war, he would go back to school and become a medical doctor like his father. He jumped out of his sack and he headed for the chief's quarters. He knocked on his compartment door and the chief cook answered. Andre said, "I have to speak with Chief Turner right away. It's very important."

Chief Turner stepped out and began speaking to him in a strong voice, "Now look Robber. Let's forget what I did for you with the captain. It's over. Now forget about it!"

Andre, flustered, interrupted him, "You don't understand, Chief. I want to go to medical school. I changed my mind. I see now that I can't be an ordinary sailor. When I was helping those wounded marines on our last invasion, I was actually enjoying myself. I felt good about what I was doing by helping the wounded. Everyone of you could see that doctoring was my natural profession, but I couldn't. It took losing a girl that I cared for deeply to straighten me out. I'm certainly no gunman, that's for sure. I'd be more worried about saving some wounded soldier's life than killing a Jap. Hell, I don't think I could even kill a Jap."

The Chief shook his hand and said, "Great. I knew you would come to your senses one of these days. Now that you've decided to become a corpsman, I can tell you what I told the Captain. Even though you deserted your post, I convinced him that the work you did by helping Chief Smith in the sick bay had saved at least 30 marines from dying. He agreed not to punish you if you'd become a corpsman. Now that you've decided to become one, I'll work out the details for ya. You will be sent back to San Diego to be trained as a Pharmacist Mate. I can't promise that you'll come back to this ship, but the navy needs men like you."

"I understand, Chief. I didn't expect to be back. Thank you for everything, including bailing me out with the skipper. You're really not a bad guy. I'll always remember what you did for me."

Joseph Francis Panicello

The chief quickly turned his head to the side. He couldn't be seen displaying emotion. A tear was rolling down his cheek. He had to maintain the reputation of being heartless and tough or he would lose control of his men.

"Dismissed," he barked, and, as Andre sped off down the passageway, the chief smiled to himself. Part of his job was getting the best out of them. With a sense of accomplishment he went back into his compartment. He never realized a little girl from New York had made the difference.

19. The Next Island

Now that Rendova had been secured, the Munda Island invasion began on July 2. Operating from Rendova with amphibious craft, two army regiments landed six miles east of Munda using transports, LCMs, LCVPs and LCPs with PT boats as escorts. Unfortunately, the Japanese were prepared for them and their shore batteries began firing at the transport force. Japanese fire lit up the sky, making it seem like there was a bright full moon, and several transports were destroyed by artillery.

Cruisers and destroyers bombarded Japanese defenses around Munda from July 9 through the 25th. After the bombardment was completed, Munda was assaulted by marines and soldiers, using only small craft. Johnny and Bob did not participate in this attack because LSTs were not involved. When the troops secured the island, an Amphibious Force gunnery officer discovered that the bombing actually did not penetrate the deeply dug bunkers. His conclusion was that night bombing was too uncertain and should be delivered during daylight hours. The success of Rendova and Munda was a great feat for Admiral Turner but his command was turned over to Rear Admiral Theodore Wilkinson in July 1943.

After Rendova and Munda were under U.S. control, the new commander, Admiral Wilkinson, set his sights on a smaller, unnamed island, just 50 miles northwest of Munda. He wanted to maintain a continuous assault on the Japanese throughout the Solomons. Four LSTs, three APAs, and two destroyers were assigned the task of assaulting this unidentified island and LST 142 was chosen to be a participant in this invasion. It was now July, 20, 1943.

When the ships arrived, all but the destroyers had anchored about a half-mile off shore. The destroyers began their usual barrage of cannon fire on the beach to soften it up. They cruised across the shore line, back and forth, bombarding the beach for four hours. The APAs and LSTs then launched their small landing craft with 3,000 troops and 10 tanks. Now that LST 142 had only one LCM left on board, Johnny and Bob manned it by themselves because a major counterattack was not expected. They went over the side with 50 marines and, after they picked up a tank from an APA, they headed for the beach with the rest of the LCM Flotilla.

The opposition from the Japs was a mere 300 men compared to the thousand that were on Munda but they did cause sufficient damage on the assaulting party. Bob's boat reached the beach first, with Johnny spraying the shore line using the port machine gun. The ramp was dropped and the tank disembarked, followed by the 50 marines scampering up the beach, hiding behind the advancing tank for protection.

The return gunfire was somewhat brutal and several marines didn't make it. The rest of the Flotilla reached the shore with twenty more tanks and the rest of the 3,000 marines swamped the shore with gunfire. The 300 defending Japanese troops were quickly disposed of. The wounded marines were taken back to an APA for treatment and, as usual, the dead would be taken out in the deep water and buried at sea, after their dog-tags and personal property were removed.

The LCMs began beaching themselves, disembarking more tanks and trucks ashore, along with several tons of supplies. A marine Major surveyed the area on a Jeep and later reported to Admiral Wilkinson by radio.

He said, "The island has been captured and it seems that it is uninhabited. It doesn't seem to pose any further threat to our troops. I recommend that the island not be considered as an aircraft landing strip because of it's narrow width and it's horseshoe shape."

Meanwhile, Johnny and Bob had left the LCM, and as they wandered up the beach, they passed some dead marines on the beach. Bob had had some reservations about assaulting this island and said, "Sometimes, I don't think it's worth going after

A Slow Moving Target, The LST of World War II

every Goddamn island. This island could have been by-passed and these marines would still be alive."

Johnny's reply was, "Olly. We can't worry about these things. War is hell and many people die as a result. Let's just do our job." They both carried 45-pistols in a holster.

Bob noticed that two of the dead marines had "Tommy" guns laying alongside of them. He quickly said to Johnny, "Why don't we confiscate those guns. There's no sense leaving them here to rust out and we could sure use them. We don't have any on board our LST."

Without hesitation they appropriated two Thompson machine guns, removing several clips from the jackets of the dead. The two went further up the beach and above the tree line, to investigate the island themselves. They came upon a cottage that was half destroyed. Johnny slowly moved closer to it while Bob covered for him with his Tommy gun.

The place was empty and Johnny waved Bob to join him. They went into the half destroyed house slowly and it appeared to be empty. Bob said, "I guess the Major looked at this cottage and decided it was in pretty bad shape and of no use to us."

Johnny agreed and said, "Sure looks like we made a mess of it with our bombs."

Bob began investigating further and discovered a trap door, under a rug, in the center of the main room. He opened the trap door and carefully went down several steps. He called out to Johnny to come down and see what he had uncovered. To their amazement they found a large storage area in the basement that was loaded with can goods of food.

Unknown to Johnny and Bob, back at the beach, Admiral Wilkinson ordered the Flotilla to evacuate the island and return to Munda for further orders. Johnny and Bob weren't aware of this last order and continued their exploration of another cottage that was completely destroyed. There they again found a trap door and more canned food in the basement. It seemed that the provisions were there to feed the Japanese troops.

Joseph Francis Panicello

Johnny said to Bob, "We better go back and report our find to the Major. There's enough food here to feed a Japanese Division."

When they returned to the beach they were shocked to see that the Flotilla had vanished but much of the supplies remained on the beach. Their LCM was the only remaining boat.

"What happened?" was Bob's first reaction. "I wonder why they left in a hurry?"

"Maybe they heard the Japs were coming," answered Johnny.

Johnny noticed that the Flotilla had left drums of diesel oil, gasoline, cans of water, and some munitions on the beach. One truck was stranded, with a flat front tire, and another truck was completely destroyed, laying on its side.

After the initial shock was over Bob said, "Our LCM could never make the trip back to Munda unless we took on board some of those diesel oil drums and strapped them down. The Major must have realized that we were still here so he left the boat for us to return to Munda."

"I guess you're right, Olly. They left in such a hurry they didn't have time to bring this cargo back on board the boats."

The weather was becoming foul and Johnny said, "It looks like we're in for a good one. We better wait for the storm to subside. Those waves out there look pretty nasty. Why don't we see what the rest of the island looks like before we attempt that trip back to Munda."

"It's okay with me, Macaroni, but I think we should replace the flat tire on this truck with a good one from the other disabled truck. We can use the truck to explore the island a hell of a lot faster. There are at least twenty 5-gallon cans of gasoline left on the beach which we can use."

"I agree, Olly. But we better get inside that cottage right now, or drown in the rain." Raindrops had started to fall.

They ran to the cottage that they had discovered initially. It was large and it did provide shelter. One side of the house was blown out but the living room area, kitchen and two bedrooms

A Slow Moving Target, The LST of World War II

were intact. There was plenty of food available and, as far as they could tell, they weren't in any danger.

They stayed the night and the next day and after the rain subsided, they replaced the flat tire on the truck. Five of the gasoline cans were placed in the back of the truck and were tied down with a box full of canned food and two 5-gallon cans of water. They were prepared for a long expedition. Bob drove the truck along a dirt road while Johnny held his Tommy gun at the passenger side, ready for action.

After thirty minutes of driving Johnny spotted another village and said, "Hold it, Olly. The village looks uninhabited but we better check it out first."

Johnny climbed out of the truck and began approaching the village slowly, running from tree to tree, similar to a halfback in a football game. Suddenly, gunfire began hitting the tree trunk that was protecting Johnny. He laid on the ground, wondering how many Japs were there.

Bob quickly climbed out of the truck, carrying his Thompson machine gun, and proceeded to fire his automatic weapon at the cottage where the gunfire was coming from. He heard a terrifying scream coming from the cottage, then an eerie silence.

Both Johnny and Bob remained at their positions awhile longer. Johnny then motioned to Bob that he was going forward. He ran quickly to the next tree for cover. There was no return gunfire. Bob also approached closer and again there was no enemy gunfire. Bob waved to Johnny to approach closer to the cottage. In a crouching position he went to one side of the cottage and approached an open door on his knees. He then immediately jumped in front, ready to blast anything, or anyone, inside. He was shocked at what he saw. Inside there was a group of young children, cowered in a corner, staring at him with wide open eyes, afraid to move.

Johnny waved back to Bob to come over and see what he had discovered. When he entered, the first thing he saw was a dead Jap soldier lying on the floor and a dirty, young woman, in

Joseph Francis Panicello

a torn dress, standing in front of the children, protecting them. In a French accent she asked, "Are you Americans?"

Bob, letting his guard down, lowered his gun. He replied, "Yes, we are. Are there anymore Japs here?"

"No. You killed the last one." Feeling secure, Johnny lowered his gun.

"What are you doing here?" asked Bob.

"I'm a French missionary taking care of orphaned children who have been displaced because of the war. I came here with my father. He was a pastor here for many years. He was killed by the Japanese because he wouldn't abide by their rules. If you are truly Americans, I'm happy. Please come in and sit at the table. We have no food but I can offer you a cup of tea."

Johnny was still a bit uncertain about the situation and asked again, "Are you sure there are no more Japs around?"

"Yes, I'm sure. The rest of the Japanese went down to the shore to fight against you, but this one was a coward and he alone remained behind. He got what he deserved," she said bitterly, with a resentful expression on her face. "He was one of the men that tortured and eventually executed my father."

Johnny grabbed the dead Jap and pulled him outside and out of sight. He then went to the truck and brought back an armful of canned goods and laid them on the table. The French missionary and the children were delighted.

She spoke first. "Thank you, monsieur, for your gift. We haven't had much to eat for the past few days. My name is Lovette Bavour, pronounced *Bavo*, in French. We have 23 orphaned children here and, as you can see, some aren't doing very well. This food will surely help. My name Lovette is French, meaning love."

Bob introduced himself as Robert Olsen and Johnny as John Maroni. She immediately called Bob "Robier" and John "Jean."

She proceeded to open up some cans and the aroma from the food in the cans aroused the sick. The children were now wide-eyed and anxious to eat. She heated the meat and fish in separate pots and the vegetables in pans. When the food was ready, the

A Slow Moving Target, The LST of World War II

children lined up, each with a metal plate, and Bob helped distribute the food. He placed a spoon full from each pot on to a child's plate until every plate was full. There was a variety of beef, tuna fish, corn, potatoes and green beans. Johnny also brought in a five-gallon can of water. He figured that the village water might be contaminated.

As the children began eating Lovette excused herself. She felt grubby and self-conscious. She washed her face, combed her hair and changed her dress. When she came out again Bob and Johnny were amazed. She was a very pretty woman.

Lovette Bavour was born in a small town outside of Paris. Twenty-two years of age, she had spent most her young life in French Indo-China and on various islands in the Solomons. Lovette's mother died five years before of jungle fever. Lovette was devoted to her father, and replacing her mother, helped him continue his work to support the orphans in the mission. Her father was a Calvinist Protestant, the reformed religion originally lead by the French theologian, John Calvin, in 1533.

When the Japanese invaded the island she begged her father to leave with the children, but he was a stubborn man who thought he could get along with the Japs. He was also a sentimental man who didn't want to leave the mission which had taken him ten years to build.

Lovette was average in height, about five-foot four and 118 pounds. She had a very shapely body and was extremely attractive. She had a small round face with a straight, small nose and a medium size mouth with attractive lips. Her long reddish hair laid softly on her shoulders. When she smiled her white teeth sparkled and her large brown eyes radiated enthusiasm. She was a very appealing young lady. Bob couldn't keep his eyes off of her and couldn't do enough for her.

Bob had a good looking face, was tall, with incredibly blond hair. He towered over everyone in the cottage. Johnny had never thought of Bob as anything but another swab doing his job, but when he saw how Lovette was watching Bob he had to admit that he wasn't a bad looking guy. Johnny suspected that there

Joseph Francis Panicello

was an attraction blossoming between them. He grinned to himself. "Love and war somehow seem to go together," he thought.

After the kids were fed, Bob said to Lovette, "We can't stay here. This island has been abandoned by the U.S., and it won't be long before the Japs return. I want all of the children to get into the back of our truck as soon as possible. We are leaving right now."

She was reluctant to acquiesce. She wanted to continue her work there but Bob insisted. "Lovette, you and the children will get into the truck now, or I will have to carry them, and you, to it. Do I make myself clear?"

She looked into his determined blue eyes and was impressed with his firmness. She realized she had no choice. She then helped the children gather their gear and climb onto the back of the truck. She climbed into the front cab and sat between Bob and Johnny. It began to drizzle again but the canvas cover over the bed of the truck protected the children.

When they came back to the beach they noticed that the LCM was still there with its ramp down. Bob dropped the children next to the cottage and had them scamper into the cottage to get out of the rain. The rain turned into a full-scale tropical storm.

That night Johnny decided to sleep in the cab of the truck and stand guard with his Tommy gun. After the children were put to sleep inside what was left of a fine cottage, Bob and Lovette sat outside, on a bench, under the porch eaves, protected from the wind and rain.

Lovette told Bob more about her life as a missionary, describing the people she'd met and the many places she had been.

"Don't you miss Paris?" he asked gently.

"Oh, no, cherie," she smiled. "Each place I have been has been beautiful in its own way. Paris, to me, is just the place I was born."

A Slow Moving Target, The LST of World War II

Bob described Boston, his home, and when he spoke of the sea and ships it brought a sparkle to his eyes. Lovette noticed and said, "It is a wise man that does what he loves and so it is with women too. I admire that in a person, Robier."

Bob placed his hand on hers, "I admire you Lovette. The work you have done, what a gift to give to others. I think I'm falling in love with you."

She smiled with understanding. "Robier, please. You just met me. You feel this way because you are lonely and far from Boston and your sweetheart at home."

He replied adamantly, "I have no sweetheart at home and it's not because I'm lonely. You are a very special person. I sensed it immediately. I want to know you better. Do you feel the same way?"

"I do, Robier," she answered softly. "But it is foolish to..." The pressure of his lips on hers cut off her reply. She responded to his kiss and wrapped her arms around him.

When they separated, as they gazed into one another's eyes, they whispered, in unison, "I love you."

They talked quietly about the future until, an hour later, Lovette, suppressing a small yawn, admitted that she was very tired from the day's events. "We should join the others."

Bob agreed. "It will be a busy day tomorrow," he said, and, hand in hand, they went in and joined the children sleeping peacefully, scattered over the cottage floor.

The next day the storm subsided and Johnny and Bob went out to the beach. They were able to roll several barrels of Diesel oil onto the LCM and carried the remaining cans of water on board. They lashed the drums and cans down securely to prevent destruction if the sea got rough.

Bob loaded the truck with food and told the children to get into the back of the truck again. Lovette joined him in the cab while Johnny waited in the LCM. He kissed her and assured her that they would make it just fine. "I'm a good coxswain and I will get us there safely, believe me." She was convinced that this man could do anything he set his mind to do.

Joseph Francis Panicello

He drove the truck down to the LCM and backed it up over the ramp and onto its deck so that the front of the truck faced the open sea. Johnny began lashing down the truck to the deck with chains and rope. The children were told to remain in the truck bed throughout the trip because it would be safer there.

Bob told Lovette, "It's going to be a 50 mile voyage and, with this weather, it will probably take us all day to reach Munda." He assured her again, "We have plenty of fuel, food and water to get us there safely, so you don't have to worry." Proudly, she watched him making the final preparations for the long trip ahead.

Johnny fired up the engine, lifted the ramp and secured it. Bob moved the LCM out slowly and onto the open sea. Johnny went back to his post as engineer and the long, grueling trip began. Even though the storm had subsided, the sea was unforgiving. The waves were high and choppy. Lovette had joined the children. Many of them were seasick and all of them were scared.

The waves, at times, were so high they engulfed the boat and almost washed Johnny and Bob overboard. They began fastening themselves down to the boat and tied their bodies together with a rope. If one went overboard it was hoped that the other could haul him back.

After the LCM traveled for two hours Johnny noticed that the fuel in the tank was getting low. The LCM's fuel tank contained enough fuel to travel thirty miles in a calm sea. In a hostile sea the fuel was consumed much faster. Johnny called out to Bob, "Slow down, Olly. I've got to refill the fuel tank." He now remembered that he should have topped off the fuel tank before they left.

Johnny had to run a hose, connected to a hand pump, from the drum to the fuel tank. To do this, he had to untie himself from the boat and crank the pump. Suddenly, a large wave hit them. Johnny found himself over the side, hanging on to the only life line he had left, which was, fortunately, still tied to Bob. Bob stopped the boat and began hauling Johnny back in.

A Slow Moving Target, The LST of World War II

Bob yelled out, "Hang on, Macaroni, I've got you." He pulled and pulled and was finally able to bring Johnny close. Lovette, watching from the back of the truck, asked if he needed help. Bob yelled, "Stay put or you'll be washed overboard too." Bob, by now, was exhausted and didn't need another problem.

As Johnny finally came on board he was breathing hard and all he could say was, "Thanks, buddy. I owe you one."

Still breathing hard, Johnny went back to pumping diesel oil into the fuel tank. After awhile he called out, "Okay, Olly. It's full, shove off." Johnny had to refuel the tank once more before they spotted Munda but by now the sea was calmer.

As they approached the island a PT boat came out to investigate and, after recognizing who they were, escorted them back to shore. When the LCM landed and the ramp was lowered, Bob drove the truck full of children up to one of the newly installed Quonset huts that were put together by the Seabees. Twenty-three children, ranging from two to twelve, climbed out of the truck and began forming a single line, holding hands. They were led by Lovette, carrying the toddler, as they were led to a temporary headquarters that was set up for Admiral Wilkinson.

At least 100 marines promptly assembled around the hut's front door to observe the procession of these small children being guided into the hut by a pretty woman. There was total silence. They were amazed and a bit melancholy at the sight of these young children, with smiles on their faces, walking in a single file toward the hut. It was as though they had never seen children before. This might be the last time for some of them to ever see any children at all, for tomorrow the fighting would begin anew. After a brief conversation with the Admiral, Lovette and the children were escorted to another Quonset hut where they were to remain until they could be evacuated to Hawaii.

Bob was told to write a report for the Admiral explaining the **status of that island, and how he'd happened to acquire these children.** With the report completed, Bob went over to the Quonset hut to visit Lovette. He explained to her that he might

Joseph Francis Panicello

not see her again for a long time. He had to return to LST 142, anchored out in the bay, but he would write to her regularly. She cried in his arms and held him tight for a long while. He kissed her goodby and left her, with tears in her eyes.

For their bravery, the Admiral recommended that Maroni and Olsen receive the Silver Star. The information in Bob's report about the island turned out to be beneficial and Admiral Wilkinson decided to use that island as a radio relay station to assist in the invasions of other islands.

20. Sicily, July 1943

On Monday morning, Danny Bletcher reported to the Saint Albans Naval Hospital in Queens. He had to take the 142nd Street bus from South Ozone Park to Jamaica and transfer again to a Hill Side bus and out again to North Central Queens to Saint Albans. It took almost two hours to make the trip, even though the actual distance from South Ozone Park was less than five miles.

On Tuesday he had to see a navy doctor about the condition of his left arm and, after the examination, the doctor said, "It's healing fine Bletcher, but you need therapy to strengthen that arm. Your arm was shattered pretty badly and it's going to take awhile to get your strength back. With about a month of therapy you should be able to go back to duty."

Danny was delighted that he could have another month with Angela, less ecstatic about the prospect of going back to duty. Every liberty weekend he was granted he would spend with his wife. They were extremely happy. He was definitely a changed man. His mother and father came out to Queens from New Jersey to visit one day and they noticed the enormous difference in their son's attitude. He was calm, considerate and was even talking about going back to school after the war was over. Angela had changed his disposition completely and the Bletchers could see that they were truly in love. They were proud of their once unruly son.

After the month of therapy was over Danny was dismissed from the hospital and reported to a Chief Yeoman at the naval base next to the hospital.

The Chief said to him, "Here are your orders, Bletcher. You're to report to LST 85, now docked at the Brooklyn Navy Yard, where it is being modified with evaporators."

Evaporators were being installed on the LST to give it the capability of creating its own fresh water from sea water. This would provide the ship with a greater range to travel over the

Joseph Francis Panicello

Atlantic Ocean as far as Eastern North Africa. The LST carried 186 thousand gallons of Diesel oil and 120 thousand gallons of fresh water. It had a range of 15 thousand miles, traveling at eight knots, but the water supply would give out much sooner. Showers by the crew were forbidden when traveling long distances on LSTs without evaporators, which are used to desalinate the sea water.

At the shipyard the personnel officer on board LST 85 reviewed Danny's papers about his experiences in the Pacific. He immediately filed the papers to transfer him to his own ship. He also made a recommendation to LST 85 Captain Gerrad, to promote Danny to 3rd Class Boatswain Mate. The crew on this ship were all new recruits and Danny would need a rate with authority to teach them all he knew about the landing craft operation.

Danny reported to the Chief Boatswain Mate Kelly of LST 85 who said, "So you're Daniel Bletcher? Here are your new stripes. You've been promoted to Third Class Boatswain Mate. I hope we didn't make a mistake." He sounded skeptical.

Danny was surprised and replied, "Thanks, Chief. This is going to mean more money for my wife. I won't disappoint you."

They went down to the crew's quarters together and when Danny met the seamen he knew right off that he had his hands full. The crew were very young and looked like they should still be in high school.

Chief Kelly said to him quietly, "If you can do anything with that lot I'll recommend you for the Congressional Medal of Honor. I gave up on them while we were in Norfolk, Virginia."

"I'll do the best that I can, Chief. I can remember when I came out of boot camp myself. I was just as young and inexperienced as they are." The Chief simply walked away, shaking his head. He wasn't expecting too much.

The destination for LST 85 was Algiers, which was now under the Allied command, after defeating the Vichy French. It was April 15, 1943, when the ship left the Brooklyn Navy Yard for North Africa. They had no cargo on board, which allowed the ship to run at its cruising speed of 10 knots. Unfortunately, the weather wasn't ideal and it took them 18 days to reach their destination.

During the trip Danny gave instructions to his young crew on the different duties they would have to perform in the process of a beach landing. He explained how every man had to be able to handle more than one task in the event that someone is incapacitated. As usual, he started with the rear anchor operation, then operating the blowers, and later, how to lower a landing craft over the side. He even instructed them on how to fire the 40mm guns from the bow and the guns on the small landing craft. Finally, he began instructing them on the different tasks required to open the main bow doors and lowering the ramp.

He tried to instill in them the fact that communications between the various stations and the bridge were crucial and every operation has to transpire at the proper sequential time, especially when the ship is being beached.

As he was giving instructions to the recruits, Danny realized that one of his sailors was not paying much attention. He looked at this recruit and recognized the similarities between them. This sailor had the same attitude that he'd had and was just as big.

Danny just grinned and said to himself, "I think I've found my seaman first class to help straighten out these yokels. All he needs is a little encouragement."

He proceeded to give this recruit, whose name was Harry Winter, special responsibilities. Putting Harry in charge of a task made him feel important and it wasn't long before he became more interested over the ship's operation, and how important the landing craft was to the war effort.

When they reached Algiers on May 17, 1943, they met up with several other LSTs that were being loaded with cargo, tanks, trucks, and artillery. Captain Gerrad of LST 85 finally received his orders that day. It was to support Colonel William O. Darby and his rangers in the invasion of Sicily.

Joseph Francis Panicello

Colonel Darby had already gained considerable renown in the North African campaign. Unfortunately, a full third of his present command were neither rangers nor infantry men, but rather an untested 1st Battalion, the 39th Combat Engineer Regiment, with no combat experience at all.

Major Stanley Dziuban, who was the commander of the 1st Battalion, was ordered by Darby to transfer his command to the port city of Oran, which is located 100 miles south. There they would perform military functions and have to undergo a two-week period of intensive training in infantry tactics. The reason for relocating the engineers was purposely done to keep the operation secret throughout their training period.

On May 3, 1943, a new plan was accepted by the Joint Chiefs which was clearly General Montgomery's idea, even though he was considered arrogant and vain by the American brass. It was a maneuver of simultaneously landing three American and four British divisions across a 100 mile-wide invasion front of Southern Sicily. The plan was for the Americans to land left of the British flank on the southwest coast of Sicily. Montgomery's troops would land on the southeast coast near Syracuse.

Admiral Hall's Task Force, which consisted of the 1st Infantry Division and Rangers, were told to attack the city of Gela, and then, under Patton, they would work their way around the west coast through the cities of Marsala, Trapini, Alcamo, and to the capital city of Palermo by July 22. From there they should march east and meet up with Montgomery in Messina with his army coming up the east coast. Montgomery would be there waiting for them in Messina. Patton, of course, had other ideas. Messina is the city located on the northeast coast of the Messina Strait, which is a narrow body of water between Sicily and the toe of the Italian mainland and the Provence of Calabria.

Sicily is the largest island in the Mediterranean with an area of 9,925 sq. miles, making it larger than the state of New Jersey and about the same size as Vermont. It has a population of four million people. Sicily is sometimes referred to as "The Island in

A Slow Moving Target, The LST of World War II

the Sun." Much of the island is mountainous, with an active volcano, Mt. Etna, which peaks about 10,750 feet.

The original Sicilians were members of the Italic tribe, the same people that migrated to Rome from central Europe. Because of the many wars in the Roman area, several groups of these Italic people migrated south and eventually ended up in Sicily.

These Sicilians were later driven into the mountains by the Greeks, who invaded the island in the 8th Century B.C. After that the Phoenicians, Carthaginians, Romans, Byzantines, and German Vandals created colonies on the island, before being conquered by the Saracens from Africa. They, in turn, were ousted by Roger I, the Norman Viking conqueror who became the first Count of Sicily. He was followed by his son, Roger II, who then became the first king of Sicily and of Southern Italy. In turn he was followed by others, such as the German Emperor, Frederick II, the French Angevin of Anjou, and the Spanish Aragons. Sicily was later conquered by Garibaldi who lead his "Red Shirts" to victory in 1860 over a French Bourbon King who had controlled the two Sicilies (Sicily and Naples). Garibaldi was the major figure to help unify Italy as a country in 1871.

The distinguished Greek mathematician and physicist, Archimedes, (287-212 B.C.) was born and died in Syracuse, Sicily. He worked on 'areas' and 'volumes' of conic sections and determined the value of 'pi' which is used today in geometry and other mathematical equations. His Archimedes' principle founded the science of hydrostatics, which is the reason our large steel ships are able to float today. His principle states, basically, that the force acting to float a ship in water is equal to the weight of water it displaces. In physics he was the first to prove the law of the lever.

Ernie Pyle, the author and correspondent, described the Flotilla that assembled off the shores of Sicily on July of 1943, as the biggest amphibious operation in history at that time. It involved 3,300 ships and seven Allied Divisions.

Joseph Francis Panicello

Ernie Pyle was known as the "GI journalist" and "soldier's best friend" in World War II. He walked through mud and crunched in foxholes, and even thumbed rides in jeeps, tanks, and aboard ships. He didn't file his reports from safe posts, but hammered them out as bullets whistled overhead and shells exploded close by. Ernie Pyle was killed on April 18, 1945, by a sniper's bullet on Ie Shima Island during the invasion of Okinawa, just before the war ended. On the spot where he fell a Memorial was built by the 77th Inf. Div. to honor him.

Before the decision to attack Sicily, there were deep disagreements between the British and Americans on the next operation. U.S. Chief of Staff, General George C. Marshall's approach was to mount a massive force in England and send it across the Channel, through France and against Germany. Going up through Sicily, as far as Marshall was concerned, was "a suction pump" that would draw troops from the main effort.

The British saw it differently. After hundreds of years of fighting wars in Europe, they favored Churchill's approach of nibbling away at the Germans, by constantly providing a blockade, bombing and attacking them, until the opportunity arose to deliver the mortal blow. Going through Italy would definitely weaken the Germans and might even encourage Italy to surrender. There was a large Partisan guerrilla force in Italy that was against the war and fought the Germans and Mussolini's blackguards from underground. It was the Partisans that finally killed Mussolini and his girlfriend.

Roosevelt and Churchill met in Casablanca, Morocco, January 14, 1943. Churchill persuaded FDR to follow up the North African campaign with an invasion of Sicily and then Italy, aiming at the so-called "soft underbelly" of Hitler's Europe. In truth, Churchill wanted the Western Allies rather than Stalin's Russia to oversee the postwar reorganization of Europe. Churchill won out, again.

The tactical plan for the invasion of Sicily was for General Sir Bernard L. Montgomery to land on the southeast corner of the island with the British 5th, 50th, and 51st infantry divisions, the 1st Canadian infantry division, and two Royal Marine Commando units. The American 7th army, under General George S. Patton Jr., would land on Montgomery's left using the U.S. 1st, 3rd, and 45 infantry divisions, and later the 2nd Armored division. Montgomery's plan was to drive up the coast through the cities of Augusta, Catania and finally to Messina.

The American commanders were ruffled over this plan because they were now regulated to a secondary role. Montgomery would receive all the credit. The Americans intensely disliked Montgomery who had expressed the thought that the Americans were not good fighters. General Patton, however, was not to be denied.

On July 5, the engineers, along with the rangers, were taken to Algiers and only then did Dziuban and his officers learn of their mission. His rangers were now known as Force Dime.

Admiral Hall's orders to Major Dziuban were that he should take the port city of Gela located nearer the central southern side of Sicily. Gela was a quaint fishing city with a population of about 32,000. Its capture and defense were critical to the success of the whole operation now named Operation Husky, the largest invasion thus far in military history.

Gela is an ancient city that was founded by the Dorian Greeks in 689 B.C. The city is at the mouth of the river Gela. "Gelo" means freezing, in Italian, and the river was so named because the waters coming down from the mountains were relatively cold. Gelato is the Italian word for ice-cream.

Eventually, the city was controlled by the Greek leaders of Syracuse, and in 405 B.C., the Carthaginians conquered Gela, but one hundred years later it was recaptured by the Syracuse army. In 282 B.C., the city was completely destroyed by a Syracuse leader, and remained that way throughout the Roman Empire. In 1233 A.D., the German (Swabia) Emperor Frederick II, who became the king of Southern Italy, Sicily and Germany, rebuilt the city as it stands today. Frederick was the nephew of both the Norman King Roger II, the first king of Sicily and Southern Italy, and Frederick Barbarossa of Germany.

Joseph Francis Panicello

Dziuban and his officers began looking at a map of Gela, which showed that the town sat on a 150-foot-high mound extending three miles along the coast and 4,000 yards inland. They also learned that the Italian 429th Coastal Battalion had established defenses all around, using concrete pillboxes and barbed wire. The beach front was about 1,000 yards long and divided in half by a 900-foot concrete pier at the center. The left side was designated by the American invaders as the Red Beach, and the right side the Green Beach. Both beaches were roughly 80 yards deep. Because there were several local fishing boats beached on the shore the American officers assumed there were no mines on the beach.

The weather was not very favorable, which slowed the departure of the ships from Algiers and, at midnight, July 9, 1943, it was decided to proceed with the plan. When the order came over the loud speaker system to prepare for the landing, the army quickly gathered their gear and began filing out onto the open decks of the different transports. The men moved to the transport's port side, the leeward side, and descended rope ladders onto the Higgins LCVP that waited below.

The LCVPs moved to their assigned staging areas and, in a circle, waited for their orders to be given to head for shore. The grueling half-hour wait caused many men to become seasick from the turbulent sea.

The orders were given to attack on July 10, 1943, and less than two months after North Africa's liberation, 180,000 Allied troops and an armada of 1,375 amphibious ships arrived at Sicily and proceeded to make their journey to shore. It was the largest amphibious force ever assembled, up to that time, making the first full use of LSTs in the Atlantic.

Rough seas, however, forced many of the landing craft to be pushed out of position, causing confusion among the coxswains. There was no communications between the Higgins LCVPs, which didn't help the situation. Then came a barrage of artillery fire from shore directed at the oncoming LCVPs. At this point

A Slow Moving Target, The LST of World War II

the destroyer, *Shubrick*, opened fired at the shore and knocked out two search lights.

Intense gunfire erupted from both sides and the skyline was ablaze with tracer bullets crisscrossing in wild patterns, followed by many explosions. Machine guns from shore were hitting the landing crafts and several others took a direct hit from mortar rounds. Approximately 100 yards from the beach a sandbar was discovered. When several landing craft struck the sandbars they prematurely dropped their ramps and the men were ordered to inflate their Mae West life preservers and make for shore as best they could. The Rangers came under heavy machine-gun fire which caused the loss of a whole platoon.

On the east coast the British were celebrating an easy successful landing near Syracuse. Montgomery, quick to make headlines, made an announcement that it was a spectacular victory for the Brits. However, he hadn't seen the worst of it.

At Gela, before the American attack, the Italian General Guzzoni, had designated one mobile Italian division and two other groups with tanks to counterattack the American forces along with a German division that was commanded by General Paul Conrath, but there was a mix up between them due to the bombing from the Allies and Conrath never received his orders to fight together with Guzzoni. Being separated, Guzzoni had to go it alone. Somehow, ten of his tanks got through to Gela.

After the Americans reached shore they ran into heavy machine gun fire, concentrations of barbed wire, and unexpected mines. Apparently, the fishing boats were just decoys. Initially, the American troops got the worst of it. A young ranger, Lieutenant Colonel William O. Darby, lost his patience after firing 300 rounds of 30-caliber ammunition at one of those Italian tanks and watching the bullets bounce off of it harmlessly.

Col. Darby quickly jumped onto a jeep and went down to the shore where he saw the soldiers bringing out an anti-tank 37 mm gun from an LST, so he took the anti-tank gun and its crew back with him to town and began firing at a tank. They completely demolished the Italian tank. Because of the destruction the rest of the Italian tanks withdrew quickly. This action saved many American lives. Darby received the Distinguished Service Cross for his act.

Kesselring, in Rome, was not happy with either the Italians or Conrath's performance, and ordered them to attack the next day. This time Conrath linked up with the Italians but when they attacked they were met with naval gunfire from Captain James B. Lyle on the light cruiser, *USS Savannah*. The *Savannah*, using 66-inch guns, released 500 rounds at the attackers.

In the onslaught the Americans captured 400 Italians who were dazed, staggering, wounded or killed. They could hardly comprehend what had hit them. The gunfire had been devastating and Captain Lyle reported that, "there were human bodies hanging from the trees."

Dziuban ordered his men to proceed with the assault, but they ran into two pillboxes that pinned them down for a long while. A brave Sergeant Gilbert ran up to the nearest pillbox and tossed a grenade through its firing hole. After the explosion there was silence, then the second pillbox raised a white flag. From this point on the Italians gave only a half-hearted resistance. Before long every pillbox surrendered.

Many Italian prisoners showed up with white flags, causing an unexpected swell of POWs. A makeshift POW camp was set up and was filled to capacity. Many Italians prisoners remained outside the camp because there was no room inside but they had no desire to escape. Why should they? They seemed to be delighted that they were captured and out of an unpleasant war, led by the German puppet, Mussolini. Most Italians were against the war in the first place.

Due to the loss of the concrete pier, all LSTs were diverted to a beach six miles east. It was absolutely necessary to bring in the heavy equipment because they expected a counterattack, not from the Italians, but from the Germans.

Lieutenant John Pacer of Company B, who was in charge of the LSTs operation, went on board LST 85 and directed the

A Slow Moving Target, The LST of World War II

unloading of M2 halftracks that were badly needed back at Gela. At 10 a.m. while unloading the half tracks, three German Messerschmitt Me-109 fighter-bombers suddenly attacked the beach area, dropping two bombs on the LST. Deadly shrapnel flew everywhere. Unfortunately, Pacer was unable to provide any halftracks to Gela at this time, which disappointed Major Dziuban.

Danny Bletcher, who was manning the forward 40 mm gun on LST 85 at the time, was blasting away at a German bomber. The bomber managed to drop his bomb on the deck close to Danny. Danny was hit in the arm from shrapnel and was thrown overboard into the water from the concussion. Fortunately, his wound was only superficial. He swam to shore, jumping into a fox hole which contained two dead American soldiers. He was horrified, seeing his comrades laying there dead in the line of duty.

As he lay there defenseless, he was shocked from an enormous explosion coming from LST 313 that was stranded on the sandbar near Gela. It was set ablaze by enemy bombs. Army troops and sailors were abandoning the LST as quickly as possible. The blaze of fire coming from LST 313 lit up the sky. By that light Danny found a safer fox hole. He then watched LST 312 being hauled off the beach by a tug, after it had broached. When the bombing subsided he worked his way back to his own ship. He found considerable damage on board but LST 85 was salvageable.

As was expected, the German counterattack began. A heavily armed battalion of Hermann Goring's tank division began advancing toward the 1st division at the north edge of Gela. Fortunately, Lieutenant Pacer was finally able to bring his halftracks to support Dziuban. Also, several medium tanks that came off LSTs were now forward and in position. Additional field batteries had also arrived during the night. The attack from the Germans was strong, with heavy artillery bombardments. The Americans stood their ground, beginning a barrage of cannon fire at the enemy. The German advance was halted as the engineer-led halftracks overwhelmed them.

From a nearby position, Captain Hanson had a spectacular view of the decimation of the enemy. Arriving at Hanson's position, Lt. Gen. George Patton also witnessed the scene. Patton was annoyed with Hanson's hesitation to advance. Patton ordered Hanson to personally destroy the enemy completely. Hanson proceeded with his men in halftracks, firing their 50-caliber machine guns, raking the area with bullets and shells, killing many German soldiers ruthlessly. "Orders are orders," he reasoned, to rationalize the overkill.

General Patton originally wanted to hit the beaches with his men on D-day, July 10, 1943, but thought it best that he remain on the flagship. The next morning he went ashore and noticed that two DUKW amphibious trucks, with the capacity to carry twenty-five men, were knocked out of action. That was a close call because he would have been on one of them had he gone ashore on D-Day.

Instead of visiting General Allen, Patton ordered his driver to turn off the road to visit first with Colonel Darby. Fortunately, the detour saved his life a second time. Had he continued down the road he would have run into several German tanks firing at the Americans.

For the moment Patton was safe. When cannon fire erupted from other enemy tanks in the streets near him, he spotted a naval officer with a radio and roared, "If you can connect with your God-damn navy, tell them for God's sake, to drop some shell fire on the road."

The navy complied, launching a barrage of 6-inch shells from the cruiser *USS Savannah*. The General was pleased with the results. The shelling destroyed several tanks, the rest withdrawing to safety.

East of the city, a battle with German armor continued, backed up with German air attacks. There were many casualties among the Americans but finally they were able to subdue the enemy. At 0300 hours on July 12, the battle for Gela ended.

A Slow Moving Target, The LST of World War II

After Gela fell, Danny wrote to his wife, Angela. He told her he was alright but couldn't mention anything about the battle for security reasons. He did tell her that he was slightly wounded in the arm but was fixed up by the ship's corpsman.

When he mentioned Gela in his letter, Angela's father was elated and said to her, "That's where I was born. I still have relatives there. Quickly, my dear Angelina, write to him and give him my sister and my cousins home addresses. They will be honored and delighted to see him."

Angela did write to Danny about the family. She also told him she was pregnant. When Danny received her letter a month later he went absolutely ape. "I'm going to be a father," he yelled out.

Montgomery's British 8th army became a battering ram. Kesselring decided that the east side of Sicily was more important to counterattack, so he ordered many Italian and German troops to move to the east, reducing the number of defenders in the west. Montgomery's movement north was now slow and costly. He definitely wanted to be in Messina first.

While the British were stalled on the slopes of Mount Etna the American Seventh Army was going up the west coast.

On the way to the Capital city, Palermo, the Americans had to capture the city of Trapini and then Marsala. Trapini wasn't badly hit by the Americans but the famous wine city of Marsala was bombed badly by several hundred American bombers on Garibaldi Day, May 11. There had been ample warning for the 30,000 people to leave the city when Allied planes dropped thousands of leaflets, but many wouldn't leave and died. On July 24, 1943 American GIs marched into Marsala. The next city north, *Alcamo, received the Americans with cheers.

The people of Palermo were so anxious to surrender to the Americans that they sent a delegation of prominent citizens to seek out Gen. Patton at Alcamo and offered him the keys to the

---

* Alcamo is the birth place of the author's parents.

city. Palermo was a prime prize because it was the capital of Sicily and a major port for American ships to dock.

After Palermo, the Seventh and Eighth Armies headed east for Messina. Messina had no longer anything worth bombing. It was a pile of rubble. Gen. Patton entered Messina in August, 1943, at 1045 that morning. The end might have come sooner if Patton hadn't been given a subordinate position in the overall plan. As it turned out, Patton and his Seventh Army beat Montgomery into Messina by a few hours. Montgomery told Patton, "It was a jolly good race. I congratulate you."

Lucky Luciano, the notorious American Mafia Chief, made a deal with the U.S. government. If he were freed from jail and deported to Italy, he would assist in providing tactical information about Sicily and help persuade the Sicilians to support the Allies. After what happened at Gela, it seems he wasn't completely successful but many of the Italian soldiers did surrender easily, and through his efforts, Luciano was able to persuade the people of Sicily to welcome the Allies with open arms. He did supply tactical information to the Americans that proved to be very valuable to the Generals so his release was not completely unwarranted.

The intense rivalry between Montgomery and Patton continued until the end of the War, stemming, in part, from Montgomery's low opinion of the fighting ability of American troops. This attitude was shared in the beginning by Hitler, who thought Americans would not be much of a fighting force. It seems they both learned a lesson, although Montgomery would always feel that the British army was the main force of the Allies.

Hitler and the Japanese both, for some reason, thought Americans were soft and could not be disciplined into becoming a fighting force. The Japanese myth about Americans in their training manuals read, "Americans are very haughty, effeminate and cowardly—intensely dislike fighting in the rain or in the dark." In Hitler's opinion, Americans were "just gangsters" and had no desire to fight.

They both obviously miscalculated America's perseverance and discovered that Americans were great fighters and innovators who could produce many tanks, ships and aircraft in short order. The Americans did fight unconventionally but they were relentless in their attack. Patton's army of topsy-turvy soldiers were first to arrive in Messina, which removed all the glory expected by Montgomery. It was a personal and satisfactory victory for the Americans and taught the Germans to respect the American fighting force.

Joseph Francis Panicello

21. Letters to Angela

Dear Angela:

Johnny asked me to write and catch you up on events. Things are happening so fast. We all miss Danny but were pleased at his promotion. Your marriage is the best thing that ever happened to him. You must be quite a girl.

I'm glad he's okay. When Johnny read your last letter we were afraid his arm would put him permanently out of action. Getting hit twice in the same arm is sure a coincidence.

Johnny and I each received the Silver Star. We rescued a missionary woman and 23 children. The woman's name is Lovette and if I survive this war I intend to make her my wife.

Things sure happen fast in the Navy!

Johnny's getting leave soon. He intends to go to California. He wants to see Dolores, of course, but Rich Hienman's wife, Mildred, hasn't written in almost 2 months. Rich is very unnerved. Johnny wants to make sure everything's all right. Between the two of us, Rich is a straight-arrow about his marriage but us Phibies aren't so sure about Mildred.

Next time you write let us know about Andre. We haven't heard anything since he left the ship for Corpsman's school.

By the way, Johnny was thrilled to learn that he will be an uncle by next year. Congratulations. Danny must be crowing like a rooster.

Sincerely,
Bob Olsen

My Angel:

I can't believe it! I ran all over the ship shouting to everyone I passed, "I'm going to be a father!" It's the second best thing that ever happened to me. You make sure you take care of yourself, get plenty of rest. I wonder if it will be a boy, or a girl, just as pretty as you. If it's a boy he'll probably be a hellion.

A Slow Moving Target, The LST of World War II

I tried to contact your father's relatives but there was so little time. The Navy keeps us on the move. I can't even let you know what's next. I just don't know.

I miss the Phibies. Please keep writing them. The only news about them I receive is from you. Only three are left on LST 142. Who knows how long that will last.

The crew here on LST 85 has turned out to be a pretty good one, even with the raw recruits. Still it's not the same. I even miss Robber. In answer to your question, no, I don't mind if you continue to write to him. If I were the one you hadn't chosen I'd miss your letters too.

I miss you everyday. Pray for me.

Love,
Danny

Dear Angela:

Danny's a lucky man. It's still hard to believe that you and Danny are married, and a baby on the way!

I have to admit this all shook me up. You know how I feel. I guess I should say felt. I need to put my feelings for you away and become the faithful family friend. If you should ever need anything, Angela, just ask. I will always care for you, and that big ox!

Because of you, Angela, I've transferred from LST 142 to go to Pharmacist Mate training. It's the best thing I could have done.

In Hawaii, waiting for a transport to San Diego, the navy put me to work in the hospital. I was assigned to the operating room. The wounded were arriving by the hundreds each day. I caught on pretty fast. One doctor thought I was already a medical corpsman. He said he had never seen anyone so efficient and capable at stitching, setting broken bones and digging out bullets and shrapnel.

Penicillin has helped immensely in cutting down the death rate from infections because of battle wounds. It's much more

Joseph Francis Panicello

effective than sulfa, which is all we had at the beginning of the war. It was discovered accidently in 1928, by a man named Alexander Fleming, in England and is now used as an antibiotic medicine. It's made of fungi. It wasn't until 1940 that the product was able to be manufactured by Howard Florey and Ernst Chain.

As you can tell, I've been learning on the job, and fast! When I reached San Diego, after hitching a ride on a PBY aircraft I immersed myself in my studies.

The hard work paid off, Angela. After twelve weeks of training I graduated at the top of my class, posting the highest marks of any student that had ever attended there. My Dad was really proud. So was my Mom.

At graduation, the commanding officer, after receiving my records and "my exceptional record of service at the hospital in Hawaii" is the way he put it, recommended I become a First Class Pharmacist Mate.

I will be here at this address working at this base hospital until I get my orders. Please write me soon and catch me up on the activities of the other Phibies.

With love,
Andre

22. Macaroni Goes Home

Within two months Andre received orders to pick up LST 153 in the Solomons at Renova. The previous chief Pharmacist Mate of LST 153 was killed while tending a marine on shore.

Andre was excited. He knew that LST 142 was operating in the Solomons and after settling in on LST 153 he set out to locate the other Phibies. He discovered LST 142 was anchored in a bay off of Renova and, with the help of a few dollars, coaxed a coxswain into taking him to the ship in a motor launch.

When Andre arrived he asked the officer on watch for permission to come aboard. He was allowed to pass without the proper boarding papers because the officer recognized him and was glad to see him again. Security was now becoming an important issue because several ships had been sabotaged by spies dressed in sailor suits.

Andre went into the crew's quarters and yelled out loud, "Phibies." Johnny jumped out of his bunk and ran over to Andre and grabbed him. He was followed by Bob and Rich. The questions came pouring out, "Where have you been? How did you get those stripes?"

"Doesn't Angela write to you?" asked Andre.

"Of course," Johnny replied, "to just about all of us, but with her letters and our letters bouncing all over the world, lines are bound to get crossed some times."

As they were chatting away, swapping sea stories, trying to out do each other with their jokes and jibes, Chief Turner came in, interrupting the reunion.

"Hello, Robber. I see you got your stripes. Congratulations. I knew you'd make a great Pharmacist Mate and a first Class at that." The chief turned to Rich, "Hinny, you're to report to the Captain immediately," and abruptly walked out.

When Rich entered the Captain's quarters he stood at attention, mystified. The Captain said, "At ease, Hienman." After examining a paper in front of him the Captain looked up

Joseph Francis Panicello

and reluctantly announced, "I have good news for you, Hienman. You are being promoted to First Class Gunners Mate."

Hienman, a little startled, simply replied, "Thank you, Sir." The Captain, however, didn't appear pleased.

The captain continued, "That's the good news. The bad news for us is, you are being transferred to the flagship destroyer, *Cony,* under the command of Admiral Wilkinson. I knew this would happen some day. Every time I get a good cook or a good gunner they steal them from under my nose, the bastards. Well, that's the way it is in the navy, so good luck to you on your new assignment and keep shooting down those rotten Japs. I understand there's a motor launch tied to our port side and going ashore soon. Be on it. That is all. You're dismissed." He was very blunt, not revealing his dismay.

As Hienman left the captain's office he was happy, but reluctant to leave the other Phibies. He was proud of the promotion, however, going from a Third Class Petty Officer, skipping Second Class, to First Class. It meant some prestige for him but practically, more money for him and his wife. He sure hated to leave his buddies, though.

When he returned to the galley table he broke the news to the others. At first there was silence, then Johnny stood, extending his hand, and said, "Well, congratulations, Hinny. You're going up in this navy. We'll sure miss you, especially at the guns." They all smiled and shook his hand.

"Thanks guys. I'll miss you clowns too. Is that motor launch tied up on the port side of the ship for you, Robber? If it is, I'll be going ashore with you as soon as I can get my gear together."

"No sweat, Hinny. We have plenty of time. It cost me ten bucks to con that coxswain to bring me out here," replied Andre. "Keep in touch with us through Angela, will ya, Hinny?"

Hienman had never written Angela but promised to start. He went to his locker to transfer his gear into his seabag. As he packed, he thought, "At least I'll be in the same Flotilla," as though that would be consolation.

A Slow Moving Target, The LST of World War II

As the Phibies shared a last cup of jo together, each was lost in their own thoughts. The news of Rich's transfer had put a damper on the party mood.

Again, Chief Turner interrupted, "Damn Navy!" he grumbled. He handed Johnny an envelope and, without a word to him, started out.

Johnny was afraid to look at the contents. Bob couldn't stand the suspense and, as the other Phibies watched, grabbed the envelope, opened it, and read silently. He looked up, paused, then said quietly, "It's a new assignment. You are to return to New York, to train recruits on Diesel engines, especially those used on LSTs and other amphibious craft. If you have leave coming you may take two weeks before reporting for duty.

"Holy smokes." cheered Johnny. "I'm going home. Wow! Maybe I can stop on the way and see Dolores in Los Angeles. This is great news." Johnny was absolutely thrilled.

Bob said sadly, "Hell, it looks as though each of us will be all alone out here."

Johnny immediately packed his gear into his seabag and left the ship, using the ship's motor launch which had to be lowered into the bay. A PBY aircraft had landed in the bay to deliver mail and three new officers. It had anchored that morning and would be leaving for Hawaii in the evening with mail and personnel.

Andre and Rich boarded the "rented" motor launch and headed for shore. Bob could only watch the two launches move away from the side of the ship, in opposite directions. He felt a lump in his throat.

As Johnny, in his launch, taxied over to the PBY and made ready to board, the other launch approached, Rich calling to Johnny to wait.

When Rich came close enough he yelled out, "Macaroni, if you get to Los Angeles, will you look up my wife for me. I don't know what's going on there. I haven't heard from her in over two months. She may be in trouble. I don't know if she needs money or what. Tell her I have five months back pay coming and if she needs it, I'll send it to her."

Joseph Francis Panicello

"Sure, Hinny. I'll do what I can."

As Rich's boat came closer and alongside he added, "Are you going to see my sister, Macaroni? Well, if you do give her my love. I suppose you're getting serious with her. I will say this, Macaroni, if you marry her I will be proud to have you as my brother-in-law. I think you'd be a great guy for my sister."

Johnny wasn't expecting this and said bluntly, "I'm sorry, Hinny, but marriage is out of the question right now. You see, I have other plans. I love Dolores, but I can't marry her, not yet. When this war is over I intend to go on to college and become a Mechanical Engineer, and I can't marry until I can support a wife. If Dolores wants to wait for me until after I'm settled and have a good job, I will definitely marry her."

Rich returned with, "Gosh, Macaroni. I'm sorry you feel that way. I didn't wait and I'm happily married." Johnny had no answer for that. He couldn't share his suspicions with Rich.

That was another reason Johnny didn't want to marry, but he wouldn't tell that to Rich. He always liked him and he didn't have the heart to tell him that his wife was probably fooling around. Dolores had written to Johnny about her. It was very disturbing when he found out that Mildred was dating other GIs.

Johnny arrived in Hawaii with no problem. He went to the naval base in Pearl Harbor to receive his final orders. He was told to see a Captain Markus Jones, who was commander of the engineering school for the Pacific fleet.

Johnny stepped into his office and stood at attention. Captain Jones, at first, looked him over curiously. He wasn't quite sure what this Petty Officer would look like but, it seemed, he approved. He finally said, "At ease, Maroni, have a seat. I've been reviewing your background in civilian life as well as your experiences in the navy. You're a fine sailor, Maroni, and I'm proud of you.

"Your record shows that you had good marks in high school in the subjects of math, science, physics, and chemistry. You also had experience as a automobile mechanic's helper. Your navy entrance test (The Eddy Test) has recorded you as above

A Slow Moving Target, The LST of World War II

average in math but just average in English. Your record in the Pacific is commendable, and I understand you received the Silver Star. Have I left anything out, Maroni?"

Johnny was astonished at all the data the captain presented about his background and answered, "No, Sir. You covered it all. I didn't know the navy kept such records."

Captain Jones grinned and said, "Well, you'd be surprised at what we do. When we find an outstanding sailor we reward him. This brings me to the point of why you are here. Because you are an outstanding mechanic on Diesel engines, you and ten other motor mechanics have been selected to become instructors on Diesel engines throughout the country. You will first have to attend a special six week advanced class at a navy school in New York City to become an expert in this field.

"After you've completed this course you will be given orders on where your first teaching assignment will be. The problem is, the U.S. is producing thousands of amphibious craft each year, not to mention destroyers and submarines, that use Diesel engines. We need men badly to service these craft. That is why we are setting up this program, to support our Amphibious forces. Are there any questions about your duties, Maroni?"

"No, Sir. Except... Is it possible for me, on my way to New York, to stop over in Los Angeles and visit with my girl?"

"No problem, Maroni. We have transport planes that fly into LA every day. I'll make the arrangements for you."

"Thank you, Sir," Johnny replied.

Johnny flew into the Los Angeles airport and took the Red Car to the L. A. downtown Union-Pacific train station. It was 1800 hours that evening when he called Dolores. When she picked up the receiver she was completely surprised that Johnny was in town. She immediately jumped into her car and went to the train station to pick him up. When she saw him she threw her arms around him and kissed him over and over again. They stopped at a coffee shop for a quick bite and then went to her apartment.

Joseph Francis Panicello

As they entered her apartment Johnny noticed that she was alone and asked, "Where's Mildred? Isn't she rooming with you any longer?"

Dolores didn't want to discuss the situation but said, "No, Johnny. We had a big fight. I didn't like the way she was carrying on with other GIs, with her being married to my brother. I got mad, so we split."

Actually, Johnny already knew about Mildred's escapades from her letters but didn't know how serious it was. For the moment he wanted to forget about Mildred. He was with his girl on her couch together and they began necking. Within minutes Dolores was asking him to stop. Johnny by now wanted her very much and didn't want to stop. She pushed him away.

"Johnny, quit that!" She was adamant.

Johnny pleaded, "Come on, Honey. I need you. I can't go on like this. We've been apart so long."

She stuck to her guns and replied, "I'm sorry, Johnny. I'm not going to be a sailor's one night stand. If you love me you can wait until we are married. I'll marry you right now if you want!"

Trying to be reasonable he said, "I can't, Dolores. With this lousy war going on, I don't know what will happen to me. I don't want to leave you a widow, with a kid, if I'm killed. I even told your brother that. When the war is over I intend to go to college and make something of myself before I marry anyone. Don't you see, Darling? It would be better that way for the both of us."

Stubbornly she replied, "No, I don't. You want me to be your lover tonight and what about tomorrow or next month. Am I supposed to just sit around here when you might have an affair with a girl in every port you visit. No thank you. If you want me, I'll say it once again. Marry me today or leave me."

Johnny just sat there, bewildered. He didn't know what to say. He was sure that Dolores would see it his way and wait for him. He tried once again, "Dolores, my darling, please listen to me. I do love you very much. I can't live without you. Please be reasonable. If you don't want to make love with me unmarried, okay, forget it. But don't give me a marriage ultimatum. If I leave, I'll never be back. I can't marry you now. It just wouldn't work."

"Then leave!" She was firm.

Johnny felt stupid. How could he just walk out of her life. He'd thought of her for months. He was tempted to agree with her but then he remembered about Hinny and the trouble he was having with Mildred. He was afraid that it would happen to him. It was too much for him to accept. He picked up his white cap and simply walked out, without saying another word. He just could not marry her now.

He had promised Hinny he would look up Mildred and see if she needed any help. When he was down to the street he hailed a cab but, before he climbed in, he looked back once again at Dolores's apartment. He saw her watching through the window. He was tempted to go back, but then he slumped into the back seat, slamming the taxi door. As Dolores watched the cab pull away, she began to cry.

Johnny tried to remember the name of the apartment building where Mildred was now living. Dolores had mentioned it earlier that evening. "Stratford Arms," he thought. That was it. He asked the cabby if he knew where it was.

"Stratford Arms, buddy? Yeah, I know it," the cabby replied.

"Well, take me there, and hurry," Johnny demanded.

Ten minutes later, getting out of the cab, Johnny stared up in amazement at one of the most exclusive apartment buildings in Burbank. "How can she afford this on Rich's pay?" he wondered.

Johnny walked into the vestibule of the building and ran his eyes down the list of tenants. Mildred Adair was listed on the second floor, #6. Adair was Mildred's stage name.

He climbed the stairs, located #6, took a deep breath, and knocked on the door. Johnny was surprised when a soldier opened the door. "What do you want, sailor? The lady's busy."

Johnny overcame his shock and answered, "I'm looking for Mildred Hienman."

Joseph Francis Panicello

The soldier replied, "Well, there ain't no Mildred Hienman here, but there is a Mildred."

"Mildred Adair?" Momentarily, Johnny had forgotten her stage name.

"Yeah. But it's like I said. We're busy."

Johnny was getting irritated and said firmly, "Now listen, buddy. I want to see her right now and if you refuse to let me in I'm going downstairs and bring back a bunch of MPs, capish?"

The soldier finally conceded and remarked, "Okay, okay. Come in and join the crowd."

When Johnny entered he was shocked at what he saw. There were three other soldiers sitting around in their shorts. They turned around and looked at him nonchalantly and appeared to be unfazed at his entrance. Johnny noticed that a bedroom door was closed and walked over to it. He cracked it opened slightly and peeked in. Mildred and a man, nude, were locked in an embrace.

Johnny quietly closed the door, turned around and faced the soldier he first met. Johnny wasn't stupid. He had been around. He asked the soldier, "How much does she charge?"

The answer was astonishing, "Twenty bucks."

"That's quite a bit," Johnny said, considering a sailor's pay is only 21 dollars a month. "Hell. I can go down the street and pay five. What's the big deal with her?" he inquired.

By now the soldier was getting perturbed with this sailor and said, "Listen. It's like this. She's special, see. It's twenty bucks per man but we can go back for seconds. She also gives us the 'around the world' treatment, if you get my drift. If you don't like the price, go down the street and pay your five bucks."

That was Johnny's cue and he said, "You got it, buster. I'm outa here."

Johnny was furious when he went outside. He stood around for awhile pacing the sidewalk, pondering over the nerve of that girl making money as a whore while her husband was fighting for his life. He was extremely irate. He noticed a Shore Patrol

A Slow Moving Target, The LST of World War II

Chief standing in front of a corner market. He walked over to him and began a casual conversation with him.

He finally asked, "What's the penalty for soliciting in this neighborhood, Chief?"

"It's jail time for the girl. We are trying to stop these broads from sticking it to our sailors. We catch a few now and then."

Johnny thought about it for a moment and decided to turn her in. It serves her right for messing around on one of his buddies, he reasoned.

He said to the chief, "Well, I know where a party is going on right now."

The chief became interested and asked, "You do? Where?"

Johnny was quick to reply, "You see that apartment up there. There are four soldiers paying big money for the services of one girl. She charges twenty bucks a man. And not only that, she is married to a sailor who is fighting the Japanese in the Pacific while she collects his allotment."

"Wow! You're kidding? She charges that much, huh. What's the sailor's name?"

Johnny told him and the chief wrote it down on a pad. The chief was visibly disturbed, especially when he heard that she was two-timing her sailor husband.

He began speaking into a walkie-talkie and a few moments later two jeeps drove up. One carried two SP sailors, and the other contained three MPs. The Chief talked with them for a moment and then pointed to the second floor. Then the six military policemen, including the chief, went up the stairs and entered the apartment.

Moments later, Johnny witnessed four soldiers, half dressed, leave the building in a hurry. They were followed by the MPs, who allowed the soldiers to leave the building without any charges. Shortly, a Burbank police patrol car drove up. Two police officers entered the building and within moments the Burbank police and the SPs came out with Mildred in handcuffs. Johnny remained in the shadows and witnessed the whole episode. He watched as the SPs climb back into their jeep and

Joseph Francis Panicello

drove away with the chief who would, undoubtedly, report the entire incident to the navy command.

Johnny didn't like what he did but he knew he had to do it. He knew it would hurt his buddy, Hinny, but Johnny knew it was best for Rich to find out now. A woman cannot easily divorce a man in the service, especially when there is a war going on, but there are certain circumstances when a divorce is justified.

Johnny wished he could be back there to console his buddy when Rich was made aware of the situation. "There's nothing else I can do about it," he thought, knowing Rich would be better off.

One week later, on the destroyer, *Cony,* Hienman was personally escorted to see Admiral Wilkinson. A marine guard came over to his bunk and acted as though he were under arrest. Rich was confused. The marine's orders were simply to bring First Class Gunners Mate Hienman before the Admiral, and on the double!

In the admiral's cabin Rich was told to sit down. At first the admiral began casually questioning him about his wife. "I understand, Mr. Hienman, that you are married to a Mildred Adair. Is this so?"

"Yes, Sir. Adair is her stage name. She's in the movies and becoming a star," answered Rich somewhat proudly.

The Admiral continued, "When was the last time you heard from your wife?"

Rich answered, "It's been close to two months, Sir," wondering why he was being interrogated about her.

The Admiral continued with his questions, "Do you and your wife have a good relationship?"

He answered quickly, "Yes, Sir. We sure do. We love each other very much. I don't understand why she hasn't written, however. I asked a buddy of mine, Macaroni, I mean Maroni, to look her up and see if she needs any financial help. I was going to send her some extra money if she did."

The admiral paused for a moment as he began scanning a paper in front of him. "She wouldn't be needing more money," he thought. The admiral wasn't sure how to proceed. He decided to have it out quickly and said, "Mr. Hienman. I have bad news concerning your wife. She is okay physically, but it's just... well, she was picked up as a prostitute."

Hienman was startled. "It can't be. She gets plenty of money from my allotment and she works in the movie industry. She doesn't need more money, especially like that. She wouldn't do that."

"I'm sorry, Mr. Hienman, but it's true. She is now being held in a Federal Court in Los Angeles and is expected to receive two years in prison for soliciting money from military personnel. You see, it's a Federal offense. She's been doing this for over a year now while you were out here fighting for your country.

"Under these circumstances, you may be able to ask for a divorce through the military. I will personally help you with this. I have already drawn up the necessary papers and all you have to do is sign here on the dotted line."

Rich wasn't convinced and asked, "Is there a chance I could phone her, first, Sir? I've got to be sure. There could be a mistake."

The admiral anticipated this request and said, "Yes, you may. I'll have my yeoman contact her immediately." He pressed a buzzer and the call was completed. The admiral handed the ship to shore telephone to Hienman.

"Mildred. Is that you? What happened? Is it really true that you were picked up?"

Mildred's answer was strong and loud when she said, "So what? You're nothing. Who needs you? I've had better lovers off the street. I never want to see you again."

Rich instantly hung up the receiver. Holding back tears in his eyes he immediately signed the divorce papers.

Rich was numb as he walked back to his quarters. He couldn't think clearly and her words echoed in his ears.

He joined a card game already in progress at the galley table.

"Hell," he reasoned, "there are many more pebbles on the beach. I'm still in the war and now the only thing I have to

Joseph Francis Panicello

concentrate on is killing Japs." He lowered his head and began staring at his playing cards, not paying attention to the game. He felt a tear begin trickling down his cheek. He stood up, throwing his cards on the table, and walked to his bunk. He began crying softly. His marriage was over. He would not mention Mildred's name to anyone for a long time.

23. Pacific Offensive

After February, 1943, when the Allies had regained Guadalcanal, the Japanese navy reverted to a defensive posture, and the United States navy continued their offensive island-hopping throughout the entire Japanese controlled perimeter.

On March 1, 1943, the Allies spotted a convoy of 16 Japanese ships coming from Rabaul steaming toward Lae to reinforce the Japanese garrisons on New Guinea. This was the beginning of "The Battle of the Bismarck Sea." Several U.S. B-17 bombers attacked the convoy, sinking a transport and four destroyers. The battle was an important victory. Years later an incident in the battle became known as the sinking of PT-109, which was commanded by our future President, Lt. John F. Kennedy.

On April 18, 1943, Allied code breakers had learned Adm. Isoroku Yamamoto would be flying near the Solomon Islands. A fighter squadron of P-38s, led by Lt. Col. Thomas G. Lamphier Jr., downed Yamamoto's plane, killing the man who planned the attack on Pearl Harbor.

Now that Munda was secured, Nimitz suggested to Halsey that they bypass Kolombangara and target the smaller island of Vella Lavella. It was then planned to land on Vella Lavella on August 15, 1943. Before the assault it was necessary to provide up-to-date intelligence on the conditions of the island. A scouting party landed on Lavella July 21. They did not sight any Japanese. On the scheduled day 4,600 soldiers, marines, and seabees made the assault. The landing was unopposed but the next day there were numerous air raids from the enemy.

The LSTs did a fine job of fighting off the Jap bombers. One captain expressed in his action report how grateful he was for the help of the 35th combat team of soldiers and marines who manned the extra guns on his LST 395, fighting off the Japanese. The Japs, however, scored a direct hit on another LST while it was supplying cargo on the beachhead. An internal explosion

Joseph Francis Panicello

and fire completely destroyed the LST. Many of its crew members were killed. The engine crew were hardest hit.

Rich Hienman, recently transferred to the destroyer, *Cony*, from LST 142, personally shot down three Japanese bombers and two fighters. Admiral Wilkinson was delighted with his new gunner. By day's end Wilkinson's ships transported 6,305 men and over 8 tons of cargo to the island. After the successful capture of Vella Lavella by the Americans the Japanese forces abandoned the nearby island of Kolombangara.

A usual collection of APDs, LSTs, LCIs, and LCTs were again put to the test in the invasion of Lae on September 1, 1943, located in the Hunon Gulf, New Guinea. As five destroyers barraged the beach front, Australian infantrymen headed for shore, with little opposition. As the ships approached the shore, a flight of Japanese bombers flew in and attacked the ships.

A Japanese bomber dropped a bomb on LSI 336, destroying it completely. Andre's LST 153, was also hit but not seriously, and with the few casualties on board Andre ably cared for them.

A Jap bomber torpedoed LST 471 and both LST 473 and LST 142 sustained bomb blasts. Bob Olsen was on the forward gun of LST 142 at the time and was hit with shrapnel, breaking his left leg. He continued to man his gun, however, and was able to shoot down a Jap bomber before he collapsed.

Casualties were heavy but by mid-afternoon, 7,800 troops and 1,500 tons of supplies had been transported on the shores of Lae. Bob was transferred to an LST-converted hospital ship, located just south of Morobe, which still had fifty open beds. He was later shipped to Hawaii.

Priscilla Preston Scanzani of Beverly, Mass., said, "I was an Army nurse stationed in New Guinea when an Australian ship was bombed by the Japanese and some of the navy casualties arrived at our hospital. They were badly burned and their bodies were wrapped like mummies. Only their lower extremities were exposed.

"One day after administering to one of these patients, I felt a pinch on my buttocks. I quickly turned and caught a twinkle in his eyes. I wasn't mad because these guys had just gone through hell. I never knew what became of these men, but this memory has remained with me. It exemplified the resilience and spirit of the fighting men and women of World War II."

Phillis T. Galeaz of Lynn, Mass., a Army nurse who served in New Guinea evacuation recalls, "Bombs began dropping like rain. I ran to the hospital tents intending to reassure the patients, only to discover that they too were worried about the nursing staff."

In September of 1943 Admiral King's offense on the Solomons in the South Pacific was about to begin. The plan called for an invasion of Finschhafen, then Bougainville. A task force of twenty-six small amphibians would assault the beach at Finschhafen while ten destroyers would be used as escort to provide gunfire support.

On September 21, the task force departed for Finschhafen. Andre's LST 153 was among them. After the destroyer's continuous bombardment of the shore, the first two waves of soldiers landed from LCIs. There was opposition but the Japanese were, eventually, driven back from the beach by gunfire from the destroyers.

The LSTs then began bringing in their major cargo, at a rate of 50 tons per hour. More than 850 tons of supplies, 5,300 men, 180 vehicles, and 32 artillery cannons were landed by September 23. Finschhafen fell on October 2, 1943. The Japanese countered with an air assault and mounted their own beach landings on October 16, but were again defeated. Admiral Halsey next launched an attack on Bougainville, a Japanese stronghold in the Solomons.

Bougainville was not going to be as easy as Finschhafen. It is the largest island in the Solomons, mainly used by the Japanese to defend Rabaul. There was a large Japanese garrison on the island of Bougainville waiting to mount a counterattack, having several airfields with sufficient air power to fight off any

Joseph Francis Panicello

Allied invasion. It was estimated that there were 35,000 Japanese troops ready to defend the island, down to the last man.

Halsey decided not to assault where expected, but instead landed his troops farther north on a relatively unguarded beach. He decided to peck away at the Japanese, little by little, using air power to continuously bomb all the islands, including Rabaul, Treasury Island and Bougainville. He called this assault Operation Dipper.

The plan was to have 1,000 troops land on Bougainville the first day. Within 66 days 6,200 tons of ammunition, rations, and heavy weapons would have to be transferred to shore. A convoy of LSTs, the 37th Infantry Division, would be brought in.

Admiral Wilkinson transferred his flag ship to the *George Clymer* transport. With him came his staff, and an inconspicuous sailor carrying a sea bag. It was Hienman, the Admiral's prize gunner. The Admiral now ordered the bombing from his ships on Bougainville. As usual, destroyers pounded the beach with bombs but none of the bunkers that were spotted behind the lines took a hit.

It took thirty-seven minutes for the *Clymer* to unload its troops onto small boats. As they approached the beaches a wave of Marine aircraft fighters and bombers pounded the beaches with gunfire and bombs. It had little effect on the waiting Japanese.

The Japs began their counterattack with a 75-mm gun and immediately blew up a LCVP. Thirteen other boats took a hit and three were sunk. The marine assault continued but the men were being hit as they landed. As LST 153 approached the beach she became a slow moving target for the Japs. After she beached and her doors were wide open, the ramp came down, allowing tanks and trucks to come ashore. The counterattack was awesome.

Andre was watching the assault from within the tank deck and saw many men being hit by enemy gunfire. Two corpsmen on shore were trying to assist the wounded but there were so many of them in need of help. In a situation like this, corpsmen

A Slow Moving Target, The LST of World War II

are essential because many deaths are due mainly to loss of blood. If the corpsmen can get to the men quickly, most of them could be saved. But there were only two of them.

Instead of waiting for the wounded to be brought on board his ship for treatment, Andre grabbed his medical supplies and run down the ramp to help the corpsmen. He went from one man to another, using tourniquets, bandages, IVs, and morphine. When he came to a marine dying he had to leave him. He had to tend those who had a chance to survive. When he looked up to see how the other corpsmen were doing he found, to his surprise, that they had both been hit. Andre ran to the one closest to him. A stream of blood ran down the corpsman's arm. Andre stopped the bleeding and applied a bandage.

He asked the wounded corpsman, "Can you continue to help?"

"We're on our own. I'll try," he answered weakly. "Ron's dead."

Andre left him, hoping he could indeed help because there were so many wounded that needed attention. Andre secured the assistance of sailors on LST 153 to carry on board the men already attended. He instructed, "Get blankets and lay the wounded on the side of the tank deck so they will be out of danger."

Andre noticed that the other corpsman had collapsed. Andre quickly gave him an IV of blood plasma and had one sailor hold the IV bottle while two other sailors carried him on board on a stretcher.

Andre moved from one wounded man to the next. When he ran out of medical supplies from his own bag he confiscated the medical supply bag from the dead corpsman. Hours passed. He managed to save 50 marines. Many died because he couldn't get to them in time. This bothered Andre deeply. Somehow, he had to get the message to high command that more corpsmen are needed during a beach assault. Men were dying for lack of prompt treatment.

Joseph Francis Panicello

While Andre was assisting the wounded men on the beach, his captain watched with his field glasses from the ship. After the wounded were on board he ordered the ship to leave and anchor 2,000 yards from shore.

Captain Miles, of LST 153, went down to the tank deck to see how the wounded were doing. Andre was busily working on the men, trying to make them comfortable. He watched Andre stumble from exhaustion, then move on to administer to still another marine. At that point the captain commanded several sailors to help Andre in any way they could.

Captain Miles went back to the bridge, tears of anger in his eyes and radioed the hospital ship for help. He did not mince his words either, when he said, "Get your Goddamn ship over here. I've got over 100 marines that need immediate attention and my only corpsman is dragging himself off the ground to keep these guys alive. Hurry!"

The captain on the hospital LST answered, "Sorry, Skipper. We have our orders not to come near the shore to pick up survivors until the beach is secured. As soon as we get the all clear signal, we will proceed to help you. It shouldn't take much longer."

It did take longer, because the Japanese mounted another aerial counterattack. Rich Hienman's AA gun on the transport was now ablaze, firing at the enemy, and he was able to shoot down four Jap bombers. During the onslaught twelve of Admiral Wilkinson's smaller Amphibs were able to unload most of their supplies. A warning came in that the Japanese had sent a force of cruisers and destroyers to counterattack the invasion. The Amphibious fleet were ordered to leave the area and they departed for safety.

In the sea battle that followed, one Japanese cruiser and one destroyer were sunk. Americans lost one cruiser. A destroyer was torpedoed but saved. In spite of the attacks by the Japs, more than 33,000 men and 22,000 tons of supplies were transferred to the beachhead, using bulk unloading procedures, with trucks, from the LSTs. LST 395 carried a pontoon trestle bridge to

A Slow Moving Target, The LST of World War II

Bougainville and the army engineers put together a 45 foot structure to help the unloading in the swampy waters.

The enemy was not ready to concede Bougainville. They carried out more than ninety air raids during November. One method the Amphibs used to deter the Japs was to release a barrage of balloons. LST 354 reported that a Jap torpedo bomber was brought down trying to avoid the balloon wire cables.

By mid-December, there were 44,000 troops on Bougainville and the campaign in the Solomons was almost over. Captain Miles on LST 153, recommended that Andre receive the Navy Cross for his efforts in saving many wounded men under enemy fire.

The fighting for Treasury Island was also violent. The destroyers did their usual bombing to soften up the Japs but the Japanese were well fortified. Before the landing party made their assault, two LCIs that were converted to gunboats, LCI(G)s, came close to shore to provide gunfire after naval bombardment stopped. When the assault began, LST 399 received two hits from mortar-fire, killing three sailors. As her bow doors opened and the ramp dropped, the first four soldiers coming down the ramp were shot.

LST 399 took a beating from a Japanese pillbox located at its port bow. The LST raised its ramp to protect the crew from a volley of bullets coming into the tank deck, ricocheting off the side walls packed with soldiers, marines, and seabees. A seabee, Aurelio Tassone, MM 1st Class, mounted a bulldozer, ordered the ramp to be lowered once again, and charged with the blade raised. With his bulldozer he worked around to the opposite side of the pillbox. Lieutenant Turnbull, while laying on the ground, covered for Tassone and distracted the Japs by firing at them through the apertures in the pillbox. The Japanese saw the bulldozer and their machine gun bullets began bouncing off the blade. It seemed that Tassone didn't have a chance of surviving. Timing it perfectly, he dropped the blade and plowed the pillbox into the ground, burying 12 screaming Japs that were in it. The

Joseph Francis Panicello

28 year old Italian-American seabee, Tassone, was awarded the Silver Star for his heroism.

The attacks on LST 399 were not over. Mortar fire continued to slam the ship. Her bow soon became a ball of flames. The fire was put out and the captain decided to leave the beach even though he still had 20 tons of cargo on board. She headed for Guadalcanal for safety but on the way a Japanese bomber dropped two bombs on her and rendered her helpless. Her cargo and her entire crew had to be transferred to small craft. The navy later was able to repair and restore the ship which was then used in the assault of Guam and Iwo Jima, receiving 5 battle stars for World War II.

24. Salerno

When Sicily fell, Mussolini was ordered to present himself before King Victor Emmanuel on July 25, 1943. Standing before the king, Mussolini looked dejected and humble, his future uncertain. He knew that the Allies were getting closer and the men in his army were surrendering in great masses.

King Emmanuel was adamant, "Mussolini, you are a disgrace to all of Italy. Because you have sided with that imbecile *Todesca,* Hitler, you have caused our great Italian nation to be reduced to ashes. You have destroyed history here in Italy, forever. I was leery of you from the beginning. Now you have proved me right. I couldn't stop you then. You were too powerful. Now parliament is on my side.

"To restore and preserve our country's art and unity I have appointed Field Marshal Pietro Badoglio to replace you. I am negotiating a surrender with the Allies before there is any more destruction to our nation."

Mussolini could only mutter, "Then my ruin is complete."

Mussolini was taken under guard to a place in the mountains for his own protection from the partisans. The Italian underground partisans, who fought gallantly against the Germans and Mussolini's personal Black Guards, would surely have killed him for all of the crimes he had committed while in power.

When Hitler heard that Mussolini was dismissed he was so outraged that his first impulse was to seize Rome, the King, the Royal Family, the Badoglio government, and even the Pope. His generals dissuaded him, but he instructed them to find out where Mussolini was imprisoned, to rescue him and bring him to Germany.

The rescue was successfully accomplished and Mussolini was taken safely to Germany. He was later restored as a puppet power in Italy by Hitler and returned to Rome. After the Allies took Rome and were pushing north, he tried to escape to Germany but was captured and killed, with his girlfriend, by the

Joseph Francis Panicello

partisans. They were both hung upside down in a town piazza, representing slaughtered pigs. The local Italians, angry because of his war crimes, threw stones at their bodies.

The King's concern of Italy was genuine. Two developments precipitated Mussolini's downfall. On July 19, the Allies dropped bombs on a railroad yard in Rome, killing and wounding 4,000 Italian civilians, hitting the venerable Basilica of San Lorenzo, and, unfortunately, plowing up graves in the Compo Verno cemetery. The second major loss was the invasion of Sicily. It was clear that nothing could prevent the Allies from overrunning the island. Mussolini had to be deposed of and the alliance with Germany dissolved or Italy would be dragged down to complete ruin.

Paul A. Thomsen wrote, "As the war in Europe neared an end, the Nazis garrisoned in Rome were ordered to begin deporting Jews. Pope Pius XII and his clergy quickly moved the refugees to new hiding places, saving the lives of countless Jews. Thousands of safe houses throughout Europe were established to hide Jews and condemned diplomats.

"According to the post-war International Tribune at Nuremberg, 2,700 members of the clergy died for practicing their beliefs, and more than 860,000 Jews were saved through the resistance efforts of Pope Pius XII and many of his Roman Catholic clergy. In the words of the chief rabbi in Rome about the Holocaust, `No hero in all of history was more militant, more fought against, none more heroic than Pius XII.'"

Eisenhower, at first, thought that now would be the time to seize the islands of Sardinia and Corsica. Winston Churchill was against this approach and said, "Why crawl up the leg like a harvest bug from the ankle upwards?" He continued, "Let us rather strike at the knee." Roosevelt reluctantly agreed with him.

On September 3, 1943 the British crossed the straits of Messina and into Calabria under General Montgomery. The object now was to attack the Germans in Southern Italy and drive them out, and support the Allied forces on the assault against Salerno farther north.

A Slow Moving Target, The LST of World War II

The problem was that the British advance to the north was so slow that they couldn't help General Mark W. Clark in the battle of Salerno. Montgomery's quick advance from the south was slowed to a crawl by a strong German resistance under Commander In Chief Field Marshal Kesselring and his commander in the south, Colonel General Heinrich Von Vietinghoff.

The final invasion plan was decided upon by General Eisenhower. His plan to attack Salerno was to use a convoy of 600 ships that came from Oran and Palermo, Sicily. This convoy was comprised of slow moving Amphibious forces, followed later by faster transports and cargo ships. The slow moving ships were escorted by destroyers and PT boats, while several civilian-manned hospital ships would follow behind the convoy to help with the wounded.

The Gulf of Salerno offers a beautiful panorama of the sea. Longfellow praised the bay, referring to the gulf as, "The blue Salernian bay with its sickle of white sand."

To the north, the blue-green Sorrento peninsula can be seen with its jewel-like towns at its base. About eight miles away is the Gratto di Smeraldo, named after the eerie emerald glow of its stalagmites and stalactites.

Today, Salerno is a big, busy port that was once famous for its Schools of Medicine. In the temple of Duomo is the tomb of St. Mathew, and its museum contains an early medieval alter-front, embellished with 54 ivory panels, the largest work of its kind.

Regardless of the security measures the Allies took, the Germans knew that the Gulf of Salerno would be the Allies next target. The 16th Panzer Division was ready for the assault with 17,000 experienced German soldiers deeply entrenched in barricades.

On September 3, 1943, the Italian government surrendered to the Allies. Unfortunately, this announcement had a negative effect on the Allied troops because they assumed there would be no resistance on shore and relaxed. The Germans remained in

Joseph Francis Panicello

full force. The American men thought that they would be going home. Instead they would face a massive counterattack soon.

Allied troops were singing army songs and one soldier said, "I'll be going ashore with an olive branch in one hand and an opera ticket in the other." The senior officer knew it wasn't over and tried to damp the celebration, but with little success.

Most of the Italian soldiers had thrown down their arms but the Germans took over their artillery. The German soldiers were ordered to confiscate all Italian weapons but one die-hard old Italian general, Don Ferrante Gonzaga, refused to give up his pistol. He was shot dead by a German officer.

There were some drawbacks in the landings. A sand bar wall divided the beach because of two separate rivers entering the sea, the Sele and the Calore. This meant that the Allied forces would be separated by eight miles in their respective landings. In addition, the mountains that enclosed the beachhead would be a major obstacle to negotiate after troops secured the beaches.

The Germans allowed the first wave of Allied troops to reach the beach before they opened fire. It was a planned maneuver to allow an easy landing and make the Allies feel there would be no opposition. It paid off for the Germans and a bitter fight followed. Many Allied soldiers were killed and wounded on the beach because they were unprepared for the counterattack. Small boats equipped with rockets helped slow down the German attack.

W. J. Burke was a Seabee who came onto the British sector to clear the beach. He saw eight Tommies building a fire and boiling water. One of them yelled out, "Say chappie, come on and have a spot of tea."

As Burke started toward them a land mine, ignited by the fire, exploded. The explosion knocked Burke flat on his back. All eight Tommies were killed.

As an LCT was approaching the beach with two tanks on board, the first tank received a direct hit from the Germans. It was set ablaze and the explosion killed the coxswain. The second tank was used to push the disabled burning tank overboard, then driven ashore. Bombs were exploding everywhere, at sea as well as on the beach. Many small craft didn't make it to shore.

In spite of the massive counterattack, slowly but surely the Allies were able to get troops and tanks ashore. There were many landing craft destroyed but the overall operation continued, and a steady flow of cargo was landed on the beaches. Enemy fire was intense and other landing boats, including DUKWS (amphibious trucks) kept circling in the water off shore, unable to land because of the sunken craft just off the beach.

After six hours of waiting many small craft began dumping their cargo on the water line of the beach and leaving quickly to get out of danger. Eventually, there was a wall of cargo on the water line which prevented the rest of the Amphibious craft from unloading their cargo.

Mine fields were another deterrent. LST 386 struck one mine while approaching the beach and the explosion blew her pontoon causeway up. The skipper of the LST gave the orders to retract the ship because it could not unload its cargo on the beach. He was finally given permission to transfer his cargo into LCTs out at sea.

As German tanks arrived on the scene several were demolished by destroyer gunners. Luftwaffe airforce swooping down on the ships caused considerable damage. They began strafing the beaches, sinking a tug boat, and killing many Allied soldiers. Fortunately for the Allies, the enemy fliers couldn't see their targets well because of the smoke screen produced by the destroyers and the patrol boats including LCVPs, that were equipped with oil-fired smoke generators. This capability saved many American lives.

By mid-day the shore was under the control of the Allies. The LSTs were now given permission to begin landing their ships onto the beaches even though they were still being fired upon. Because the beach had a high slope it was difficult for the LSTs to stay on the beach. They had to drive themselves into the beach at 8 knots and when they reached the beach they had to pump their ballast forward to weigh the bow down onto the sand.

Joseph Francis Panicello

Several LSTs couldn't get close enough to the sand and pontoons had to be used in order to unload their cargo.

The nickname given to the LST, *"Large Slow Target"* proved to be true in this assault. The LST 385 was hit three times. Narrowly missed by an aerial torpedo aimed at the bow, LST 385's crew watched as the torpedo come to rest on the beach without detonating. The LST 375 was hit twice by artillery and once by an aircraft bomb which killed fifty crew members. The LST 85 was also involved in this landing and, even though it was being attacked by the Germans, Danny and the other gunners on board were able to destroy enemy tanks on shore with their cannons.

By September 10, 1943, all the troops and most of the vehicles were on shore, but the unloading problem still existed. Without enough labor troops to unload the large cargo from the LSTs, Admiral Hewitt had to order his amphibious sailors to come ashore to help unload the supplies. The Admiral was disgusted with the army because they had no plans for unloading supplies.

The Germans were fighting back and began shelling the beaches at both the Sele and Calore. General Clark ordered Hewitt to evacuate the LSTs from the beaches even though they were still fully loaded and to move the 36th Infantry Division to another sector.

Hewitt tried to dissuade Clark. Explaining, he said, "Sir, under normal circumstances, when an LST is loaded it has no problem beaching by ballasting the ship's weight aft, and after it is unloaded the bow is now light enough so that the ship can be easily withdrawn. If the cargo and tanks are still on board, the ship is too heavy and the bow is now entrenched into the beach sand. It is difficult to retreat under those conditions."

Clark still insisted, so Hewitt drew up plans for the evacuation, but when General Alexander came ashore, he informed Clark that no evacuation would take place. Backup troops were coming from Sicily and 1,300 paratroopers from the

A Slow Moving Target, The LST of World War II

U.S. Airborne Division would be dropping inside the enemy lines.

The 36th Artillery Division fired more than 4,100 rounds and the 45th Division another 6,687 rounds at the Germans. The navy fired 11,000 tons of shells to support the troops on the Salerno beach. Brig. General John Lang sent a message of praise to the admiral, "Thank God for the fire from your bluebelly Navy ships."

Help also came from Eisenhower when he ordered the African forces to relieve the ground forces in Salerno. Then, on September 14, hundreds of B-25, B-26, and B-17 bombers began blasting the Germans.

In this short battle of nine days, the Americans lost 500 soldiers killed, 1,800 wounded, and 1,200 reported missing. The British suffered much heavier losses with 5,000 killed, wounded, and missing in action.

Admiral Hewitt was frustrated with the poor procedure of unloading cargo from the Amphibious craft. He concluded it should take no more than 30 hours to unload all the LCMs and LCTs. He also thought that the bulk-loading cargo should always be the last to be unloaded from LSTs. In this operation the LSTs were committed too soon, making them vulnerable.

On Danny's ship, LST 85, many men were wounded or killed. They lost several gunners, bow door operators, other seaman, and two officers. Danny was short of men to operate the ship properly after this fierce assault. He made up a list of needed replacements and submitted it to the captain who filled the positions left open with survivors from ships that had been destroyed.

On September 8, 1943, Italian warships had been reluctant to engage the Allies in battle. There were 206 Italian ships in the area which could put up a serious fight. When the truce was signed by the king, the Allies terms dictated that the Italian ships on the west side of Italy were to steam south to Algiers, Africa. The ships to the east of the peninsula were to sail to the British held island of Malta. The Allies were concerned that the Italian ships might be confiscated by the Germans and used against them.

On September 9, three Italian battleships, with three light cruisers and eight destroyers, escaped from the Germans. Their escape enraged the German command, precipitating raids on various towns. Italian captains who were in the process of getting their ships underway were shot. That afternoon, the Italian battle ship *Roma* was attacked and sunk by German bombers, with a loss of 1,000 men. The rest of the Italian ships made it to Algiers and to the island of Malta.

25. Johnny in New York

Johnny's plane landed on a hot August night in 1943, at La Guardia airport, located on the north side of Queens, New York. He caught a bus which took him into Manhattan, then a subway back out to the south side of Queens, to Jamaica. He then grabbed a cab which took him to South Ozone Park. Johnny had forgotten a bus crossed the Borough of Queens. A trip of 9 miles had taken over two hours. In his excitement at being home, he wasn't thinking clearly. The New York International Airport, now know as JFK, was not yet completed.

In the cab, the driver kept up a continuous stream of conversation, bragging non-stop about a son in the army, in Europe, winning the war single-handedly, to hear the cabby tell it.

Johnny barely listened. It had been almost 2 years since he had been home. It was good to see New York again. As Johnny left the cab and entered the street in front of his home, he noticed how hot and muggy the night was. His whites were clinging to him. He knocked on the door, waiting for a joyous welcome.

No one answered. He sat on the stoop. "Damn," he said. He had no key. He felt the humidity closing in on him. "A cold beer would taste good," he thought. He shoved his ditty bag up against the door, deciding to walk over to a saloon located on the corner at Foch Blvd. and 143rd street.

The place was fairly busy. Some GIs and several girls were drinking beer at the bar. At one table there were a couple of girls drinking beer and chatting. They were nice looking, he thought, and wondered if they were waiting to be picked up. He wouldn't mind meeting either one of them. With the jukebox playing Jimmy Dorsey songs, Johnny sat on an empty stool at the bar and ordered a beer. One of the girls sitting at the table stared at him for a moment, as though she recognized him. She finally got up, walked over to him, and said, "Hi, Johnny."

Johnny was startled, then asked, "Do I know you?"

"Probably not," she answered. "We went to the same high school but I was a couple of years behind. My name is Megan O'Brian."

Johnny, relaxed but hopeful, remarked, "Hi, Megan. I guess I missed something. I never saw you in school." He tried to be charming.

She smiled and said, "Yeah, sure. You were so popular in school. You wouldn't have noticed me, not with all those pretty girls hanging on you. Are you on leave?"

"Yeah. I just pulled in but no one's at home. I'm killing some time until my parents show up."

She then offered, "Why don't you bring your drink over to my table. We can talk more comfortably." Johnny was delighted at the prospect.

The other girl at the table was named Tammy. When Johnny was introduced she casually got up and left for the bar, allowing Megan some privacy with this good looking sailor.

After they settled down Megan asked, "How long will you be home, Johnny?"

"I have a couple of weeks leave, then I will be teaching Diesel mechanics in Manhattan to some mechanic strikers. New recruits, to you. So, I may be around a whole year, which is okay with me. I saw all the action I want to see."

Megan sympathized with him and said, "I guess it was pretty rough out there. Where were you, in Africa or in the Pacific?"

"In the South Pacific, below the Equator. Fortunately, I didn't get hit."

She smiled, "I have three brothers in the service. One enlisted in the Navy but the other two were drafted into the Army. My oldest brother was wounded somewhere in the Solomon Islands but I don't know which island."

"Hey! I just got back from there. Maybe I saw your brother. Was he a soldier? What's his name?"

"William Ryan. He's very tall, about six-four, and has blond hair like me. Yes, he was in the Army."

"Ryan, eh? Why the different names?" Johnny was a bit puzzled.

She quickly responded, "O'Brian is my married name. My husband is somewhere in Italy and the last time I heard from him was over a month ago. I don't even know if he's still alive."

At first Johnny wanted to leave. He didn't want to get involved with a married woman. Even if she was very pretty.

At this point Megan called to the bartender and ordered two more beers. "Coming right up, Megan," was the quick reply from the bartender.

Johnny thought a little and decided he might as well finish the next beer, especially if she was buying. He had nowhere to go, anyway.

"Thanks, Megan. I really should be going after this."

"I understand, Johnny. I'll bet your parents can't wait to see you. How's your sister, Ann, doing? I heard that she's pregnant. Ann and I were good friends. We were in the same class together. I never met her husband."

Johnny was becoming curious about her. He couldn't help but ask, "You hang around here often? I mean... do you have friends here? That's not what I mean." His words weren't very complimentary.

"I understand what you are implying, Johnny. You think I'm bar hopping, waiting to be picked up. Well, it just so happens that I own this place. It belonged to my husband before I ever married him. That's why I'm here. Does that help explain everything?"

"Yeah, I mean, sure," he said, somewhat embarrassed.

He felt a little uncomfortable and wanted to leave but she was very pleasant. After breaking up with Dolores it was refreshing to meet another girl. Since she was married, he figured, she wouldn't be asking him to get married. He wondered if she would be willing to have an affair with him while her husband was away. Probably not. She's just being friendly. So he downed his beer, got up and said, "Thanks for the beer, Megan. I'll see you around."

Joseph Francis Panicello

"I'm glad that we met, Johnny. Anytime you want to talk to someone, I'll be right here. Say hello to Ann for me." She gave him an alluring smile which puzzled him.

When he arrived home he noticed that the lights in the living room were on. He rang the bell and when Angela answered she yelled out, "Johnny!" and threw her arms around him. She then began crying.

"Hi, Sis. You miss me?" Johnny was half smiling and a little tearful himself over the reunion. He was really happy to see her. He took one hand and twirled her around, "You look beautiful, little sister," he grinned.

As they entered the living room he asked, "Where's Mom and Pop?"

Angela said, "They went to Brooklyn to stay the night at Aunt Jenny's home. If they knew you were coming today they would have never left. Mom is worried sick about you. With all those Gold stars popping up in the windows it seems our boys on the front are dying like flies."

Johnny nodded his head and said, "I know, Ann. It's pretty rough out there. We lost a lot of men. Those Japs are putting up a good fight. I don't know anything about the European conflict.

Sadly, Angela asked, "What about Danny? Don't you know anything?"

Johnny shook his head. "You'd know more than anyone, Ann."

"I'm afraid, Johnny," she answered. "He tries to make everything sound matter-of-fact in his letters, like he was across the state, instead of across the Atlantic, fighting."

Johnny tried to reassure her, "Danny is strong as a bull and twice as stubborn. He's fine. He'll be back, believe it! You and me and Danny and the baby and the rest of the Phibies are going to have a reunion none of us will ever forget!"

Angela smiled and wiped away the tears that had slipped from her eyes. "You're right and I'm being silly," she said, laughing a little.

"Hey, I met a friend of yours a little while ago," Johnny said, changing the subject quickly, while she was still smiling. "Her name is Megan."

Angela again became despondent. She said, "Oh, poor Megan. A soldier who served in Sicily is dating a friend of mine. He saw Megan's husband, Jim, in a hospital there. He said Jim is paralyzed and might not make it. The news hasn't reached Megan yet, but I can't be the one to tell her, Johnny. It will break her heart."

Johnny sighed, "I'm sorry. Megan seems like a really nice person. We had a nice conversation," he added.

"I'll bet," Angela laughed. "When we were young Megan had a huge crush on you. Did you know that, brother?"

Johnny was touched. "I didn't know. I don't remember her."

"What did she say to you, Johnny? Was she happy to see you? What do you think of her? Pretty good looking, heh?"

"Well, as I said, I don't remember her, but I'll admit, she sure is pretty," he grinned. "I wish I had known her before she was married. We might have hit it off."

As Angela went to the kitchen to prepare dinner for the two of them, Johnny sat mulling over what Angela had told him about Megan.

Throughout dinner his thoughts kept wandering back to the bar, wondering when Megan would get the news about her husband and how she would handle it.

"Any more, Johnny?" Angela asked, rising to clear away the dishes.

"No thanks. That was great, Ann. Your spaghetti sauce is as good as Mama's, and the meatballs were perfect." He patted his stomach as he got up and stretched. "I think I'll take a walk around the neighborhood, okay?" he asked her.

"Oh yes, go ahead," she assured him. "I have letters to write. Keeping up with the Phibies is a full time job," and laughing softly to herself, she headed for the kitchen. "Lock the door on your way out?" she called to him.

Joseph Francis Panicello

"Night, Ann, and thanks," Johnny said as he pulled open the door and shut it gently behind him. Once on the stoop, he half-ran down the steps and immediately made his way back to the bar.

When he entered he noticed that Megan wasn't at the table where he had left her. He was disappointed as he stepped up to the bar and ordered a beer. He casually asked the bartender, "Where's the boss?"

The fifty year old bartender replied, "Oh, you mean Megan. She's in the back room having her dinner before the crowd gets here. That's where she lives. You're Johnny, aren't you? She did mention that if you dropped in again she'd like to see you. I have to go back there and bring her a beer. I'll tell her that you're here."

"Thanks," said Johnny, feeling pleased.

When the bartender returned he said to Johnny, "She wants you to go back. Take your beer with you, on the house."

Johnny walked through a large, dark, empty room. He assumed it was probably used for engagements or weddings. He noticed there was light seeping through a partially closed door at the rear of the room and wandered over toward it. He knocked on the door and a soft voice from within called, "Come in, Johnny."

Megan had changed into an appealing blue dress that heightened the blue of her eyes. Her blond hair hung loosely. She was slim, with a lovely figure.

Johnny whistled softly and Megan laughed.

"Thank you," she said. "I thought you might be back. Please sit down."

As he approached, Johnny smiled. "You look beautiful, Megan. I probably shouldn't have come, though."

"I wanted you to," she confessed, looking at him steadily. "I've always been infatuated with you," she said with a smile.

"I'm married, you know," she continued. "My husband, Jim, is twelve years older than I am. He's a good man, with a promising future. At least it was, until the war came. He owns the bar, and a small grocery store in the neighborhood. He made me feel safe and secure so I married him. Now, I don't know where he is, whether he is alive or dead." Megan paused for a moment.

Johnny listening intently, understood what she was trying to convey. He desperately wanted to tell her about Jim but just didn't know how. Standing up, Johnny took hold of Megan's hands and gently pulled her up close to him.

"Nothing has to happen right now," he whispered softly. "If you need me, I'll be here."

He kissed her, softly, and as each could feel the response in the other, they slowly parted.

Without another word, Johnny left the room. He moved out of the bar onto the sidewalk and started down the street, still thinking about Megan. He wished like hell that the other Phibies were with him.

Abruptly, he turned and headed down Rockaway Boulevard, entering another saloon. He strode up to the bar, slapped a fiver down in front of him and explained to the startled bartender, "Five shot glasses, fill them with Scotch, and keep the change."

The bartender watched in amusement as Johnny raised the first glass.

"To Belcher," he said, and swallowed.

"To Robber," and gulped the second shot.

"To Hinny," and the third shot went down.

"To Olly," wiping a tear from the corner of his eye.

"To me, Macaroni," and choked down the last shot.

As he turned to leave, the bartender grabbed his arm, "Hang on, buddy." The bartender reached for another shot glass, filled it, raised it in Johnny's direction and said, "To all of you!" and drank it down.

Johnny, grinning, gave a smart salute in return, and leaving the bar, slowly made his way home.

Joseph Francis Panicello

26. Central Pacific

The Gilbert and Marshall Islands were next on Admiral King's agenda. The Gilbert Islands consist of Makin, Tarawa, Abemama, Abaiang, Maiana, and Nauru. The Marshall Islands consist of Majuro, Kwajalein, and Eniwetok Atolls.

Admiral Nimitz was instructed by the Joint Chiefs of Staff (JCS) to assault the Marshalls no later than November 15, 1943. Nimitz, however, suggested that the Gilberts should come first to protect his southern flank from enemy aircraft that were now stationed in the Gilbert Islands. The JCS agreed and gave permission to Nimitz to take the Gilberts first, in November, and the Marshalls in January, 1944.

Vice Admiral Spruance, the newly appointed commander of the 5th fleet, would head the Gilbert invasion. The major problem he faced was a dispute between the two men directly under him, Rear Adm. Kelly Turner, commander of the 5th Naval Amphibious force, and Lt. General Holland Smith, commander of the 5th Army Amphibious Corps.

Adm. Spruance demanded strict adherence to military protocol from both himself and his men and though Smith and Turner wrangled over who should command the assault on the Gilberts, Spruance wasn't worried. To his chief of staff he said, "Don't worry about them. They'll do as they are told."

On the positive side, Admiral Spruance had a powerful fighting force for the next two assaults. He had 17 carriers, 13 battleships, many cruisers, a score of destroyers, two LSDs, 38 LSTs, 11 LCIs, many LVTs, and nine merchant ships loaded with troops.

The Gilberts consist of a group of 16 atolls in the Central Pacific ocean and they lie northeast of Australia. The equator runs through the center of the group. They were discovered by Captain Byron of England in 1764, and in 1892 the islands, including the neighboring Ellice Islands, were made a protectorate of Great Britain. The Japanese overran the islands in

1941. After World War II was over, the British, from 1975 to 1979, colonized the islands. The islands later gained independence as the Republic of Kiribati.

The Marshall Islands consist of 33 major island units. They were discovered by the Spanish explorer Alvaro de Saaveda in 1529, but were renamed by the British sea captain, John Marshall, in 1788. The weather is hot and humid and the chief commercial product today is copra.

An atoll is classified as a island surrounded by coral reefs. They can be shaped like a doughnut with water in the center, a three quarter circle, or even half moon in shape. The Makin Atoll, in the Gilberts, wouldn't require a major assault because it was estimated that there were only 500 Japanese troops defending that island. Many of them were Korean laborers.

The Tarawa Atoll, in the Gilberts, would require a major assault because it was well fortified. Galvanic was the code name given for the attack on Tarawa and Makin in the Gilberts. On November 20, 1943, Air Force bombers began raids on Tarawa, followed by many rounds of shells from cruisers and battleships. It was the opinion of Holland Smith that nothing could survive the shell firing, but they discovered later, as they did on other assaults, that it did little damage to the fortified Japanese. Japanese pillboxes were constructed with reinforced concrete to withstand heavy bombardments.

The invasion force was divided into two attack units. The northern group, Task Force 21, under the command of Admiral Turner, was to capture Makin. The southern section, Task Force 53, under Admiral Harry W. Hill, was directed to seize the atolls of Tarawa and Abemama.

The LST Task Group 54.5 on Tarawa, under Lt. Commander R.M. Pitts, consisted of LSTs 34, 242, and 243, each carrying an LCT. They were escorted by DD-598 *Bancroft*. Task Group 54.7, under Lt. Commander B.B. Cheathham, consisted of LSTs 478, 20, 23, 69, 169, 205, 218, 484, carrying two LCTs. They were escorted by DD-606 *Coghlan*.

Joseph Francis Panicello

On Makin, the LST Task Group 54.6 was commanded by H.A. Lincoln, consisting of LSTs 476, 477, 479, 480, 481 and 482, carrying two LCTs. They were escorted by DD-605 *Caldwell.*

On Abemama, the LST Task Group was under Lt. Commander P.A. Walker, consisting of LSTs 19, 240, 241, and 244, carrying three LCTs. They were escorted by DE-19 *Hastings.*

Rear Admiral Turner, commander of the Amphibious forces, requested that a photo reconnaissance be made by the *Nautilus* submarine, under Commander William D. Irvin. The photographs were to be taken through the submarine's periscope. Submarines are usually loners and have to fend for themselves. There's an old navy saying, "Submarines have no friends," and the submarine *USS Nautilus* found out the hard way that this was true.

On November 19, the *Nautilus* sent the following message: "Planes were seen coming from the north and south off of Tarawa." Shortly thereafter, Task force 53 began bombardment of the Tarawa Atoll.

After that bombardment, the *Nautilus* captain radioed, "We were being shelled so we dove and raised our periscope to 15 feet. Our photo shows that the Japanese built a six to eight foot wall along the seaward beach. These walls were untouched by our bombs." Because their batteries were running low the submarine had to surface.

The Amphibious landing force that was headed for Tarawa were escorted by two destroyers, the *USS Ringgold* (DD-500) and *USS Gansevoot* (DD-608). The problem was that when one of these destroyers saw an unidentified sub, its captain thought that the *Nautilus* was a Jap sub. The captain of the *Ringgold*, Commander Thomas F. Conley, reported his finding by radio to the other ships in the area and immediately sounded his own general alarm. No answer came from the subs IFF (Identify, Friend or Foe) so it became a case of, "Shoot first and ask questions later."

A Slow Moving Target, The LST of World War II

The *Nautilus* captain became concerned and ordered battle stations himself, because his IFF was not working and he didn't know if the destroyer was friend or foe, either. Commander Conley fired two torpedoes at the sub but one ran wild and the other missed. Then friendly attack came from another ship, the *Santa Fe*, which began firing its 6-inch batteries at the assumed sub target. The *Ringgold* had expended a total of 69 rounds of 5-inch shells and the *Santa Fe* fired 77, 6-inch shells at the target. One shell ripped into the *Nautilus's* superstructure but did not explode. It was a dud.

The *Nautilus* dove for safety. It began taking on water and, unfortunately, they had to surface again. They limped away to the island of Abemama and on the way the captain decided he might as well complete their reconnaissance mission.

The marines on board the submarine were anxious to get off because the torpedo rooms didn't make satisfactory foxholes for them. The one hundred or so marines were allowed to go ashore on Abemama and managed to kill the few hundred Japs and Korean workers left on the island. The marines refused to return to the *Nautilus* and were later picked up by a destroyer. They had had enough of that confinement.

Through it all, the *Nautilus* captain learned a hard lesson. In a friend or foe situation the submarine has no friends at all unless it can make contact with other ships using its IFF. Shoot first and ask questions later is a scary situation when one's equipment doesn't work.

The Tarawa invasion was later to be called, "The Assault into Hell." First of all, landing craft were late, taking considerable time transferring the LVTs from the transports to the sea, and because there was a reef between them and shore, LVTs had trouble crossing them, taking many hits.

What happened next would be considered the most violent killings of World War II. Both sides suffered huge casualties. Many LVTs were sunk and the few marines that survived had to struggle to reach shore with heavy packs on their backs, carrying their weapons high. Then the Higgins LCVPs came in but

Joseph Francis Panicello

because the tide was low they were caught eight hundred yards out and shelled unmercifully. Japanese bullets were killing American men by the hundreds.

The resistance was fierce on Tarawa. The Japanese had 5,000 well dug in troops waiting for the Marines as they waded in over a half mile of coral flats. A predicted high tide failed to materialize, stranding the Marines' Amtracks far off the beach.

Landing craft could not cross the reefs until the tide rose again to unload their cargo. They had to circle aimlessly outside the lagoon waiting for a higher tide. LVTs were finally able to cross the reefs and kept delivering troops to the beaches but the marines, by now, didn't need more troops. They needed ammunition, cannons, tank, medical supplies, food and water which were on board the LCVPs and LSTs that were being delayed by the tide. When the tide rose the LCVPs were able to land but unloading supplies became a sequence of mass confusion and chaos.

"We need help... Situation bad," radioed the Marine commander, Col. David Shoop, as he was taking cover next to a Japanese blockhouse. After days of fighting Shoop, eventually, drove inland with his men to finally control the island. For Shoop's heroism on Tarawa, he earned the Medal of Honor.

It was also a difficult task to care for the wounded on Tarawa. The wounded had to be removed as quickly as possible so as not to diminish the morale of the newly landed marines. Seeing dead marines all over the beach could be devastating, so a casualty station was set up on the beach and a surgical team was sent to shore. Because of the reefs, LSTs could not land at all on Tarawa, even with a high tide. They had to transfer their load to LVTs at sea. The seriously wounded had to be transported to the hospital wards in the transports that were anchored out in the bay.

Many of the wounded were brought to LST 153 where Andre administered medical first aid. Another corpsman was assigned to Andre's ship to assist him. Andre was becoming very skillful at saving men by performing surgical operations.

A Slow Moving Target, The LST of World War II

The corpsman yelled to Andre, "Robber. We can't take any more in. There's no place to put them and we're running out of plasma."

Andre, busy operating on a marine with a bullet in the chest, wearily instructed the corpsman, "Put them in the passageway on any mattresses you can find. These guys are dying right in front of us. We have to try to save as many as we can."

Every time a wounded marine was patched up on the makeshift operating table another was promptly put on the table. Cleanliness at the operating table was lax. Andre didn't have time to wash his hands between operations. Saving their lives was of the utmost importance to him right now. Infections could be handled later he figured, if the men survived.

When the assault on Tarawa was finally over Andre's captain recommended that he be promoted to Chief Pharmacist Mate for saving so many lives. This promotion would give him the authority he needed to perform minor operations on the spot, even though he was already performing major operations on board LST 153.

Of the 2,619 Japanese on Tarawa only 17 were captured alive. Of the 2,217 Korean laborers on the island, only 129 survived. The American casualties consisted of 1,113 U.S. Navy and Marines killed, three missing, and 2,290 wounded. The Army had 66 killed and 187 wounded soldiers.

The mistakes made in the assault on Tarawa began to drift back to the States. The Army generals were complaining about the marines. They did not believe that any Marine general was qualified to command the troops. Marine Gen. Holland Smith was proud of his marines but was bitter toward the navy. He said that the navy should have let the marines run the show. He was especially mad for not having enough gunfire from the ships, feeling they should have bombed the shores over a longer period to soften up the enemy. Admiral Turner was faulted for gambling on the low tide. The finger pointing became intense between all three commanders. In the end a lesson was learned from this assault which did help futures offensives.

Joseph Francis Panicello

Conflicts between General MacArthur and the navy continued over the Amphibious operations. In January, MacArthur sent a letter to the Secretary of War saying that the Tarawa assault was a tragedy and that he should be given the command of the entire war in the Pacific. He also proposed a plan that diverted ships from the Central Pacific and bypassed the Marshall Islands. He mainly wanted to remove control of the fleet from Nimitz.

In January 1944, a major conference was held at Pearl Harbor with regards to future strategy in the Pacific. MacArthur's chief of staff made a presentation for him about an attack on the Marianas which Nimitz thought would be too costly. MacArthur also sent a representative to Washington. Admiral King's judgement of MacArthur's plan consisted of one word, "Absurd." The Marshall Islands would remain the target in the next operation.

Nimitz's subordinates were also arguing against him. Holland Smith, Spruance, and Turner didn't think that Kwajalein in the Marshalls should be the next objective. Nimitz was stern and said, "If you don't want to do it, I'll find someone else to do it." It didn't take long before they all agreed with their stubborn Texan boss.

27. Kwajalein and Eniwetok

In January, 1944, Andre's slow moving LST and Hienman's faster cruiser went out to sea at different intervals. Their destination was the Marshall Islands. Admiral Spruance, on the cruiser the *Indianapolis,* followed behind the carriers, along with the task force that would assault the Marshalls, a Japanese stronghold since World War I. A newly formed 4th Marine Division and the 7th Infantry Division would make the assault. Included in the complement of ships were 75 transports, 11 carriers, 75 destroyers, 7 battle ships, 12 cruisers, and close to 200 Amphibious ships and boats.

Admiral Turner was in charge of the Amphibious fleet set to attack Kwajalein, which is the largest of the islands. The other atolls in the Marshall Islands that were to be assaulted were Roi, Namur, and Eniwetok. In the previous month of December, carrier aircraft began their raiding of the islands by destroying pill boxes and artillery guns. Army Aircorps Bombers that came from the Gilberts continued the raids to soften up the enemy. On January 30, the various ships consisting of cruisers, destroyers and battleships began their artillery firing on the islands.

On January 31, twenty five minutes before the landing craft began their approach, the ships sent a barrage of heavy explosives onto the beach. The plan was for the cruisers to stop their bombing when the amphibious boats were within 1,000 yards of the beach, the destroyers at 500 yards. The various LCI converted gunboats would stop whenever they deemed it was safe for the landing party.

Regardless of the training the 4th Marine Division had on San Clemente Island, off the California coast, as the assault began many problems cropped up. During training there was little teamwork between the LSTs, the Marines, and the troop ships. It was mass confusion. In the assault on Kwajalein, the disorientation continued. Somehow the Americans landed and

Joseph Francis Panicello

were on the beach with artillery and DUKWS. There was no rest for the Japanese and many chose to die rather than be captured.

On February 1, the soldiers and marines began disembarking from the transports into Higgins LCVPs. After they were in the water several of these men had to go back up rope nets onto LSTs from the LCVPs to man the LVTs that were sitting on the main deck of the LSTs.

The LSTs that did have LVT tractors on their main deck were stuck with other problems. The LVTs were very heavy and too long for the elevator. An incline ramp had to be rigged to allow the tractors to be passed down the elevator shaft. LST 226 had mechanical problems with the bow doors and its ramp could not be lowered. The doors were finally strapped open with ropes and chains, which permitted its ramp to be lowered to allow 17 LVTs to come ashore.

Robert H. Stickney on board LST 29, related the following story on the invasion of Kwajalein: "The night before we approached Kwajalein, I had the 12 to 4 watch in the main engine room and had gone almost 20 hours without any sleep. The next morning at 7 a.m., February 1, the invasion of Kwajalein began in earnest. The battleships Mississippi, Pennsylvania, and New Mexico, along with the cruisers Minneapolis, New Orleans and San Francisco, also eight destroyers, began firing point blank at the beaches. In addition the aircraft carriers Enterprise, Yorktown, and Belleau Wood flew more than 40 sorties against the port city of Kwaji in Kwajalein. LST 29 transferred thousands of tons of supplies from deep draft transport ships in the bay to the Green Beach-4 on Kwajalein western end."

The assault troops on Kwajalein were being hampered by enemy shells so Admiral Turner radioed two battle ships harboring out at sea, directing them to, "Come close to shore to within 2,000 yards and blast away at the enemy." This act proved to be the final blow on the batteries of Japanese, which, in turn, allowed the troops to land.

A Slow Moving Target, The LST of World War II

The marines and soldiers destroyed the Japanese in one day on the islands of Roi and Namur. It was discovered later that 75% of the enemy were killed from American bombardment. These assaults were much better than that of Tarawa and the Marshall Islands were now in American hands. Rai, Namur, and Kwajalein cost the lives of 313 marines and 173 solders, and over 850 wounded, in comparison to 4,900 enemy defenders killed and 70 taken prisoner.

On February 17, 1944, the assault on the Eniwetok atolls began. As usual, small islands outside the atolls were quickly seized to provide artillery bases that would be used to bombard the three main islands. Engebi was first to be hit with 7,000 artillery shells and the marines quickly took over the island with relatively few causalities. The Japanese losses were heavy, with only 19 out of 1,200 surviving. A major loss for the Americans was an LCM carrying a tank. The LCM was sunk and the crew inside the tank drowned.

The assault on Eniwetok was not easy. The Japanese put up strong resistance and the 106th Infantry assigned to the task were not penetrating. It took a battalion of marines to assist the army assault and the resistance was finally subdued.

Robert H. Stickney discussing LST 29 said, "On February 15, 1944, LST 29 was loaded with Army troops that had secured Kwajalein and more supplies headed toward Eniwetok atoll. On February 17, LST 29 entered Eniwetok atoll, taking many infantry troops to the beach in our LCVP. Pat McCafferty was the coxswain and I was the Motor Mach. On our way to the beach you could hear the whistle of naval shells over our heads.

"About 100 yards from the beach you could hear the sound of small arms from the enemy fire overhead, some were hitting our steel bow ramp. We all had crouched down, except Pat who had to see where we were headed. I was talking to an Army private who had a radio strapped to his back and after we hit the beach and the ramp was down I saw that poor Army soldier lying face down on the beach. I never saw him move after that! The next day our LST beached itself to unload heavy equipment."

Joseph Francis Panicello

Parry Island, the next objective, was thought to have 2,462 Japanese defenders. It was discovered that Parry Island's defense was bigger than expected so the Admiral and the General decided to bombard the island an extra day. Friendly fire was one of the disasters that occurred. There was so much smoke close to the beach an LCI was hit by an American destroyer's bomb, causing 13 sailors to be killed and 43 others wounded by our own ships. In another case of friendly fire, American naval gunfire, making a grave mistake, landed their shells right in the center of our assaulting marines on the beach, wounding many before the guns could be called off.

When the fighting was over 4,500 Japanese were killed, in comparison to 348 Americans. The four more remaining islands in the Marshalls were by-passed and the Japanese on those islands did not surrender until after the war.

After the Marshall Islands victory, Nimitz recommended that Rear Admirals Spruance and Kelly Turner be promoted. Later, against Nimitz's advice, Marine commander Holland Smith was given a third star by Admiral King. There were always conflicts between Nimitz and Smith, but King could not justify promoting Spruance and Turner and not Smith.

While the securement of the Marshall Islands was completed the fight to save the wounded continued.

The hospital ship *Solace* arrived to accept 951 wounded Americans. Andre's LST 153 accepted the first fifty and after providing first aid to those badly wounded they were transferred to the *Solace*. The captain on LST 153 was again proud of his men, especially Chief Andre, who saved the lives of at least twenty of those badly wounded.

Andre initially had mattresses and blankets placed on each side of the tank deck and had the ship's welder make up several stands that were used as IV blood plasma holders. When LST 153 landed and the tank deck was emptied of its load, Andre immediately went out onto the beach carrying a makeshift red-cross flag.

A Slow Moving Target, The LST of World War II

He yelled out to the army medics and navy corpsmen, "Bring the wounded onto the LST." In no time at all, soldiers began carrying the wounded on stretchers with a medic or corpsman walking along side holding an IV bottle. Andre then yelled out, "Bring the serious cases in first."

As a medic passed him, he said, "Chief, they're all serious." Andre stopped his yelling and instead just directed the traffic.

When the sides of the tank deck were filled he had the most seriously wounded moved up to the crew's quarters, using the same bunks previously emptied by the vehicle drivers and foot soldiers who had gone ashore.

Andre had to dodge some bullets once himself. A Japanese aircraft came swooping down, strafing his ship. He yelled out, "Holy smokes," and left the red-cross flag standing. He ran up the ramp as fast as he could and into the tank deck for protection. The bullets were banging against the open ramp, ricocheting against the bow doors and into the tank deck. Missing Andre completely, a stray bullet did hit a sailor in the leg. It seemed like there was no place to hide.

When the plane was finally shot down he noticed that both a medic and a soldier, who had been carrying a wounded soldier up the ramp, had been killed from this latest raid. Luckily, the wounded soldier that remained on the stretcher was still alive. Andre called out to two sailors, "You swabs, carry that poor soldier on aboard."

When he went down the ramp again he began looking for his make-shift red-cross flag. He found it was completely destroyed by gunfire. Had he remained there he would have been annihilated.

The problem that Andre now faced was bringing in more wounded after the tank deck was emptied. The trucks and tanks on the main deck had to be lowered by elevator to the tank deck, which interfered with his moving the wounded on board. As the elevator came down he had to stop the wounded from being brought on board or they would have been run over by the trucks on their way out.

Joseph Francis Panicello

As the elevator hit bottom the truck driver had only one thing on his mind, and that was to get his vehicle ashore as quickly as possible and out of harm's way. After each truck rolled out and onto the beach the procession of wounded renewed.

Andre knew there would be plenty of time before the elevator was able to bring down the next truck and during this interval he ordered the wounded to be brought on board as quickly as possible. Raising the heavy elevator back to the main deck was a very slow process. To unshackle the next truck from its position on the main deck, and driving it to the elevator to be tied down and lowered, took up precious time.

The navy learned a hard lesson in amphibious unloading from the main deck during a earlier assault. Previously, when an LST landed on a beach the crew would unlatch all the vehicles on the main deck to be ready for a quick departure down the elevator. This was a great idea under a normal assault landing.

In one situation, however, the captain ordered a retreat of the ship because of enemy fire. The vehicles on the main deck were now loose and began colliding with each other. Many had to be pushed over the side to save the ship. As a result of that calamity, the new procedure was not to unshackle a truck until the elevator was up and ready to receive it. This method slowed the removal of trucks from the main deck but was much safer and it did provide Andre the additional time he needed to bring in more wounded up the ramp and onto the ship.

The weakness with saving the wounded on many of these assaults was that the Hospital ship would not come into the area until the next day or when the island's beach was secured because they were very vulnerable to enemy attack. They were not allowed to have AA-guns on board to protect themselves. They were hopeful that the Japanese would honor the ship's hospital markings but couldn't depend on it.

The second problem was that the LCVPs that were used to transport the wounded to the Hospital ships had to be refueled close to the beach, which meant bringing oil tankers in close,

A Slow Moving Target, The LST of World War II

leaving them open to attack. The Hospital ship and the oilers refused to come close enough until it was safe. So the wounded had to wait, suffering on the beach. Some would die in the interim.

This is why Andre set up his LST as a temporary first aid station. He knew that many lives could be saved if immediate attention was given to the wounded and he did save many wounded using this procedure.

A third problem involved the traffic jam of LSTs backed up, waiting to unload cargo. At one point the Captain of LST 153 was ordered away from the beach by the flag ship. The captain was forced to comply. The many wounded still on shore had to be transferred by LCVPs from shore to a hospital ship at sea, losing precious time.

The situation of attending the wounded during and after an assault was so deplorable the captain authorized Andre to draft a new procedure. "I will direct your recommendations to Admiral Spruance, himself!" declared Captain Miles.

Andre wrote an impersonal prelude to his list of recommendations. It read, "There are not enough doctors and nurses here to care for the wounded. I received the Medal of Honor for saving over fifty men on the battlefield. Most of the wounded marines and soldiers would have died from loss of blood if I wasn't there to assist them. We need more combat medical men close enough to the front lines to render immediate attention to the wounded. By the time the wounded are brought out to the Hospital ships it's too late, and many marines and soldiers die on the way due to lack of blood or by not getting immediate aid. I therefore recommend the following:

1. Hospital ships are too late to administer first aid to the wounded. Use LSTs as first aid stations after they unload their cargo. The wounded can later be transferred to the hospital ships using small craft.

Joseph Francis Panicello

2. Each LST should have at least three corpsman to help tend the wounded. It is essential that first aid be provided quickly to save those that are wounded badly. Loss of blood is the number one cause of men dying.

3. At least one LST should be used as the lead first aid station and should have a medical doctor on board.

4. Each LST should carry additional medical supplies, especially blood plasma, to supplement the army medic and navy corpsmen's supply on the beach. These medical men on shore can only carry a limited amount of medical supplies on their backs and they run out rather quickly.

5. More medics and navy corpsmen are needed during an assault. That first hour of an invasion is the most crucial time to save lives.

Admiral Spruance was now using the heavy cruiser *Indianapolis* as his flagship. Hienman had been transferred to this cruiser, with a recommendation from Admiral Wilkinson, as a top gunner to support and defend Spruance against air attacks. Hienman followed Spruance's entourage carrying his gear but this time with a 45-pistol in a holster at his side. His second duty on board was to be Spruance's personal bodyguard. Because Rich was never assigned any duty on board he was able to go ashore anytime he wanted to, except when the Admiral went ashore himself. Then he would accompany the Admiral as his personal bodyguard and chauffeur. When he was on board he would practice his gun draw. He became exceptionally fast at it. He was deadly with that 45-pistol. Fortunately, no one ever tested his expertise.

When Andre's message arrived at the *Indianapolis,* Rich intercepted it. Since it wasn't listed as an emergency he couldn't

A Slow Moving Target, The LST of World War II

interrupt the admiral, who was heavily involved in conducting the assault. Rich put the request in his Pea-Coat pocket and would give it to the admiral later. Meanwhile, at his gun turret, shooting down the enemy, he was again magnificent, downing four more Japanese aircraft. After witnessing Hienman's performance, the admiral was pleased with his appropriation from Admiral Wilkinson.

A few days later Rich remembered the message in his coat and read it. He yelled out loud, "It's from Robber, wow." He took the message to the admiral and was quickly admitted into his cabin.

The admiral was first to speak, "I saw what you did to those bastards. Good show, Hienman. Now, what's so urgent that you have to see me?"

"It's about a message, sent from LST 153. I delayed giving it to you because you were busy with the invasion and I didn't think it was an emergency. It was written by a good buddy of mine, through his captain."

The admiral reviewed the letter and then paused for a moment. He then said to Hienman, "How well do you know this Chief Robbier."

"Very well, Sir. He'll be a great medical doctor after this war is over. I understand he received a medal for saving many lives under fire. Whatever he says, you can bet Robber, I mean Robbier, knows what he is talking about."

"Very well. Have my Chief Yeoman come to me at once. I will have him type up an order to satisfy that Robber friend of yours. You're dismissed."

From then on all LSTs in the Pacific had ample medical supplies on board and three new medical corpsmen were assigned to Andre during the next assault. There was a shortage of medics and corpsmen, so more help could not be given on land during an assault as requested. Andre would have to be satisfied with having three more corpsmen on board.

Joseph Francis Panicello

28. Letters to Angela

Dear Ann:

I've arrived in England and am looking forward to my new duties. I can't say more.

I hated to leave Megan. Despite my attempt to stay at arms-length with her, when she received the news about Jim I couldn't stay away. I saw quite a lot of her in the couple of months I was home. The shock of seeing him again in that condition unnerved her. She was visiting him every day in the VA hospital in Long Island.

Jim keeps insisting she get a divorce but her sense of loyalty can't allow her to do it. You know as well as I do the Catholic Church is opposed to divorce and Megan's as Catholic as we are.

I feel like a heel for saying it but Megan's a young, beautiful woman. What will life be like for her? I know she and I could be happy together if she would listen to reason but she refuses to discuss the subject of her and I. She says even seeing me makes her feel guilty.

It all seems a hopeless situation. The day I left she cried in my arms. I know she loves me but I don't know what I can do about it.

Please don't worry about Danny. I know he'll be okay. Take care of yourself and keep writing.

          Love, Johnny

Dear Angela:

If not for your letters I wouldn't know anything about the other Phibies.

I have some news of my own for you to share with them. Lovette and I were married in Hawaii.

A Slow Moving Target, The LST of World War II

When I got to the island the doctors at the hospital found out, along with my fractured leg, I had internal injuries in my abdomen. They operated, and between that and the leg I was laid up for almost a month.

The minute I could hobble around I got permission for liberty. I got a lead from a Christian Missionary on where Lovette was staying. She's been transferred to a mission on Maui.

I guess I don't have to tell you I high-tailed it over to Maui in a fishing boat I scrounged up. When I arrived and located the mission my heart was pounding. There she was, surrounded by the kids, having some sort of a game in the yard. I was laughing, and she was crying, as we embraced. The kids were all clapping their hands.

We were married two days later in Maui. There isn't a better place in the world for a honeymoon.

Someday I hope you can meet her. I read your letters to her. She thinks the world of you already.

I have some more news but don't share it with Andre and Rich. I received my orders. I'm to report to LST 153. I'll be seeing them and I want it to be a surprise.

I'll close for now. Take care of yourself.

Fondly, Bob

Angela:

I don't know if, when this letter reaches you, Johnny will still be in New York.

I received a letter from my sister, Dolores. Her career is going well. She's getting better parts and is very happy but she would like to contact Johnny. She regrets the misunderstanding they had and would like to patch things up. Let him know, would you?

Joseph Francis Panicello

I saw Andre recently. He visited my ship while we were docked in Australia. He has made a real success for himself in the navy. He'll be a real doctor by the time he's through.

We double-dated but I don't think his girl made much of an impression, though she is very pretty. Do you think he might still be carrying a torch?

I want to thank you, Angela, for your supportive letters. When I couldn't talk to anyone about Mildred it was a relief to sit down and pour out my thoughts on paper and send them on to you. Your letters help more than you know and all of the Phibies appreciate it.

By the way, I met an Australian girl I like very much. Her name is Lucy. She's very intelligent, a teacher. She isn't movie-star pretty like Mildred but there is something very appealing about her. I enjoy her company very much. I never thought I'd feel that way again.

We've discussed my divorce and Lucy understands I'm not anxious to jump into another hot, heavy romantic situation. From now on I take it <u>slow</u>, like an LST.

With regards, Rich

Dear Angela:

Thanks so much for the letter. It's nice to have someone at home to share my achievements with. Medicine is becoming more important to me than I would have ever thought possible. Your interest is an inspiration to me.

I have decided that after the war is over I will definitely go to college and become a full-fledged doctor. I can't think of a more rewarding and fulfilling profession to devote myself to. And since the most beautiful girl in the world was stolen from me, I'll have plenty of time on my hands.

Congratulations on your wonderful news. I can hardly believe Danny is going to be a father. He's a lucky devil! You - and baby, too.

Please don't worry so much. I'm sure Danny is fine. You will probably hear from him any day now. Take good care of yourself and with your prayers, say one for me.

Love, Andre.

29. Anzio

Bari, Italy, is a city of 200,000 people which juts out into the Adriatic Sea. It boasts famous landmarks such as the Castello (Castle) Svevo, a medieval fortress dating back to Norman times, and the Basilica San Nicola, which contains the tomb of St. Nicholas. When the Southern Italian King, Roger II, conquered Bari in the 11th century, the area had been under the control of the Byzantine Empire for several hundred years. After the empire was defeated, King Roger II, the son of the Norman Count of Sicily, allowed the Greeks to stay and keep their possessions as long as they remained faithful to his kingdom and became Italians. The Greeks had been there for several generations and they decided to stay.

In 1942, the city of Bari was under the control of the Allies. Unexpectedly, there was a surprise attack on Allied merchant ships and LSTs in the Bari Harbor. The surprise *Luftwaffe* raid on the Adriatic port city sank several ships and left thousands suffering in the wake of the deadly poison, mustard gas. The German attack on Bari was dubbed "The Second Pearl Harbor." Bari was under the jurisdiction of the British and was used as the main supply base for Montgomery's Eighth Army. At the time of the attack the Allies believed that the *Luftwaffe* in Italy was relatively weak and could not mount a major effort against them. The Allied leaders discovered how wrong they were.

After the invasion of Sicily in July, 1943, by the Allies, and the capture of Messina, the Italians were virtually out of the war.

As the Allied forces fought their way up the Italian mainland the German forces in Italy fought back. In August, Allied air raids smashed Foggia, a German air base in Italy and in September, after the Italian surrender, the British forces took the naval base of Taranto, while the American forces invaded Salerno.

On October 1, 1943, the city of Naples fell to Montgomery and the Allies, but the push north thereafter toward Rome slowed

A Slow Moving Target, The LST of World War II

to a crawl because the Germans had the advantage of having nine more divisions than the Allies and the protection of the mountains, which German Field Marshall Kesselring called "God's gift to gunners."

The next invasion would be Anzio, Italy, close to the capital city of Rome.

Anzio is in the Province of Rome, and is just 33 miles south of the capital city. It stands on the site of ancient Antium, the birthplace of two Roman emperors, Caligula and Nero. The fishing town fell into decay in the Middle Ages, but was restored in the 18th century. The present population of Anzio today is about 30,000 people. Rome, of course, was the ultimate goal for the Allies, using Anzio as a port of entry.

In January, 1944, Generals Mark Clark and Frank Lowry were setting up the amphibious assault on Anzio. The problem Clark had was that he was given orders from the Allied Chiefs in England to transfer many of the needed amphibious forces to England to support Overlord, the invasion of France. If he did there wouldn't be enough amphibious craft to make an assault on Anzio. The code name for this assault was called 'Shingle,' which was still being pushed by Churchill.

Mr. Churchill had to use all his charm and his great influence with President Roosevelt in order to have 'Shingle' accepted. "How can we take Rome if we don't assault Anzio first," was his argument. "Montgomery's troops are too slow coming up from the south. Rome must be taken as a moral victory."

The core of the struggle to launch an attack on Anzio was the availability of LSTs and, of course, the other landing craft as well. There were all types of craft now in service, some designed to land on the first wave, anti-aircraft boats for protection, rocket launching craft, and craft to make smoke screens. Churchill knew that one of the most important keys to success of an invasion was the LST.

Without enough LSTs, there could be no invasion and no landing in Anzio. These ships were in great demand but in short supply in Europe. Every commander tended to hoard these "*Slow Moving Targets.*" They used any scheme to keep them. Before each assault the distribution of LSTs was argued over, and a commander possessing one jealously guarded it. Churchill complained that the whole business of LSTs had become an obsession by some military leaders. When he addressed Eisenhower he said, "The truth of the matter is, Anzio cannot be taken without these prize ships."

Selecting which LSTs should go where became a strain on the war machine. The European commanders felt that too many LSTs were in the Pacific and not enough were allocated for the Atlantic theater, which they felt was more imperative. Memorandums were being sent in all directions for LSTs, and finally Churchill convinced Roosevelt by saying, "Mr. President, if many of the LSTs that are now in the Atlantic were made available there would be a sufficient number of them to assault Anzio."

Eisenhower finally agreed and gave General Clark permission to keep 68 LSTs in the Anzio theater until January 25, 1944. The original plan presumed that the British 5th Army Division, marching north under Montgomery, would be close enough to Rome to support the Anzio assault. But, as it turned out, the 5th Army was again being delayed by strong, stubborn German forces and could not advance close enough to Rome.

Clark then advised Eisenhower to cancel the invasion, but Churchill intervened again and pressed for the plan to continue. Eisenhower didn't want to jeopardize Overlord by not having enough LSTs available. Even Churchill recognized that the LSTs had to leave the Mediterranean by January 25, or endanger the Overlord schedule.

The plan finally agreed upon was to have those 68 LSTs available on the assault of Anzio, but after the LSTs dropped their initial cargo they would immediately leave for England. The problem with this plan was that there wouldn't be any LSTs available for the follow-up delivery of essential supplies to support the troops on their march from Anzio to Rome. This

A Slow Moving Target, The LST of World War II

would have to be done with small craft which can only move one tank at a time. Another problem cropped up. The prospect of bad weather expected in two days demanded that unloading had to be accomplished within 48 hours of the landing.

General Alexander was the commander of the entire Italian operation, and General John P. Lucas was given command of the 6th Corps of General Mark's 5th Army. Lucas's assignment made him the most controversial figure in the Anzio affair. Clark chose Lucas because he had proved himself fighting with the 6th corps in his advance through the mountains against the Germans. His one flaw was that he was a cautious leader. Lucas wrote in his diary, "I must keep from thinking of the fact that my order will send these men into a desperate attack."

General Patton, who was on his way to England after being grounded in Sicily for slapping a soldier, didn't give Lucas much encouragement either. He said to General Lucas, "John, I'd hate to see you get killed. You can't get out of this alive. Of course, you might be badly wounded. No one ever blames a wounded general!" He then said to Lucas's aides, "Look here, if things get too bad, shoot the old man in the backside, but don't you dare kill the old fellow!"

The plan began thirty days before D-Day when ships were first loaded in Naples. The commanders were; Rear Admiral Frank Lowry, commanding the naval forces, and Maj. Gen. John Lucas, in command of the army. The American 3rd Infantry Division and the British 1st Infantry Division would make the assault on Anzio.

After the usual shelling of the beaches by destroyers and cruisers, the LSTs and the other smaller amphibious craft headed for the beach. It was January 22, 1944, when General Lucas said, "This is it! There can be no turning back!"

To be able to get close enough to the steep sloped beach, the LSTs had to lighten their load at the bow. This was done by allowing the DUKWs to disembark first, but it was still necessary to use pontoons to unload the tanks and trucks from the LSTs. The Amphibious fleet had to land 40,000 troops and

Joseph Francis Panicello

because the LCIs couldn't get close enough to the beach, many of the troops had to be off-loaded onto LCVPs. Fortunately, the invaders had caught the Germans completely by surprise. DUKWs were also coming ashore from the big Liberty ships out at sea.

On an LST, coming from Naples to Anzio, a nurse asked MO/MA 1st class Bill Nackovina, Cleveland, "Is the water on board soft?...I'd like to wash my hair."

Bill was stunned by the question and all he could say was, "Yes." This was proof enough that women were now part of the war.

When the Allied soldiers finally went into town they found that the city of Anzio was deserted. The Germans had cleared the people out and left nothing but waste. Suddenly, six German aircraft came swooping down, dropping bombs, strafing the Allies. There was a large explosion by the beach. The Germans had hit a LSI (Landing Ship Infantry), killing all those aboard. By midnight 36,000 troops had landed with 3,000 vehicles and plenty of supplies.

One LST was hit by a torpedo and Bill Brinkly said, "It was like running into a stone wall." The second torpedo, ten minutes later, broke the ship apart and the crew abandoned the LST, with men jumping into water flaming like a torch.

By January 24, the assault force had secured a 10 mile deep beachhead. LSTs, LCTs and LCIs began unloading their supplies as quickly as possible. On the 2nd day a major gale came in and broached one LST, 7 LCTs, and three causeway sections collapsed. On the 4th day, the beach was clear enough to allow 5 LSTs to unload their cargo at the same time. However, another storm began brewing and it struck the beach with such force that it broached 12 LCTs and destroyed the remaining pontoons.

Field Marshal Kesselring was waiting. He established his defenses with Panzer tanks, anti-aircraft batteries, and thousands of hard-core soldiers. He ordered the German shelling to increase. They began their aerial attacks, using torpedoes and their new glide-bombs. These remote controlled glide-bombs

A Slow Moving Target, The LST of World War II

were frightening, as well as devastating. The bombs were guided by a mother aircraft well out of danger but the Allies quickly learned that by jamming the airwaves they could cause some of the glide-bombs to fall harmlessly into the sea. Even so, several bombs did get through. One hit the British destroyer *Janus,* which sank in twenty minutes, losing 150 men. At Anzio, the German guns found the LSTs easy marks.

Ben Dauria MoMI/c on Coast Guard LST 326 recalled; "The beaches at Anzio were shallow, with many sand bars, making beaching an LST virtually impossible. Our LST 326, along with other LSTs carried 100-foot metal pontoons mounted on both sides of our ship and when installed together they formed a causeway, making a 200-foot dock to the beach.

"On January 29, 1944, while anchored in the Bay of Anzio, we were raided by Dornier 217s and tanker 88s aircraft carrying glide bombs, which were radio controlled from mother planes. We felt secure knowing that there was the British cruiser *Spartan* nearby, firing at the planes and the glide bombs.

"All of a sudden, a glider bomb struck the *Spartan's* forward magazine and there was a tremendous explosion. The *Spartan* rolled over in a matter of minutes. It was a ghastly sight to see but we did pick up many survivors."

The Germans also hit and sank a hospital ship, *St. David,* out at sea fully illuminated in accordance to the Geneva Convention. All the wounded on board died. This act infuriated the Allied commanders. The desire to capture Anzio became almost an obsession.

The 34th infantry fought brilliantly but the division took a beating, losing 2,000 men. Some rifle companies lost 75% of their combat strength.

When the VIPs came visiting, the GIs referred to it as "Swanning." The term came from swans' habit of making short flights over water without any serious purpose. On one occasion, General Mark Clark made a PT-boat trip to the Anzio beach, accompanied by his usual entourage of correspondents and photographers. After posing with a GI while holding K-rations,

Joseph Francis Panicello

General Clark gave the K-rations back to the GI and said, "Here, son, eat it," and left. Word got around to the rest of the GIs that K-rations were good enough for the GIs but not good enough for the General. It certainly wasn't a moral booster.

On D-Day 2, Danny's LST 85 was approaching the shore. Its rear anchor was dropped at the proper time and its bow doors were being prepared to be opened. Danny and three of his men were down in the bow manhole to undog the bow doors. Then, a continuous rapid gunfire from German Luftwaffes began straffing the LST. Danny could hear the bullets hitting the main deck, just above his head, ping, ping, ping.

Even under attack, his orders were to continue to open the bow door and lower the ramp to 45 degrees. Danny's LST 85 would beach itself despite the latest German strike. The captain was determined to unload his cargo to support the troops that were waiting on the beach for munitions, tanks, and backup artillery.

When the door was finally opened and the ramp lowered, Danny and his men climbed up the ladder back to the main deck. He looked over at the port side and saw another LST receiving a hit by a torpedo that was launched by a German plane. The men on that ship began jumping into the sea as it began to sink.

There was a loud burst on the port side of his own ship. A radio controlled glide-bomb had managed to get through and hit his ship. It produced a large hole on the top port center but did not cause enough damage to sink the LST. A German fighter now came into play and attacked the port side, shooting his machine guns at them. Danny took cover behind the port bow turret and again began hearing the ping, ping sounds of bullets hitting the steal turret. As the plane passed he looked into the turret and saw that the gunners mate and his apprentice were killed.

Danny scrambled over the turret and took over the forward port gun, yelling at one of his own men to load the AA-gun. As the next German plane came in, Danny began blazing away at it with his Anti-Aircraft gun. He was able to destroy one German

A Slow Moving Target, The LST of World War II

plane. He heard the order on the intercom from the captain to retreat the ship. Danny and his apprentice abandoned the guns, returned to the manhole, retracting the ramp and closing the bow doors. Danny and his striker went back to the port guns to resume shooting at any German aircraft that might still be on the attack.

They didn't have to wait long. The German planes attacked again, passing through a continuous barrage of AA-gun fire coming from other LSTs and destroyers. Somehow, one German plane got through the battery of gunfire and sent a few rounds at Danny's ship.

Danny's gun kept blazing away at the intruder but in his attempt to shoot the aircraft down he was hit. He slumped to the deck, and lay there, unable to move. His wound was not fatal but he was bleeding profusely. He tried to raise himself to resume his cannon fire but fell over, flat on his back. Both his right arm and left leg were wounded. Danny's striker, after seeing him go down, took over the gun but was unable to help Danny because he was busy concentrating on shooting at the attacking German aircraft.

Danny was bleeding excessively now and needed tourniquets around his upper right arm and left leg to stop the flow of blood. Even if his bleeding were stopped he would still need blood plasma to save his life. Other sailors on the ship were also too busy defending themselves against the attacks and were unable to help the injured.

Danny tried his belt as a tourniquet, using his left arm, but was unable to fasten it. He was helpless. He then stuck his thumb into the wound, hoping to stop the flow of blood. It helped, but by now he was too weak to do anything further. As Danny lay there he began thinking of Angela. Her lovely face appeared before him momentarily, then slowly faded away. His eyelids became heavy and began to close. He tried to fight off the inevitable, but he was becoming weary and weak. He gave out a desperate, last minute call for help but his voice was drowned

Joseph Francis Panicello

out by the AA-gunfire. He slumped over, falling into a deep sleep.

Danny died in the gun turret, due to loss of blood. Had there been a medical corpsman available he might have been saved. At the time Danny needed assistance, the only corpsman on LST 85 was on the bridge administering aid to an officer who had also been wounded.

Despite German attacks the beachhead was held until May 25, when contact was made with the United States 5th Army and they all headed for Rome. On the drive to Rome, Gen. Alexander's massive offense had succeeded, but at a terrible price. The casualty count was 40,000 dead, wounded and missing, the Germans lost 38,000 men. The remaining LSTs headed for England to support `Overlord.' They were now a month late, but they would still be ready for the invasion of France, which was expected in June.

Many German and Italian prisoners were captured in this assault. The Germans referred to Anzio as, "a prison camp where the inmates feed themselves." The Anzio prison had some 70,000 Italian and German prisoners and to feed them, there was a continuous parade of LSTs going back and forth to Naples, a distance of 120 miles. It took almost a day for this trip using these "Slow Moving Targets."

30. New Guinea

The Joint Chiefs finally decided to give MacArthur the go ahead to begin his long awaited return to the Philippines on January 15, 1944.

The first assault would be the Admiralty Islands. A reconnaissance party went ashore on one of the smaller islands, Los Negros, and discovered the island is "lousy with Japs" but the report did not reach the task force. On February 29, 1944, MacArthur decided to assault the Admiralties just north of New Guinea.

The seizure of Admiralty Islands was a move to seal off the large collection of Japs on Rabaul. The Admiralty Islands stood at the entrance to the Bismarck Sea, which provided a path for the Japanese to supply troops and cargo to Rabaul, and from Rabaul, to New Guinea.

Rabaul is a city port on New Britain Island which lies off the northeast coast of New Guinea. Rabaul contains Admiralty Island's largest community. In the 1937 and 1994 volcanic eruptions this port city suffered tremendous damage. Many people were killed.

In 1700, the English explorer, William Dampier, reached New Britain and gave it its name. In 1884, it became a part of the German Empire, but Australian forces took over the island after W.W.I., by a mandate from the League of Nations. Japan captured New Britain in 1942. In 1975, New Britain became part of the newly independent nation of Papua New Guinea.

Rabaul was the main base for Japanese warships and carriers that were used to launch attacks on the Allies in the South Pacific. Because of this, Rabaul became the target for many air raids by the U.S. Airforce, the Royal Australian Airforce, and New Zealand Airforce. Though the Allies concentrated their assaults on other islands they continued to bomb Rabaul relentlessly, but never invaded it. When aircraft returned to their bases and carriers with bombs left on board they would release them on Rabaul, just for good measure.

On November 2, the fifth Air Corps, flying North American B-25s, were escorted by Lockheed P-38 fighters. They attacked Rabaul but were intercepted by 112 Zeros. The loss of 9 B-25s and 9 P-38s earned this raid the nickname "Bloody Tuesday." The Japanese lost 18 Zeros and numerous ground installations were destroyed.

American air men, downed at sea, were picked up by LCI-70. LCT-68 was damaged by the Japanese. LCI-70 and PT-167 escorted the LCT back to Treasury Island. A Japanese B5N, flying very low, struck PT-167's radio antenna with a wing. The plane fell into the sea, but dropped a torpedo, undetonated, into the boat's bow. Fortunately, there was no loss of life. LCI-70 then received a series of attacks from Japanese torpedo planes but because of its shallow draft three torpedo passed under its keel.

No LSTs were scheduled to take part in the invasion. A task force of APDs, small craft, and eight destroyers would be used, with LSTs later providing supplies for the invasion forces.

The Admiralty Islands are part of Papua New Guinea. Manus Island is the principle island in the group. The Dutch navigators, William Schouten and Jakob le Marie, were first to discover the islands in 1616. The people they found there were dark skinned with curly, black hair. Australia captured the islands in World War I, but Japan occupied them in 1942.

When the Americans invaded, the Japanese batteries began shelling the beach. In response, American destroyers came within 2000 yards of shore to bomb and silence the Japanese artillery. MacArthur, on the light cruiser *Phoenix*, observed the assault and was satisfied with the results. The 1st Cavalry Division met no opposition. The Japanese commander expected the Americans to come through Seeadler Harbor and had 4,399 troops waiting there. Unpredictably, MacArthur avoided the heavily mined waters of Seeadler. Instead, he landed his troops at Hyane Harbor, located on the east coast of Los Negros.

A Slow Moving Target, The LST of World War II

In Australia LST 153 was taking on cargo slated for delivery to the Admiralty Islands.

Andre was enjoying his first liberty in many weeks. Rich Hienman had been transferred to LST 153 a few days before. Admiral Spruance had returned to Hawaii. The new commander of the *Indianapolis* disapproved of the favored treatment Rich had received, due to his expertise as a gunner, and the commander had no need for Rich's service as a body guard.

The two Phibies had shared a joyous reunion, staggering back to LST 153 late one evening, with their arms around each other. As they entered the crew's quarters a familiar voice rang out, "Hinny, Robber! How ya doing, Phibies?"

Andre caught a glimpse of Bob Olsen's face before he slumped onto the floor. Rich staggered to a vacant bunk, laid back and promptly began snoozing.

Bob crouched down next to Andre. Andre opened his bleary eyes, shook his head slightly, and asked, "Olly, is it really you? How did you get here?"

"Easy, Robber. Let's get some jo. I've got a lot to tell you."

As they sat at the galley table, Bob related the story of his stay in Hawaii and his reunion with Lovette. When Bob told him he was married to Lovette, Andre was visibly pleased, shaking his hand, and congratulating him over and over again.

"Robber, there's something else. I received a letter from Angela." Bob's face was troubled. "Belcher is dead. He was killed at Anzio."

Andre was stunned. A tear slipped from his eye. "Poor Angela. She must be heartbroken. How is she?"

"She's devastated," Bob continued. "The news turned her world upside down. The baby was born prematurely. It's a boy. She named him Daniel."

Andre stood up suddenly. "I need to write to her. I'll take care of her and the baby. I've always loved her. It will work out."

Bob grabbed his arm, pulling him down. "Wait a minute, buddy. Now is not the time. Whatever you feel, keep it to

Joseph Francis Panicello

yourself for awhile. Let her get used to the idea of Danny being gone. Give her some time."

Andre listened quietly, then nodded his head in agreement. "You're right. I'm only thinking of myself. As if I could make her forget Danny."

"Come on Robber," Bob said softly, "let's get some sleep. We're heading out in the morning."

In silence the two men left the galley.

The attacks on Rabaul by the Allies continued into March of 1944, which kept the Japanese under fire. With Rabaul's Japanese airfields, and 98,000 troops isolated, MacAthur's march to the Philippines continued. As Admiral Nimitz put it, "Henceforth, we plan to give the Japs no rest." Even though Rabaul was not invaded, it was still a threat with its airfields and the many troops located there. By constantly pressuring them with bombs they were virtually out of the war.

By March 20, the seizure of the Admiralty Islands was complete. With the fall of the Bismarck Islands on April 3rd, MacArthur decided to bypass the mass of small islands in the area and make a gigantic leap of 500 miles, targeting Hollandia, located on the north coast of New Guinea. Hollandia's capture would make it possible to seize points farther west along New Guinea's coast, to use as a stepping stone to reach the Philippines southern-most island, Mindanao.

New Guinea is a large tropical island, north of Australia. It is the world's second largest island. Only Greenland is larger. Most of the natives are dark skinned with black, wooly hair. The earliest settlers migrated to New Guinea thousands of years ago from Asia and Indonesia.

In 1826, Jorge de Meneses, the Portuguese governor, was the first European to visit New Guinea. The Dutch claimed the western portion of New Guinea in 1828. In 1884, Germany claimed the northeastern part of the island, while Britain claimed the southeastern part. Britain gave their territory to Australia in 1906 and, after W.W.I., Australia was mandated the northeastern

German section of the island. In 1942, Japan seized the northeastern part of New Guinea.

There was a continuous dispute between MacArthur and Nimitz as to where to hit next. The Joint Chiefs solved some of their differences by instructing Admiral Nimitz to lend support of his powerful Pacific Fleet to MacArthur's invasion of Hollandia and Mindanao. In return, MacArthur was to send heavy bombers from Hollandia to soften up the Palaus Islands for Nimitz.

Nimitz met MacArthur in Brisbane. Many of the staff officers expected a major clash between the two. Instead, Nimitz came bearing gifts from Hawaii. He presented rare orchids for MacArthur's wife and Hawaiian play clothes for their six-year-old son Arthur. Compromises were made on both sides and the Hollandia invasion was scheduled for April 22, 1944.

Through radio intercepts and code breaking, the Americans knew that the Japanese General Adachi expected the invasion to take place at Wewak, 200 miles away. To reinforce this belief General MacArthur ordered several false attacks at Wewak, using destroyers to bomb its shores, having reconnaissance planes make simulated fly-bys, and dropping dummy parachutes in the area. An invasion armada of 217 ships was assembled, carrying 50,000 combat troops and 30,000 support personnel overall. This armada represented the largest amphibious operation yet undertaken in the South Pacific.

MacAthur fooled the Japanese again. He first headed the armada northeast away from Hollandia, then, in the middle of the night, had the ships swing southwest, steaming straight for Hollandia. The scheme worked. The invasion was a success, catching the Japanese by surprise. One Japanese officer explained ruefully, "The morning we found out the Allies were coming to Hollandia was the morning the harbor was filled with American transports and battleships."

The initial operation cost 19 American lives versus 525 Japanese dead. The greatest coup of the invasion was the capture of three major airfields, a network of roads, supply dumps, and barracks, all Japanese constructed, which the Allies could immediately put to use.

LST 153, heavily laden with cargo from Australia, made their landing amidst a rain of Japanese fire power from overhead. Rich Hienman was at his best. He shot down four Zeros and one bomber before being grazed by a bullet from another Zero.

Bob Olsen, manning a 40 mm gun in the second turret amidships, saw Rich go down. After downing a Zero, Bob immediately called Andre on the main deck to assist Hinny.

Later, in the sick bay, Andre said, "That was a close one, Hinny. A couple of inches to the right and I might be putting you in a bag. The Japs are getting too close."

Uneasily, Rich answered, "You're right, Robber. The Japs got through and played hell with us. I can't stop them all. There are too many. The other gunners need to bag a few. When we get back to Australia I'm going to give a crash course on shooting accuracy. Thank God Olly's good with the guns. It's the others I'm worried about."

When LST 153 left New Guinea, headed back to Australia, they were short four sailors and one officer. The loss of life at Hollandia totaled 152 Americans and 3,300 Japanese. Six hundred Japanese were captured, while another 500 fled into the jungle towards Sarmi, a Japanese base.

A Slow Moving Target, The LST of World War II

31. Overlord

In January, 1942, the first American ship to arrive in England in World War II was the U.S.S *Albatross*, a fishing schooner converted into a minesweeper. A week later, our first troop convoy came to northern Ireland. England is no bigger than the state of Iowa with a population of 40 million people.

By 1942 the German blitz claimed 44,000 British civilians, another 50,000 were seriously wounded, and 375,000 people were left homeless in London alone. By 1944 it had doubled.

In January, 1944, Johnny cruised to England on board the English luxury liner, *Queen Mary*. But the liner wasn't considered luxurious at this point in time, not with the thousands of servicemen on board, parked anywhere they could find a spot, whether on the main deck or inside the ship where they could find a place to be comfortable and out of the foul, cold, winter weather. Many slept under their canvas pup tents to protect them from the splashing waves and the rain. If a soldier was lucky he was able to find a spot inside the ship, laying on the deck with full pack. When a soldier wanted to go to the head he stepped carefully, over men parked side by side like sardines.

Johnny was lucky. He was assigned, along with eleven naval officers, to share a compartment which normally accommodated only two civilian passengers. The compartment was converted to sleep twelve men, having three separate sets of bunk beds that were stacked four high, right up to the overhead. The major advantage of being in a compartment was that it had its own head and it was warm and dry.

Two days into the trip Johnny fell into conversation with a young Lieutenant. His name was Maurice Pillard, of French extraction. His parents had been born and raised in Toronto, Canada, and moved to Detroit before Maurice was born. He was six feet tall, with straight brown hair, and handled himself gracefully. He had once considered boxing as a profession. When he wore his dress blues he looked very distinguished.

Joseph Francis Panicello

His father had encouraged him in his studies and with the help of a first cousin from Illinois, a member of Congress, he was recommended to Annapolis in 1939. U.S. Representative Jason Pillard, owner of an auto parts firm, had promised Maurice a high position in his firm after the war.

After he had introduced himself, Maurice said teasingly to Johnny, "You must be pretty important, an enlisted man bunking with us officers. What gives?"

Johnny shook his hand and said, "I don't know why, Sir. I'm First Class Motor Mechanic Johnny Maroni. My orders are to teach men to repair Diesel engines in England, especially on amphibious ships. I've been doing just that in New York for the past six months. I understand that a lot of amphibious craft are out of commission, sitting in the English harbors because they don't have enough mechanics or spare parts to repair them. Well, that's my job, to train Englishmen and Americans to become Diesel mechanics and to put those ships back into the fleet."

Lieutenant Pillard was impressed and said, "Well, Maroni, you are right about that subject. I was in Italy six months ago and it was pitiful to witness damaged LSTs, LCIs and small craft that had to be towed away and left stranded or anchored in the bay because they had nobody to repair them and not enough spare parts to fix them. It took months, in one case, to repair an LST that was anchored in the harbor because they had to wait for parts to be delivered from the States. LSDs can support the smaller amphibious boats but not the larger LSTs."

At the end of 1943, the first Landing Ship Dock (LSD) entered the service. Their mission was twofold, to carry small craft to the assault area and to provide a repair station as a floating dry dock. Its dimensions were 457 feet long, 72 feet wide, and 17 feet above the water line. It could carry two LCTs, 36 LCMs, or 41 LVTs, and a landing crew of 263 troops. The crew on board required 254 men. Its top speed was 17 knots.

It cannot beach itself like an LST but it could launch small craft by lowering itself into the water with its ballast. Its main purpose was to provide a repair station or dry dock by allowing

A Slow Moving Target, The LST of World War II

the small craft to drive into its center and then the LSD would raise itself with its ballast and bring the small craft completely out of the water ready for repair.

Johnny agreed with Pillard over his comments on disabled LSTs and replied, "You're right on that score. I was in the Pacific campaign and we had the same problem. It's funny how Admirals will order many ships and boats to support an invasion but they forget that the amphibious ships need plenty of back-up. Parts and a good maintenance crew are essential in keeping these ships afloat. Sometimes it's not the enemy that can knock out a ship but the failure to provide essential spare parts and a maintenance crew. This alone could cripple them before they are even available for combat."

The *Queen Mary* took six days to cross the Atlantic, resorting to a zigzag course to avoid U-Boats. Two destroyers escorted the Queen but they had a hard time keeping up with the liner, able to cruise at 40 knots even under high seas. If a U-Boat was spotted the *Queen Mary* simply out-ran the German submarine. Speed was its greatest defense. The top speed of a U-Boat is only 12 knots. There were over 200 U-Boats prowling the Atlantic, sinking 7.9 million tons of Allied shipping in 1942 alone, a fearful toll.

The *Queen Mary* landed in Plymouth, England, in February, on a cold rainy day. Thousand of troops disembarked that first day. Johnny and Pillard had to wait until the next day to go ashore because of the mass confusion created by all of those soldiers going ashore at the same time, carrying their heavy gear, not knowing which way to go. The next morning, Johnny and Pillard were given permission to disembark.

Johnny shook Maurice's hand and wished him luck.

Maurice grinned, saying, "So long, Maroni. Maybe I'll see you in London."

After Johnny gathered his gear and pushed his way to the street he noticed a cab driver holding a sign with Johnny's name on it. "What goes," Johnny muttered to himself, as he made his way over to the cab.

Joseph Francis Panicello

As he climbed inside he was startled. Maurice, already settled there said, "I guess I just can't get rid of you, Maroni."

In London Maurice was dropped off at a fancy Charing Cross hotel which had been converted to officers quarters.

When Johnny arrived at the enlisted men's quarters he was given his orders by the chief manning the front desk. "In two days you are to report to 1st Division of Repair Facility in London, commanded by Captain Welch. At 0900 hours, tomorrow morning, you will be fitted with chief uniforms. You have been promoted to a temporary rate of Chief Motor Mechanic," the chief conveyed in a monotone voice.

As he notice the stunned look on Johnny's face, the chief chuckled, "It's only for the duration of the war, buddy. You'll probably be busted back when the war's over. Normally it takes ten years of service to make chief. Enjoy it while it lasts."

The following morning Johnny was fitted for blue and white dress uniforms, with two sets of grey and tan khakis.

On his second morning in London he reported to 1st Division of Repair Facilities. He was surprised to find Maurice waiting for him. "You again," Johnny exclaimed. "What are you doing here Sir?"

"You're to report to me," answered Maurice, grinning. "I'll oversee your entire curriculum. I will be attending your classes myself, to learn, in a matter of practical fashion, what I learned at Annapolis about Diesel engines." He paused for a moment looking over Johnny's new dress uniform and said, "By the way, now that you a chief, I don't mind being seen with you. Looks like we're going to be buddies."

"Well, buddy," Johnny answered, with his own wide grin, "Let's get to class. You've got a lot to learn."

In the winter of 1943-1944, the Allies were preparing for an assault on France, code-named Overlord.

The plan was to simultaneously land on two main beaches; at St. Laurent-sur-Mere, on the northern coast of Calvados, and at Varreville, on the east coast of the Peninsula, with two airborne divisions dropping somewhere inland the night before.

A Slow Moving Target, The LST of World War II

The British and Canadians would come in north of Caen at La Havre.

In December of 1943, General Montgomery was given the command to direct the landing force for Overload. Eisenhower would be the supreme commander, with Aircorps Chief Marshal Arthur Tedder as his deputy commander. The operational commanders for Overlord were Montgomery, directing the Army, Chief Mallory, directing the air forces, and Adm. Ramsey the naval forces. Subordinate to Montgomery was Omar Bradley for the army. The naval commander under Adm. Ramsey was Rear Adm. Kirk, assigned to coordinate with General Bradley. They had worked together in the Mediterranean and were glad to renew their association on this endeavor.

The main problem for the naval planners was assembling enough landing craft. It was difficult to nail down the number needed. Experienced planners doubted there could be enough. Admiral King knew he didn't have enough landing craft and ordered a 35% increase in production, but best estimates insisted that this increase wouldn't be sufficient. Because of this shortage a planned simultaneous assault on Southern France had to be delayed. They couldn't spare the LSTs for both offenses. The invasion of Southern France would have to wait.

The second problem was overloading the landing craft. There was a limit to what the ships could carry. For such a huge incursion as Overlord, a vast amount of equipment and troops would be needed, sacrificing safety for necessity. On one LST, for example, planned for the movement of 400 troops, 600 men were packed together on deck and in every available compartment. Fire power was a third issue. Naval support would consist of three American battleships, three heavy cruisers, and thirty-one destroyers.

The airforce concluded that 5,000 Allied aircraft would make German interference insignificant and acceded to Eisenhower's request for air support. The Allies' continuous bombing over the European Continent in the early months of 1944 did much to clear the way for the invasion plan, initially set

Joseph Francis Panicello

for early May. The German Luftwaffe was considered incapable of stopping the Allied aircorps from the invasion.

Tension was high as the Allies waited through the months of May for more favorable weather conditions. The Joint Chiefs of Staff of America had informed Ike, "Land on the coast of France and thereafter destroy the German guard forces." It wasn't that simple.

Approaching D-Day, waiting on the weather were 17 British, 3 Canadian, one Polish, one French and 20 American divisions. Air support consisted of 5,049 fighters, 3,467 heavy bombers, 1,645 torpedo bombers, 698 combat aircraft, 2,316 transport aircraft, and 2,591 gliders.

Readied for the sea were 233 LSTs, 835 LCTs, 6 battleships, 22 cruisers, 93 destroyers, 159 PT boats, 255 mine sweepers and mine layers, and 72 LCIs. Over 6,000 naval vessels were on hand, overall. The Allied main strength, officers and troops, totaled 2,876,500 men.

On June 4, 1944, Group Capt. Stagg of the Royal Air Force predicted there was a fair weather cell northwest of Spain, drifting eastward and expected to be over France by June 6. With this information, Eisenhower made his plan available on June 5, the day before D-day.

The final decision was made by Eisenhower that Overlord would take place on Monday, June 6, 1944. All principals were present at the final meeting, held at St. Paul's School, including King George VI and Churchill.

Churchill said to Eisenhower at the conclusion of the meeting, "General, if by the coming winter you have established yourself with your thirty-six Allied divisions firmly on the Continent and have the Cherbough and Brittany peninsulas in your grasp, I will proclaim this operation to the world as one of the most successful of the war."

Without a doubt, it was the largest military operation ever planned, a concentrated effort of vast proportions. Everyone held their breath and waited.

32. Normandy

In the months following their arrival in England, Johnny and Maurice were very busy. Something was in the works. The brass were encouraging Johnny to push his trainees as fast and as hard as he could.

In their off hours, Johnny and Maurice would sit drinking warm beer in a small pub near the theater district, talking over the latest war news, trying to fit the puzzle together.

"Something major is going to happen, Maroni," Maurice said somberly. "This island is about ready to sink from the weight of material and men. Tension is so thick that you could cut it with a knife."

Johnny looked doubtful. "You think invasion, maybe?" he asked.

Maurice glanced around to see if he'd been overheard. "What else?" he whispered. "Look Johnny, the Russians are pushing in from the east. They've pushed the Germans back to the Polish border. Now that the Allies have taken Cassino in Italy it's only a matter of time before Rome falls to us. That will be it for Italy."

"My brother-in-law died at Anzio," Johnny said quietly. "His name was Danny. My sister, Angela, is in New York. She had a baby son. Danny never even got to see a picture of him. He died before the baby was born."

Maurice looked sympathetic. "Damn, that's tough. Hell, this war has taken a lot of good men. We need to push in from the west, Johnny. Squeeze the Germans from all sides. They can't fight the world."

As the men left the bar and joined the people in the street they walked in silence, each lost in thought.

A female voice called out, "Johnny Maroni, what are you doing here?"

Joseph Francis Panicello

Looking up, Johnny caught sight of a beautiful blond woman, twenty feet away, standing at the edge of the curb. "Dolores! God, look at you," Johnny said, as he rushed up to her.

Maurice held back, watching curiously.

"You look great," he continued. "What are you doing here?"

"I'm starring in a play, in a little theater not far from here. I've been in England about a month. What about you? Are you an officer now?" she asked, noticing the change of uniform.

"I'm a Chief Mechanic," he replied. "Temporarily, anyway. You must be doing well, Dolores, starring in a play and all."

"My agent thinks I will make it really big in Hollywood. The parts are getting bigger and better all the time. I've changed my name to Dolores Harman. I'm already making $1,000 a week, under contract, and it runs another five years. Money's not everything, though," she added flirtatiously.

She paused, watching Johnny's reaction to her last remark. Johnny felt as attracted to her as he used to but something had changed. He wasn't sure weather it was her or himself but something wasn't quite right.

"I'd love to get together with you, Johnny. I've missed you. Nothing's changed. It will be like old times," she finished, giving him an inviting smile.

Suddenly, Johnny realized what had changed. Everyone he knew, really knew, had changed since the war. Danny was gone, Angela mourning him, with a baby who would never know his father. The other Phibies out in the Pacific, seeing battle. Johnny thought of Megan, sticking by her man with love and commitment, while many other women were betraying that commitment. Men too. Johnny thought of Rich and Mildred. With a flash of insight, a new maturity, he realized that the war had not affected Dolores at all. She stood before him, a beautiful, shining image. She had changed. She wasn't Dolores Hienman from a ranch in Texas. She was Dolores Harman, from Hollywood.

"I don't know if that's possible, Dolores. I'm kept busy and I don't even know when new orders will come through," Johnny said quietly, but firmly. "Take care of yourself. Please say hello to Rich when you write."

He leaned over and kissed her quickly on the cheek, turned and rejoined Maurice who was out of hearing distance. As they moved down the street, he turned his head slightly to see her gazing after them, a look of bewilderment on her face.

With a small sigh of relief, he smiled and said to Maurice, "That was Dolores Harman, the movie star."

Maurice whistled out loud. "Don't I know it! Where'd you meet her?"

"Oh, her brother is a good friend of mine. One of the five Phibies," Johnny said carelessly.

"What did she want?" asked Maurice.

"She wanted to go out with me, but I refused," answered Johnny, "It's better that way."

"Now Admiral, will you kindly tell me where the invasion should take place?" Johnny said, forcing a grin, trying to change the subject. Breaking with Dolores hurt him, but he knew it had to be done. It wouldn't work between them.

The following morning, the first of June, Johnny and Maurice were called to Captain Welch's office.

"Men," began the captain, "I'm reassigning you to the LST 182, which is now harbored at Dover. When you join the ship it will proceed to Slapton Sands near Plymouth, to pick up a commanding general of ground forces here in England. Lieutenant Pillard will be officer in charge of the engine rooms. Chief Maroni, you will be his second in command. The ship will be crossing the English channel, therefore we require experienced engine men to safeguard the voyage from any mechanical difficulties."

The captain paused, then more casually, continued, "Men, I can't explain more fully, except to say these orders are directed from the highest command. It's an important assignment. I know you'll do your best. Dismissed!"

Joseph Francis Panicello

As Maurice and Johnny left the captain's Quonset hut, Maurice was excited. "This is it, Maroni! I knew something was up."

Sure seems that way," replied Johnny grimly. "We better hope for the best engine gang we've ever seen. We haven't got much time to pack our gear and get the hell out of here. We'll leave first thing in the morning."

"Hey!" protested Maurice., "who's the Lieutenant and who's the Chief here?"

"Who cares," laughed Johnny. "Let's get going."

When Johnny and Maurice arrived at Slapton Sands an unfortunate incident was related to them, which reminded them of the dangerous undertaking they were about to become involved in.

Weeks before D-Day, eight other LSTs were to meet at Slapton Sands on April, 18, to join the ever increasing fleet of LSTs. They were newcomers to the theater and had never worked together as a Flotilla. Unfortunately, the British left only one corvette to protect the flock of LSTs and, unknown to them, German E-Boats were lurking out in the channel. One slipped through the single convoy protection at night and LST 507 was torpedoed at 0200 hours. In the confusion, two more LSTs were torpedoed, causing the death of 700 amphibious sailors and officers. The *Slow Moving Target* was obviously no match for German submarines.

Arriving at Plymouth, LST 182 prepared for the assault on France. Johnny began inspecting both the main and auxiliary engines. He first proceeded to fire up both main engines and let them run for an hour or so while monitoring the different meters, especially the temperature gauges. He then varied the RPM of each engine quickly, from slow to fast, to see how fast the engines responded with no load. The governors were working perfectly. He then went through the log and saw that it had been awhile since the engine oil had been changed.

He ordered a fireman, "I want you and the other fireman to change the oil immediately in both of these engines!"

A Slow Moving Target, The LST of World War II

The fireman looked somewhat bewildered and replied, "Gee, Chief. I never changed oil before. I don't know how."

Johnny called a meeting with the engine crew and began explaining to the six firemen on board and to three Third Class Petty Officers the procedure of changing oil in the main engines. None of them had ever changed oil on an LST with GMC engines before.

He started with, "I want three of you firemen to assist me in this demonstration. There is an output valve under the crate here, right below and near the engine which is marked 'Oil Output.' You should open this valve fully as I'm doing. Now one of you firemen go over to the Sump Pump and open the valve that is marked 'Input.' I will now remove one of the crank case covers on the side of this engine and each of you should notice that the oil level in the crank case is marked 'Full.'

"I will now power up the Sump Pump with this switch. Notice that the oil is being sucked out from the engine crankcase and into the Sump Pump reservoir. Observe how the crankcase oil level is going down, slow but sure. When the crankcase is empty, which it is now, I will turn off the Sump Pump power. Now you men can close off those two valves we opened.

"The next step is to pump clean oil back into the crankcase. This is done by opening the valve marked 'Oil Input' in the engine bilge as I am doing. Now one of you men open the 'Output" valve on the clean oil storage tank. By turning the main transfer pump on, as I'm doing, the clean oil will be transferred into the crank case until the 'Full' level is reached again. Okay sailor, stop the pump when you can see they are full. Now you other men close off the valves.

"There is one more step involved here, and that is to transfer the old oil from the Sump Pump to the exhaust storage tank so that the Sump Pump can be used again to remove the oil from the second engine. This is done simply by opening the Sump Pump 'Output' valve and opening up the exhaust storage tank 'Input' valve. By powering up the sump pump again it will transfer the old oil into this tank which will be ready for disposal

Joseph Francis Panicello

when we are out to sea. Two of you Motor Mechanics go ahead and do what I have just explained."

One Third Class Motor Mechanics asked, "Why don't we use the main pump to do all of the transferring of oil instead of the sump pump?"

"The reason we use the sump pump instead of the main pump to transfer old oil is to keep the input lines to the engine clean. We don't want dirty oil going back into the engine."

After they completed the exchange Johnny continued, "When the Sump Pump is empty shut the main pump down and close off all of the valves again. This same procedure is to be used all over again with the second engine. The whole procedure on both engines should take no longer than two hours."

While the crew continued the procedure of changing oil Johnny explained a few other tips for troubleshooting the GMC Diesel engine.

"This engine," he explained, "is not the same as your conventional V-8 auto engine, where one head is used to cover four cylinders on each side of the V-8 block. On the GMC Diesel V8 engine each cylinder has its own individual head, bolted down to the main block with four large bolts. Each cylinder has a liner or sleeve that the pistons travel up and down in and is cooled by running fresh water through its jacket.

"Sometimes these liners crack and the water seeps into the crankcase. The question that is usually asked of me is, 'How does one know when a liner is cracked and has to be replaced?'

"Generally, what happens is, the engine fresh water temperature begins to increase dramatically because there is water in the oil which has seeped through the cracks in the liner. Also, the engine may sound like it's missing and not running on all cylinders.

"If this problem is detected while the ship is under way, the captain must be informed immediately that one engine may have to be shut down for repairs or it will overheat and eventually burn out.

"Before you stop the engine, however, a compression test should be performed at the port on each of the eight cylinders. If one cylinder shows a very low compression the chances are its cylinder liner is cracked. The engine then should be shut down, even though the ship is under way. The ship can still run with one engine, but it will only be able to travel at half speed or lower.

"To remove the head one must first remove the four large bolts from each corner of the head. These bolts require large sockets and it may take two sailors, using a four foot long 2-inch pipe to extend the wrench, to provide the necessary torque to crack the bolts loose. One must be careful not to break a bolt shaft, though this sometimes happens."

"What do we do if we break a bolt, Chief?" a Motor Mechanic asked.

Johnny answered, "If that happens you now have a major problem. First pull the head off anyway. Now with the broken bolt exposed, it can be removed by drilling a one inch hole into the center of the broken bolt, then using a large easy-out tool to remove it. If that doesn't work you'll have to drill a larger hole entirely through the bolt and use a hack saw or a power saber saw to cut through one side of the bolt. Then chisel the bolt out. If it still doesn't come loose you may have to hack saw the other side of the bolt as well.

"Under normal circumstances, after the bolts have been removed, attach a chain driven pulley to the overhead and the other end to a cylinder head using an eye bolt that is installed at the top of the head. Raise the head off of the block slowly. Remember these aluminum heads are awkward to handle because they are about a two feet square at the bottom and one foot high. They weigh over fifty pounds, so it will take two men to guide it up and out.

"The liner can be removed by attaching screws and a plate over the top of the liner and again using the chain pulley, lifting it out of its cylinder. It should come out fairly easily.

Joseph Francis Panicello

"These V8 Diesel engines were originally manufactured by the Grey Marine Company who were later bought out by General Motors Corporation. Fortunately, the initials 'GMC' didn't have to change.

"When the temperature of the fresh water is rising, it may not be due to a liner being cracked. A liner doesn't usually crack until the engine temperature is extremely high, which could be caused by some other problem.

"When the temperature is rising see if the salt water pump is air bound or disabled. In your average automobile engine at home, the fresh water coolant is cooled by a fan passing air through a radiator and, of course, with the movement of the auto. But on this ship the engine's fresh water is cooled with sea water, using a heat exchange tank. If the sea water becomes air-bound as a result of the ship rolling and raising her input port above the sea water line, it will suck in air and the sea pump could become air-bound which will cause the fresh water temperature to rise. Usually, this will clear by itself but sometimes it doesn't, and then it becomes necessary to manually bleed the air out of the salt water pump by opening this petcock above the pump until the air is removed and only water comes out."

Johnny continued with his lecture until the oil was replaced in both engines. Johnny was now satisfied that the two main engines were ready to make that important excursion across the English Channel and be part of the invasion. He reported to Maurice that the engines were ready for the trip, and, in turn, Maurice reported it to the Captain.

At the hour of 2200, several jeeps pulled up to the pier alongside of the ship. Johnny was on deck and got only a glimpse of the General as he was coming up the gangway. His view was obscured by an entourage of officers surrounding the general in the dark. When the general was at the bridge, he gave the orders to the captain to prepare to get under way and adding, "This is it, Skipper."

Normandy was the goal of Overlord. It's ironic that William the Conqueror, the Viking from Normandy, invaded England in 1066 and became its king. Now the situation was reversed. William the Conqueror was just two generations removed from his ancestors in Norway, whose grandparents came to the northern European shores in the ninth century, sailing with their dragon long boats up the Loire and Seine Rivers, then conquering and looting the lands in Northern France.

It was around the year 880 when Ralph (Rollo), the son of the King of Norway, was banished from the kingdom for defying a royal ban, and sailed to what is now Normandy with many other Scandinavian outlaws. Ralph, now in charge of thousands of fierce criminals, plundered the towns in France for the next thirty years. In 911, King Charles of France conceded lands to Ralph to stop the pillaging, awarding him the title of Count.

Later, many thousands of Norwegians, both male and female, migrated from Norway to Normandy to gain their fortunes in this new land of riches, but after it became overcrowded the Vikings moved on and began pillaging Spain and Italy. These fierce warriors were merciless in their conquests as they confiscated enormous amounts of wealth, and slaves were brought back to different ports and sold. Some of the slave girls were kept by the Vikings for their own enjoyment.

The son of one of these great warriors, Roger II, became the first King of Southern Italy and Sicily in 1154. His father, Roger I, fought with William the Conqueror over lands in France, but instead of going to England against the British, he and thousands of Norsemen, went south for booty and fought against the Saracens, Byzantine Greeks, and German Lombards to free Southern Italy and Sicily in 1072. Roger I, became the first count of Sicily.

In England, Eisenhower stared out of his office window and all he could see was rain, rain and more rain. At 2145 hours on June 4, 1944, he said to his subordinates, "I am quite positive that the order must be given."

Joseph Francis Panicello

With that statement, Admiral Ramsay left the room to set the ships in motion. The slow landing craft of LSTs and LCIs were the first to leave which included Johnny's ship, LST 182. They were followed later by faster fire-support ships. At 0400 hours of the next morning, Eisenhower made the final decision and said, "O.K., let's go."

The Germans were sure that no invasion was imminent because a German naval weatherman said the conditions in the channel made it impossible to cross. As a result of that report, General Rommel left his headquarters on June 5, to go home to Germany for his wife's birthday. Other generals also left their divisions to practice war games, preparing for an inevitable invasion. While this was going on, Allied paratroopers had already begun dropping beyond the invasion zone.

Rommel always felt that Normandy would be the target, but Hitler disagreed and the bulk of German strength, the Fifteen Army, remained at the Pas-de-Calais area. From Pas-de-Calas to the English coast was a distance of only 22 miles. Instead, the invasion targeted a sixty mile wide area of the continental peninsula, on the Normandy coast.

At the same time, a phantom army was created in Scotland, and a second, under the command of Gen. George C. Patton, in Kent, southwest of London. This second phantom army convinced Field Marshall Gen. von Rundstedt, the overall German commander in the West, that the attack was coming in his direction of Pas-de-Calais because, he assumed, only a great fighting general such as Patton would lead the invasion. A German commander who respected Patton once said, "Patton would even make a good German General." That was indeed a compliment.

Over 200 mine sweepers led the way, laying buoys and providing a path for the assaulting ships by marking the lanes. These were followed by transports and landing craft. The transports had to lay back about eleven miles from shore in case of a retaliation from shore artilleries. This meant that the troops

A Slow Moving Target, The LST of World War II

had to make that long eleven mile journey to shore in small craft, a rough ride for the infantry.

When the lanes were cleared by the mine sweepers, firepower ships passed through the lanes to bombard the shores. The Air Force bombers were supposed to deliver bombs from the first minute but because of the weather they delayed their flight. When air cover began, Allied planes commanded the skies. The ships began their bombardment at 0536 hours.

The German counterattack was so heavy the troops had to seek shelter any way they could. The few early tanks that reached the beach were quickly put out of commission by antitank guns. LCTs were used to drive onto the beach, each carrying three tanks that eventually made it to shore.

LST 543 was outfitted in Evansville, Indiana. It sailed down the Ohio and Mississippi rivers to Louisiana and was commissioned on March 6, 1944. It then sailed to Europe and participated in the invasion of Normandy at Gold beach. It subsequently made 25 trips between England and France. After V-E Day it sailed to the Pacific and was involved in the invasion of Okinawa. When the Japanese war ended LST 543 carried Korean and Chinese civilians from Japan back to their home countries. It was awarded 2 battle stars for World War II invasions.

The men participating in an invasion on an LST, waiting below decks, were in a very lonely place. One sits and sweats and doesn't say anything, because there is nothing to say. He looks around wondering who will be dead after the invasion and an awful thought comes to him when he realizes it could be himself.

Clarence A. Johns wrote about his experience on another LST that participated in the invasion. "We crossed the English Channel to land at Omaha Beach. The ship in front of us sank. There were no survivors. As we approached the shore, a tank on our left rolled over into deep water. It was bedlam with the noise of the battle, with the wounded and dying soldiers screaming for medics, and the dead lying like scattered sticks of wood. We

Joseph Francis Panicello

rode a jeep into cold water as officers screamed their orders, 'Keep moving!' I remember going up that hill and never looking back. It was a terrible, frightening experience and our first taste of combat."

On Omaha beach, everything was in confusion. Units were mixed up. Boats were burning, and vehicles had nowhere to go. Many boats hit mines on their way in and, if they got ashore, their supplies were wet and disorderly. Only six out of sixteen tankdozers reached the beach. The beach resembled a junkyard. It got so bad that the beach-commander radioed the ships to stop sending in any more vehicles.

Destroyers played an important role, coming dangerously close to shore and directing a heavy fire at the enemy. There was a price to pay for coming too close, though, as four destroyers were demolished from undetected mines. One of the biggest responsibilities for many landing craft, and not anticipated, was pulling survivors out of the sea after they had discharged their own loads on land.

A whole company of floating tanks sank like rocks, along with their crews. Gen. Omar Bradley considered an evacuation.

It was chaos and Col. George Taylor yelled to his men on the beach, "Two kinds of people are staying on the beach, the dead and those who are going to die. Let's get the hell out of here!"

Also on the beach, Col. Charles Canham yelled out to his men, "They're murdering us here. Let's move inland and get murdered there."

Years later, Marion R. Adams recalled how LST 491, on around June 9, 1944, returned to Portland, England with many casualties from the Normandy beach, including wounded German prisoners and men from a DD that struck a mine and sank. "On June 11, 1944 we returned to the Normandy beach and the Germans staged a major air raid but they missed us. We were stuck on the beach, literally, because the low tide was 18 feet below the high tide. When the tide came up again we left for England with 19 German prisoners and 60 U.S. Army casualties.

A Slow Moving Target, The LST of World War II

"On June 16, LST 491 went past the Straits of Dover. This was the first night the Germans used their secret weapon, the V-1 Buzz Bomb. The V-1 left a trail of light from the exhaust and when they ran out of fuel they crashed on London and exploded."

On the morning of June 6, LST 182 approached the shore at Omaha Beach. The General on board insisted that they not delay his going ashore any longer. "My men need me," he told the captain, who was reluctant to obey because the mine fields were not completely cleared out. However, he complied with the General's wishes.

As they approached the shore the captain gave the orders to drop the rear anchor as usual and to open the bow doors. As they partially lowered the bow ramp they hit a mine. There was an enormous explosion, opening a gaping hole on the port side, down by the main engine room. Johnny was at his post in the engine room at the time, near the throttles, which was amidships. He was thrown down from the explosion, and, as he raised himself, he witnessed a fireman being washed under by the onrushing sea water.

There was nothing he could do but save himself. He scuttled up the ladder on the starboard side as fast as he could. He had practiced this escape route many times. The practice proved to be worthwhile. While he was at the top of the ladder, the ship received another sudden jolt from a second explosion. His left arm got twisted and caught in the rungs and almost threw him off the ladder and into the water below. He heard a crack in his left arm and assumed it was broken. He managed to climb up the rest of the ladder, one-handed. As he reached the passage way he joined sailors and soldiers running pell-mell, trying to escape the inevitable.

Johnny saw a sailor laying on the deck in the passageway who was unconscious. He'd been knocked down by the panicking sailors, trampling over him in their flight to abandon the ship. After they passed, Johnny grabbed the sailor with his good arm and helped him through a hatch and out onto the main deck. He knew the ship would sink because the inrushing sea water would eventually cause the main engines to explode. When he reached the railing on the main deck he tossed the sailor overboard, immediately following, broken arm dangling.

In the water he could hear the ship's loud speakers blaring away, over and over again, "Abandon ship, abandon ship." He tried wading as far away from the ship as possible, his life jacket keeping him afloat. He saw many sailors jumping into the water. In the chaos he watched the captain and the general abandon the ship. He guessed there were probably another one hundred soldiers and sailors still on board. As the ship slowly slid down into its aquatic tomb, stern first, he felt his own tears mingle with the salt spray of the sea.

The sea water was very cold and it was hard for Johnny to maneuver with one arm. He was becoming exhausted and floated in the water for over an hour. He tried dismally to yell for help, but he was too weak to be heard.

The life jacket, according to the navy, was only functional for a few hours. He was sure his life was over. Suddenly, the sailor he had rescued earlier recognized him and swam over to him. "Hold on Chief. Don't give up," he said, and began yelling for help. It was pitch black. Fortunately, men on a small craft heard the sailor's outcry and came close.

They yelled back, "We got you, sailors. Don't panic." The craft had emptied its cargo on the beach and was headed back to its mother transport, which was eleven miles away. Johnny and the sailor, Leroy Jones, were saved.

Leroy Jones was a black Stewards Mate Third Class. Before the explosion, Jones was carrying two trays of food to the Chief's quarters when the first blast occurred. It knocked him down, food flying in all directions. As he tried to get up, several sailors and soldiers, whose bunks were located on the starboard side of the ship, came poring through the passageway and, in their panic, knocked him down again. He hit his head on the deck, losing consciousness.

The main lights went out but the emergency battery lights came on. When Johnny saw his body lying helplessly on the deck he proceeded to help him up and out through the hatch. Jones woke momentarily, long enough to catch a glimpse of his savior, before he was thrown into the water.

The next day many LSTs made shore at Omaha beach with supplies, tank, artillery, and trucks. The Germans were still shelling them and a few craft were hit and disabled. The LSTs had to come ashore at high tides to allow their cargo of vehicles to drive directly onto the beach. The only problem that now existed was that the LSTs, including LST 533, could not leave the shore until the next high tide making them vulnerable to German artillery. It was a "turkey shoot" for the Germans.

The British Broadcasting Company (BBC) announced the invasion of Normandy to the world on the afternoon of June 6. Just in case, Eisenhower had two announcements prepared. One, that it was a success, and the other in case the invasion failed. Fortunately, he only had to announce the first.

Thousands of casualties were evacuated from the front lines and brought to hospital transports. Ninety-five LSTs carried the wounded to England. LST 288, a medical ship, as it was heading for England, passed the British LCI-525. Her deck was overcrowded with casualties, many in serious condition. The LCI came dangerously close, in the choppy waters, in order to transfer many of the wounded to LST 288. In the opinion of the doctors on board LST 288, the majority of the 22 men that were brought on board may not have survived if the transfer had not been made in time for the wounded to receive blood plasma.

Immediate attention with blood plasma was necessary to save the wounded from dying. This was a major weakness during the many assaults made by the Allies. The preparation for the attack was always the main consideration for the Admirals and Generals. Saving lives was secondary or wasn't considered at all in their planning.

The amphibious operation Overlord provided the element of surprise and, though the enemy outnumbered the Allies on shore,

Joseph Francis Panicello

it was an advantage to the Allies for amphibious forces to strike anywhere, surprising the enemy.

In a documentary on the History Channel entitled "Onto Rugged Shores: Voyage of LST 534," the veteran newsman Howard K. Smith recalled his experience in Germany in 1940, as Hitler was contemplating an invasion of England. He said, "I watched the Germans moving every kind of boat, including coal barges, to ferry their mighty army to Britain. In sea trials those boats all sank or broke up under heavy loads, in turbulent waters. Hitler had to give up the English invasion because the idea of a true landing craft had yet to be perfected." If Hitler had had a fleet of LSTs and other Amphibious craft he would have invaded England in 1940.

LST 534 saw action in Normandy and Okinawa.

On D-Day Adolf Hitler slept through the early hours of the invasion, not believing it would take place. He joked with his generals, lunched with the new Hungarian prime minister and ordered Gen. von Rundstedt to stay where he was. Hitler was still sure the major invasion would be at Pas-de-Calus.

At the end of the first day, "the longest day," the Allies had 55,000 troops dug in on the beaches along with thousands of vehicles and tons of material. The fighting in Normandy wiped out 40 German divisions, killing or wounding 240,000 men, while the Allies lost 36,976 dead. By June 10, Omaha and Utah beaches were under control, and Cherbough fell to the U.S. forces on June 27, although the Germans had blocked its harbor so skillfully it was not usable until August. By July, the Allies had landed one million men and a half-million tons of supplies on the Normandy shore. Overlord was a huge success.

33. Mariana Islands

During 1944, Japan was under blockade by sea and bombardment by air. American sea power had grown tremendously. New ships ready for battle included 8 battleships, 92 carriers, and 513 destroyers. Submarines, laying mines and using torpedoes, made fantastic inroads on Japanese shipping. In 1944, 492 Japanese ships were lost to the American Navy. The Japanese economy was coming apart, suffering inadequate food supplies and a critical gasoline shortage.

In the initial stages of the war, when America was on the defense in the Pacific, she was, conversely, gaining control of the air. This allowed the air cover necessary to support and sustain marine and army forces moving forward from one group of islands to the next.

It was March 12, 1944, when Admiral King decided that the next assault would be the Mariana Islands which were 3,500 miles from Pearl Harbor but closer to Tokyo by 1,400 miles, well within the range of the new B-29 bombers. King received support from "Hap" Arnold, who was ready to use his squadron of B-29s against the Japanese homeland. MacArthur and Nimitz were not convinced that the Marianas should be the next step. King then had to use his authority, ordering Nimitz to proceed with the attack by June 15, 1944.

The Mariana Islands were discovered by Ferdinand Magellan in 1521. Spain ceded Guam to the United States by the Treaty of Paris at the end of the Spanish-American War in 1898.

Guam is the largest island in the Mariana Islands and is located on the southern tip of the Marianas. It is volcanic in origin and rises steeply from the ocean floor, located just a short distance from the deepest ocean depth in the Pacific. Coral reefs fringe much of the coast. Its highest peak is Mt. Lamlam which rises 1,334 feet. Its average rainfall is 80 to 100 inches, occurring mainly in May and June. It is 30 miles long and 10 miles wide.

Joseph Francis Panicello

To capture Guam the Japanese bombed and invaded the island, using their airforce from Saipan, four heavy cruisers, four destroyers, and eight transports carrying 5,000 men. There were only 350 American marines to defend the island of Guam. Their heaviest gun was a machine gun. Japan took over the island on December 10, 1941.

The operation to invade the Marianas was called Forager. The assault would begin first with the island of Saipan on June 15, followed by Guam on the 18th and lastly Tinian, on July 15. Admiral Spruance would be fleet commander, Kelly Turner would direct the Amphibious forces, while Holland Smith would have overall command of the landing forces.

The difference in composition of these islands compared to others they had assaulted was that these were not flat atolls but hilly, and up to 300 miles long. Also, the Japanese garrisons were much stronger on the three Mariana Islands. The amphibious force assigned to this assault would be the largest yet required in the Pacific.

Turner immersed himself in the myriad details of the invasion, drinking heavily, pushing himself to the point of exhaustion. The Saipan assault would require 85,000 marines, 42,000 soldiers, and another force of 38,000 troops, just for the amphibious operation. There were 535 ships involved, compared to the 71 used on Guadalcanal. Many LSTs would be used. The small craft required were on the order of 1,000 LVTs and 21 chartered merchant ships, which had to be enlisted for this operation. The amount of ammunition alone was unimaginable. Food and other supplies were even more inconceivable. Tanks, DUKWS, and LVTs were all preloaded, to reduce the amount of ammunition to be handled on shore, which would be supplemented later by small craft.

A new practice was attempted, which involved loading LVTs from the open sea onto LSTs. The idea was that an LVT would approach the LST's bow and run up the ramp with its tractor wheels. One problem was that the LSTs would rise from the swells and cause the LVTs to have to go up the ramp on a

A Slow Moving Target, The LST of World War II

steep incline. Rope lines had to be used on the oncoming LVTs to steady the approach. Eventually, the LVTs were brought on board. The LSTs then headed for shore where the LVTs were able to disembark right on the beach.

Because there were so many troops involved, LSTs had to double up as troop carriers. The additional load for each LST was 300 more troops. Many had to sleep under the LCTs that were stowed on the main deck. Turner's ships would be carrying 320,000 tons of supplies to the Marianas.

The plan was to have twenty-five LCIs lead the assault to the beach on the first wave, followed by 100 LVTs carrying troops in tractors and tanks. To protect the main troops each assault battalion had a destroyer to provide fire support and twenty-six aircraft carriers provided air coverage that began bombing the beaches.

The first casualties of the Forager invasion involved a group of LSTs in Hawaii that were scheduled to be part of the assault. From the L.S.T. Scuttlebutt, Douglous F. LeVere, who was aboard LST 274, near the tragedy, said, "Six LSTs, each loaded with gasoline drums and ammunition, were tied together, in tares, at West Lock, Pearl Harbor on May 21, 1944. LST 353 was being loaded with mortars.

"Suddenly there was an explosion from LST 353. It was followed by an enormous blast coming from its remaining ammunition that sent flames and fragments over eight LSTs in tare 8 as well as other ships moored there. There was mass confusion among the sailors who fled from the scene in panic. Admiral Turner, who was in Hawaii at the time, boarded a fireboat tug and took part in the fire-fighting effort."

Six LSTs were lost, 163 men were killed and another 396 were injured. The LSTs that were either totally lost or required major repair were LST 353 with LCT 963 on board, LST 179, LST 43, LST 39, LST 480, and LST 69 which had LCT 961 on board.

None of the men had ever experienced any combat. The cause of this accident was never resolved. In 1946, the Secretary of the Navy awarded LST 353 the Navy Unit Commendation for its service in the LST Flotilla Five campaign during the Solomon Islands invasion. It also was awarded 3 battle stars.

On May 29, 1944, aerial photos showed that there were 187 guns positioned on Saipan with 32,000 Japanese troops on the island. The Japanese had a plan called A-Go. In their plan, Japanese aircraft from the Marianas would attack the American fleet, reducing its number. Their carrier aircraft would finish the job, which would leave the amphibious forces helpless. With the American fleet destroyed the American troops that had already landed would be annihilated. The Japanese over estimated the power of their plans. The approaching Japanese navy fleet would be no match for the Americans.

On June 15, 1944, LSTs began unloading LVTs by the dozens into the water off Saipan. As the first 96 LVTs headed for the beach LVI(R)s began saturating the shore with 45-inch rockets and 40-mm fire. When the LVTs were within 1,000 yards of the beach Japanese artillery and mortars were filling the air.

The LVTs were to proceed toward land, providing depth for the beachhead. It wasn't easy. Enemy fire knocked out dozens of LVTs, causing heavy casualties. The American forces had not envisioned such a massive artillery defense by the Japanese. It was chaos. Tanks tried to reach the beach but drowned out trying to cross the reefs. Spruance's carriers fought to protect the amphibious forces, rather than move out and meet the approaching Japanese fleet head-on.

An LCI that was lashed down on an LST's main deck broke loose, crashing overboard. Nineteen marines on board drowned.

Evacuating casualties was a nightmare. The numbers were much larger than anticipated. Two LSTs, including LST 153, stood off the beaches and served as clearing stations for the wounded while a third stood by in reserve. After taking on board at least 100 casualties on each LST, they moved them out to a transport ship for further treatment. Getting the injured to the transports required considerable effort and many casualties had to endure being transferred from a LVT to a LCV, spending hours lying on the small landing craft deck before they could receive medical attention.

Andre had left Australia for the Marianas with three new recruit corpsmen on board LST 153. He attempted to prepare them for the realities of an actual invasion. After the initial assault the casualties lay on the beach waiting for help. A few corpsmen and army medics attended the wounded, limited in capability because of the sheer number of wounded and the fact that the only medical supplies available were carried in packs on their backs.

After LST 153 hit the beach, tanks and artillery moved down the lowered ramp, followed by the troops. Andre rushed his corpsmen after them, shouting instructions as they ran. With blood plasma, tourniquets and morphine, the most essential supplies, they hurried from man to man, intent on saving as many as they possibly could, yet knowing they faced an insurmountable task.

On board LST 153 Rich Heinman and Bob Olsen were having a field day shooting down Jap planes. American sailors later dubbed it the "Marianas Turkey Shoot." Rich shot down 19 zeros and four bombers. Bob got five zeros, but received a wound in his left arm, though he did not give up his gun.

Holland Smith said, "Turner's men unloaded an average of 4,683 tons of supplies daily from June 15, until July 20, 1944. The most important consideration of the attack was the cannon gunfire support from the naval ships. The downing of enemy aircraft was a sight to behold."

A Japanese prisoner stated that the naval gunfire was the greatest single factor in the American success. Without the fleet guns he said, "We could have licked the Americans."

With the cargo unloaded, LST 153 moved back out to sea. Andre and his corpsmen worked around the clock. They received a new batch of wounded from a LVT as fast as they transferred a batch to a hospital transport waiting out in the bay.

Joseph Francis Panicello

The wound Bob received was more serious than he had realized. He begged Andre to do something for him but Andre became adamant. "Olly, you need to get to a hospital where they can give you proper attention. You don't want to lose your arm. I'm not equipped to deal with your injury. Look around!" Andre said. "There are more wounded on board than my men and I can deal with now."

Bob boarded the hospital transport reluctantly, while Rich and Andre watched.

"Hey, Olly," Rich called out, "say hello to Mrs. Olsen for us!"

At that remark, Bob grinned. "You bet I will," he yelled back. "Take care of yourselves, Phibies."

The Americans completed the invasion of Saipan in July 9, 1944. The loss of American life was 3,000 men, with 11,000 wounded. It was estimated that 27,000 enemy soldiers were killed, with thousands more entombed in caves.

As LST 153 was leaving Saipan a horde of Japanese fighters came swooping down like a swarm of bees. Hienman immediately went to work at his gun, downing five of them. One Zero had his machine gun blazing away at Hienman. He was hit in the side and in both legs. His striker got on the intercom, asking for help. Fortunately, Andre showed up in time to stop the bleeding and provide him with an IV containing blood plasma. "Hinny. You're going home," Andre said quietly.

Rich's eyes widened in surprise.

Andre looked at his buddy with sad eyes and said, "Sorry, Hinny. You're going home. You're in pretty bad shape and most of the cases like yours always go back to the States." Andre didn't want to tell him how serious his wounds really were. Rich was shipped out immediately.

The invasion of Guam was initiated July 21, 1944, with 20,000 3rd Division marines and the army 77th division. After 20 days of fierce fighting Guam fell. On August 10, American forces pronounced Guam secure. The Japanese lost 17,000 men,

A Slow Moving Target, The LST of World War II

with about 500 surrendering to American forces. The United States listed 1,214 dead and 6,000 wounded.

Tinian was a small island, 38 square miles in size, shaped like Manhattan, with steep cliffs surrounding it, a disadvantage to amphibious forces. It was nicknamed "The Rock" by American troops.

It was estimated that 10,000 Japanese troops occupied Tinian. The two major beaches were heavily mined and guarded. Two smaller beaches, the larger only 150 yards wide, were chosen for the assault by the Americans.

On July 24, arriving from Saipan in LSTs and smaller craft, the Americans took the Japanese totally by surprise. The two small beaches were lightly defended by the Japanese. American forces, by the end of the day, had progressed two miles inland and had managed to land most of their tanks, an extra battalion, and had four howitzer batteries in place.

Tinian was declared secure by the American forces one week later, on August 1, 1944. The invasion was a success. Japanese dead numbered 6,000. American suffered 300 dead, with 1,500 casualties.

The battles for control of the Marianas was some of the bloodiest fighting seen in the Pacific so far. Many military men saw it as a prelude of what was ahead. Plans for the invasion of the Philippines, then Japan itself, not only had to include a count of ships, planes, ammunition and other supplies that would be necessary for success. The number of troops, and probable losses of those troops, would also be estimated and those losses would be prohibitive, fighting against an enemy that preferred death to surrender.

Joseph Francis Panicello

34. London

Through the summer months of 1944 Allied forces fought bitterly to capture France. They fought mortars, machine guns and rifle men, advancing slowly but relentlessly. Cherbough was captured by American infantry on June 27, but the major breakthrough occurred July 25 when the First Army, led by General Omar Bradly, broke through the German defense lines. Patton's Third Army slipped through the gap, capturing Auranches on July 31. Four days later American tanks blocked the Brittany Peninsula.

On August 15, the invasion of the Mediterranean coast had begun, gaining new ports, and insuring new Allied supply lines while the American 8th Army, starting from Italy, invaded southern France in operation Anvil.

In the L.S.T. Scuttlebutt newspaper, Marion R. Adams writes, "On August 12, 1944, Secretary of the Navy, James Forrestal, came aboard the LST 491. He was accompanied by Admiral Hewitt for consultation with Commander Blair, who was in charge of the 36 LST convoy."

Adams continues, "Before he left, the Secretary chatted with the troops that would be making the assault on Southern France. Not famous at that time was the most decorated soldier of World War II, Audie Murphy, who was in the 36th Division.

"On August 15, 1944, we arrived at a Southern France beach and lowered LCVPs. After we were beached German bombers began bombing the LSTs. LST 282 was struck just forward of the conning tower by a bomb that was controlled by a mother plane. There were few survivors. The ammunition on board the LST 282 exploded from the intense heat of fire and the burning ship ended up on the rocks.

"We were but 500 feet away from the LST 282 so our captain, Robert Fahnestock, ordered our LST 491 off the beach to assist LST 282. Since we had just beached it was impossible

A Slow Moving Target, The LST of World War II

to retract because we still had a full load of cargo on board. We could only pick up survivors with our small boats.

"On August 23, 1944 we left Southern France en route to Naples, Italy, but our convoy was held up to transfer a sailor from LST 551 to our ship. He had acute appendicitis and was operated on while underway at the aft end of the tank deck that had been set up for emergency surgery for casualties during the invasions."

By August 17, the German 8th Army was caught between Argentan and Falaise, which broke the German defenses. By August 20, Paris was surrounded by Allied troops and by August 25, Paris belonged to the Allies.

Johnny woke up in a London hospital, three days after Leroy and he had been rescued. His arm, now in a cast, had been fractured in two places but a bone had pierced the skin, causing loss of a good deal of blood. That, and the hours he and Leroy had spent in the cold water, had weakened him.

An efficient nurse bustled up to him. "Finally," she said with a smile, "You're awake. My name is Ellen. How do you feel?"

A shadow of a grin crossed his face. "O.K., I guess. Weak. How bad off am I?" he asked hesitantly, fearing the worst.

"You're taking up a bed a sick man could use. Your friend is already up and around. Are you going to let him best you?" she said, chuckling. "I understand the two of you rescued each other." While she talked she had been taking his pulse, listening to his heart and checking his eyes, moving with the quickness of experience.

This time Johnny really grinned, a big, wide smile. Leroy was okay. Johnny was relieved. Memories of the events at Normandy were rushing back, with them the realization that so many other men had been lost. Slowly, Johnny's smile faded. "What about the others, are there others?" he asked quietly.

The nurse looked at him sympathetically, "I don't know about that," she answered. Just as quietly she said, "Leroy has come every afternoon." She continued more cheerfully, "Do you

Joseph Francis Panicello

think you could eat something? Maybe we can get you on your feet before he arrives."

Johnny realized he was hungry. "I sure could!" smiling at her.

"O.K., beautiful eyes, hang tough. I'll be back," she said, leaving to see another patient.

When Leroy arrived he asked, "How'er doing Chief?"

"Fine, Leroy. Have you heard anything about Lieutenant Maurice?"

Leroy had a sad expression on his face and finally said, "I think he went down with the ship."

Johnny laid there in silence, shaking his head. He'd lost a good friend.

Johnny was discharged from the hospital a week later, Nurse Ellen sending him off with a motherly hug.

He was directed to report to Captain Edwards for new orders. He stood quietly before the Captain's desk. There was an Ensign present, standing in a corner.

The Captain asked, "How are you doing, Chief Maroni? You're well I'm told. Ready to go back to duty?"

Johnny wasn't sure he liked the idea of going back to duty. He remained quiet, however.

The Captain continued, "I'm told that you are an expert on diesel engines and were an instructor here in England and in New York. Well Chief, now that the Normandy invasion is over we have discovered that there are many LSTs here in England with their diesel engines disabled and in need of repairs or overhaul. Some LSTs will be needed here in the Atlantic to furnish equipment and supplies to our troops as they march through France and Germany but the Japanese war is hot and Admiral Turner is demanding more LSTs to be transferred to the Pacific campaign.

"I'm ordering you to go over every LST in the English ports and provide me with a detailed damage report and what it will take to repair these ships so that they will be ready for action in the Pacific. You will be given ten able men to assist you. Your own selection, if you wish. Are there any questions?"

Johnny shook his head, "No sir."

"To make your job a little easier I'm promoting you to the temporary rank of Lieutenant JG. You can go to the ship's store and draw out your new clothes. Ensign Smith here, will help you get started and will assist you in keeping records on whatever you find. Good luck."

Johnny was excited by his next assignment, though not by the idea of a promotion, even if it was to Lieutenant JG. The captain did say that it was temporary. It didn't matter to Johnny. He had no intention of making the military a career. Johnny loved being part of the fleet of LSTs, though, huge monsters that had made the impossible, possible.

Johnny had his team assembled in less than two weeks. Leroy Jones was his first choice for Second Class Motor Mechanic. Johnny instructed Jones personally to get his stripes.

Johnny and his team spent weeks assessing the damage of the LSTs in several ports. Of the one hundred LSTs or so that they investigated, four could not be immediately overhauled or put into action. The damage from bombs was too severe on those four ships and their engines had to be completely replaced.

Johnny's report to the captain stated that 40 LSTs could make it to the States, as is, to be overhauled there, and ten could be used immediately in the Pacific with minor repairs. The 50 that were left had to be overhauled in England. This would mean that many spare parts would have to be shipped to England from America as soon as possible.

Johnny estimated that it would take two months to train British and American mechanics and another six months to overhaul the ships. The Captain gave orders that the ten good LSTs were to be sent to the Pacific immediately, to assist in the Iwo Jima assault. The rest, optimistically, would be ready for the Battle of Okinawa. It was now July 15, 1944, enough time to support both the Iwo Jima and Okinawa invasions.

Joseph Francis Panicello

Johnny worked around the clock teaching American civilian mechanics who were already living in England and several British mechanics about overhauling American diesel engines. After they became proficient he had them overhaul the engines of the 50 LSTs located in different ports. To Johnny's surprise, Leroy learned fast. He could see that Leroy had a natural talent as a mechanic and all he needed was a chance. Johnny was pleased with Leroy's progress.

The work required was typically the same as on most standard gasoline engines but on a much larger scale. It involves removing all the heads. grinding the four valve seats on each head, installing new valves, removing the pistons and replacing the rings, replacing any damaged liners, replacing main and connecting rod bearings as needed, replacing head gaskets, overhauling the two starters, and finally replacing or overhauling all of the fuel injectors. This was a tedious task that was slow going because of delays caused by shortages of spare parts, due to late deliveries from the States.

Captain Edwards called Johnny every day to assess the situation, with Johnny insisting each time, "We need more parts, Sir, if I'm to meet your schedule." The Captain occasionally ordered some critical parts to be flown in, rather than using slow ships to transport them.

Finally, a day before Thanksgiving of 1944, the last LST was heading out into the Atlantic and eventually to the Pacific. They would first land in the States for supplies and a new crew. Then the LSTs would go to Hawaii to pick up their cargo of tanks, artillery and troops. Several LSTs took another path by going around South Africa to the Pacific directly, because they had received their supplies and experienced crews in England.

Johnny, along with Ensign Smith, reported to Captain Edwards in December. Smith was a statistical expert and kept impeccable records. He rattled off countless numbers of parts on the ship's inventories to the Captain until the Captain had to stop him, "Thank you Ensign. I'm very impressed with your records. You are dismissed."

A Slow Moving Target, The LST of World War II

He said to Johnny, "That man could bore you to death with his records, but he's a good accountant. First of all, I want to thank you, Lieutenant Maroni, for your hard effort in getting those LSTs ready for combat again. I knew you could do it. Now that your task is over, what shall I do with you? Any suggestions?" The Captain was toying with him. He knew exactly what his next assignment would be.

Johnny didn't know what to say.

The Captain continued, "I'm going to need you in the Pacific. Your job is going to be bigger than ever there. I have decided to make you the maintenance officer of all Pacific LSTs and you will be based in Hawaii. You will set up a repair depot there that will have the capability of repairing at least five LSTs at a time. You will take Ensign Smith with you to keep the records again."

The Captain went on, "I'll be joining you in Hawaii. You and your team will remain under my command. I want all of you in Hawaii by December 12th, 1944. Pick up your official orders from my Chief Yeoman tomorrow morning. You've plenty to do. You are dismissed."

Johnny was dazed as he left the Captain's office. Hawaii! He and his crew would have to cross the United States to reach Hawaii. No chance of a leave. There just wouldn't be time if they had to be in Hawaii by December 12. "What's the rush," Johnny muttered to himself. He stopped in mid-stride. He thought of his friend, Maurice Pillard. Maurice had known, long before Johnny, that the Allies would have to launch a huge offensive in the Atlantic to turn the tide on German occupation of Europe.

Johnny recalled the bloody battles of the Pacific already fought in the past few years. One inescapable fact had emerged. The Japanese would never give up. Die, but not surrender. He began walking again, moving quickly. He knew what the hurry was, as if Maurice were striding along beside him, explaining the strategic facts of life. "Japan, Johnny. It's the only way. We'll have to invade to finish it." Johnny walked faster.

Joseph Francis Panicello

35. The Philippines

The Philippines are part of a large, submerged mountain range made up of over 7,000 islands, though less than 500 are larger than one square mile in size. The two largest are Luzon and Mindanao. Each of these boasts a large volcano; Mount Mayon in Southern Luzon rising 9,000 feet, and Mount Apo, the highest point of the Philippines at 9,600 feet. The islands split the South China Sea from the Pacific Ocean, and measure over 1,100 miles in length. Much of the land is mountainous and covered with forests.

Ferdinand Magellan found the islands in April, 1521. Though he was killed by the inhabitants of Cebu Island, his ship continued to circumnavigate the world. Other Spanish ships followed and, in 1565, colonization began. The natives were named "Filipinos" after Prince Philip of Spain.

For three centuries native resentment grew over the oppression of Spanish rule. An open revolt was interrupted by the United States defeating the Spanish fleet at Manila in May, 1898. Americans occupied Manila by August 13, and the Treaty of Peace ended the Spanish-American war. On April 11, 1899, America owned the Philippines and Spain was 20 million dollars richer.

America became the focus of Filipino insurrection. Two years later, on July 4, 1901, after hundreds of engagements, an American government was formed. The first governor-general of the Philippines was William Howard Taft, later President of the United States.

By 1935 a Commonwealth government had been enacted with a promise of independence set for January 4, 1946. General Douglas MacArthur was assigned to prepare, defensively, the Philippines for their eventual independence.

Douglas MacArthur followed in his father's footsteps. Arthur MacArthur served in both the Civil War and the Spanish-

A Slow Moving Target, The LST of World War II

American War. He was military governor of the Philippines and was also a general.

Douglas MacArthur graduated West Point achieving the highest record in 25 years. He was wounded twice in France in World War I, becoming the youngest divisional commander in the Army. After the war he became the youngest man ever appointed superintendent of West Point, at the age of 39. President Hoover made him the youngest full general, at 50, in American history.

After retiring from the service in 1937, MacArthur remained in the Philippines, working with Commonwealth president Manual Quezon. In July 1941, he was called back to the service and made commander of United States forces in the Far East.

Ten hours after the attack on Pearl Harbor, Japanese aircraft, in a single raid, demolished half the American bombers and two thirds of the fighter planes located at Manila airfields in the Philippines.

In the weeks and months that followed Japan's offenses in the Far East, Guam and Wake Islands fell. Hong Kong was captured. February, March and April of 1942, brought the surrender of Singapore, the East Indies and Burma.

For five months American and Filipino troops, total number around 47,000, resisted the Japanese invasion of Luzon. Trapped on the Bataan Peninsula, lacking supplies, air support and reinforcements, the men fought on.

Anticipating an invasion of Australia, Roosevelt ordered, in February 1942, MacArthur's relocation to Australia as Supreme Commander of the Allied forces in the South Pacific. General Jonathan M. Wainwright was given his Philippine command.

Four PT torpedo boats carrying MacArthur, his wife, son, and staff, eluded the Japanese blockade. MacArthur promised he would return. On May 6, 1942, the Philippine Islands fell.

In July, 1944, in a meeting between MacArthur, Nemitz, and Roosevelt, at Pearl Harbor, MacArthur fought to keep his promise. Roosevelt asked MacArthur, "Where do we go from here, Douglas?"

Joseph Francis Panicello

MacArthur quickly replied, "Leyte and then Luzon."

Roosevelt then asked Nemitz, "What's your opinion, Chester?"

Admiral Nemitz had brought his naval forces thousands of miles across the Pacific from Hawaii to the Marshalls, then the Marianas, to Saipan, Guam and Tinian. Nemitz said bluntly, "Formosa. If we take it the island will be in closer range of Japan and we can launch a continuous air attack from that country." Nemitz knew his superior, Admiral King, was set on Formosa. He was reluctant to agree with MacArthur.

MacArthur knew the Navy's preference. He turned to Roosevelt and with visible emotion said, "Mr. President, you cannot abandon 17 million loyal Filipino Christians to the Japanese in favor of taking Formosa and returning it to China." He chose his next words carefully. "American public opinion will condemn you, Mr. President, and it would be justified."

"I'm inclined to agree with Douglas. The Philippines are more important at this time," Roosevelt concluded.

Nemitz then struck a bargain with MacArthur. In exchange for an Amphibious task force to protect MacArthur's progression to Leyte, the invasion must be scheduled no later than October 20, 1944. MacArthur agreed.

In September, the American forces landed on the Western Carolines. The Caroline Islands lie between the Marshall Islands and the Philippines. The group extends more than 2,000 miles consisting of five large island groups; Kosroe, Pohnpei, Turk, Yao, and Palau, and 32 atolls.

Spain originally claimed the Caroline Islands in 1885, but sold them to Germany in 1889. After W.W.I., the League of Nations gave them to Japan. In 1978, the U.S. Government agreed to give the Carolines self-government, which divided the islands into two groups - the Palau Islands and the Federal States of Micronesia which consists of Turk, Yap, Kosroe, and Pohnpei.

MacArthur and Nimitz both agreed that the Palau Islands must be seized to prevent the Japanese aircraft based there from attacking the right flank of MacArthur's sea approach to the Philippines. Halsey disagreed with Nimitz, saying, "I believe that the cost would be too great." Nimitz was not swayed and issued orders for the seizure of Peleliu and Angaur, two of the smaller islands of Palau. Palau is at the western part of the chain.

The Japanese began sending reinforcements to Palau, early in 1944 to beef up the defenses of Peleliu and Angaur. The Americans estimated that Peleliu and Angaur had garrisons of 10,500 and 1,400 men respectively. The 1st Marine Division under Maj. Gen. William Rupertus, would take Peleliu and the 8th Infantry Division under Maj. Gen. Paul Muller would go after Angaur.

For weeks Navy craft patrolled the central Pacific while aircraft ranged over the Philippines and Formosa.

The assault on Peleliu began on September 15, 1944. Earlier bombardments killed many defenders. The Japanese had to leave their safe bombproof caves and shelters to man their cannons. They began blasting the assaulting troops and many American craft were blown to bits. The firing from the Japs at the American troops on the beach killed many of the men. It disabled tractors, which then cluttered the beaches, along with the dead and wounded. One Japanese battery delivered sixteen four-gun salvos per hour onto the beachhead for twenty-two hours straight before being knocked out by American artillery.

The most difficult part of the invasion was providing medical assistance. With the beaches clogged with tractors and small craft, Andre, on board LST 153, could only wait in frustration. There was no room for the LST to land. Andre had to wait for smaller LCVPs and other craft to reach the beach. Once there corpsmen would load the wounded and transfer them to his LST. In three days 700 casualties were transferred in this manner, too late for many of them.

The glut of LCVPs, LVTs, and DUKWS picking up wounded slowed down the flow of supplies.

Providing water to the troops on land became a serious problem. It was discovered that the drums that contained the

Joseph Francis Panicello

water were contaminated so the seabees went ashore and began drilling for water, using distilling gear to produce fresh water.

Bad weather arrived, making it impossible for the smaller craft and cargo ships to continue. Transferring loads onto LSTs in heavy seas from other, smaller craft was no easy feat, but six LSTs were loaded this way, and with the beaches cleared somewhat, delivered needed supplies to the troops.

The struggle for Peleliu was costly. It claimed the lives of 1,252 marines and 277 soldiers, with 5,274 marines and 1,008 soldiers wounded in battle. The Japanese lost 10,000 troops. The majority of Americans in the states never heard of Peleliu because there was very little reporting by the press on that assault. MacArthur was the big news.

Halsey said, after the war, "If military leaders were gifted with the same accuracy of foresight that they are with hindsight, undoubtedly the assault of the Paleliu would never have been attempted."

Admiral Fort believed that Peleliu was "the most difficult amphibious operation of the Pacific." He recalled after the war, "The only difference between Iwo Jima and Peleliu was that at Iwo there were twice as many Japs on an island that was twice as large, and they had three Marine Divisions to take it while we had only one to take Peleliu."

On October 20, Lieutenant General Walter Kruger's 200,000-man Army invaded Leyte.

MacArthur had intended to follow the first three waves of men to the beach by docking at a pier. The famous photograph of MacArthur, wading knee-deep through water to shore in pressed suntans, braided hat and sunglasses was an accident.

The beaches were so crowded on A-Day (Attack Day) the stubborn beachmaster would not allow MacArthur's boat to reach the pier. He didn't even realize who he had shunted aside. The busy beachmaster simply said, "Let him walk." MacArthur later announced in a broadcast to the Philippine people, "I have returned," in a typically dramatic fashion.

A Slow Moving Target, The LST of World War II

When General MacArthur landed at Leyte in October, 1944, the Japanese hoped that a bold strike might dislodge American forces once again from the islands. In desperation, they devised Operation Victory, "Sho-Go", a massive naval plan that included all that remained of Japanese air and naval power.

Split into three parts, the Japanese Fleet was comprised of a North fleet to decoy Admiral Halsey. Led by Admiral Ozaua Jisaburo, this fleet numbered only 18 warships. Four were huge aircraft carriers. Halsey had no choice but to take the bait, leaving Leyte for the oceans north of the Philippines, arriving with six battleships, ten aircraft carriers, eight cruisers and forty-one destroyers.

The second component of Operation Victory was the South Fleet, led by Admiral Nishimua Teiji. He was to lead his ships, in a round-about fashion, to MacArthur's beachhead, hoping to break through American forces that would be waiting for them. The South Fleet was made up of only 7 ships. It was a suicide mission, another feint to draw American forces south, leaving Leyte defenses weakened.

The two decoy Fleets supported the Central Fleet, consisting of 5 battleships, 12 cruisers, and 15 destroyers. Admiral Takeo was instructed to bring this fleet through the San Bernardino Strait, waters difficult for even a fishing boat to navigate, and fall upon Leyte.

At three in the morning, on October 25, the battle of Leyte began. The South Fleet, in single file, one after another, moved from a narrow strait into open waters to find an American Fleet of 6 battleships, 4 heavy cruisers, 4 light cruisers, and 28 destroyers, led by Admiral Oldendorf, strung out in a formidable line. This formation was referred to as "crossing the enemy T," considered fatal, and so it proved to be.

Six of the seven South Fleet ships were lost. Admiral Teiji went down with his ships. Not one American ship was lost.

In the north, Admiral Halsey and his force fell on the Japanese, inflicting so much damage that by late afternoon it was apparent that the North fleet would be demolished by Halsey's ships. The four huge carriers had already been sunk. Before the American fleet could complete their task, Halsey was apprised of the situation taking place at Leyte.

Admiral Nemitz in Hawaii recognized that MacArthur's position was threatened by the oncoming Central Fleet. A message from Nemitz, which Halsey interpreted as an admonishment, forced Halsey to turn away from certain victory over what he now recognized as inferior forces. Halsey realized the North Fleet had been a ruse and, by snapping at the bait, he had left MacArthur vulnerable. Though he felt he would be probably too late to change the course of events, he moved his fleet back to Leyte.

Though suicidal, the North and South Fleets had accomplished what was intended.

On the morning of October 25, the Central Fleet confronted an American force vastly inferior to their own. No battleships, no cruisers, no large aircraft carriers and no destroyers. The American force consisted of 16 small aircraft carriers, 9 mid-size destroyers and 12 destroyer escorts.

Some of the destroyers moved out to attempt the first offense against the Japanese fleet, with smaller escorts following, acting as decoys, to allow the destroyers a chance to withdraw, after firing their torpedoes.

The bombardment from the Central Fleet was intense and the smaller craft of the American fleet dodged this way and that, attempting to evade the salvos that filled the air. The heavy ammunition of the Japanese that were so useful against heavy armored American battleships cut through the thinner walls of the small American carriers without detonating, causing few casualties, though ships were left with gaping holes.

With inadequate ships against the major firepower of the Japanese, the Americans put up a hell of a fight. American aircraft from the small carriers filled the air, attacking the Japanese ships.

Wm. J. Russell recalls in the L.S.T. Scuttlebutt magazine, "We were two hours out of Leyte, in the Philippines, when our

A Slow Moving Target, The LST of World War II

LST 695 was hit by two torpedoes on October 24, 1944. Twenty-four shipmates were buried at sea and 57 were wounded in a sinking LST. But the ship was saved by the crew of LSTs 170 & 986 who dropped out of the convoy to assist us, with a doctor. They were in a small boat with a crew of 170 men and were able to retrieve a crewman who was blown overboard. We were towed to Palau Island but for the next 10 months we went through a typhoon, suicide subs, and bombings. We did survive those attacks, with K-rations we were sure the Army didn't miss!"

During the invasion. Leo C. Gavitt of Sheridan, Mich., said, "Our task force was attacked in a battle off Samar by a Japanese fleet of 4 battleships, 9 cruisers and 14 destroyers. With many of our ships sunk, hundreds of our young lads were in the water, gulping oil, and dying. They hadn't yet learned what life was about. As we picked them up, we received orders from the captain over a bullhorn, `Just the live ones, boys. Just the live ones.'

"We picked up over 150 on our little destroyer escort, the *USS John C. Butler.* As the dead lay there in the water, their oil-soaked eyes shut, and mouths open as if to say, `I did my best,' we took their dog tags and said, goodby, buddy, and God bless."

Inexplicably, with the small American force anticipating complete destruction, the Japanese Admiral, Kurita, gave orders for retreat of the Central Fleet.

The battle of Leyte Gulf is considered the largest naval engagement in history. Sixty-nine Japanese ships were involved, with a loss of 28, a death knoll for the Imperial Navy. American ships numbered 144, losing the carriers *Princeton, St. Lo* and *Gambier Bay*, and the destroyers *Hoel, Johnstone*, and *Samuel B. Roberts.*

Leyte was finally secured by mid-November by Gen. Robert Eichelberger's Sixth Army. Only 5,000 of the 70,000 Japanese soldiers who fought there survived.

36. The Four Phibies

On a hospital ship, in the middle of the Pacific ocean, Rich Hienman had his leg amputated at the knee. The doctor said it was so badly shattered it couldn't be repaired and though Rich begged him to hold off until they reached Hawaii, he was sedated and operated on against his wishes.

After surgery, when he awoke, he was violent, having to be restrained by the corpsmen. He contemplated suicide, feeling half a man, a cripple, imagining a look of pity in other people's eyes when they looked at him.

He thought of Lucy, of the time they had spent together in Australia. He realized, too late, that she meant more to him than he had been willing to admit.

The first night they met they had walked along a river front, quietly talking, exchanging details of their lives, in the shy way men and women do when they are strangers.

Lucy had been sincere in her interest, not the least coy, and Rich felt comfortable with her. He found himself divulging all the thoughts and feelings he'd kept pent up inside. At some point, talking of Mildred, he started to cry. Lucy held him as she would a child, patting him on the back. As he pulled away he saw tears on her face and slowly, surprised at himself, he kissed her. She kissed him back and that had been their beginning.

LST 153 put into port many times to pick up cargo for the island campaigns in the Pacific. Rich spent most of his free time with Lucy and the relationship blossomed. Rich felt himself more drawn to Lucy each time he saw her. She was gentle, and kind, and she always had a smile on her face. She was giving and loving and Rich responded, wondering sometimes why he had not met Lucy before Mildred had made him a victim of the old adage "once bitten, twice shy."

Rich recalled, with anguish, the last time he and Lucy had seen each other. It had been just before LST 153 left for Saipan.

Cuddled on Lucy's couch, listening to the radio, talking the nonsense lovers do, Lucy had suddenly straightened up. Slowly, she put a hand on each side of his face and, looking directly into his eyes, whispered, "I love you, Richard."

She pulled him closer to her and before he could answer she continued, "I will wait for you, as long as it takes, but tonight I want to love you. We don't need to talk about it. We'll talk about it the next time we meet."

Rich kissed her in silent agreement.

The following morning she had sent him off, refusing to talk about the future until the next time they met. She held him tightly for a moment, then stepping back, gave him a brave smile and snappy salute, "Go get 'em, Gunner!"

On board the hospital ship, Rich buried his head in his hands at this memory. How could he go back, a cripple. Lucy deserved more, so much more. Rich remembered he'd never even told Lucy he loved her. Fear had held him back and now it was too late.

Rich thought of his future. He knew a discharge would be forthcoming. Then what? He could go back to the ranch. He knew, realistically, there was still plenty he could do to keep the ranch going. Maybe he could go to California, become an assistant to Dolores, help her career in some way. Rich shook his head. No, that wasn't for him. From her letters it sounded like Dolores had "gone Hollywood" as they say. Rich wasn't sure he knew or liked his sister anymore.

Rich remained quiet and aloof on the trip back to Hawaii. He spent several weeks in an island hospital. He started several times to write to Lucy. Though unwilling to tell her the truth of his situation because he didn't want her pity, he was even more unwilling to make up some lie. He could not bring himself to hurt her. Instead he did nothing.

When Rich was discharged from the hospital he decided to visit with Bob and Lovette before he made arrangements to go back to the States.

Joseph Francis Panicello

Bob was fully recuperated, waiting for his orders. He and Lovette were very happy. Although Rich was initially self-conscious of his crutches, Bob and Lovette greeted him with so much genuine pleasure he soon forgot his disability.

They caught up on the activities of all the Phibies but eventually the conversation turned to the subject of Rich's plans.

"Hell, I'm okay. It's not the end of the world, Olly." Rich said in answer to Bob's question. "In a few weeks I'll be a civilian reading about you guys fighting in the Pacific. I've got plans, so don't worry about me," Rich finished, with a bravado he didn't feel.

"What about Lucy?" Lovette asked. "Have you heard from her?"

"I haven't written." Rich replied. For the first time Bob and Lovette noticed the sadness in his eyes. He looked at the two of them helplessly. "I just can't," he finished quietly. "I can't burden her with a one-legged man. When I finish therapy and get my artificial leg, maybe I'll feel better about all this. Maybe I can find the words to explain it to Lucy, but not now."

"She's here, Rich," Bob said. "Not here in the house," he said quickly, noticing the stricken look on Rich's face. "She's in Hawaii. Andre wrote her right after he put you on the hospital ship. It took weeks for her to make the arrangements to get here. She's a very sweet but very persistent girl," Bob finished with a grin.

"She wouldn't come to the house to surprise you," continued Lovette. "She didn't want to put you on the spot or make you uncomfortable. She said she's come thousands of miles and if you want her she's only several hundred feet away. What do you say, Rich?"

Rich was dazed. He looked up at Bob and Lovette, both smiling assurance, coaxing him to reach out and accept this gift.

"Come on, Hinny. I don't know if that girl can wait forever," Bob said.

"Attention!" said Lovette suddenly. Bob and Rich stood up, laughing. "Fall out!" she ordered and the three of them, with Rich in the lead, headed out the door.

Rich and Lucy were married three days later. They planned, eventually, to head back to Australia but remained on the island temporarily to continue Rich's therapy and enjoy an extended honeymoon. Lucy had been saving money for years. She wanted to give Rich time to get "his sea legs back." This always made Rich laugh, but not with bitterness. He felt he was truly the luckiest man alive.

Early in January on a balmy Hawaiian morning, LST 153 docked for maintenance and repairs. As LST 153 docked, Andre, up on deck, noticed an officer on the pier obviously waiting for the ship to drop its gangway. As the officer started up the ramp Andre, recognizing him, shouted out with pleasure, "Macaroni!"

Johnny, startled at seeing Andre, ran up the gangway, saluted the stern flag as was customary, then threw his arms around Andre. "What are you doing here?" he demanded, with a grin. "I wasn't sure I'd ever see you again."

Andre, laughing, said, "What about you? Where did you get those stripes? Who did you bribe?"

Johnny proudly explained his promotion and assignment.

"My job today, Robber, is to insure that the engines on your ship are up to snuff and ready for further combat. I will go through the logs and discuss any problems about the engines with your Chief Motor Mechanic. I suspect your engine will need a complete overhaul. From what I've read you've been out to sea a long time, running up a lot of hours on those engines. If that's true you'll be in Hawaii for at least a week. I certainly didn't expect to see you here. After I get through talking with the Chief, how about you and I going to town?"

Andre was delighted and said, "You're on, Macaroni."

"Hey, I almost forgot," Johnny practically shouted. "We've got to tell Olly and Hinny you're here. My God, Robber, you've been away from us a long time. There's so much to tell you," he finished.

Joseph Francis Panicello

"I know more than you think I do," Andre said mysteriously.

"We'll see," replied Johnny with a mischievous grin. "Meet me at the `Lanai Hawaii' about 1600 hours," he commanded, as he moved towards the ladder leading below deck.

Andre spent the morning and early afternoon hours roaming the docks, visiting with other corpsmen on different LSTs, discussing their shared concerns about improving medical treatment for the wounded, such as securing more medical supplies, especially plasma, and increasing the speed in which they get to the wounded on the crowded beaches so more could be saved.

Unfamiliar with Honolulu, he was twenty minutes late arriving at the crowded bar. He stopped to accustom his eyes to the dim interior. A group of five people at a nearby table caught his attention and, with a start, he recognized the three men, but only one of the two ladies.

"Olly, Hinny," he called out.

As he moved towards them, Johnny, standing up, pulled a chair from an adjacent table, and with a sweep of his arm, directed Andre to it, saying, "Our guest of honor has arrived."

Andre sat down, speechless, as all five young people began babbling at once.

Johnny watched with a grin as Andre slowly regained his composure. Rich and Bob were shaking his hand in welcome as the women, Lovette and Lucy, both touched by the scene of the four Phibies reunited, laughed and cried at the same time.

Lucy had met Andre in Australia and if not for him, she wouldn't be with Rich now. She leaned over and whispered, "Thank you for my husband," and kissed Andre on the cheek.

"That goes double for me, Robber!" Rich exclaimed, gazing at Lucy for a moment, with a mist in his eyes.

Andre reached for the drink that had been placed in front of him moments before. Holding it aloft, he spoke softly, "I knew you two were meant for each other the first time I saw you together. Congratulations, and all the happiness in the world."

The six drank in unison, and as Johnny motioned to the bartender for another round, Bob stood up.

"Robber, I would like to introduce my wife, Lovette."

Andre turned to the lovely woman seated at his right side and, taking her hand in his, said, "It's a pleasure after all this time, Lovette. You are as pretty as Olly said you were," and lifting his glass he said, "To Olly and Lovette," and they all raised their glasses and repeated the toast, "To Olly and Lovette."

Bob continued, "Another announcement, Phibies. I am going to be a father." Everyone at the table was surprised, including Johnny.

He felt a twinge of annoyance, thinking of Dolores, and what might have been if, in the early days of the war, he had been willing to commit to marriage. He thought about Megan and what could never be. He shook these feelings off and raised his glass, "To the baby," he said joyously, meaning it, as they all drank.

They talked and laughed, drank and danced for hours that evening. They discussed the Hienmans' plans for going back to Australia. Bob and Lovette planned to make Boston their home when the war ended. Andre spoke of his love of medicine, gratefully acknowledging that if the navy hadn't given him a chance, he might have passed up a career he was completely suited for.

Johnny stated boldly, "I will go to college and become an engineer and settle down."

"What's your plan, Macaroni?" Rich asked teasingly.

"I don't know." Johnny replied, shrugging his shoulders. When the group burst into laughter, Johnny laughed loudest of all.

Andre knew he was heading back to the Pacific. The invasion of the islands was continuing. Bob knew that he was to report to LST 145 and would soon be joining Andre there. Johnny's assignment in Hawaii would continue, probably as long

Joseph Francis Panicello

as the war lasted. The group tried not to dwell on these facts as they finished their last drinks before parting.

In a last, quiet moment, Andre stood up. The group looked up at him expectantly. "I would like to remember the two that are missing from this wonderful reunion tonight. To Belcher and Angela," he proposed. The group quietly touched their glasses together, then finished their drinks in silence.

As Johnny and Andre left the "Lanai" to head back to the base, Andre asked abruptly,, "Macaroni, how's Angela doing?"

"She's fine, just fine. The baby's growing fast. He looks just like his Dad, she says," Johnny answered.

"You know that I love her, Johnny," Andre confessed sadly. "I tried to meet other girls but they don't compare. I've poured my heart out to Angela in my letters. No, not so much about my feelings for her," he assured Johnny, as Johnny looked at him curiously. "All through the war she's the one I've shared my thoughts with, through the letters. When the war is over, I know it probably sounds silly, I want to go home and take care of her, and the baby."

Johnny stopped and sat on a low wall. "Sit down for a second, Robber," he said. "Look, what happened to Belcher was probably the saddest thing that Ann ever had to deal with. You haven't been able to forget her. Well, she can't forget him. Ann is a bright girl, a practical girl. She continues to write you, as always, because you matter to her. Hinny told me he advised you to, well, lay low about how you feel and he was right. I don't think Ann could stand to lose you like she lost Belcher," Johnny paused.

"I've hoped for that," Andre answered. "The idea that when the war is over things will be different. Do you think so?" he asked, unsure.

Johnny grinned, with a twinkle in his eye. "Do you know what she named the baby, Robber?" he asked.

Confused, Andre answered, "Sure, Daniel Bletcher."

"Daniel A. Bletcher," Johnny corrected him. Johnny watched tears come to Andre's eyes. Putting a hand on Andre's shoulder, he said quietly, "A, for Andre. Hang on, Phibie. We'll be home soon and everything will work out. Be patient." Johnny began laughing and said, "I told you that you didn't know everything."

Joseph Francis Panicello

37. Iwo Jima

By September 1944, Allied troops in Western Europe had crossed the German border and Germany had unleashed a new weapon, the V-2 or Vengeance weapons 2., a guided missile. More advanced than its predecessor, the V-1, it was recognized by some civilians and military personnel as an innovation that would reshape the art of air warfare.

Over 3 thousand V-2s were fired at France, London and Belgium. In France very little damage was caused, but in Antwerp, Belgium, V-2s left the important port city in ruins. The damage in London and elsewhere in England could not be compared to the aerial bombing the country had suffered throughout the war from the Luftwaffe. Edward R. Murrow in London predicted that, "German science has again demonstrated a malignant ingenuity which is not likely to be forgotten when it comes time to establish controls over German scientific and industrial research."

In December, German and Allied forces fought the "Battle of the Bulge." With the Germans defeated the combined American and British forces moved halfway across Germany eastward, while the Russians took Budapest in February and Vienna in April. Mussolini was killed April 28, in Italy, by partisans, with the Germans surrendering the next day. By the end of April Allied forces had Berlin surrounded. Hitler committed suicide on the night of April 30, 1945. Germany surrendered unconditionally on May 7, at 0241 hours in a little red school house in Reims, France.

A German woman who came from a small town outside of Berlin and had migrated to America after World War II, said, "When I first saw the American soldiers coming into our town waving at the girls, smoking cigarettes, with dirty and unkempt uniforms, and in no particular formation, I said to myself, "How could these unruly soldiers beat our disciplined and powerful

A Slow Moving Target, The LST of World War II

German Army?" Unruly or not, she admitted, "I finally realized they proved to be an exceptional fighting machine."

In the Philippines, MacArthur's forces moved on to Luzon. Most resistance ended in February, 1945, though it took several more months to rout out isolated pockets of fanatical Japanese resistance.

Admiral King felt that Formosa should be the next island to be invaded but the Joint Chiefs were convinced that Formosa would be too costly to assault at this time because they were massively fortified. On January 20, 1945, they ordered Admiral Nimitz to seize Iwo Jima. He then explained to the other "Mad Monks" that the timetable after Iwo would be "the Tokyo Express." Nimitz's staff was dubbed by reporters as "The Mad Monks of Makalapa."

Iwo Jima is part of the Bonin chain which includes 97 volcanic islands. Chichi Jima is the largest, covering 15 sq. miles. They were first charted by a Spanish sea captain, Bernard de Torres, and later visited by an English explorer who called Iwo Jima "Sulphur Island" because it reeked of the vile-smelling mineral. In addition to Iwo, the Bonin chain consists of Haha Jima and Chichi Jima. Japan called the Bonin Islands Nanpo Shoto, meaning Volcano Islands. The Bonin Islands were later colonized in 1830, by the Polynesians from Hawaii, and in 1875 Japan claimed them. After the war they were occupied by the U.S. until 1968, when they were again returned to Japan.

Iwo Jima is located 600 miles south of Japan and north of Saipan. It's a small island of only eight square miles in area and five miles across its widest point. It is basically a volcanic rock with no natural water. Why, then, was this island so important to the Allies and fought over so relentlessly?

The main reason the Americans fought for it so violently was because it lay within the shortest route B-29 bombers would take to bomb Tokyo, coming from the Marianas. Using Iwo as an American airstrip, fighters flying from this base could be used as escorts for the bombers as they passed over. The way it stood, the Japanese Zeros flying out of Iwo Jima's three airstrips could intercept American Boeing B-29 formations and cause considerable damage to the bombers. In addition, if Iwo were under the Allies control, the Americans could use Iwo as a stopping point for any disabled bombers returning from a raid on Tokyo. Iwo Jima would give the U.S. a forward air base at the front door of Japan.

Nimitz had a Japanese counterpart, the brilliant Admiral Isoroku Yamamoto, Commander in Chief of the Imperial Fleet. He had said, "Unless the American fleet is put out of action by 1942, the balance of power will shift to the United States and that will be the end."

Yamamoto presented his strategy for victory to the Imperial War Council by saying, "Impart a fatal blow to the Hawaiian Islands, capture Midway Islands, invade the Aleutians at the tip of Alaska, and be ready to make landings on the West Coast of the United States." Yamamoto concluded, "If this is done the United States will have to negotiate a peace treaty and leave Japan a free hand in China, Southeast Asia, and the Pacific Ocean."

On December 7, 1941, the day of the attack of Pearl Harbor, the Japanese had 1,400 troops on Chichi Jima and Iwo Jima. Iwo became the headquarters and focal point because it was the only island suitable for an airfield. After Kwajalein and Eniwetok were seized in February, 1943, Iwo's build-up accelerated. Hirohito's hand-picked general was Tadamichi Kuribayashi, who came from five generations of ancestors that served in the armies of six emperors. Kuribayashi spent much time in the United States and could speak English fluently.

Kuribayashi wrote a letter to his brother about Iwo Jima which said, "I may not return alive from this assignment, but I will fight to the best of my ability so that no disgrace will be brought upon my Samurai father."

By 1943, Iwo was armed to its maximum and had a garrison of 25,170 Japanese troops. It's airfield had 52 first-line fighters. The island had 14 large coastal guns, 13 heavy artillery, 4,652 rifles, over 200 light and heavy machine guns, and 32 twin-

A Slow Moving Target, The LST of World War II

mounted anti-aircraft weapons. They were ready for the worst that the U.S. could give. Kuribayashi's orders from the Emperor were to fight to the last man. If Iwo fell, Japan would be in grave danger.

A Japanese Admiral, by 1945, realized that all was lost, but the War Council disagreed. They felt America could never take the Japanese homeland. It was well fortified with reenforced concrete bunkers and a network of underground military facilities. The emperor was well protected in a fortified cave in the mountains with his generals and administrators. With the people ready to die rather than surrender they could last ten years of resistance. Emperor Hirohito was informed that Iwo would be next and he ordered an all-out build-up on Iwo Jima.

The American preparation for the invasion was colossal, with 73 Liberty and Victory transports ready to haul troops and combat supplies. Each ship would carry enough rations for sixty days, 6,000 five-gallon cans of water, gasoline for twenty-five days, 5,263 pounds of grease, plenty of ammunition and weapons for the troops, communication equipment with spare parts, and thirty days of supplies for the troops. The Fifth Division carried 100 million cigarettes and enough food to feed a major city in the States.

On December 8, 1944, the attack on Iwo Jima began with B-29 Super-fortresses and B-24 Liberators bombarding the islands for seventy-two days, including heavy naval shelling from offshore. Eleven days into January, 1945, the attack continued as bombers hammered Iwo with 15,000 tons of bombs. The battleship *Indiana,* on January 25, began firing 1,300 sixteen-inch shells into Iwo, and four cruisers slammed another 1,300 eight-inch shells into the island. It seemed that nothing could exist after such a punishing avalanche of bombs. However, General Smith said the air strikes and Navy shelling were virtually meaningless.

Smith wrote, "The airfields were destroyed, but the main body of defense not only remained physically intact but were strengthened markedly."

Joseph Francis Panicello

Nearly five hundred ships were anchored off Saipan in February 1945, waiting to sail the six hundred miles to Iwo Jima. Seventy LSTs, including Andre's LST 153, were carrying tanks and amphibious tractors, while 30 transports were loaded with men with their combat gear. Four communications ships loaded with radio equipment were also carrying generals and admirals that would be commanding the invasion.

On February 16, the enemy began their air defense of Iwo from Tokyo, hoping to intercept the American ships, but because the weather was near perfect American carrier planes were able to counter their attack and knocked down 117 interceptors. The net results announced by Admiral Nimitz were 332 enemy planes shot out of the skies, 117 planes destroyed that were on the ground, an aircraft carrier left burning, a destroyer and five merchants ships sunk. The American losses were forty-nine planes. Nine pilots were plucked out of the water and saved.

On D-Day, February 19, 1945, the amphibious assault on Iwo Jima began when Higgins boats approached the Iwo shores. Admiral Spruance, on his flag ship *Indianapolis*, had arrived during the night to take command of the assault. At 0300 hours, reveille was announced on the loud speakers and the Marines had their last breakfast of steak and eggs before the attack. At 0630 hours, Admiral Turner gave the now familiar order, "Land the landing force!"

Troops on the LSTs, who would be in the first wave, climbed aboard amphibious tractors known as Amtracks that would carry them to the beaches. As the LSTs approached the shore with their bow doors wide open the Amtracks clanked over the partially lowered ramps and into the water, under heavy Japanese fire. They then circled back to meet with other Amtracks and wait for the signal to attack, forming abreast a heavy band ready to assault the beach.

Navy men that were originally in the invasion of Normandy described the American bombardment of Iwo Jima as mightier than D-Day in Europe. It seemed that its volcano was erupting

A Slow Moving Target, The LST of World War II

and one sailor said, "Maybe the goddamned thing will blow up and sink into the ocean, and then we can all go home."

Nineteen year old Bill Hudson described his experiences in the landing on Iwo Jima. As a member of K Company, 25th Marines, 4th Marine Division, Hudson left Maui, Hawaii in January, 1945 on an LST.

"On the morning of February 19, 1945, after having the traditional pre-invasion meal of steak and eggs, we got into landing vehicles, tracked (LVTs), and waited for the signal to begin the invasion.

"After the way we bombed Iwo over the last month it seemed there couldn't be any life left on the island. The coxswain on our LVT yelled down to us, 'You guys will be back for noon chow. There ain't no Japs alive on that island.'

"When I landed on Iwo Jima, I had my BAR (Browning Automatic Rifle), Kabar, plenty of ammunition, two canteens of water, two grenades, a gas mask, chocolate D-ration bars, and an entrenching tool. We also had a big box of ponchos with us.

"I knew why we needed ammo and water, but I didn't know why we had to carry ponchos. I soon learned the ponchos were to be used to cover dead bodies.

"I did not actually see any Japs the first day," he remembered, "I only saw dead and wounded marines. All the officers in my company were killed or wounded during the first six hours. By 1800 hours our battalion of 400 men was reduced to 150 men.

"Prior to the invasion, Kurabayashi had his men construct 750 gun emplacements and dozens of concrete blockhouses, with walls five feet thick. The Japanese had huge 240 mm mortar that fired from a deep cave. Its shells looked like 50-gallon oil drums. Fortunately the mortar made a loud noise when fired, and we could track the course of the shell and, if possible, take cover. The marines dubbed the Jap mortar as,'Screaming Mimi' or 'The Ash Can.'

Joseph Francis Panicello

"I was eventually wounded by shrapnel from a Jap grenade and was treated in a field hospital. I had my first undisturbed sleep in 26 days."

In November 1945, Hudson was awarded the Bronze Star Medal for his actions on Iwo Jima. He later enrolled in the Marine Corps' V-12 program and became an officer.

The job of the first wave of Amtracks was to smash any enemy positions they could find on the beach and to cover up to fifty yards inland to set a defense position for the landing force. No assault troops were on these Amtracks—only a three-man crew to operate it and another four men to man a 75-millimeter howitzer and three machine guns. The second wave of Amtracks would carry 1,360 marine riflemen, at 300 yards apart, and each wave would land at five-minutes intervals. Hundreds of Higgins boats would follow with thousands of troops. There were more than 500 landing craft used in this invasion.

Troops carried their weapons and two heavy packs of gear on their backs. Corpsmen that would go ashore on the third wave carried fifty pounds of battle dressings, morphine, sulfa, blood plasma, and a small kit of surgical knives and scissors.

Andre, the sole Phibie in the Pacific, was prepared to administer first aid to the marines on the Iwo shores and supply the corpsmen on the beach with extra blood plasma. He stationed himself with two of his corpsmen close to the bow doors and when they opened the doors he observed the beaches being bombarded by the American guns. He couldn't believe any Japanese soldier could survive. Horrified at the grim scene confronting him, he wondered momentarily if anyone would survive. Shaking off this dark thought, he made ready to move out.

Ten minutes before H-Hour a final assault of bombardment from B-24 Liberators was made and at 0847 hours the Naval bombardment stopped. The first wave of Amtracks was now 400 yards inland from shore, too close to continue the bombing.

At 0902 the announcement came, "Boats on the beach!" From 0911 to 0919 hours the Red, Yellow, Blue, and Green

A Slow Moving Target, The LST of World War II

beaches swarmed with troops, where the resistance was moderate, with mortar fire from the Japanese.

Japanese General Kuribayashi's plan was to let the marines land and suck them into a gigantic ambush. He waited an hour after H-Hour, when the Navy gunfire had to stop to avoid friendly fire, and then he would cut off further landings with his own artillery and mortar fire. His plan was to slaughter the marines on shore and push the invaders off of Iwo. The trap was triggered at 1000 hours.

It was hell on the beaches. By now 6,200 men were pinned down on the beaches and boats were still trying to land but there was no room to drop the new men. Seven landing craft were sunk with tanks, trucks, and ammunition. General Kuribayashi's ambush was working but he waited too long. It gave the marines enough time to get their Sherman tanks and artillery into position to fire back and move forward up the beach and across the island.

Many LVTs were hit, as well as LSMs that were bringing tanks ashore. The Sherman tanks continued the onslaught, with their cannons and machine guns firing at the enemy, allowing the troops to move forward. It looked like the resistance was waning, then Kuribayashi made his second move, with extensive machine gun and mortar fire coming from concealed positions. American casualties were mounting, and any attempt to take the wounded back drew even heavier fire.

In the water, Higgins boats and LSTs were ready to land reinforcements, tanks, artillery, ammunition, trucks, cranes, medical supplies, bulldozers, fuel, and fresh water. But the beaches were cluttered with wreckage and only a few boats could make it ashore. LSTs 201, 807, 891, 779, and many more finally were able to land on D-Day plus two. It wasn't easy for the LSTs and LSMs because of the gauntlet of enemy fire and they had to weave their way around debris cluttering the beach.

General Smith on the *Eldorado* said to news correspondents on board, referring to General Kuribayashi, "I don't know who he is, but that Jap general running the show is one smart bastard."

As the LSTs and LSMs approached, they would drop their stern anchor, as usual, to help steady the ship on the beach, but, unfortunately, the anchors would not hold on the soft bottom, making it difficult to hold the ships without broaching. The weather became so bad that nothing but an LSM could even approach the beach, delaying the unloading even more. The LVTs and the DUKWs took up the slack by shuttling supplies from the transports to the beaches and bringing casualties back on the return trip.

Hitting the beach, Andre swung into action. Frantically he moved from man to man, doing what he could to patch them up or, at least, relieve the worst of their pain. With tears in his eyes, he administered to a young boy, no more than 19 years old. Knowing that the boy was only minutes from death, Andre, while alleviating the boy's pain with a shot of morphine, tried to comfort and reassure him.

By evening more than a thousand casualties had been evacuated, but hundreds were still on the beaches waiting for help. Many would die before they could be removed to hospital ships in the morning.

Louis Bianco, a marine, was wounded on Iwo Jima and required blood. The package that contained the blood had the name and address of the woman donor. When Lou was brought back to the States and in a hospital, he wrote to the lady and thanked her for her blood. After the war was over he visited her. She lived in the Midwest and was married, with children.

The casualties mounted even out on the water. The carriers that remained became a primary target for kamikazes. They put the fleet carrier *Saratoga* out of commission and sank a CVE. Several other ships took major hits but were not sunk.

General Kuribayashi reported to Japan that he was slaughtering the invaders by the thousands, with little cost to his own men.

A Slow Moving Target, The LST of World War II

At the White house when President Roosevelt was told about the invasion of Iwo Jima and the casualty count, novelist Jim Bishop wrote, "It was the first time that anyone had seen the President gasp in horror."

In three days there were 4,574 American men killed and wounded. The beach was secured in D-Day plus 4. It was only the beginning. It took the marines 30 days to take Iwo in the longest battle they have ever fought over an island. The battle for Iwo Jima ended March 18, 1945.

In anticipation of the landing on Iwo, LST 779 was in Pearl Harbor for extended training maneuvers. Lieutenant JG Alan Wood was serving as the LST's communications officer and said at the time, "It was our first operation and we were a little excited because Iwo Jima was so close to Japan."

During the ship's stay in Hawaii, Wood visited a Navy salvage depot for no apparent reason. Lt. Wood, who was also responsible for LST 779's flags recalled, "I was just rummaging around looking for anything that might be of use, when I found this brand new flag in a duffel bag with some old signal flags. It was a large flag, and I was glad to find it because we were out of large flags on board." He didn't know its origin but said, "We carried the flag on board during our long trek to Iwo, and it flew several times from our gaff on Sundays."

After they stopped at Saipan, LST 779 set out on its last leg for Iwo Jima. On board were a company of Marines with their 155-mm howitzers, reserve ammunition and high-octane gasoline.

Lt. Wood described his first impression of the battle of Iwo Jima in a letter to a friend which is now in the Congressional Record, which said, "On the 19th of February, a clear, cool, beautiful day, we rolled up to Iwo, which by now was a mass of smoke and dust. The big ships of the Navy circled the island and were leisurely pumping a steady barrage of shells at it. Overhead our planes buzzed and roared as wave after wave dove at the beaches and at Mount Suribachi. It didn't seem possible there could be a living thing left on Iwo when the Marines got there. It

Joseph Francis Panicello

looked like a pushover. But that afternoon, as we cruised around, we could see, by looking through binoculars, that the Japs were doing a lot of fighting back."

Lt. Wood was dismayed as he watched the Japanese mortars and artillery brutally pummeling the marines that were pinned down all along the beach. A call came in for help. The howitzers were desperately needed, so LST 779 headed for the beach.

The letter to Wood's friend continued, "The beach was a mad house of men, supplies, and noisy vehicles. Suribachi was a few thousand yards down the beach. Jap mortar would explode with a shattering burst right on the beach in the midst of all the men, supplies and machines."

Unloading LST 779 took the afternoon and most of the night, a night Wood declared he would never forget. In the early morning hours, a Japanese mortar barrage threatened his LST, which was still loaded with gasoline and ammunition. Wood said in his letter, "How we missed being hit I don't know. If we had been hit the results would have been disastrous.

"By this time the skipper decided to pull out. After two days at a safe distance, our LST was again beached but this time closer to Mt. Suribachi. It turned out that LST 779 was the first LST to be beached on Iwo Jima."

Late in the afternoon of February 23, the marines managed to secure Mount Suribachi and raised a small flag. But the little banner seemed insignificant to properly acknowledge the Americans' momentous accomplishment. A battle-weary Marine came on board LST 779 and asked Wood if he could borrow a large American flag.

Wood asked him, "What for?" and the Marine responded, "Don't worry. You won't regret it." Wood then got approval from the skipper for the loan, which later became a donation that replaced the smaller flag.

Wood recalls that the marine was barely over 18, but looked like an old man. He said, "When I saw Joe Rosenthal's Pulitzer Prize winning photo, I looked for that same marine but I didn't recognize any of the men who raised the flag."

Today the flag is displayed in the U.S. Marine Corps Museum in Quantico, Virginia. In that famous photograph were: Ira Hayes, Ariz.; Franklin Sousley, Ky.; Michael Strank, Pa.; John Bradley, Wis.; Rene Gagnon, NH.; and Harlon Block, Texas. The original flag raisers were never found.

Iwo Jima proved to be the bloodiest battle of Marine Corps history, with close to 6,000 deaths, 23,000 casualties, and approximately 450 missing in action. Japanese losses totaled 22,000 killed, including General Kuribayashi. Only 1,200 Japanese prisoners were taken.

The invasion of Okinawa followed quickly and proved bloodier still.

Joseph Francis Panicello

38. Okinawa

Okinawa is the largest and most important island in the Ryukyu Islands, covering 554 square miles. Possession of the island would be a perfect springboard for the American airforces to attack Japan. The Japanese southern tip is only 350 miles away from Okinawa, and 840 miles to Tokyo. The island had been under control of the Japanese government for over sixty years, and it now contained the largest Japanese garrison of any island assaulted thus far. Okinawa was the last island in the war to be assaulted and the worst for the Allies.

The island is very important strategically to the United States, even today. It is located within easy flying distance of China, Hong Kong, Japan, the Philippines, Taiwan, Korea, and Vietnam. China originally claimed Ryukyu Islands until 1874, when Japan took possession. In 1972 the U.S. returned the island back to Japan with the condition that U.S. military bases remained on Okinawa. They are still there today.

Okinawa is 60 miles long and was inhabited by mixed races. The Chinese called the island "Shurei No Kuni," a Nation of Constant Courtesy, because they were a more easygoing people than the Japanese.

This invasion, at first, was planned with only Army personnel, but it was later decided by the JCS that the marines would also be involved in the assault. Lt. Gen. Simon Buckner was in command of the Army. His subordinates were Marine Maj. Gen. Roy Geiger, commanding the III Amphibious Corps, and Army Maj. Gen. John Hodge. Spruance would command the naval contingent, while Kelly Turner remained in command of the amphibious forces.

The assault, planned for April 1, 1945, required 15 attack transports (AP), 6 attack cargo ships (AK), 25 LSTs, 10 LSMs, and one LSD. Kamikaze planes would be kept at a distance from the landing craft by planes from the Fifth Fleet carriers.

A Slow Moving Target, The LST of World War II

Included in the fleet was LST 534, built in an Evansville cornfield, and LST 641, which received 2 battle stars.

Taking Okinawa would be a dress rehearsal for the expected landing on the mainland of Japan. More than 500,000 soldiers, marines, sailors and airmen would participate in this last island invasion of the war. If the Okinawa invasion was successful Japan would follow.

The human cost was expected to be huge on Okinawa. That became obvious when six hospital ships and eight medically equipped LSTs were assigned to support the invasion. Finally the Pentagon realized the important role medical ships have during an invasion, especially medical LSTs that could be beached and provide immediate assistance to the wounded. So instead of allocating one or two hospital ships as they normally would, the Pentagon assigned fourteen for this invasion. Andre, of course, had been right about not having enough hospital ships and medical LSTs for support, but it had taken a long time for the planners to realize it.

The Japanese, of course, would defend the island even more so than they did on Iwo Jima. The command for the defense of Okinawa was given to Lt. Gen. Mitsuru Ushijima, a competent and energetic officer. He knew he couldn't keep the Americans from landing so he ordered a different defense scheme to stop the invaders. He put 80,000 regulars and 30,000 local militiamen to work like ants burrowing 100 miles of tunnels throughout the island's southern end. He had his men dig out bunkers and reinforce them with steel and five-foot concrete walls. The Americans would have to face the heaviest concentration of artillery ever accumulated. The Imperial Navy was also ready for the invasion with a plan to overwhelm the American fleet with kamikaze pilots. Ushijima and his men were prepared to die with honor rather than surrender.

On March 22, 1945, Adm. Raymond A. Spruance's Fifth Fleet opened a massive, 10 day bombardment of Okinawa, the last stepping stone to Tokyo. Hundreds of kamikaze pilots dove their planes into the largest American fleet ever assembled in the

Joseph Francis Panicello

Pacific, with 1,000 warships carrying 180,000 soldiers, sailors and marines. It was a minor victory for the Japanese as kamikaze pilots sank 36 American ships. Another 368 ships were damaged.

Charles J. Adams Jr. recalls in the L.S.T. Scuttlebutt newspaper, "My ship LST 281, was loaded in Guam with fog oil, 80 octane gasoline, and headed for Okinawa. Upon our arrival we were attacked by kamikazes but LST 281 was lucky as all around us ships were being sunk or damaged. We helped rescue men from LSTs 534, 808 and an APD."

Also from the Scuttlebutt, Richard A. Ramsey recalls that his ship LST 947, was launched on October 15, 1944, at the Hingham Shipyard, MA., and headed for Norfolk and the Chesapeake Bay. It was involved in the invasion of Okinawa with 1,400 other ships. On D-Day at Okinawa they launched their LCT, and beached the ship, getting rid of 300 tons of ammo.

The morning of April Fools Day, 1945 and Easter Sunday, was calm, and Admiral Turner issued his now famous orders again, "Land the landing force," at 0400 hours. It took another four hours to load the troops and to set the formation of the landing craft.

At approximately 0800 hours the leading Amtrack headed for the beach. The first wave landed on Okinawa just a little after 0830 hours. Opposition was light and troops were transferred from Higgins LCVPs into LVTs because there was a reef blocking their entry and the amphibious tanks could drive over them. The other larger Amphibious ships, such as the LCMs, LSMs, and LSTs brought the troops close enough and onto the reef so that the troops could wade ashore. More than 75,000 soldiers with tanks and artillery landed that first day.

The casualty figure was low that first day and it was hard to believe that the Japanese were not putting up a fight, but they were waiting in the interior with their strong defense. They allowed the troops to land with all their supplies. It turned out that this assault was the smoothest of all, as LSTs, LCMs, and LCTs had no trouble beaching to begin unloading their cargo.

Ushijima was ready with 80,000 troops and 39,000 natives waiting for the precise time to execute his counterattack. The Americans got a taste of things to come when kamikaze pilots hit three carriers and the Amphibians suffered their greatest attack.

On April 6, the real test for the fleet began when the Japanese launched a multitude of kamikaze planes which destroyed one LSM, one LST, and the transport *Henrico*. None of these attacks were expected by the fleet commanders, nor was the massive ground attack from Ushijima's troops, which was just about to begin. The Japanese massed an unbelievable 700 aircraft just for their kamikaze attacks. On the afternoon of April, 6, the major ordeal of Okinawa began.

The mightiest kamikaze was to have been the world's biggest Battleship, the *Yamato*. According to the Japanese plans, she was to drive herself into the American Navy fleet, then ground herself and become a floating battery. Fortunately, she was spotted early and sunk before she could do any major damage. This was particularly disturbing to Emperor Hirohito, who was bewildered and asked in disbelief, "She's gone?"

On previous invasions of the islands in the Pacific the American ships didn't always do a satisfactory job of bombarding the Japanese. The problem was that these large ships, such as cruisers and destroyers, had to remain far out at sea when they bombed the shores and had to cease their bombing when the marines or soldiers came close to the beaches. The military realized that the bombing needed to continue longer to protect the invading forces, but because of the fear of friendly fire which had previously killed American men in other invasions, they had to stop too soon. A vessel was needed that had a shallow draft that was well armed which could operate closer to shore and continue to bomb the enemy after American troops hit the beaches.

The navy's solution was the conversion of the LCI (landing craft, infantry) to several types of gunboats. Thus, during the

Joseph Francis Panicello

Marshall invasion, these newly converted LCIs became available. They were reclassified LCI(G) for gunboat, LCI(M) for mortar, LCI(R) for rockets and LCI(D) for demolition. Their success demonstrated the need for a newer and larger vessel that would incorporate additional firepower, and that's when the LCS(L) for landing craft support (large) was born.

The new vessel, an expanded version of the LCI, had an overall length of 157 feet, with a beam of 23 feet. It had a draft of only 5 feet 9 inches, which allowed it to operate close to shore. It had no bow doors or a ramp. It was strictly a gunboat that could bring devastation on the enemy close to shore. The LCS(L) had an impressive array of armament. Some mounted a 3-inch naval gun on the bow. Others either had a single manually operated 40mm cannon or a twin 40mm mount operated by a Mark 51 director. Behind the bow gun on each vessel were rocket launchers of ten 4.5-inch Mark 7s, their main offensive weapon. Each vessel also carried four 20mm mounts and two twin 40mm director-controlled mounts aft. Finally, there were four 50-caliber machine guns, two on the port side and two on the starboard side. The LCS(L) proved to be a devastating force.

During the invasion of Okinawa these new vessels were invaluable. Not only did they provide firepower to the shores, protecting our troops as they landed but they also were a strong force at shooting down those dreaded kamikaze attackers. Their other duties included convoy escort duty, laying smoke screens, fire-fighting, rescue work, towing, and mine destruction duty.

The first set of Japanese kamikaze attackers came in low, just barely over the water. The Americans greeted them with a barrage of flak, but many got through. At day's end they'd sunk three American destroyers, two Liberty ships, and an LST. In addition, twelve more ships were so badly damaged that they were out of the war. The kamikaze pilots were wreaking havoc on the fleet.

The destroyer *Abele* received a rocket-powered Okha bomb midships from a Japanese plane with such force the destroyer sank in two minutes. LSMs 189 and 190 was able to rescue 258 men from the destroyer. The Captain of LSM 189 had to repeat the rescue mission several times when eight more amphibious ships were sunk. General Ushijima's plan worked, and forced the Americans into a slow advance upon the well dug-in camouflaged positions of the Japanese.

The LST 884 was attacked by a kamikaze pilot and it was burning fiercely. It had to be abandoned by its crew and the 300 marines that were assigned to the ship. But because of the help from LCS(L) 115, 118, and 119, they were able to douse the flames, saving the ship and incurring few fatalities.

LCS(L) 51 and the destroyer *Laffey* were fighting for their lives. The captain of LCS(L) 15 was Lieutenant Howell D. Chickering. The destroyer had already been hit by three kamikazes and Chickering moved his vessel closer to pick up survivors and fight off the kamikazes. Chickering gave an excellent description of life aboard his ship during the attack in his log.

He wrote, "I clearly remember worrying about my crew. They were so young and the situation looked hopeless. There was no glory in this kind of warfare, just terror, despair, hopelessness, rage and exhaustion."

Chickering had nothing but the highest praise for his crew, especially the gunners. He continued to write, "Their combat performance was excellent. They were merely youngsters, teenagers and 20-year-olds."

For the Okinawa operation the LCS(L)-51 received the Presidential Unit Citation, and its valiant skipper, Chickering, was awarded the Navy Cross. His ship, the LCS(L)-51, was able to destroy many kamikazes planes as they approached and saved several ships from being destroyed.

It was a costly struggle but by May 17, Spruance declared the amphibious phase of the battle was over. It was June 21 before the island of Okinawa was completely secured. When the American casualties were counted, 12,500 soldiers, marines, and sailors were killed in action. Another 36,631 men were wounded. The Japanese toll was 107,000 bodies counted but many more

Joseph Francis Panicello

died inland, buried in their now famous tunnels. The number of civilians that died were 150,000.

Caught in the middle of the war were 450,000 natives who were pressed into service. Many killed themselves, believing the Japanese tales of American atrocities. They embarked on a panicky frenzy of mass suicides and murder. A native boy on Tokashiki Island, off Okinawa, recalls the death of his mother at the hands of her family, "In the end they must have used stones to her head."

Life in the caves was a madhouse of rotten dead and moaning wounded. Terrified civilians surrendered, afraid of the American flamethrowers. A woman survivor remembered, "The sea water was dyed red." A soldier said, "The Japanese were running to the cliffs to jump to their death. It was like ants when their nest had been dug up."

It had taken 4 months and a combined total loss of almost 300,000 people, both Japanese and American, military and civilian, to secure Okinawa, an area half the size of America's smallest state, Rhode Island, 1214 square miles in size. Within reach, only 350 miles away, was Japan.

A Slow Moving Target, The LST of World War II

39. Invasion of Japan

With Okinawa secured, raids on Japan became a daily routine. B-29 Superfortress made 1,200 flights a week, while the Third Fleet bombarded targets from the coastal waters of Japan.

Though the Japanese realized the war was lost, the unconditional surrender terms the Allies offered were rejected by the Japanese military leaders. With the invasion of Okinawa the Japanese Emperor had appointed a new premier. Both he and the Emperor worked towards mediation through the Russians, hoping to keep Japan a sovereign nation and an influential force in the world.

The Japanese military leaders won the day. An invasion by the Allied forces would be too costly in terms of lives lost and casualties suffered, possibly extending the war another 18 months to 2 years. A refusal of the unconditional surrender would force the Allies to reconsider, the Japanese thought, and offer terms closer to an armistice.

They couldn't have been more wrong. On May 27, 1945, MacArthur and Nemitz were ordered to ready their forces for the invasion of Japan. MacArthur naturally felt he should be supreme commander of the invasion. Admirals King and Nemitz objected. A compromise was reached by the JCS. MacArthur would command the land and tactical air forces, while Nemitz would retain command of the naval force. The Joint Chiefs would keep overall command of the invasion.

The Joint War Plans Committee had submitted an invasion plan to the Joint Chiefs as early as September, 1944. A second plan, Operation Olympic, was chosen instead. It called for a 13 division assault on Kyushu, at the southern tip of the mainland. The attack was planned for October 1, 1945. A second invasion would follow at Honshu on December 31, 1945. The initial invasion would include 7,200 aircraft and 3,000 ships. It was estimated that approximately 60,000 American deaths and casualties would result from the assault on Kyushu beaches alone.

With the invasion imminent, the Japanese Imperial Army Headquarters sent reinforcements south to Kyushu. Strength was increased from six to fourteen divisions. An estimated 300,000 Japanese troops were ready for the invasion. Millions of civilians were drafted for the home defense and suicide missions.

The Japanese designated thousand of planes, torpedo craft and explosive laden boats for kamikaze tactics. All troops were instructed to fight to the death. The leaders of the Japanese force were willing to forfeit lives rather than suffer defeat. The only remaining doubt was the willingness of the Japanese people to die for the Emperor and the homeland they revered.

On April 12, 1945, President Franklin Deleno Roosevelt died of cerebral hemorrhage in Warm Springs, Georgia.

Selwyn Baer Malone, of New York, wrote in the American Legion magazine Sept., 1991, "In 1945, I was 18 and serving in the Coast Guard as a radio operator aboard the cutter *Rariton*, off the coast of Greenland. While on duty the following un-coded message came through: 'Our Commander in Chief is dead. President Roosevelt died this day.' Tears flowed as I relayed the message to our captain. I believe his passing was the motivating force behind the U.S. and Allies ultimate victory."

Harry S. Truman was sworn in as President two hours later, inheriting a mighty military force, poised for final victory on two fronts. That same evening, after holding his first cabinet meeting, he met with Secretary of War Henry L. Stimson privately, and heard for the first time, of an amazing new explosive.

On April 24, Truman was apprised of a secret weapon, under development for the past 3 years, which would probably reach completion within a few months. He was informed that a test bomb, capable of destroying a city, would be ready sometime in July, 1945. If successful, it could be an alternative to the invasion of Japan.

The weapon was the atomic bomb. Conceived, designed, and ultimately brought to completion within the Manhattan Project,

A Slow Moving Target, The LST of World War II

the largest scientific industrial endeavor in history. It involved over 200,000 people, including a core of the brightest scientists in the world, under the direction of Robert Oppenhiemer. Overall command of the project was held by General Leslie R. Groves, of the Army Corps of Engineers. The project was carried out in secret, at a cost of 2 billion dollars.

By June, 1945, after extensive discussion of the pros and cons of using this weapon against Japan to bring a swift conclusion to the war in the Pacific theater, a select committee, reporting to President Truman, recommended its use. Truman concurred. At 0530 hours on July 16, 1945, a test shot at Trinity, New Mexico was detonated, revealing the awesome power of atomic weaponry.

Truman, meeting in Potsdam, Germany with Joseph Stalin, was informed that the test was a complete success. With renewed confidence he issued an ultimatum of unconditional surrender to Japan. Acceptance must occur by August 3. Japan declined the offer.

Truman's decision to proceed was based on the number of Americans that would die in an invasion of Japan. Also, if the Russians entered the war against Japan, they would definitely claim the lands they conquered. This alone was unacceptable to Truman.

On August 6, 1945, a B-29 dubbed *Enola Gay* dropped the first atomic bomb ever used in warfare. Hiroshima was leveled. Deaths incurred from the blast reached 140,000.

The Japanese military remained unmoved. On August 9, a second atomic bomb was dropped on Nagasaki. Loss of life totaled 70,000. Russia, troops poised on the Manchurian border, entered the war against Japan August 10, 1945.

On August 14, the Japanese government, fearing further atomic warfare, surrendered unconditionally.

The celebrations by the Allies were awesome. Millions of fighting men all over the world realized they'd be going home. In the Pacific thousands of flares filled the air, like a gigantic fireworks display on Fourth of July.

Joseph Francis Panicello

William A. Emerson wrote in the American Legion magazine, Sept., 1991, "I was aboard the *USS Buchanan* about 125 miles from Tokyo. Our planes were almost over their targets when word of the Japanese surrender reached them. We heard the words of Admiral Halsey: `It looks like the war is over. Cease firing, but if you see any enemy planes in the air, shoot them down in a friendly fashion.'"

In June, Johnny was Engineering officer of LST 150, maintaining repairs, readying the ship for the invasion of Japan. The ship had to be ready by the end of July which didn't seem to be a problem. One of the main engines did not require a major overhaul, it had only a blown head gasket, but the other main engine required a full overhaul. Fortunately, the Hawaii shipyard had all the necessary parts and the shipyard workers immediately began the task to overhaul the engine. One Auxiliary engine also required a complete overhaul and another shipyard crew took charge of that one.

Now that the repairs were in the hands of experienced mechanics at the shipyard, Johnny had a lot of time on his hands. There was no need for him to monitor the repairs any longer. He dropped over at Bob Olsen's apartment. Bob now had a one week old daughter. He stayed for a spell telling Bob that he was being shipped out. Bob said the same thing, that he was to report to LST 145 in a couple of days. They both knew where they were going. Bob said it first, "It looks like this is going to be the big one."

Johnny nodded his head and replied, "I'm afraid you're right. They estimate hundreds of thousands will be killed or wounded in this one."

Alarmed, Bob whispered, "Keep it down, Macaroni. I don't want to scare my wife. I know it's going to be hell out there but what alternative do we have. Those people are brainwashed and would fight to the last person. How does one fight against someone who is willing to die rather than surrender? If we give them the terms they want, several years from now they will rebuild, just like Hitler did with the Germans. We have no choice but to demand an unconditional surrender."

Johnny agreed and said, "You're right, Olly. But it's going to be very costly. I hope and pray we both make it through in one piece and not get shot up like Hinny. Look, Olly, how about going into Honolulu and having one last fling with me?"

Apologizing, Bob answered, "No thanks, Macaroni, I'd rather spend these next two days with my family. You understand?"

"Yeah, sure. Well, lots of luck out there. I may even see you on the Kyushu beach. Who knows? I'll be seeing you."

Before he departed, Olsen had one last request of Johnny and asked, "Macaroni, if anything happens to me, I mean fatally, will you see to it that my wife and child are transported to Boston for my parents to care for?"

"Sure, Olly. You can count on me."

Olsen was visibly relieved and simply said, "Thanks. Take care of yourself, Macaroni." Johnny gave him a half-hearted smile, waved and left.

Andre's ship, LST 153, was docked in Hawaii at the time to pick up a new load for the coming invasion. He decided to double his medical supplies to be prepared for the big one, especially extra blood plasma. Late one evening Andre went ashore and instead of going to the medical depot, he took a cab into town. He knew the depot would only allow emergency withdrawals late that night and they would not fill his big order until the next day. To kill some time he took a cab to the Lanai nightclub and as he walked in he was surprised to see Johnny at the bar.

He yelled, "Macaroni! Macaroni!"

Johnny turned around, completely surprised, and said, "Robber! Where the hell did you come from?"

They embraced and Johnny lead him over to a table. They talked about everything, but the first thing Andre said after observing Johnny in uniform, "You know, Macaroni, you look

Joseph Francis Panicello

good as a officer. You plan to stay in the service when this thing blows over?"

"No sir, not me. Right now, I'm only concerned with what goes on today. I was the engineering maintenance officer of all LSTs docked in Hawaii, until yesterday that is. Because it's going to be an all out effort on this next assault, all hands are being used for the big one. The military have even decided to bring men in from Europe for this campaign. From what I heard through the scuttlebutt, all leaves have been cancelled and a massive attack is scheduled."

Andre replied depressingly, "Yeah. I know. We're going to lose a lot of men. What a waste. Don't those Japs know they haven't got a chance? It's going to be a major slaughter on both sides."

Reluctantly, the two men said their goodbyes later that evening, making a vow to meet again in New York, when the war was over. June passed into July. Johnny's LST was ready to head out to sea. Andre and Bob had left weeks before.

The gloom on LST 150 was palpable. Most of the crew were young and had not witnessed or been involved in any combat before. Another officer, an Ensign, began asking Johnny questions about how bad it was in Europe during the Normandy invasion. Johnny could tell that he was green and this would be the young officer's first assault.

He decided to ease the rookie officer's concerns and said, "The Normandy invasion was different from what we will be experiencing in Japan. First of all, the Germans had a better defensive position than the Japanese because they were sitting on a high site overlooking the sea. The Germans could continuously bomb our forces from their reinforced bunkers and sink our landing craft at will as we approached. In this invasion the most serious counterattacks that our LSTs will be faced with are kamikaze pilots.

"The marines and soldiers will take the brunt of the defensive guns from the Japanese as they hit the beaches, but there's no getting around it, our LST will receive some flak as

A Slow Moving Target, The LST of World War II

we try to beach the ship. There's no way of avoiding it. The chances are, however, when we are ordered to approach the beach it will have already been secured and the danger will be less for us.

"LSTs are not used in the first wave and sometime not even in the second wave, but generally come to the shore with their cargo of tanks and artillery on the following days to support the troops. So it won't be that bad for us."

Johnny could see the obvious expression of relief on the officer's face and felt that he had eased his apprehensions a little. He knew it was going to be hell out there when they hit the beach but why worry the young officer now? "He'll find out soon enough," Johnny thought to himself.

One evening Johnny went ashore with another officer to have a few drinks before they departed. He didn't return until 2400 hours and went directly to his stateroom to sleep. An hour later, Motor Mechanic 3rd class Kowalski knocked at his cabin door and told Johnny they had a problem in the auxiliary engine room. Johnny could see that Kowalski was concerned. The ship was blacked out except for the emergency portable battery lights in the passageway. Johnny grabbed one of the lights and when he went down the long ladder to the engine room he detected smoke and began coughing. After he hit the bottom of the dark engine room, with his flash light he saw that one auxiliary engine was completely burned out and black. There was a man sitting in a chair with his head lying on a desk.

Johnny barked at Kowalski, "Light off the other engine so we can get some light in this engine room."

After that was done he asked Kowalski, "What happened?"

"Electrician's Mate 2nd Class Robinson fell asleep on his watch. He is drunk as a skunk. It looks like the engine overheated when the coolant fresh water pump failed, causing the engine to freeze. I came down and thought Robinson was dead. Now I see he isn't. I haven't told anyone else about this yet, Sir, because I wanted to tell you first. The captain and his

Joseph Francis Panicello

Exec. are ashore so they didn't witness the lights going out, or the smoke coming out of the engine room."

Kowalski then helped Robinson up the ladder to his bunk. When he came down again he said to Johnny, "Poor Robinson. The captain will hang him for this and may even give him a dishonorable discharge. The guy is a war hero with two Purple Hearts and now he'll be busted."

Johnny then asked, "How did he get the booze?"

"Fireman Arnold brought it on board about 2000 hours and he and Robinson went back by the rear anchor for privacy and drank a whole quart of whiskey. Robinson has the 12 to 4 shift and I'm surprised he even got down the ladder in the shape he was in. What do we do now, Sir?"

Johnny thought for a moment and then said, "First of all, I want you to make a complete inventory of the spare parts and see if we have enough to overhaul this engine. Meanwhile, I want every engine man not on duty and not on liberty to report to me at once. We gotta do something to save poor old Robinson's hide."

Luckily there were enough parts on board and the five engine men that were still on board were each given a specific assignment. They began ripping the engine down as fast as they could. Kowalski then recognized a major problem. After the pistons were removed from the six cylinder diesel engine, Kowalski said to Johnny, "The king pins in the pistons for the connecting rods are frozen tight from overheating. How do we replace them?"

Johnny answered, "Have a fireman hoist one of them up to the galley freezer and lay it on the floor for an hour. The dissimilar metals of the aluminum piston and the stainless steel king pin will allow the old king pin to be pushed out easily with a new one. Try it. I'm sure it'll work."

A fireman did follow Johnny's instructions and was able to replace all king pins but he used the freezer locker without the permission of the chief cook. He knew that the cook would refuse him and would proceed to blab the whole affair to the captain. So he broke the lock on the freezer door to get in. Johnny didn't know how he did it and wasn't going to ask any questions.

The engine crew worked all night without sleep until 0600 hours and were able to fire up the engine in time for breakfast. Robinson couldn't thank everyone enough the next day. Kowalski requisitioned new replacement parts and Johnny, as the senior officer on board at the time, signed the order. No one was the wiser except maybe the chief cook who later reported to the captain that someone broke into his freezer locker. Robinson was saved, however. The only telltale sign was the paint on the overhauled engine block. It was now black instead of looking clean and navy blue as it appeared on the other two engines.

On August 4, 1945, Johnny's ship LST 150, approached Okinawa. The next stop for them would be Japan, in October, as planned. Even though Johnny was chosen as Engineering Officer this was not his primary assignment. Officers are given secondary assignment such as Navigation Officer, Commissary Officer, Communications Officer, etc., but the primary assignment for all officers is bridge duty while under way or during an assault.

There were eight officers on the LST and two are required to stand watch over the three shifts. The captain and his Exec. do not have specific watches but they are expected to be on the bridge during battles or during high seas.

Johnny was on duty in the pilot house one day when the captain mentioned to him quietly, "Lieutenant Maroni, there is something big going on. I don't know what it is, but our new orders are for us to remain in Okinawa after we land, until further notice. This doesn't make sense especially if we're supposed to meet the fleet outside of Japan in the next few weeks. It's very confusing to me. Maybe the Japanese government has surrendered, but I doubt it."

Johnny responded, "I agree, Sir. Something's amiss. I was talking with the radioman before I went on my watch and he said the communications between ships and Hawaii are not very

Joseph Francis Panicello

clear. He has never heard anything like it before. Sometimes they are jumbled and other times they are clear. I guess all we can do is wait and see."

On August 6, 1945, all radio communication stopped on Johnny's LST. It was very confusing to the radioman and he immediately asked to speak with the captain in the pilot house. The captain then went down to the radio shack and asked the radioman, "Still no radio signals?"

"No, sir. Only static."

The captain was still puzzled and said, "That is the oddest thing that I have ever heard."

They waited and waited for days. Still no communication with other ships or Hawaii. Then on August 14, 1945, the radio began blasting away about a bomb. The radioman ran up to the bridge and began shouting, "The war is over, the war is over! The Japanese surrendered!"

The celebration on board went wild. The gunners were shooting their guns into the seas. Flares were being shot into the air. The captain, however, didn't participate in the celebration. He simply went back to his cabin and wrote a letter to his wife. He was a religious man and took a moment to say a prayer, thanking God that the war was over and that many American lives would be spared.

On September 2, 1945, Prime Minister Mamoru Shigemitsu came aboard the *Missouri* in Tokyo Bay to sign the surrender papers. The Japanese war was over but the amphibious fleet still had a job to do. They had to ferry the once proud enemy Japanese troops back to their homeland in Japan from China and from the many islands that they still occupied. The Amphibs had to ship thousands of Chinese soldiers back to China, and finally the LSTs became the main transportation for shipping American troops back to the States.

Johnny's LST participated in these relocations of men. On September 6, 1945, his ship transported 300 Marines back to Hawaii, then on to San Diego.

A Slow Moving Target, The LST of World War II

40. Home Coming

By September, American servicemen were being discharged by the thousands, using a point system which depended on the many months of service and if they were reserves or drafted. If a service man had 26 points (one point per month of service) he was eligible for discharge. If he was wounded and received the purple heart he would receive 3 extra points. Those that were eligible for discharge would have a small Golden Eagle with outspread wings sewn to their uniform jumper or jacket, which was sometimes referred to as the 'Ruptured Duck.' In September 1945, there were 12.4 million Americans in the service and by 1947, these numbers were reduced to 1.2 million.

Johnny's orders instructed him to report to Norfolk, Virginia. After arriving in San Diego he took a train east with thousands of military personnel, having to change trains several times. It was a peculiar trip, crowded with sailors, marines and soldiers, sleeping in the passage way of the train. Many were sleeping up in the baggage racks above the seats. The nickname "Cattle Car" used by the servicemen certainly applied. Johnny was lucky. As an officer he was assigned a seat.

It took three days to reach Norfolk and another three days was spent at the separation center. He had to listen to many orientations about insurance transfers and they even tried to persuade him to reenlist or to join the reserves, which would give him extra pay as a civilian, retaining his rank. Johnny declined and was discharged with the rank of Lieutenant JG. One thing he neglected to do was to transfer his $10,000 insurance policy to a civilian policy. Many ex-GIs later received financial compensation from their GI insurance premiums.

It took Johnny overnight on the Greyhound bus to get to New York. He grabbed a cab all the way from Manhattan to Queens and the cabby only charged him half fare. As he stepped out of the cab he was greeted by hundreds of people including many of the neighbors. Johnny's reception at his home in

Queens was outstanding and he was smiling from ear to ear. Angela wouldn't let him go. She hung on to his arm, making sure she didn't lose him in the crowd. His mother cried for hours and ended the evening with a prayer of thanks.

Johnny's dad sat quietly. As a man, he had waited through the war in quiet worry and frustration. With his son home, his heart was filled with a proud love and feeling of thankfulness. He was content to enjoy the celebration in silence.

The following afternoon, under the pretense of looking up old pals, Johnny left the house alone. He had to see Megan. Walking briskly to the corner bar he found it closed. He went next door to a butcher shop. The owner, Otto, had known Johnny since he was a boy and was pleased to see him, shaking his hand vigorously and saying, "Welcome home, Johnny."

Johnny had other thoughts and asked the butcher, "Why is the bar closed?"

Surprisingly, Otto answered, "It's closed in mourning. The owner passed away."

Johnny was stunned. He asked Otto if he had the telephone number of the owner's wife, Megan. The butcher, bewildered by the request, went behind the counter and opened a pad, and after a moment, gave Johnny what he requested. Using the butcher's phone he called her number and a soft voice answered, "Hello, this is Megan."

Johnny's heart began pounding but he quickly responded, "Megan. This is Johnny. What happened?"

"Johnny, where are you calling from. Is this a long distance call? You shouldn't be spending so much money, Johnny, not on your salary. And..."

By now Johnny was getting impatient and tried to interrupt her, but she continued with a stream of questions. He then yelled into the phone, "Megan, please be quiet!" As she paused, Johnny composed himself and said, "Megan, this is not a long distance call. I'm right here, next door, in the butcher shop with Otto. I'm home for good, so let me in. I have to see you, please?"

Again there was a moment of silence but then he heard her excited voice yelling, "Johnny, are you really here? Oh, my gosh, I'll be right out."

Johnny ran out of the butcher shop and waited in front of the bar. When the door opened he didn't even have time to catch his breath. She came running into him colliding with such force she almost knocked him over. She was still in her mourning black but in Johnny's eyes she was still a beauty. She kept kissing him over and over again. It was a grand homecoming.

When things calmed down she asked, "Did you hear about my husband, Johnny?"

"No, I didn't know. I'm sorry for your loss, Megan."

They were quiet for a while, just looking at each other. Johnny then bent over and kissed her lips tenderly and said," I sure missed you, Megan. I do love you so much."

At home, Angela and her family were still celebrating Johnny's homecoming. By now the relatives didn't need the main guest to continue their celebration. The doorbell rang and Angela answered it. At first, she didn't recognize the figure standing before her. After a moment she gasped, "Andre," and reached out and pulled him close to her.

Andre wasn't sure what his reception would be like. She kissed him, then began crying. The first thing she asked was, "You're alright, you're not disabled, are you?"

"No. I'm fine. I just put on some weight." He wasn't kidding, either. He must have put on 30 pounds which made him look more manly and, because of the experience he had in combat, he even acted more mature. She dragged him in and sat him down on the couch.

She gave him a glass of beer and sat down next to him. She said, "Andre, I'm so glad the war is over and you are in one piece. I was so worried over you. I prayed for you at the Novena in church every Monday evening with my mom, for you and Johnny, and the other Phibies. My prayers have been answered and now you're here." She leaned over and kissed him again.

Joseph Francis Panicello

Andre, by now, was completely dumbfounded. He hadn't expected such a reception. Encouraged, he said, "Angela, let's go outside. I have to talk to you."

She was puzzled at his request but she went with him. Outside, facing her, he said, in a rush, "Angela, I know I'm being presumptuous, but I've got to know the answer right now or I'm heading home. Will you marry me?"

She looked into his eyes, smiling, and said, "Of course I will. Was there ever any doubt?"

"Did you say yes?" he asked, surprised.

"Yes, yes, yes, my darling. I will. I want to, and Danny would want it too. I was afraid you would be killed. Please forgive me for holding back. I was so afraid."

With that Andre hugged her and kissed her with all the passion that he had stored up for her over the last few years.

Andre and Angela were married at St. Clements Catholic church and moved in with his parents in Chicago while he attended school for his doctor's degree. Besides raising young Danny they had two of their own children, a boy and a girl. With all of the experiences that Andre had accumulated in the war, medical school was a cinch.

The Hienmans became ranchers in Australia. It was pretty difficult for him at first, punching cattle with one good leg but by using a jeep instead of a horse it made it much easier. They had two daughters.

Rich's sister, Dolores, continued in Hollywood, and was married three times in eight years. In her mid-thirties her career went downhill. She left Hollywood and went back to Texas with her two children. She remarried a successful farmer and settled down.

Olsen and his wife Lovette, moved to Boston and he resumed his fishing trade with his dad. The Olsens' had two more children, all pretty, blond girls.

Megan wanted Johnny to forget about college, and take over running the bar so they could be married immediately. Johnny refused and insisted on going back to school.

A Slow Moving Target, The LST of World War II

Johnny first had to repeat his high school education by taking a refresher course in an accelerated program at Rhodes Prep. School in Manhattan, and later attended Columbia University to receive his bachelor's degree in Mechanical Engineering. Johnny did exactly as he planned to do all along. He wanted to get his degree in Mechanical Engineering and establish himself with a job. He later was hired by Sperry Rand in Long Island.

It wasn't easy for them because Megan wanted to get married and he was still living at home, using the G.I. bill. She continued to run the bar and he would visit her often. After five years of schooling they were finally married by Father Donovan at St. Clements Catholic church in South Ozone Park. Megan later sold the bar and they moved to Long Island, close to his work. He took out a G.I. loan to purchase a small home in a veteran's home development.

The GI Bill of Rights was a great program dedicated to the support of the American Veterans after the war. On June 22, 1944, President Roosevelt signed the GI Bill of Rights that had been prepared by The American Legion. As the nation's veterans hope for posterity, the GI Bill sought to make the transition from the military to civilian life as easy as possible.

The GI Bill was originally drafted by PNC Harry Colmery, who outlined the medical and vocational needs of veterans on unlined Mayflower Hotel stationery and presented it to The American Legion. The American Legion was determined that what happened after World War I was not to be repeated. Those World War I GIs were left to scrounge for themselves, making readjustment to civilian life very difficult.

Passing the GI Bill through Congress wasn't easy. On May 21, 1944, a House-Senate conference committee met to iron out their differences about the bill. If the seven-member committee did not agree on the final wording, the bill would die. One member, Rep. John Gibson, was out of town at the time and the committee was deadlocked three to three about the job replacement provisions. Representative Gibson's proxy, who favored the bill, was rejected by the committee chairman who was against the provision.

If Gibson did not appear in person to cast his vote by 10:00 A.M. on June 10, the bill would fail. The Legion made a massive search to locate Gibson somewhere in Georgia. When he was found he was driven by a Legionnaire through a thunderstorm at 90 m.p.h., to Jacksonville, Fla., for a flight to Washington, D.C. He was able to cast the deciding ballot on time in favor of the bill. Through the efforts of The American Legion, the GI Bill of Rights became a statement of simple dignity for those who served the U.S. military in World War II, and later on for the Korean War and VietNam veterans.

Megan and Johnny were blessed with three children, one boy and two girls. His love for America was embedded within him. His patriotism for his country and what it stood for was still strong so he joined The American Legion to become involved and help support the wounded war veterans who were not as fortunate as he.

Once a year the Phibies, with their families, would meet. The Hienmans, because of the expense, would come every fifth year.

At the U.S. Military Academy in May 1962, MacArthur made a speech about The American Soldier. He described the devotion, courage and sacrifice of the men with whom he served in World War II. He spoke of the devotion of the service men and women who were called upon to give their lives for their country. He said, "Their resolute and determined defense, their indomitable purpose of victory, always through the bloody haze of battle, were followed by the passwords, `Duty, honor, country.'"

The *Five Phibies* would have understood.

The End

Afterward

Before the Atomic bomb was dropped, my two brothers were still serving in the army and were slated to go to the Pacific to fight against Japan. It was to be an all out effort in the invasion of Japan and the military were transferring men from all parts of the world to participate. My brother, Thomas, who had been severely wounded in the battle of the Bulge, had completed his tour of duty in Germany and was ready to be transferred to the Pacific theater. My older brother, Carl, was already in the States by August 1945, and was expected to fight against the Japanese.

I enlisted in the Navy in June of 1945, after I graduated from high school, but didn't report for duty until September 6, 1945. I probably would have been involved in the assault on the city of Kyushi, Japan, which was planned for October 1, 1945. I don't know if my two brothers and I would have survived that assault or the following invasion of Tokyo, because it was expected to be very costly. But one thing I'm sure of, had there been no atomic bomb, there would have been many more gold stars in windows throughout the country to honor the many Americans that were expected to die in the invasion of Japan. War has always been hell on both sides and the object of any war is to win with the minimum number of casualties.

I say this now with my utmost appreciation, "Thank God for President Truman who had the `guts' to drop the bomb and save many American lives."

During the period when my brothers and I were in the service, there were a few unusual incidents that transpired, which I will now describe.

My brother Carl was a Drill Sergeant in the early part of the war and was considered successful because many of his men in combat wrote back to him thanking him for being very tough and uncompromising in basic training. They told him how they appreciated his hard efforts to train them in the anticipated

Joseph Francis Panicello

battles ahead against the Axis and claimed that his rigid drilling, his guidance and fortitude in the States had saved their lives in combat.

Carl was later transferred to help guard the Panama Canal. While he was there, the army was always having problems with the San Blass Indians, who were fighting in the jungles of Panama. Carl was picked to lead a 25 man section into the thick jungle to suppress these activities, not knowing if the fighting was against the Americans. They had to carry their heavy armament such as personal rifles, heavy machine guns, ammunition, and machetes through the dense forest. The men had to cut their way through the jungle with their machetes while each man took turns carrying a water cooled machine gun with its tripod that weighed 80 pounds. Besides the misery of the heat the jungle was infested with snakes, wild animals, ants and mosquitos.

Carl's men cut their way through 5 miles of jungle which took several hours and, not knowing what was ahead, the men were ready for war, prepared to destroy the enemy, if necessary. As it turned out, the Indians were fighting amongst themselves, which was of no concern to the American Army. It took them another 3 hours to get back to their unit after that false alarm.

In another situation there was an attempt to sabotage the Panama Canal Locks. Carl was on duty at the time and noticed a suspicious vehicle parked near the main gate. He reported it to the Officer of the Day who immediately dispatched several soldiers to investigate. They found a group of civilians inside the area of the locks with explosives ready to blow up the locks. Because these civilians were overwhelmed by the many American soldiers no shots were fired and the saboteurs were arrested. Carl never found out who those civilians were but assumed they were German and Panamanian spies.

Carl was an outstanding baseball player in the States before the war and had the opportunity to play in the Canal Zone for his regiment during the war. One day, after his game ended in Cristobal, he went through the main gate to go back to the army

A Slow Moving Target, The LST of World War II

base. Then, for no apparent reason, two detectives from the town of Cristobal grabbed him. They wouldn't tell him why he was being arrested until they arrived at police headquarters. A police Captain approached him and showed Carl a picture of a girl and asked, "Do you know her?" Carl said he didn't.

The Captain then said to him, "This is my daughter. She was raped by a Staff Sergeant that fits your description and she pointed you out at the game. She has two broken ribs, her leg was twisted, and her face was black and blue from blows to the head. Where were you last Wednesday at 8:00 PM?"

Carl was dumbfounded over the accusation and responded, "I was playing baseball under the lights in Balboa, Panama at that time." He was completely astonished at the allegation.

They detained him for several hours while checking out his story and finally released him. Two weeks later Carl was again apprehended and escorted by the same detectives to the police station. He was told to sit and wait for the Captain to arrive.

When the Captain showed up, Carl was ushered into another room and, to his astonishment, he saw this man standing in the room with handcuffs on and in leg irons who looked exactly like himself. Carl thought he was looking in a mirror. The resemblance was uncanny except the man was 160 lb. while Carl was 190 lbs. The man was also a Staff Sergeant in the Army, as was Carl and being in the same regiment he had a similar insignia on his uniform. Carl never forgot the incident and was lucky to have had an ironclad alibi.

My brother Tommy, while he was still alive, revealed to me several incidents that happened to him as his company marched toward Germany. Tommy was in the second wave in the Normandy invasion and made it through untouched, which was lucky. When they were marching through France they came upon several American prisoners lying on the ground who were executed by the Germans. After seeing this assassination his commanding officer issued the order, "Take no prisoners."

Tommy was carrying a Thompson machine gun at the time and was ordered by his Lieutenant to shoot down several

Joseph Francis Panicello

German prisoners that were standing against a wall. Tommy didn't have the heart to kill unarmed men, just for revenge. It was against everything he stood for. When he delayed to follow the order another soldier grabbed Tommy's gun away from him and said, "I'll do it," and proceeded to slaughter those German prisoners. War can sometimes be very brutal.

Tommy was in the Armored Division and had learned to drive a tank during basic training. This training came in handy one day when he found an abandoned American tank off the main road in France. He didn't know why it was stranded so he climbed in and started it up. It seemed to be in working order so he proceeded to drive it back onto the road.

When he sighted the enemy he stopped the tank, loaded the cannon and fired it at them. He drove some more and every time he spotted the enemy he stopped and fired the cannon again. He then came upon an enemy vehicle and proceeded to blow it up. He was a one man operation and went through this maneuver several times, until he ran out of gas.

Running low on gas was probably the reason the original tank operators abandoned it. Tommy climbed out of the stalled tank and left it on the road. When he reported back to his company he was chewed out by his Lieutenant for leaving his squad. The Lieutenant didn't have a clue what Tommy had done. My brother didn't know how many Germans he had killed during his cannon assault but he assumed there must have been a few, especially when he knocked out that vehicle.

In the Battle of the Bulge, while Tommy and his platoon were on the march to counterattack Adolf Hitler's Ardennes offense, German Bombers came swooping down, dropping their bombs on American soldiers. It was December 16, 1944, when Tommy, in his attempt to take cover, was hit with shrapnel in his lower left side. He also broke his leg. He laid there bleeding, unable to move while waiting for medics to show up to help him. When the medics arrived they placed him on a stretcher and began carrying him to a medical receiving station.

A Slow Moving Target, The LST of World War II

Just then, German fighters came swooping down, with their machine guns blazing away. The medics panicked, dropped Tommy and ran for cover to save themselves. Tommy, realizing he was now in danger, crawled out of the stretcher and, on his belly, he slowly made it to a hole that was created by a previous bomb. After he entered the hole he could hear the bullets passing over his head and all around him.

When the planes finally left, the medics returned and carried Tommy back to the stretcher, but Tommy noticed that the stretcher was riddled with bullet holes. Had he remained on the stretcher he would have been annihilated. Tommy was bitter over this incident and could never forgive those cowardly medics for leaving him there to be slaughtered, just to save their own skins. They could have just as easily carried him to safety.

The Battle of the Bulge was named because of an assault in the Ardennes region which began Dec. 16, 1944, and created a huge bulge in the Allied lines, with two hinges at Butgenbach, on the north, and Echternach, on the south. The Ardennes is a wooded area which borders Germany, Belgium, Luxembourg, and is just northeast of France. The Ardennes assault was the last major offense by Hitler to stop the Allies from advancing into Germany. Field Marshal von Rundstedt was anxious to burst through this Butgenbach bulge and capture Liege, which was the heart of the American supply dump, with fuel and food. They were held back by the American troops.

Tommy's picture appears on page 294 with other GIs receiving mail from home somewhere in France, in the book *The GI War*, by Ralph G. Martin.

I was on LST 533 for two years after World War II and in the engine room gang. Early in 1946, we were scheduled to go into a dry dock in Portsmouth Virginia, for repairs. While we were tied up to a pier, our ship was hooked up to an electric panel on the dock that supplied us with electricity, so there was no need to have anyone on watch in the engine rooms. A fireman happened to notice that the main engine room was taking on water and called me. I went down with him and I found myself standing in four feet of water which was still climbing. Fortunately, the lights were still on which helped me discover where the water was coming in. I noticed some bubbling at the rear of the engines so we took turns diving to investigate.

We discovered that a sea water filter, used to strain the incoming sea water to cool the main engine fresh water, was ajar. We first closed the sea water input valve, replaced its cover and dogged it down. It did stop the leak and the ship was saved.

We had a lot of thoughts about how it happened but our Chief Motor Mechanic thought it was sabotage. He assumed that someone purposely loosened the filter cover in such a way that it would, eventually, come completely off and sink the ship. There was an investigation but we never found out the truth.

We pumped out the engine room and discovered, to our dismay, that all of our electric motors, including two starters, were waterlogged and had to be disassembled, cleaned out, and baked, which took the entire engine crew two weeks to accomplish. We didn't even receive a thank-you from the Captain, but the other fireman and I did receive liberty from our Chief for our efforts.

In the novel, the story of the drunken 2nd Class Electrician Mate falling asleep on watch in the auxiliary engine room and causing one engine to overheat and freeze, was actually true. I was the first one to go down to the engine room and I saw the Electrician Mate sitting in a chair with his head on a table. I thought he was dead because I had so much trouble prying his hands loose, but he was just drunk and out cold.

I was the fireman who had to carry the large pistons, one by one, up a long ladder and place them in the freezer locker to remove and replace its king pins. Using the freezer locker for this task was accomplished without the approval of the Chief Cook. I did have to break the lock to enter but was never caught at it. The Chief Cook was irate over someone breaking his freezer padlock and reported it to the captain. We did save the Electrician Mate's hide, who couldn't thank us enough. Had the Captain found out that the Electrician fell asleep on his watch he

A Slow Moving Target, The LST of World War II

would have been busted, given brig time, and possibly a dishonorable discharge.

I mentioned that I spent two years out of three in the Navy on LST 533. The other year was on a Yard Tug Boat (YTB) stationed at Norfolk, Virginia. Like the LST the Tug Boat is another one of those vessels that doesn't receive any fanfare in the media, but it also provided a very important function in the Navy.

I was on the YTB 365 which was named the *Sigrausa*. All Tug Boats have Indian names, as Battleships are named after states and Cruisers after cities.

I had many important duties on my Tug Boat where I learned a great deal about seamanship and Diesel engines. Over and above its yard duties my Tug was also used as a fire fighter. It had two powerful water guns, one main gun in front of the bridge and a smaller one above the bridge. These two water guns had enough pressure to produce a water stream that could reach a fire that was over two hundred feet away.

There were two machine gun turrets aft and on the bridge deck to fight off enemy aircraft. This meant we required at least a Third Class Gunners Mate on board with a crew of only ten men. After the war the Gunners mate had to be given other duties on board such as coxswain and radioman but he still had to maintain the machine guns until they were removed at the end of 1946.

The Tug Boat was very powerful, with two GMC Diesel V8 engines, similar to those on an LST. Its propeller was as large as any ocean going Liberty Ship. It was so powerful that it could tow a Destroyer or a Liberty Ship, by itself, in the open sea for a thousand miles using a long steel cable, most of the cable submerged in the water. This would damp any sudden jolts between the ships and not cause the cable to snap.

After the war we had to tow many ships over the Chesapeake Bay and up the Claremount River where they were anchored in the middle of the river and put in mothballs. In the one year that I was on the Tug we must have towed 100 ships.

Joseph Francis Panicello

When I first went aboard the Tug, I was a seaman and spent many hours learning to deal with towing barges, ships, and to help large ships to dock or be launched. One of the first duties my Tug had was to take a Pilot out to a ship that was coming in to a port and was waiting out in the Chesapeake Bay. The Pilot and our Captain had a code when they were docking a large vessel. If our Tug were set up to push the bow of a ship toward the pier, for example, one blast of the ship's horn meant for us to push the bow in. Two blasts was to stop and three was to pull the ship away from the pier.

We had a situation where a Captain of a destroyer refused to accept a local Pilot. He yelled out, "I've been docking my own ship for years. I don't need any assistance. Stand clear!"

Our Pilot yelled back, "You better use a Pilot. It's dangerous in these waters."

The Captain returned with, "I said stand clear! I'm coming in."

Sure enough the Captain came in but then he proceeded to crash his destroyer into the pylons, demolishing the pier and causing plenty of damage to the Destroyer's bow. Our Pilot immediately said, "Let's get the hell out of here." The Captain didn't know that the currents and tide in the Chesapeake area were unpredictable, because of the several rivers running into it.

I later transferred to the engine room gang and became a fireman. That's where I learned so much about GMC Diesel engines. In one predicament, while we were towing a barge overnight another fireman fell asleep on duty in the engine room. The salt water pump on one engine became air bound and the engine began overheating. I was in my bunk and awoke to a peculiar sound coming from the engines. I ran down into the engine room and saw that the starboard engine was smoking and its temperature was rising. I immediately reduced its engine speed and informed the Captain that it had to be shut down. The other fireman finally woke up and didn't know what was going on.

A Slow Moving Target, The LST of World War II

The end result was that a liner was cracked and had to be replaced under rough seas. That alone was an experience I'll never forget. Bouncing around, trying to remove a large head, was quite an ordeal. We replaced the liner and kept the incident hushed to save the other fireman's rear end.

Another time we were heading toward a river to pick up a small ship. Our Captain on this trip was actually a Pilot subbing for our Captain. It was dark at the time and as we approached land the Pilot asked the crew to watch out for a lighthouse. I was on the fantail at the time, drinking jo, when one sailor yelled out, "I see it Captain," pointing to the shore. I looked out and sure enough it was a lighthouse. The Pilot headed directly for it and somehow went aground. We were stuck there and couldn't back out and he had to call the base for assistance. He couldn't understand how we went aground because, according to his chart, we were still a hundred yards from that lighthouse. We were stuck overnight and the next morning we discovered what had happened. That lighthouse was not a lighthouse at all but autos going around the corner on a hillside. It sure looked like a lighthouse to me, with its light going on and off, but it was actually auto headlights. After that incident the Pilot was nicknamed Captain Lighthouse by his associates.

The most unusual thing that happened to me on that tug occurred one evening when we were tied up to a pier. On previous occasions tugs would compete with each other with their water guns. When we approached another tug in the harbor, for example, I would have my water pumps going and, as we passed them, we would spay them down pretty good. It was a lot of fun having water fights against one another with our guns and hoses.

That evening another tug came up alongside us and began blasting us with water. We had water coming in from all directions, into the galley through an open port hole, and through a hatch above the galley. Sea water was coming in through a side hatch, flooding our crew's quarters. After we shut those hatches I rushed down to the engine room and lit off the main engines and

Joseph Francis Panicello

turned on the pumps. I slowly had to work my way up to the bridge to man the water gun to fight back. I heard one sailor on the other tug yell, "Don't let him get to that gun!"

To make a long story short, I did get to the gun and proceeded to blast them with our high powered water. In the process I blew out their Bridge windows and caused glass to be embedded into those poor sailors in the bridge, which I wasn't aware of at the time. The rest of the sailors then abandoned the boat and were running down the pier for safety so I turned my water gun at them and washed one sailor over the pier and into the water. He broke his leg while being washed over.

After it was all over and the damage was assessed I ended up in the brig. At Captain's Mass my Chief spoke for me and I was lucky. I was restricted for two months, and given a lot of extra duty. I could have served big time for destroying Government property. That was close. I could never have paid for the damage.

Cheboygan County LST 533

The author's ship, *LST 533*, was laid down on September 29, 1943 at Evansville, Ind,. by the Missouri Valley Bridge & Iron Co; launched on December 1, 1943; sponsored by Mrs. H. D. Peoples; and commissioned on January 27, 1944, Lt. C. E. Hanks in command.

During World War II, *LST 533* was assigned to the European theater and participated in the invasion of Normandy in June, 1944. Following the war, *LST 533* was used as a transport to deliver equipment (planes, tanks and trucks) and personnel up and down the Atlantic coast and then performed occupation duty in Europe until February, 1953. She was named *Cheboygan County (LST 533)* on January 1, 1955, after a county in Michigan. The Landing Ship Tank *LST 533* was decommissioned in May, 1969.

LST 533 earned one battle star for World War II service.

As I was reading through the American Legion Magazine issue of Dec. 1994, I saw a picture of my *LST 533* on the Omaha beach in the Normandy invasion, disembarking tanks. It was a pleasant sight because up until then I wasn't aware of what part of the war my LST was involved in. I was proud of my ship for its contribution in the war, and the two years I spent on it after the war was now a more gratifying experience.

Joseph Francis Panicello

Inland LST Shipyards

1. Dravo Ship Building Co., Pittsburgh, PA, built approximately 160 LSTs at this shipyard up to the year 1945. They built LST 1 through LST 60 at this yard. Several LSTs were redesigned into AGPs or ARBs in 1943 such as LST 14 & 15.

2. "Our Prairie Shipyard," the Chicago Bridge & Iron Company, Seneca, Illinois, began building LSTs May 1, 1942. By June 8, 1945, it had built 157 ships. LST 197 was the first ship launched into the Illinois River at Seneca and the last was LST 1152.

3. Missouri Valley Bridge & Iron Works Company of Evansville, Indiana, built LST 533 and LST 567. They built a total of 166 LSTs at this shipyard.

4. Jeffersonville Boat & Machine Co. at Jeffersonville, ID., built approximately 95 LSTs at this shipyard. Contracts for LSTs 85 through 116 & 183 through 196 were cancelled at this yard.

5. American Bridge Co., Ambridge, PA., built approximately 48 LSTs at this shipyard. Contracts for LSTs 142 through 156 were cancelled at this yard.

Joseph Francis Panicello

Coastal LST Shipyards

1. Newport News Shipping and Drydock Company, VA., where the first LST was built.
2. Boston Navy Yard, MA.
3. Philadelphia Navy Yard, PA
4. Norfolk Navy Yard, VA.
5. Bethlehem Steel Co., Quincy, MA.
6. Charleston Navy Yard, SC.
7. Bethlehem Fairfield Co., Baltimore, MD.
8. Kaiser, Inc., Vancouver WA.

Joseph Francis Panicello

A Slow Moving Target, The LST of World War II

LSTs that Appear in Novel

LST 16,	As an aircraft carrier, 5 battle stars
LST 19,	Has LCT on main deck, Abemama, 4 battle stars
LST 20,	Invasion of Tarawa, 4 battle stars
LST 23,	Tarawa, 6 battle stars
LST 29,	In the Pacific, lost May, 1944, 4 battle stars
LST 39,	Exploded in Pearl Harbor
LST 34,	Invasion of Makin, 6 battle stars
LST 43,	Exploded in Pearl Harbor, 1 battle star
LST 69,	Tarawa, 1 battle star
LST 85,	Danny's ship in Salerno, Italy
LST 142,	The Phibies first ship
LST 145,	Olsen's ship in Pacific
LST 150,	Johnny's ship in Pacific
LST 153,	Andre's ship in Pacific
LST 168,	On the front cover, 6 battle stars
LST 169,	Tarawa, 3 battle stars
LST 170,	Saved crew on LST 695, Leyte, 7 battle stars
LST 179,	Exploded in Pearl Harbor, sunk May 1944, 1 battle star
LST 182,	Johnny's ship in England
LST 201,	In Iwo Jima, 4 battle stars
LST 205,	Tarawa, 4 battle stars
LST 218,	Tarawa, 4 battle stars
LST 226,	Door problem in Pacific, 2 battle stars
LST 240,	Abemama, 2 battle stars
LST 241,	Abemama, 6 battle stars
LST 242,	Makin, 4 battle stars
LST 243,	Makin, 5 battle stars
LST 244,	Abemama, 4 battle stars
LST 274,	In Pearl Harbor, watched explosion, 2 battle stars
LST 281,	Okinawa, 2 battle stars
LST 282,	Southern France, 3 battle stars
LST 288,	Took casualties to England, 2 battle stars

Joseph Francis Panicello

LST 313,	Exploded and sunk at Gela, Sicily, July 1943
LST 325,	Sailed from Gibraltar to Mobile, AL, 2001, 2 battle stars
LST 326,	Anzio, 3 battle stars
LST 341,	LCT on main deck, Pacific, 4 battle stars
LST 353,	Exploded in Pearl Harbor, 3 battle stars
LST 354,	Balloon cables, 6 battle stars
LST 375,	Hit by artillery in Salerno, Italy, 3 battle stars
LST 385,	Bombed at Salerno, Italy, 5 battle stars
LST 386,	Struck a mine at Salerno, 5 battle stars
LST 395,	Pacific. Received extra help from Marines, 6 battle stars
LST 397,	Pacific, 7 battle stars
LST 399,	Hit by Mortar, Guam, Iwo Jima, 5 battle stars
LST 471,	Torpedoed by Japs, 5 battle stars
LST 473,	Bombed by Japs, 5 battle stars
LST 476,	Invasion of Makin, 5 battle stars
LST 477,	Makin, 4 battle stars
LST 478,	Tarawa, 5 battle stars
LST 479,	Makin, 5 battle stars,
LST 480,	Makin, 2 battle stars
LST 481,	Makin, 6 battle stars
LST 482,	Makin, 6 battle stars
LST 484,	Tarawa, 5 battle stars
LST 491,	At Normandy, 3 battle stars
LST 507,	Torpedoed going to England, and sunk by German E-boat
LST 521,	Normandy, 1 battle star
LST 533,	Author's ship, Normandy, 1 battle star
LST 534,	Normandy & Okinawa, kamikaze damage, 1 battle star
LST 543,	Europe & Pacific, 2 battle stars
LST 551,	Southern France, 2 battle stars
LST 556,	Carried pontoons, 5 battle stars
LST 641,	Okinawa, 2 battle stars
LST 695,	Leyte, 2 battle stars

A Slow Moving Target, The LST of World War II

LST 757, Zoot Suiters, Pacific, 2 battle stars
LST 776, Used as a carrier, Iwo Jima, 2 battle stars
LST 779, Provided flag for Iwo Jima, 2 battle stars
LST 807, Iwo Jima, 2 battle stars
LST 808, Okinawa, Damaged by Kamikaze, 2 battle stars
LST 884, Okinawa, destroyed by Kamikaze, 2 battle stars
LST 891, Iwo Jima, 1 battle star
LST 932, Bob Bridgeman's ship
LST 947, Okinawa, 1 battle star
LST 986, Saved crew on LST 695, 3 battle stars

Joseph Francis Panicello

Glossary

DUKWS—Amphibious Motor-lorries (called Ducks).
LCA—Landing Craft, Assault
LCI—Landing Craft, Infantry.
LCP—Landing Craft, Personnel.
LCT—Landing Craft, Tank.
LCM—Landing Craft, Mechanized.
LCVP—Landing Craft, Vehicles, or Personnel-Higgins boats.
LSD—Landing Ship, Dock. Amphibious repair ship.
LSI—Landing Ship, Infantry. Carries 200 troops.
LVT—Landing Vehicle, tracked. Sometime called "Amtrack."
LCS(L)—Landing Craft, Support- Large Gunboat.
LCI(G)—Landing Craft-Gunboat
LCI(R)—Landing Craft-Rockets
LCI(D)—Landing Craft-Demolition
LCI(M)—Landing Craft-Mortar
LST—Landing Ship Tank- Could carry troops, tanks, artillery, trucks, and smaller Landing Crafts, especially the LCT.

Joseph Francis Panicello

Amphibious Bibliography

1. To Foreign Shores-John A. Lorelli-Many Pacific Assaults
2. World War II Mag.-Feb. 1999-Normandy, Anzio
3. W. W. II Mag.-Sept. 1999-Guadalcanal & Gela, Sicily
4. W. W. II Mag.-Nov. 1999-Rabaul & Sub. off Tarawa
5. World War II Mag.- 2000-V2 Rockets & Iwo Jima Flag
6. Anzio—by Wynford Vaughan, & Thomas
7. Island Fighting—by Rafael Stienberg, Time-Life-Books
8. The Italian Campaign-Robert Wallace, Time-Life-Books
9. LCI/LST Operations: 1944—Military History/ Videos
10. To the Shores of Iwo Jima—Military History Books/Videos
11. Guadalcanal—by Richard B. Frank
12. Naval History of World War II—by Bernard Ireland
13. Iwo Jima, Legacy of Valor—by Bill D. Ross
14. World War II Mag.—Sept. 2000 MacArthur's Return
15. The American Legion Mag.-May 2000—Higgins LCVP
16. World War II Mag.-Nov. 2000—Wake Island prisoners
17. LST Construction & Description—Military History/Videos
18. World War II Mag.-Feb. 2001, Iwo Jima, Bill Hudson
18. The American Legion 1994- LST 533
20. The Am. Legion Mag.-Sept. 1991-Remember When.
21. The American Legion Mag.-Oct. 1993- The Solomons.
22. The American Legion Magazine—May 1995- Okinawa.
23. The American Legion Mag.-Dec. 1992- The War Years
24. Am. Legion Mag.-Dec. 1993- Island Hopping
25. Am. Legion Mag.—Oct. 1994- Leyte Gulf, Sid Moody.
26. Am. Legion Mag.—June 1994- Longest Day, by Moody
27. Am. Legion Mag.—Nov. 1993- The American Soldier.
28. Am. Legion Mag.—Aug.1993- Voices of World War II.
29. World War II Mag.—Jan. 2001- Battle of the Bulge.
30. Scuttlebutt newspaper—U.S. LST Association
31. Dictionary of American Naval Fighting Ships, Volume VII—Pub., Naval Historical Center, Dept. of the Navy
32. Our Prairie Shipyard-by Chicago Bridge & Iron Works

33. Encyclopedia, on the history of the various islands in the Pacific and cities in Europe.
34. American History: A Survey - Currant, Williams, Freidel - New York: Knopf, 1966
35. Truman - David McCullough - New York: Touchtone; Simon & Schuster, 1992
36. This New Ocean - William. Burrows - New York; Random House, 1998
37. The Making of the Atomic Bomb - Richard Rhodes - New York: Touchtone; Simon & Schuster, 1988
38. Space- James A. Michener - N.Y: Random House, 1982
38. Compton's Encyclopedia - Chicago; F.E. Compton & Co., 1959

About the Author

Joseph Francis Panicello was born in Queens, New York, on October 31, 1927. He was married for 30 years to his late wife, Rose, and is now married to his lovely wife Barbara who has eight children, 3 adult boys and 5 girls. Joe has three daughters, Jo Ann, Marie, Teresa and eight grandchildren.

Joe Panicello is a World War II veteran serving in the Navy on LST 533 for two of his three years of his enlistment. He has a brother, Carl, who was in the Army during the war and is now living in Long Island. Another brother, Thomas, was also in the Army and was wounded in the Battle of the Bulge. Both Tommy and Joe's step sister, Marie, passed away in the nineties.

Prior to pursuing his writing career, the author maintained a successful 40-year career as an Electronic Engineer for Lockheed Aerospace in Burbank, California and Bell Telephone Laboratories in Whippany, New Jersey. He received his college education under the GI bill at Newark College of Engineering in New Jersey in 1959 and at RCA Institute of Advance Technology in New York in 1952.

Mr. Panicello is a member of The American Legion, The American Fiction Society, the National Writers Association, and the United States L.S.T. Association.

He has published five books thus far, two historical novels; *A Slow Moving Target-The LST of World War II* and *The Great Sicilian Norseman*, and three novels; *Vindicated, Brian's Comet*, and *The Wheeler Dealer*.

Three of the books; *A Slow Moving Target, Brian's Comet* and *The Wheeler Dealer* may be purchased through the Internet via, www.1stBooks.com, through Amazon.com, and at Barnes & Noble or other book stores. His other books *Vindicated* and *The Great Sicilian Norseman* may only be purchased from North Hills Publishers by calling (818) 894-6729.

Mr. Panicello has two more books in process; a historical novel about Giuseppe Garibaldi, *A Man of Destiny*, and *How to Become A Successful Engineering Manager.*

Printed in the United Kingdom
by Lightning Source UK Ltd.
1174